Cara Lockwood is th[...] of more than eighteen[...] *I Don't)*, which was [...] movie. She's written [...] young adults, and has [...] several languages around the world. Born [...] in Dallas, Cara now lives near Chicago, with her husband and their five children. Find out more about her at caralockwood.com, 'friend' her on Facebook, Facebook.com/authorcaralockwood, or follow her on Twitter, @caralockwood.

Taryn Leigh Taylor likes dinosaurs, bridges and space—both personal and of the final frontier variety. She shamelessly indulges in clichés, most notably her Starbucks addiction (grande six-pump whole-milk-no-water chai tea latte…aka: the usual), her shoe hoard (*I can stop any time I… Ooh! These are pretty…!*) and her penchant for falling in lust with fictional men with great abs. She also really loves books, which was what sent her down the wild path of writing one in the first place. Want to be virtual friends? Check out tarynleightaylor.com, Facebook.com/taryntaylor1 and Twitter, @tarynltaylor.

If you liked *Hot Mistake* and *Wicked Pleasure* why not try

Forbidden to Touch by JC Harroway
She Devil by Christy McKellen

Discover more at millsandboon.co.uk

HOT MISTAKE

CARA LOCKWOOD

WICKED PLEASURE

TARYN LEIGH TAYLOR

MILLS & BOON

First Published in Great Britain 2019
by Mills & Boon, an imprint of HarperCollins*Publishers*
1 London Bridge Street, London, SE1 9GF

Hot Mistake © 2019 Cara Lockwood

Wicked Pleasure © 2019 Taryn Leigh Taylor

ISBN: 978-0-263-27386-1

MIX
Paper from
responsible sources
FSC® C007454

This book is produced from independently certified FSC™ paper
to ensure responsible forest management.
For more information visit www.harpercollins.co.uk/green.

Printed and bound in Spain
by CPI, Barcelona

HOT MISTAKE

CARA LOCKWOOD

MILLS & BOON

For my husband, P.J.

Thank you for being my real-life romantic hero.

PROLOGUE

THEY TUMBLED DOWN onto the plush cushions of the pool-side lounger and she found herself on top of his hard, fit body. The shock of the impact jolted all her senses at once. The cruise ship's pool was deserted, the silver moon high above their heads. No one was around. No one could see them. All her senses came alive then, rousing needs she'd long denied. Their bodies fit together perfectly, the thin layer of clothing between them not enough to contain the heat they generated. Everything about him screamed sex: the lopsided smile, the thick muscles across his chest on display through his thin T-shirt, the barely there hint of stubble on his chin. She glanced at his hazel eyes and the way he stared at her told her everything she needed to know: he wanted her. Her heart thudded in her chest as her brain struggled to realize what her body already understood: she wanted him, too.

This was the man she'd been warned about, the man with the reputation for breaking hearts. But none of that seemed to matter now. Nothing mattered but the feel of his body beneath hers.

He waited patiently for her to make the first move. Almost challenging her as he kept still, their lips nearly touching. All she had to do was dip down to taste him. She inhaled his scent: sandalwood and something muskier, something dangerous. She wanted that smell on her, she realized. She wanted him, period. An inner voice of warning pinged in her head. Don't do this. It's a mistake. He's going to use you.

Not if I use him first, *she told the voice.*

Oh, she liked that idea. Play the player. Take what she needed...and she would. She'd denied herself for months. She'd been good for far, far too long. What had being tight-laced gotten her? Nothing. She needed this. She needed him. She was tired of being polite. What she wanted was a bad boy, someone who was off-limits, someone who wouldn't play nice.

Her inner wild child roared to life. She'd been held down too long beneath the prim and proper, the straight and narrow path she'd struggled to walk. Tonight she wasn't going to be a good girl. Tonight she was going to let the bad girl out. Her real self, finally. Wild, free, a woman who knew what she wanted and took it.

She dipped down and kissed him, pressing her lips against his, tasting the caramel-sweet sourness of bourbon. But she wanted more. So much more. Her tongue flicked out, meeting his in perfect unity, as if he anticipated her every move. Every nerve ending in her body stood on end, her blood buzzing in her veins, as she tasted him, drank him in. Her hand skipped down, running the length of his fit chest, finding him even harder, even more ready than she'd imagined.

She knew he'd had plenty of women. His reputation preceded him, after all. But she knew for a fact he'd never had a woman like her before. She reached for his fly and pressed her fingers against the length of him through the fabric and he groaned. Yes, that's it, groan for me, *her inner wild child thought.* Get ready for the night of your life.

CHAPTER ONE

Four hours earlier

THE BRIDE-TO-BE SHRIEKED with laughter. One of her would-be bridesmaids accidentally dropped a margarita glass on the outer deck of the bar of the massive cruise ship. Gabriela Cruz inwardly cringed as she heard the glass shatter. *Another one?* She silently moaned. *Seriously?* She sprinted over, exchanging her glass of hardly touched wine for a dish towel. She worked to sop up the mess. Gabriela was already beginning to regret accepting the maid-of-honor gig from Lola, but how could she say no to the woman she'd known since preschool? Lola was her oldest and most loyal friend, and if she wanted to invite fifty of her closest friends and family on board the *Royal Harmony* for a three-day wedding extravaganza, then Gabriela could certainly babysit the bachelorette party on Deck Seven.

Felicia, the buxom blond bridesmaid who'd dropped the glass, was already on her way to the bar for another one, not bothering to help Gabriela. *Figures.* Felicia had been all about Felicia since high school and, Gabriela noted sourly, little had changed.

"Don't worry about that," Lola scolded Gabriela, gesturing for her to stand. Lola's curly amber-colored hair was perfect—per usual. As was her outfit, a sweet, flower-printed short halter dress with platform sandals. She wore silver eyeshadow across her blue eyes, making them pop even more. Gabriela always thought Lola was like a Disney princess: hair and makeup always perfect. And she had a heart of gold.

Gabriela felt not-quite-as-adorably sexy in her sleeveless, festively printed, flowing long jumpsuit, the humid Atlantic air wrecking havoc on her long, dark waves. But then again, who was she trying to impress? These were her Miami friends. They thought she was the buttoned-up Gabriela of high school, the by-the-book, no-breaking-the-rules, no-alcohol-tolerance honors student. They had no idea about the Gabbie living in New York for the last five years and Gabriela wanted to keep it that way.

"Someone else will clean it up," Veronica added. Of all the friends from high school, she was the most traditional. She'd married when she was twenty-four and had had two babies in four years, the last of which was only six months old. She was the mother of the group. Veronica gestured to a baby-faced busboy who was already on his way over with a mop. "See? What did I tell you? Gosh, I love cruise ships. Wish I had a staff at my house."

"Come on," Lola implored, grabbing Gabriela by the hand. "Have some fun, please?"

Lola caught Gabriela's eye and grinned. This had been Lola's harebrained idea: take her entire wedding party, and heck, her entire wedding, on board a four-day cruise to Mexico. She planned to have her bachelorette party, wedding, wedding reception and honeymoon all in one sweep. Lola deserved this happy-ever-after and Gabriela was going to do her best to give it to her.

She realized she'd lost her clipboard and glanced around the bar for it. The clipboard had all her notes for the party—the games she'd planned, the cruise-ship-sanctioned activities and, of course, the ever-important *schedule*. If it was one thing Gabriela hated, it was falling behind schedule. She grabbed the clipboard from a nearby table as Lola led her to the bar.

"We should calm things down a bit," Gabriela suggested. "It's only nine and…"

Her cautious words were drowned out by Felicia shouting, "Shots!" at the bar. Gabriela looked up to see a row of tequila shots—one for each bachelorette partygoer at the mahogany bar.

"Time for this mama to get her groove on," Veronica joked and then headed to the bar.

"You coming?" Lola glanced at Gabriela, who hesitated. Lola shot Gabriela a sharp glance. "I *know* you don't act like this in New York."

"We're not in New York," Gabriela muttered. "And…you promised not to…"

"I'm not going to tell anybody *what I know*," Lola said. "Not that they'd care. They might even like you more. And you know Veronica. She just had her second baby, so she's looking to live vicariously."

"Yeah," Gabriela sighed as she looked at Felicia offering up her chest for a body shot for the tanned, hunky bartender. "That's what I'm afraid of."

Lola squeezed her hand. "If you want me to talk to Felicia, I will. I know she's kind of crazy, but you know she's been through a lot…what with her divorce…"

"Which was completely her fault." What did she expect, sleeping with her brother-in-law?

"Yes, but…come on. We all make mistakes." Lola gave her the wounded puppy dog look and Gabriela inwardly felt herself melting. Lola was the kindest, most generous, judgment-free friend, which was exactly why Gabriela loved her so much. It was also why she'd have to smile and put up with Felicia and her antics.

"True." Even though Felicia seemed to make more than her share of them.

"Come on, have a shot with me," Lola said, linking her arm through Gabriela's and dragging her to the bar. "You're more fun when you have tequila."

"More dangerous, you mean," Gabriela retorted, thinking about the last time Lola had come to visit her in New York and the trouble a few rounds of margaritas had gotten them into.

"Please?" Lola batted her thick, dark eyelashes and Gabriela knew she wouldn't be able to tell her friend no. This was Lola's weekend. She was marrying the man of her dreams in two days, and Gabriela's job was to make sure everything about the cruise was perfect— even this bachelorette party.

"You know I'd do anything for you," Gabriela said.

"Tequila!" cried Felicia and handed Lola a full-to-the-brim shot glass. Gabriela noticed Felicia didn't bother handing her one, skipping right over her and giving one to Liv, her sister. Gabriela knew the snub was on purpose. She suspected Felicia had wanted to be the maid of honor and was put out a bit that Lola hadn't picked her.

Gabriela helped herself to a shot and a slice of lime. *Just ignore the toddler behavior*, she told herself. *Ignore Felicia. Do not, under any circumstances, scratch her eyes out. Not until this wedding is done, that is.*

"Here's to the bride!" cried Felicia, holding up her shot glass.

"To Lola!" the others chimed in and clinked their glasses. As Gabriela knocked hers back, the searing liquid burned down the back of her throat. She quickly quenched the fire by biting into the slice of lime. She felt the blanco tequila settle in her stomach, warming her. She was already starting to feel the tingle of a little buzz. With a little more tequila, even Felicia would be bearable.

"Now to important business," Felicia declared, pulling down on the hem of her too-snug halter dress. "Lola, you've got your man meat all settled and Veronica… you've got *yours*…but the rest of us are single. We've got to decide dibs on groomsmen."

"Is this really necessary?" Gabriela sighed.

"Of course it is," Felicia snapped, annoyed. "We'll avoid a lot of fights this way." She gave a pointed look to Liv, her younger sister who was a lot like a mini Felicia, except with blue tinges to her blond hair.

"Well, you can have them all," Veronica joked. "I've got one husband and that's enough man to take care of for me. Lola, did I show you pictures of the she-shed he built for me? Seriously—a she-shed. From scratch." Veronica pulled Lola to the side and began thumbing through the photos on her smartphone.

She-shed? Felicia mouthed then rolled her eyes.

"The groomsmen aren't even here," Gabriela pointed out. They were currently having their own stag party on Deck Ten, which was just fine by Gabriela. Handling the G Squad was enough trouble—and broken glasses.

"All the more reason to figure out who has dibs." Felicia took a breath. "Not that *you'd* care about men."

Gabriela's phone dinged, more notifications from her Spark dating app. *Sure, I don't care about men.* She almost wanted to laugh. *How little you really know me.*

"I want Marco's younger brother," Felicia declared.

Lola was so deep into Veronica's slideshow about her she-shed that she was no longer paying attention. Ugh. Gabriela hated it when Lola wasn't in the mix. Lola always calmed the Tyler sisters down in ways Gabriela never could.

"No way. I want him." Liv's lips curved down into a pout. Gabriela just stared at the two sisters, amazed. While she'd only had brothers, she couldn't imagine why on earth two sisters would be plotting how to best divvy up the single guys on a cruise ship. Besides, how could they be thinking about hookups during Lola's big wedding weekend? Then again, she knew the answer: the Tyler sisters thought about hookups all the time, so why would this weekend be any different? She was saddened yet not at all surprised that they'd grown so little since high school.

"What about Bill?" Felicia offered.

Gabriela still couldn't believe they were talking about men like trading cards. This was what she didn't miss about Miami.

"Bill is...okay," Liv said.

"Bill is *married*," Gabriela pointed out, not that it seemed to faze either Liv or Felicia. Gabriela felt like she'd dropped into the Harlot Twilight Zone.

"I'd rather have James," Liv said, ignoring Gabriela altogether as she pushed the tray filled with empty shot glasses and signaled the bartender for another refill on her now-empty margarita.

"Or maybe we shouldn't be planning hookups at all," Gabriela offered, already feeling like she needed another shot of tequila to make it through the night.

"Says the woman who is allergic to fun." Felicia rolled her eyes. "We all know *you're* never hooking up with anyone, Gobstopper." Gabriela cringed at the sound of her awful nickname from high school. She never knew how she had become Gobstopper, but the name had stuck. She hated it.

"You never do anything fun."

Not true. Not that you need to know that.

"Come on, girls, let's get along," Lola pleaded just as the bartender brought a fresh round of margaritas and a new glass of malbec for Gabriela. Both Liv and

Felicia instantly stopped. Gabriela inwardly sighed. She'd talked to Lola about them before, but Lola was loyal to a fault, and she had a habit of adopting strays. Once you were in her inner circle, she'd never kick you out. Her fierce loyalty inspired others, as well. Even though Gabriela didn't like Felicia or Liv, she knew both women would take a bullet for Lola if asked. *So be nice*, Gabriela told herself. *Don't start anything. Don't stoop to their level. Just let it go.*

"Yeah, stop picking on her," Veronica said, and Gabriela was happy for the defense. "We all know the lamest person here is me. I haven't stayed up past ten o'clock in two years."

"You have two kids under the age of four!" Lola cried.

"Exactly," Veronica said. "And I'm literally nearly drunk from half a margarita and one shot." She hiccupped as if for effect. Veronica stared at her new margarita. "Seriously, someone else should drink this or I will be asleep in, like, ten minutes."

Felicia happily took it, double-fisting her drink. Gabriela frowned. Not a good idea. "Well, you know, " Felicia added, a wicked smile crossing her face. "If I *must*, I'll take Sebastian."

Gabriela choked on her wine at the mention of Marco's best friend and the infamous best man. Sebastian Lott was not a name she'd thought about in a long time. He'd been the hottest guy in high school, the one everybody'd had a crush on at some time or another, and also the man who'd left the most broken hearts in his wake. Sensitive, he wasn't.

"No!" Gabriela said, gagging on her drink. "Are you insane?"

"Yeah, girl, don't you remember summer after high school?" Liv looked as taken aback as Gabriela felt. She thought everybody knew the rules about Sebastian Lott. The man was toxic, pure and simple.

"Well, *yes*, I remember summer after high school. The man knew his way around a body, is all I'm saying, and that was *then*. What if he's picked up new tricks since?" Felicia's eyes glazed over at the thought as she greedily sipped at one of her margaritas.

"No. Absolutely not." Gabriela shook her head. "It's a bad idea."

Felicia frowned at Gabriela. "You already spoiling my fun, Gobstopper?"

Felicia let out a sigh. "Do you think he still has that motorcycle?"

"He does, actually. A new one," Lola said. "Saw him driving it down around South Beach the other week."

"Okay, well, if he has the motorcycle…" Liv seemed to be suddenly okay with her sister dipping her toe back into the shark-infested Sebastian Lott waters.

"No, guys!" Gabriela needed to put her foot down. "From here on out, we need to think about Sebastian as Swipe Left."

"Why?" Felicia grabbed her phone and pulled up Sebastian's Instagram account. She swiped through picture after picture of a gorgeous man who seemed none too keen on wearing shirts. She stopped on one where he was astride his motorcycle, an amazing Miami sunset behind him, wearing a tight-fitting white tee and jeans that hugged his flat hips.

God, he still looked the same, Gabriela mused. Sex on a stick, that's the only way to describe Sebastian Lott. Those smoldering eyes, that washboard stomach. Gabriela felt the little tickle at the back of her throat she used to feel in high school. She wasn't immune to the man's good looks. Not that Gabriela had ever told a living soul she was fond of the broad-shouldered football player with jet-black hair and hazel eyes. Scratch that, she'd only ever told *one* person. Some good it had done. Not that he'd ever noticed her. Sebastian would've never given her a second glance in high school. She'd been the awkward kid with glasses and braces, the one who'd opted to stay home from parties to study. No, definitely not hot enough, daring enough, for Sebastian Lott's tastes.

"Oh…my." Veronica leaned in to get a closer look.

"You cannot be serious!" Liv cried. "He's Swipe Left!"

"He's hot, though." Felicia tucked a small bit of blond hair behind one ear.

"He knows it, too." Liv rolled her eyes. "I'd rather not spend the evening talking about how great he is, thanks. Look at all those half-naked women hanging all over him in all those pictures." She thumbed through them and Gabriela saw she was right. There was a new woman in each one. "Ugh… Gross."

Gabriela nodded. She needed to talk some sense into Felicia. "You can't do this. Say you hook up with him and say he says something that upsets you. Or, ignores you for the rest of the trip."

"He does tend to do that," Liv said. "He is Mr. One and…Done."

"We can't let him and his man-drama ruin Lola's big day." Gabriela glanced at her friend, who stared at her drink.

"Sebastian's not that bad," Lola offered, ever the optimist. "He'd be nice. He's…matured. He's actually pretty nice now, if you spend more time with him." Also, she was going to be Team Sebastian because he was the reason she'd met her groom, Marco. The two worked together at the same law firm, and Sebastian had introduced them at a bar on South Beach. According to Lola, it had been love at first sight.

"You're biased, Lola," Liv said. "Sebastian might be older, but you can't convince me a leopard can change its spots."

Felicia seemed to consider this. "But it's not like I want a relationship," she said. "I just want to *hit* that."

"Yeah, but why give him the satisfaction?" Gabriela offered. "Didn't he ghost you summer after graduation? After you and he were finally going to get together…" Felicia and Sebastian had been heavily flirting with each other through all of high school, with Felicia doing most of the pursuing, if Gabriela remembered right. Then, after a particularly wild party the summer after graduation the two were rumored to have made out. But after that, Sebastian had ignored her.

"That was ten years ago." Felicia's voice was flat. It was clearly a sore subject even all these years later. So why did she want to go back to drink from that same well? Seemed like it had disaster written all over it, and Gabriela's *one* job was to make sure the wedding went smoothly. Lola didn't need some brewing drama between Felicia and Sebastian to worry about, either.

"Well, it does sound like maybe Sebastian's a bad choice," Veronica said. "And we want things to go smoothly for Lola." She leaned in and gave Lola a one-armed hug.

"Yeah," Liv agreed, nodding, her blue-tipped blond hair rippling. She'd dyed it blue for *something blue* in the wedding party.

"I guess so." Felicia shrugged. "And I like James anyway." She glanced sideways at her sister, but thankfully Liv didn't rise to the bait.

"Okay, so then we all agree?" Gabriela felt a little bit of relief. She raised her glass. "To none of us going near Swipe Left tonight."

They all raised their glasses and clinked them together, and Gabriela breathed a little sigh of relief. The last thing anybody needed was for someone to hook up with Swipe Left and then have the whole wedding party sidetracked with drama.

Lola took a sip of her quickly vanishing margarita. "Seriously, though, Sebastian isn't the same jerk from high school. You should actually have a conversation with him. See what I mean."

Gabriela scoffed. No way was she talking to Sebastian Lott. She'd long since gotten over her girl crush on the guy. No need to revisit those painful days when she'd be frozen by her locker and he'd come bounding up to his, three down from hers, with a caravan of hangers-on following his every move.

"Oh, lord. Is that a cheese plate the bartender just put out? I freaking love cheese," Veronica exclaimed, glancing at the small snack nook near the end of the bar. "Lola, come on, honey, let's go get fortified. Come with me, I can't be the only one pigging out. Did I mention I love cruises? Seriously. Love them!"

"You know she's getting married in two days," Gabriela felt the need to point out. The last thing she was probably thinking about was consuming dairy fat.

"All the more reason for her to keep up her strength." Veronica tugged Lola off her bar stool and the two snuck over to see about the cheese bar.

"I'll be right back," Lola promised, leaving Gabriela with her least favorite people at the bachelorette party. Gabriela would've headed over, as well, but Liv grabbed her arm.

"You're right about Swipe Left," she said. "Thanks for reminding us."

Felicia even reluctantly nodded.

Gabriela felt perhaps a temporary truce might have been struck.

"Okay, I get it. I *get* it. No Swipe Left." Felicia shrugged, adjusting her strapless bra. The top of a tattoo at her neckline became visible for the briefest of seconds and then disappeared behind the spandex fabric. Gabriela thought she saw the head of a running stick figure. Really, Felicia? She'd just started running 5Ks a few months ago and now she suddenly got herself tattooed?

"The worst part is that I heard he's *seriously* hung," Felicia said.

Gabriela seriously did not want to know this information. She really didn't. Why were they still talking?

Felicia, however, could not read a room. "One girl told me she didn't even know they *came* that big. Like an *actual* eggplant," she whispered.

"Guess that's where the emoji came from," Liv said and barked a laugh.

"Do I really need to know this?" Gabriela protested.

"Yes, Liv, consider poor Gobstopper. You know she hates being *explicit*," Felicia teased and the two sisters burst into laughter at Gabriela's expense.

Gabriela was half tempted to confess a few of her exploits in New York. But she wouldn't. Not to these gossips. She mentioned word one and then the whole ship would know about her sexual exploits.

"Ugh, all this talk about cock makes me want some," Felicia declared, slamming her margarita glass on the bar as some of it sloshed over the rim.

Classy. Gabriela sipped at her malbec, wishing this night would come to an end.

"What are we going to do about this lame-ass party?" Liv moaned. "I'm bored."

Lame? This party was *not* lame, and Gabriela had a clipboard to prove it. A clipboard full of *activities*. Granted, they'd only gotten through the shots part so far, but they were warming up to the rest, like Friendivia. Trivia all about the roots of Lola's friendship with each bridesmaid. Gabriela had read about it online.

"We could play a trivia game. I made up one just for Lola," Gabriela began, searching for her clipboard. She had all the questions mapped out and party prizes for bridesmaids who got the right answer.

"Trivia? No way." Felicia frowned. Then she seemed to get inspired. "I know! Why don't we go crash the bachelor party?"

Liv squealed in delight, clapping her hands together. "Yes! Yes! *Yes!*"

Oh, no, no...*no!* Gabriela couldn't think of a worse idea. For one, they were supposed to have separate parties, and she'd made sure through a detailed schedule on her clipboard that they'd all be headed to different bars at different times to avoid crossing paths. Now Felicia was going to ditch all her hard work!

"No, we can't," Gabriela said. "We promised we'd stay in separate bars."

"Who promised? *I* didn't promise." Felicia smirked at Gabriela.

Gabriela thought the idea had disaster written all over it. "Seriously. What if they've got strippers there?"

"On a cruise ship?" Liv looked doubtful. "Besides, I bet Lola wants to go. Lola!" Liv raised her voice.

Lola turned after having a bite of cheese. Veronica was already stacking her plate high with tiny cubes.

"Do you want to go crash the boys' party?"

Felicia skipped over and Lola's face lit up. Pretty soon, the two were jumping up and down and squealing in delight.

"Of course she does!" Felicia called as she tucked her arm through Lola's and led her out of the bar.

"But I don't think…" Gabriela protested one last time.

"What the bride wants, the bride gets," Liv said and pushed past Gabriela on her way to the cruise ship elevators.

Gabriela shook her head. She had a bad feeling about this. A very bad feeling.

CHAPTER TWO

UP ON DECK TEN, Sebastian was desperately trying to liven up what he could only call the world's tamest bachelor party. They'd taken over the small whiskey bar on Deck Ten, with the ornate, old-fashioned, carved wooden wraparound bar, and had staked out the corner table surrounded by oversize leather chairs. The men sat in a semicircle: the groom, Marco; his brother, James; and Marco's cousin Bill, who were about as lively as a stick in the eye. The only lively attendee so far was Lola's brother, Theo, whom Sebastian had known since first grade.

So far, the men had only barely sipped at their expensive whiskeys and the most exciting conversation revolved around who took which expressway to work every morning. *Boring.*

Sebastian had to think of something to put this party back on track and fast. He was determined to make this bachelor party *the very best party of a lifetime.* If his best friend was saying goodbye to singlehood, something Sebastian himself thought was darn near close to social suicide, then he was determined to send him off with a bang. First, he needed to get these guys to drink.

Sebastian raised his glass high for a toast. "To you, Marco. Tonight is almost your last night—technically— as a single man. You crazy fool!" The others laughed a bit, but he continued. "I know that Lola is going to make you a very happy man. And no one deserves it more than you."

Sebastian meant every word. He'd known Marco since law school, where the two happened to sit next to each other in Constitutional Law. But their friendship had deepened when Marco had helped him bury his mother after she lost her battle with liver cancer. That was a sorrowful memory, but Sebastian would always be grateful to Marco for being there.

"Hear, hear," James echoed.

"Let's get this party started," cried Theo.

They all clinked glasses and took a swig. "By the way, when is it going to be your turn, Sebastian? Isn't this the fifth wedding this year you've gone to?" Marco asked.

"The answer is never," Theo interrupted. "This guy? He's not the settling-down type."

"That's not true," scoffed Sebastian. And lately he'd been thinking more and more about settling down. Sure, *marriage* sounded like pure insanity to him: one woman for the rest of his life? What was he, dead inside? Or he would be if he ever put on a ring. But, lately, he was thinking more about a woman who might be able to keep his interest for more than a week or month at a time. Lately, his parade of partners on the dating hookup app Spark was all about the quick physical connection. He couldn't actually remember the last time he'd had a decent conversation with one of them. Then again, that's not why they came over to his house at midnight, either.

"You like to play the field, huh?" Bill leaned forward and grinned, his wedding band catching the meager light. "Tell me about it."

Bill was the last person Sebastian wanted to confide in.

"He was the first guy with a dating app account in law school," Marco agreed. "He *cleaned up.*"

"He's got *game.*" Theo grinned and elbowed Sebastian hard. Sebastian mustered up a weak smile. Sure, he had to admit, it was fun hooking up with random women who weren't looking for commitment, but these days, he wanted to *take a girl out* for once, maybe even learn a single detail about her other than what position she liked best. Maybe he was getting old, or maybe he was just tired of the revolving door of his own bedroom. He wanted something *more.* Marco had showed him exactly what he wanted, actually—real companionship. Someone to talk to. Someone to care for him when he was sick. Somebody who'd just care about him *period* after the fury of the one-night stand wore off.

"Yeah, but I'm not into that now." Sebastian shrugged and stared at his glass of whiskey.

"You want to get married?" Theo asked, shocked.

"Hey, I don't know. Maybe." What was he saying? Was he really ready to shelve his riding spurs for life? Strap himself to one woman for all time? He didn't know. All he did know was that for the very first time in his life, he'd actually consider the possibility.

"Oh, please." Marco didn't believe him. Of course, Sebastian didn't blame him. Why would a player suddenly have a change of heart? Because the player was almost thirty, that's why, and realized that he'd built a life and had no one to share it with. In fact, most of the men here were married or engaged. James and Sebastian were the only fully single partygoers. "You once dated three girls *in one weekend*."

"Well, be careful," Bill said. "You know how many STDs are out there? Some of them *aren't* pretty."

Who talked about STDs at a bachelor party? Geez.

"Sounds like you know a bit too much about that, Bill," Sebastian joked. But when the man turned bright red, Sebastian realized that Bill might actually have had a few experiences at the local health clinic.

"You get in trouble, Bill?" Theo echoed.

"I'm married now," Bill said, as if that answered anything. It didn't.

The men all stared at Bill. Now they were all thinking about Bill's *issues*. How had this party got so far off track? Next they'd be asking about where his rash might be.

What this party needed was a drinking game. Sebastian knew he sure needed another drink.

"How about we play a game of Never Have I Ever?" Sebastian offered.

"Yes, let's," Theo said, leaning forward.

"Remember first year of law school?" Marco slapped the table, causing his whiskey to slosh in his glass. Beneath their feet, the boat swayed slightly, the only indication they were out to sea. "You *killed* with this drinking game."

"You *binge drank* in law school?" Bill shook his head in disapproval.

Sebastian glanced at the man's pressed khakis, super-starched, pin-striped, short-sleeved, collared shirt and wingtips. Who wore *wingtips* on a cruise ship? Hell, who wore them to a bachelor party? Sebastian had opted for a tasteful Aloha shirt and flip-flops. They were headed to Cozumel and then to Key West. Nowhere in that itinerary did wingtips factor in.

"Hell, I binge drink now," Sebastian joked. *Or I will soon if this party doesn't get going.* "Come on, one round?"

"Let's do it," James said, his dark eyes lighting up a bit.

"How do we play?" Bill asked. Of course Bill wouldn't know how. He'd probably drunk wine spritzers in college. Sebastian glanced at the wingtips again. Hell, he probably drank wine spritzers now. It would explain why he'd barely touched his whiskey on the rocks.

"Everyone takes turns declaring 'never have I ever' something. If it's true for you, you drink. If not, you don't drink. Those aren't the regular rules, but it's more fun this way."

"Sounds a little silly," said Bill.

"Let's just try it." Sebastian raised his glass. "I'll go first."

"But *never* is such a strong word. I mean, does this

include all future acts, as well?" Bill asked, clearly overly concerned about the legalities of a drinking game. "Also, what if a participant lies? How will we *know*?"

Sebastian stared at the man wearing Argyle socks in the tropics. God, if there was a vampire of fun, Bill would be it. Did the guy have to be so literal? Theo frowned and shook his head, as well. At least Theo got it. The two men exchanged a what's-with-this-dude look. He guessed it just went to prove you didn't choose family.

"Well, nobody's taking an oath to tell the truth, so the only way we'll know if you're lying is if we just call you on it," Marco explained.

"Fine." Bill shook his head in disgust.

"Let's just play. Here." Sebastian put down his drink. "Okay, never have I ever..." He tried to think of something fun. "Never have I ever run down the French Quarter naked."

The other men laughed. Sebastian lifted his whiskey and took a deep drink. He noticed Marco and James did the same, while Bill barely sipped at his. This was going to be one hell of a looong night at this rate. Sebastian bowed his head.

"Okay, okay, I have one." Theo raised his glass. "Never have I ever gone more than six months as an adult without sex."

Theo tipped his glass back. James and Sebastian both drank, but Bill failed to lift his glass.

"Are you serious?" Theo glanced at Marco, surprised.

Both Marco and Bill shrugged. "Hey, anyone can have a drought," Marco said.

"Well, I haven't had sex with my wife since the first year I got married," Bill admitted. Sebastian's mouth fell open. "Just telling you, bud, things change when you get married."

"No, they don't." Sebastian wanted to derail this conversation pronto. While marriage might kill a man's sex life, the last thing he wanted was for Marco to start thinking matrimony meant never having sex again. "Lola isn't like that. She's mad for you. I don't think you'll be like…" *Wingtip Bill, who seems to be walking birth control.*

"Sebastian defending *marriage*? Never thought I'd see the day. What? You'll be getting married next!" Theo exclaimed.

"If I find my person, you bet I will." Sebastian was surprised by his own forcefulness. Since when was he so open to the idea of marriage? Or was he just playing the part for Marco? Keeping the man's spirits up? *Hey, I'm just walking the man to the guillotine here, trying to remind him things don't look so bad.*

"Really? And how are you going to find your person sleeping with everyone?" James asked.

Sebastian stared at his glass and frowned. "Hey, how do I know unless I try them all?" The other men at the table chuckled at the joke.

"If you're really serious about this," Marco said, "you'll get serious about dating."

Was Sebastian serious? He could be, he reasoned.

"There's no way this conversation is even happening," Theo said, shaking his head. "Come on, get serious. *I've* had longer relationships with yogurt in my fridge than this guy's had his whole life."

"Not true." Sebastian was getting a bit defensive. "Besides, what does that have to do with finding the one?"

"You can't find Mrs. Right if your bed is crowded with Ms. Right Nows," Marco pointed out. "I'd been hookup free for a full month before I met Lola. It was nice not to have all that other noise when we started dating. I didn't have to keep my phone away from her or worry about awkward run-ins with dating-app hookups."

"You're going to ask *Sebastian* to be celibate for a whole month? Not possible." Theo shook his head so vigorously, he sloshed a little whiskey out of his glass. "Heck, even a *week* would be too much. Or weekend!"

"I could be celibate for a weekend," Sebastian protested. Of course, come to think of it, he hadn't been celibate for a whole weekend in a long, long time. But so what? He could do it anytime he wanted. All he had to do was shut off his Spark profile. "I'll bet I can be celibate this entire cruise."

Marco and Theo laughed. "We're stuck on a boat, so that feels like cheating."

"Stuck on a boat with thousands of attractive women. Uh-huh. Not exactly so easy," Theo offered.

"Look, I'm not a sex addict," Sebastian maintained, wondering why on earth he had to defend himself for getting some often and just the way he liked. "But what do I get if I do it? What's the wager?"

"Bragging rights?" Marco offered.

"Why would I brag about *not* getting any?" Sebastian joked. Somehow he'd dropped out of this reality and into a dimension where men had seemingly lost all their hunting instincts.

"Fine, then, a nice bottle of bourbon," Marco said.

"Hardly enough for a weekend of blue balls," Sebastian said.

"What? You not man enough to take it?" Theo nudged Sebastian with a sharp elbow.

"Oh, I'll show you what kind of man I am." Sebastian flashed a wicked smile. "Give me five minutes alone."

Theo laughed. "I don't need my ass kicked today, thanks very much. You win."

Marco raised his glass. "To Sebastian, and his vow of weekend celibacy."

"We're seriously going to toast celibacy at a bachelor party?" Theo asked, quirking an eyebrow. "Besides, he's never going to last the weekend."

"I could last the weekend," Bill offered.

"Your wife isn't even here, Bill," James pointed out.

Sebastian cleared his throat. "Okay, you nut jobs. Here's to celibacy." He lifted his glass reluctantly as he glanced around the table.

"Your celibacy, not mine," Marco joked, and the men laughed and clinked glasses.

Just then a shrill cackle of voices hit them like a wall of noise. Sebastian turned in time to see their man cave whiskey bar being invaded by…bridesmaids… and the bride.

What the…?

"Baby!" cried Lola as she ran into Marco's open arms. "Is it okay that we dropped in?"

"Is it okay? It's more than okay," Marco said and clearly meant it. He swept her up and gave her a fierce kiss, worthy of a chick flick. Lola gave the kiss her all, as well, wrapping her finely manicured hands in his thick, brown hair. Sebastian felt a twinge of envy then. Their love was the real deal. Anyone could see that.

Sebastian glanced at the bridesmaids, the first time he'd seen them since boarding the ship that afternoon, and recognized Felicia, who'd seemed to have had a rough ten years since high school. Why did she look ten years older than the rest of them? Somehow she'd etched crow's feet into her crow's feet. Her sister, Liv, looked exactly the same, except for the blue streaks in her hair.

Felicia and Liv saw him and frowned. It looked like they weren't going to let bygones be bygones. This was going to be awkward. Granted, he'd not exactly been the most sensitive guy in high school, but then what guy was at sixteen? Of course, this would make his vow of weekend celibacy that much easier to keep. They beelined for James, Marco's brother, practically ignoring Sebastian. He supposed he deserved that.

Veronica came in next and gave him a happy little wave. Well, at least there was Veronica. She was nice to everyone. It was a good thing, because Sebastian knew he would have his hands full this weekend. He'd known coming back to his hometown would mean swimming with his exes, who were more unpredictable than sharks. But he'd do anything for Marco. His best friend. Hell, he'd introduced him to Lola, and watched as the two had fallen madly in love. Marco deserved that kind of happily-ever-after, though.

He glanced up and saw a striking woman in a flowing, halter-top jumpsuit. Who was this beauty? She looked vaguely familiar and yet he couldn't quite place the face. Was this a new friend? Somehow outside the high school circle? *No...wait a minute. Wait a damn minute. That's...Gabriela Cruz.* He was sure of it. She was the only other bridesmaid it could be. Yet…how?

He racked his brain. Gabriela Cruz, the shy, nerdy and very smart salutatorian at their school. She'd always gotten As, always known all the answers. But he never, ever, remembered her having a body like that. The flowy jumpsuit hinted at her ample curves and the halter top seemed to be holding itself up. Her skin was amazing, too, and those dark, smoky eyes. Oh, mama. He'd remembered a wiry girl with braces. But she was all grown up now.

Sebastian finished his drink, put it down on the table and stood. Looked like they had some catching up to do.

CHAPTER THREE

GABRIELA TRIED NOT to panic. Sebastian Lott was coming her way. Surely that was a mistake. No way the golden boy of high school with those amazing hazel eyes meant to pay her any attention.

Stay calm, Gabriela. She held her clipboard like a shield. *Just stay still and he'll pass on by, just like he did in high school.*

"Hello." Sebastian almost sounded tentative. She glanced up so quickly she almost gave herself whiplash. His hazel, not quite green, not quite blue eyes, focused on her. Gabriela froze for a nanosecond, feeling like the awkward girl of high school burdened with glasses and braces her sophomore year, the one boys like Sebastian Lott looked right through. Except he wasn't looking through her this time. He was looking right at her. Intently. On purpose.

"Uh...hi." She smiled, feeling the awkwardness bubbling up in her. Why did the man look so good? The ten years since high school had been very kind to him. He'd always been striking, but now he was even more...manly somehow. More grown-up. The just barely there hint of stubble on his squared-off chin made her want to put her hands on his face. Feel the roughness beneath her fingers.

Snap out of it, Gabriela. Geez. *This isn't high school. You're not boy crazy. This is* Sebastian Lott. *The last guy on earth you should even consider touching.*

"Gabriela...right?"

"Uh, yeah."

"You look good enough to eat. I just wanted to tell you that."

"R-really?" Her reply came out as a squeak. Was Sebastian Lott, the guy who'd never given her a second glance in high school, calling her gorgeous?

"Can I buy you a drink?"

"Oh, I don't know." She hesitated. She was still clutching her clipboard, still hoping she could convince the other bridesmaids to leave. "We shouldn't be here that long. Sorry about crashing the bachelor party. I tried to convince them..."

"Don't worry about it." Sebastian smiled, a gleaming, white, toothpaste-ad-ready smile, and Gabriela felt her insides melt a little. The charisma was real. She could feel his charm washing over her in waves. No wonder so many women fell for Lott. All you had to do was get lost in those warm hazel eyes, that deep baritone voice. *Stop it, Gabbie. He's trouble and you know it.* Hadn't she just convinced Felicia to avoid him?

"I'm glad you're here," he murmured.

She felt the words in her toes. Sebastian Lott was glad to see her. Her heart sped up a little. Could it be that maybe she'd been wrong all these years she'd assumed Lott thought she was invisible? Could it be possible that even during her awkward high school days of glasses and braces, that somehow he'd seen her? All those years she thought her school-girl crush was unrequited, could it be that he had feelings for her, too? But why would she care? He was toxic, she reminded herself again. Completely and utterly toxic.

"Uh…" Gabriela felt all her college vocabulary leave her head. She was a successful CPA, but now she felt like a stammering, no-social-skills teenager all over again. She inwardly shook herself. Come on, she wasn't an awkward teenager anymore. She was a successful woman who had men pinging her dating app every weekend. Sometimes more than once. So what if her first serious crush of all time was finally, after a decade, paying attention to her? She could handle this.

"Let me buy you a drink." Sebastian waved to the bartender, who nodded as he finished the round of drinks he was pouring for Felicia and Liv. "What does the lady want?"

Sebastian raised his eyebrows, his attention like a beam of warm sunshine. Suddenly, Gabriela felt hot. Sweat broke out on the small of her back. What was wrong with her? He was just a man and yet she felt so flustered, he might as well have been a celebrity. Then again, she reminded herself, he was a celebrity at Culver High.

"Vodka soda," she managed to say.

He nodded swiftly and proceeded to order her cocktail with the most expensive vodka offered on the menu. He ordered himself a whiskey on the rocks. As the bartender put the two drinks down in front of them, Gabriela glanced up to find Felicia staring at them, frowning. She'd noticed Sebastian paying her attention.

"So, what are you doing with a clipboard at a party?" Sebastian nodded at it, resting on the bar.

"I just like to be organized," Gabriela said. "Someone has to keep the party on track."

"Not too spontaneous, are you?" Sebastian's eyebrows shot up. "Let me guess. You sort your underwear drawer by color?"

Gabriela felt heat rise in her cheeks. Actually, as it turned out, she was exactly one of those women. Not that she'd ever let him know that.

"You are!" Sebastian laughed. "So, how about you show me that drawer sometime?" He laughed a little, to show her that he understood how cheesy that line was. That was the charm of Sebastian Lott. He was an unapologetic player, but he also knew it.

"You think I'm going to invite you over to look at my underwear drawer?"

"I was hoping you'd model some underwear for me." He grinned.

"Has that line worked on any woman ever?" Gabriela cocked her head to one side, dubious.

"Not yet. But there's always a first time." The man's ego and confidence were out of control and, Gabriela noted, somehow all that swagger worked. He seemed to know his lines were cheesy but he didn't care. That was the amazing part. But then again, Gabriela was sure the man could pick up a woman reading a Chinese take-out menu.

Felicia and Liv had sidled over to their side of the bar. "What are you doing, Lott?" Felicia barked, not even bothering to hide her derision.

"It's nice to see you, too, Felicia," Sebastian said, barely giving Felicia a glance before focusing his attention right back on Gabriela. "If you must know, I'm having a drink with a beautiful woman."

Gabriela felt the tops of her ears burn. At least her hair covered them, she thought. Beautiful...really?

"Beautiful?" scoffed Liv.

"You can't be serious," Felicia said.

Now it was Gabriela's turn to be offended. She might have been awkward in high school, but she'd grown into her forehead, and had long since had the braces off. She knew she wasn't a runway model, but she felt she could hold her own. The guys in New York weren't complaining.

"Jealous?" Sebastian asked Felicia, whose mouth fell open.

"Me? No way. She can have you."

"Well, Felicia, that's indeed her decision to make. So, if you'll excuse us," Sebastian said.

Gabriela felt a creeping unease. This was not the way to avoid drama at Lola's wedding. Gabriela knew Felicia still had a thing for Sebastian and the very last thing she wanted to do was to create some kind of odd-ball love triangle. *I'm not interested*, she told herself even as she caught a glance at his strong, bare forearm. *He's toxic, remember? Keep it together, Gabriela.*

"Excuse *you*?" Felicia's mouth dropped open.

"Actually, no, I…" Gabriela was going to come up with an excuse, something to get her out of Felicia's line of fire. *Seriously, I am not trying to make you jealous.*

"Why don't you just butt out, Felicia? Gabbie and I are talking here."

Gabbie? Nobody except her New York friends called her Gabbie. Did he know one of them?

"Why'd you call me that?" she asked, suddenly suspicious.

"I think the name fits." He smiled. Wow, but he was a whole hell of a lot nicer than she remembered. Was he always this nice? Or was he just this nice to *her* because she was the only available single person here who didn't outwardly hate him?

"Why are you being nice to her?" Felicia asked.

Gabriela wanted to ask the same thing.

"Why *not* be nice?"

God, the man was just all sex. Everything he said sounded like an innuendo somehow. Gabriela felt her pulse tick up a notch. Was it getting hot in here? She fanned her face.

"Why not? This is why." Felicia grabbed her phone. "I've got access to the yearbook online. Let me pull up her picture…"

"No!" Gabriela shouted, louder than she intended. "Felicia, don't do that." She lunged for the phone, but Felicia skipped out of her way. The last thing Gabriela needed was for her to dredge up her horrible high school yearbook photo. One eye was half-closed and she was wearing a full set of braces. When would Felicia finally stop sabotaging her? Seemed like the answer was never. "Felicia, don't show him—"

"Here it is!" Felicia cried, triumphant, holding up her phone for Sebastian to see. He glanced at the picture and then at Gabriela, who could feel her face burning. He studied the photo a bit, but said nothing. He didn't point and laugh. Didn't tell her how ugly she'd been ten years ago, either. For that, she was grateful.

"Look at her!" Felicia said, tapping her phone. "That hair! Those braces."

"I wasn't that bad," Gabriela protested. She knew she'd been nothing special in high school, but now it was a point of pride. She hadn't been an ogre in high school. Sure, she was more manicured now, more put together, and she wore makeup now and she'd learned how to wax her eyebrows, but still.

"I think you're kind of dorky adorable, actually. Look at those pretty brown eyes." He seemed entirely serious. Could he be?

"Are you kidding me?" Felicia looked like she might explode at any moment. Not good.

"She's got a great smile," he added.

"The braces?" Felicia barked.

"The dimples," he corrected.

Felicia let out an exasperated-sounding sigh.

Rival feelings fought in her heart. Gabriela was glad Sebastian had finally noticed her yet felt ashamed for *liking* the attention. Why did she care? Why did she want him to notice her at all? Hadn't she felt at some level him ignoring her was a blessing in disguise?

He grinned at her now, eyes almost teasing and she felt her brain buzz with the attention. *Don't get sucked in by the nice-guy routine. You get close enough, he bites. You know he does.* She had a flash of a memory, a mortifying memory, standing by his locker.

"Well, thanks? I think?" Gabriela snuck a look at Felicia, who stewed in her jealousy. Not ideal. She felt color rush to her face and turned away, looking for Lola. Best thing to do was leave, and let Felicia have Sebastian. Lola was sitting in a tiny booth with Marco across the room. She'd have to go break up the love-birds.

"Gabriela, wait." Sebastian reached out and touched her arm. His hand felt warm there. "Where are you going?"

"Let her go," Felicia demanded. "We'll have more fun without her."

She and Liv cackled with laughter then. Gabriela thought she was long done with getting kicked around by them, but part of her felt like that awkward fourteen-year-old again.

Gabriela put down her drink and snatched her clipboard off the bar. She walked to Lola, even as behind her, Felicia and Liv closed the gap, pinning Sebastian against the bar. Good, she thought. Less for her to have to deal with.

Lola saw her coming and a small frown line appeared between her eyebrows. "What's wrong?" she asked, pulling her attention away from her groom-to-be.

"Nothing," Gabriela said. "But, uh, maybe we should

go? We've got activities." Gabriela thumped the sheet on her clipboard.

"No! Don't go," Marco cried, throwing his arms around his bride in an exaggerated effort to keep her in place. "You just got here!"

"Yes, but it's your bachelor party. We're crashing it," Lola pointed out.

"I want you to crash it." Marco pulled her closer and nuzzled her neck. She giggled. "Stay longer!"

"But don't you need a guys' night?" Gabriela asked, hopeful. "It's tradition, right?"

"I don't care about tradition," Marco said. "I want to be with my bride." He hugged her closer and Gabriela's heart sank. Lola sent her a minuscule shrug that said, *what can I do?*

"What the groom wants, the groom gets," Sebastian said, appearing beside Gabriela.

Was he going to follow her around this party? In high school, she'd have to set herself on fire to get his attention, and now she couldn't get rid of him. What the hell? She hugged the clipboard closer to her chest and considered her escape, eyes darting to the two exits. Could she conceivably hide in the bathroom? God, that would be prom all over again. She cringed.

"Why not ditch the clipboard?" Sebastian asked, tapping the silver clip at the top. "You taking attendance? Keeping track of tequila shots?"

"Just trying to keep organized," Gabriela said. "How else am I going to keep the party on schedule?"

"There's a schedule?" Sebastian laughed.

"There *is* a schedule and this little excursion is ruining it." She hugged the clipboard tighter, hoping it would act as a shield against Sebastian's knowing eyes.

"I'd say if your party had a *schedule* then it was already ruined." Sebastian shook his head. "Good thing you guys came to us or this bachelorette party would be DOA."

"Excuse me?" Anger pulsed in her veins. Was he implying she *couldn't* throw a party? That she wasn't any fun? "We were having plenty of fun without you."

"Not as much fun as you'd have with us. Anyway, we're staying as long as the bride and groom want us to stay. It's *their* weekend, right?" Sebastian flicked a look toward the groom, who had his arm draped around Lola's shoulders. The two looked blissfully happy, and that *was* what this weekend was all about.

Suddenly the lights in the bar went dark and Gabriela heard a loud shriek from Felicia. What was happening? The bartender turned up a thumping bass and, before Gabriela could blink, two men and a woman suddenly appeared: all wearing hardly any clothes. Each of them jumped on top of a separate table and began dancing.

What on earth? Who organized this? Then, in a split second, as Gabriela glanced at Sebastian with a big grin on his face, she immediately knew. This was his doing.

CHAPTER FOUR

WELL, *THIS* IS A SURPRISE, Sebastian thought as he watched the two men and one woman dance together on top of three conjoined tables. Granted, he could do without the oiled-up men, but, hey, this technically wasn't his party. He glanced over and saw the other men from the bachelor party looking stunned. He doubted Bill had ever been to a party like this in his life. Or, hell, even a strip club. He didn't seem the adventurous type.

"That's it, put on a show!" cried Felicia as one of the men unbuttoned his shirt. In that moment he knew she'd done this. It had Felicia written all over it: from the excessive spray tans to the sparkling Speedos the men wore. Sebastian threw back his head and laughed as Felicia jumped up on the table next to the tall, blond stripper and began dancing right next to him. He'd considered bringing in strippers, but the cruise line had balked, and he hadn't wanted to cause trouble for Marco. Felicia, however, seemed to have somehow gotten around the rules—per usual.

"What do you think you're doing?" Gabriela demanded at his shoulder. "Get rid of these people right now before we get in trouble—"

"Me? Why do you think I hired them?" Sebastian studied her. He still absolutely could *not* get over how gorgeous she'd become. How on earth had he missed *this* beauty in high school? She had the most adorable heart-shaped face and warm brown eyes. Had she always had such amazing skin? he wondered. Like toasted caramel. He had the sudden urge to run his fingers down the nape of her exposed neck. Find out if it was as soft as it looked.

"Of course you brought them here. I want you to get rid of them."

"Look, if *I* had hired them, they wouldn't be keeping their swimsuits on," he said, nodding at the dancers. "*And* there'd be more women up there. Not that I have an issue with men—everyone has their thing— but *my* thing is not men. Also, I'm not the one groping them right now."

He flicked a finger toward the dancers and Gabriela's eyes widened in new understanding as she saw Felicia shimmying next to one of the shirtless men.

Gabriela let out an exhausting sounding sigh. "Felicia."

"Exactly." Sebastian glanced at Gabriela's nearly empty glass. "Want another?"

"I want these strippers out of here. The cruise ship has rules." Gabriela gripped her clipboard tighter. She was clearly still a person who hated rule breakers.

He still couldn't believe this was *Gabriela Cruz*. She'd been the one at parties who was always telling them to stop drinking so much, to keep the music down. She'd been an awkward braces-wearing girl from what he remembered. Smart, too, but not on his radar in terms of a girl he wanted to date. Did that make him a bad person? No, he decided. Just short-sighted. Goodness but she had an amazing ass. When had that appeared? Had it been there all along? He barely remembered Gabriela Cruz, but if she'd looked like *this* in high school, he would've made it his business to remember.

Of course, he'd just gone and insulted her clipboard. He'd have to work doubly hard now.

But if he thought about it, Gabriela was exactly the kind of woman he'd want to settle down with: whip-smart, opinionated and not afraid to speak her mind. Not that he'd really pursue anything this trip. He did bet Marco he'd be celibate.

He glanced at Gabriela.

"I don't think the bartender cares about the rules," Sebastian said, nodding toward the man behind the bar who was clapping and enjoying himself. Sebastian noticed, too, that the busboys had closed the bar doors and had most likely placed a private party sign outside. Felicia had paid them all off, clearly.

"I care about the rules."

"I seem to remember that," Sebastian said.

"Really?" Gabriela's dark eyes flashed with doubt. God, the flush of those perfect cheeks. He almost wanted to keep pushing her buttons.

"How could I forget you yelling at me to put pants on when we were *skinny dipping* in Felicia's pool?"

"That wasn't Felicia's pool. That was her neighbor's pool, and I was trying to make sure nobody got arrested." Gabriela lifted her chin in defiance.

"We weren't arrested."

"Because *I* got us out of there before the neighbors got home!" Gabriela glared at him. Felicia was now grinding against the blond dancer on top of the table. Gabriela glanced over and groaned. "I've got to stop this before somebody gets hurt."

"Felicia has a pretty solid hold on the dancer, so it might be too late." Sebastian sipped his drink and watched as Gabriela ignored him and marched up to the dancers balancing precariously on the tops of the tables.

"Felicia!" she called, clapping her hands like a middle school gym teacher. "Come on. Get down."

Felicia ignored her, putting her hands on the man's now-bare shoulders. He grabbed her lower back and the two of them put the dirty in dirty dancing. Sebastian had to bark a laugh. Felicia might not be the kindest woman but the girl knew how to party.

"Seriously, guys! Come on. We're going to get kicked out."

"Of the cruise ship?" Liv said doubtfully. "Come on. Let them dance."

The other male dancer and the female dancer then jumped down off the table and moved over to the bride and groom. Lola's eyes grew wide as the male dancer, whose ample chest muscles shone with a thick layer of oil, took her hand and led her around in a little waltz. The female dancer, tall and thin with strawberry-blond hair, grabbed Marco's hand and all four of them danced together in a little circle.

Gabriela noticed the couple seemed to be having a good time, but soon enough, as the music switched to a new song, one with a slower beat, the groom and bride disengaged from the dancers and found each other once more.

That was true love, Sebastian thought. Everyone in the room could tell the couple only had eyes for one another. *That's what I want.* The desire rose up in him, surprisingly strong. *That's exactly what's missing from my life. A partner I can truly share it with. Or, hell, a woman who'd hold more than a five-minute conversation with me.*

He glanced at Gabriela, who was still trying in vain to get Felicia off that table. Hell, that was not happening now that Felicia had found her spotlight. If it was one thing she hated, it was sharing attention.

Gabriela had abandoned her vodka soda on the bar, Sebastian noticed. Well, the least he could do was take it to her. Judging by the scene unfolding before them, she'd need a stiff drink and soon.

"Felicia! *Get down.*" Gabriela stomped her foot on the carpeted floor of the bar. Felicia was now making out with the dancer in full view of everyone. Nice touch.

"Seriously, Gab. Come on. Ignore them. Have this drink." Sebastian tried to hand her the vodka soda she'd abandoned.

"I'm not going to let this party get so far out of hand," she snapped.

"You mean, you're not going to let people *have fun*?" Sebastian said dryly.

"Fun isn't grinding on strangers on a tabletop." Gabriela's dark eyes were fire and ice all at once. He wondered if she were as passionate in the bedroom as she was about enforcing party rules. She'd probably make a hell of a dominatrix.

"It isn't?"

"You're impossible," Gabriela cried, looking like she was about to pull her hair out. Sebastian wondered what her thick hair would feel like in his hands.

"And you haven't had enough to drink." He rattled her glass and the ice cubes clinked together.

Gabriela glanced at the drink. "Fine," she growled and swiped it out of his hand, sloshing a bit onto the carpet. She downed it in one big gulp and slammed the glass on the countertop, unfazed.

Holy hell that was sexy.

When did she learn to drink like that? And, look, the drink wasn't affecting her at all. Could she actually keep up with him?

He glanced up and noticed that Felicia was sticking her hands down the front of the dancer's Speedo.

Whoa. Okay, that was off bounds. Sebastian had to admit it was getting a little hot. Probably too hot for this audience. Bill, for one, was about to have an aneurysm. His eyes were so wide they seemed about to pop out of his head. Sebastian didn't know if he disapproved of Felicia's antics or very much approved of her short skirt. Veronica was staring, transfixed. The entire bar swayed slightly as the ocean liner cruised through the Atlantic, the low lights flickering across Felicia's face. Her eyes were already bloodshot. Too much tequila, Sebastian guessed.

She got even more aggressive with the dancer and Sebastian saw Lola notice the commotion from across the way and frown. Okay, maybe Gabriela was right. Maybe Felicia was hijacking the party. He couldn't have the bride upset, after all.

"Hey, Felicia," Sebastian called. "You might want to tone it down. Take him to your room if that's what you want to do, but we don't all need to see it."

Felicia broke free of her embrace with the dancer for a second. "Why? Jealous?"

"Hardly. But you're making a scene." Even the dancer seemed to agree, looking like a deer caught in headlights…or really, being caught with Felicia's hand down his underwear.

He glanced around the bar and everyone was looking at them, everyone except Gabriela, who had her nose in her glass at the bar, her back to Felicia.

"Rich, coming from you," Felicia snarled, but she released the dancer from her groping. "There? Happy now? I'll keep my hands up where you can see them."

"Look, Felicia, just stop before you get into real trouble. This is Lola and Marco's party, okay?"

"I'm not ruining any-sthing," Felicia slurred, swaying uncertainly on her feet. "You're ruining it."

"Ah, the whole 'I know you are, but what am I' defense. Okay, got me." Sebastian sighed. He hated dealing with women who'd had too much to drink, but it was a scene replayed a little too often lately, he thought.

"Let's go, though. Come on down off that table before you fall down." He offered a steadying hand.

"I'm not going to fall. You're going to fall." Felicia stumbled a little as she grabbed his hand and wobbled onto the chair and then the floor. But suddenly Felicia was gripping him. She felt like an octopus, and the more Sebastian tried to get away, the tighter she held him. He didn't want to throw the woman off him, but being gentle was becoming harder and harder as she wrapped her bony arms around him. The woman smelled like tequila and stale perfume. She grabbed his face and planted a huge kiss on him, right there in front of the entire party. He tasted margaritas and cigarettes as she unceremoniously thrust her tongue into his mouth. He almost gagged as he pushed her away.

That's when Sebastian glanced up to find Gabriela watching, disapproval stamped all over her face. And something more…disappointment?

CHAPTER FIVE

WELL, OF COURSE Sebastian was making out with Felicia in the middle of Lola's bachelorette party. This night was going from awful to unbearable. *It was day one of the cruise and this was where they'd landed.* She felt like she was right back in high school again, the "cool" kids doing their own thing, Gabriela forced to watch.

Felicia grabbed Sebastian by the hand and began dancing with him.

"Hey, you okay?" Lola was by her side, light blue eyes concerned as she held her elbow softly. Gabriela shimmied up on a bar stool, and Lola followed.

"What? Me? Fine." She could care less about who Sebastian lip-locked or danced with, right?

The music swelled again with some upbeat song and Felicia gyrated in front of Sebastian, making sure he focused on her hips. Why did Felicia always have to hog the spotlight? Why did she always have to make everything about her? It wasn't fair to anyone else here, most of all Lola.

Lola glanced at Gabriela a bit too long. "Hey, I know you didn't want her to get involved with Sebastian, but really, it's no big deal if they… I mean, *I* don't care… She's wild and single and…*free*. It's the time to have fun, you know? Before things change…" Lola let her sentence trail off as they watched Felicia twerk up against Sebastian. She studied her friend. "But it really does bother you, doesn't it?"

Gabriela shook her head yet somehow she knew it did. But she didn't want to think more about it. She wasn't that lovelorn girl who drew hearts around Sebastian's name on her notebook.

"You know, if you wanted to go jump on that fine man, I wouldn't stop you."

"You know I'd never do that… Not on your wedding weekend." Gabriela grimaced. "I don't like her making a scene. I think she's stealing the spotlight from you."

"I'm fine, though. Really. I don't mind sharing the spotlight." That much was true. Lola was the most generous person on the planet. She'd give you the sweater off her back if you needed it. Lola gave her friend a warm side-hug. "It's okay. I know you want to look after me, but I'm fine. I am!" She looked over at Marco, a slight frown creasing her brow. "You guys should have the time of your life. We're only young once. We only get one shot. Better use it before you settle down. Have all that fun, all that excitement."

Gabriela took a sip of her vodka soda.

"You don't really miss dating, do you?"

Lola hesitated then shrugged. She suddenly seemed a bit down.

"Are you okay?" Gabriela had known her friend forever. She knew her better than anyone.

"I think I'm getting a headache, is all. Maybe too much tequila." Lola shook her glass, now filled only with ice. Sebastian joined them then, a glisten of sweat on his brow. Somehow it only made the man look sexier, dammit. So did the flush of exertion.

"How did you manage to escape Felicia?" Lola teased Sebastian.

"I tossed some red meat doused in body spray out on the balcony and then ran."

Gabriela couldn't help it. She laughed. "Really? Seemed like you two were having quite a reunion. With your faces," Gabriela said dryly as she put her glass down on the bar.

"That was assault, pure and simple. I did *not* consent to that." The look of distaste that came across his features made the coil in Gabriela's stomach relax a bit.

"You didn't enjoy that?" Lola pressed.

"Do I *look* like I enjoyed it?" He wiped his mouth with the back of his hand and frowned.

Gabriela winced into her glass of ice.

"And, Gabriela, you were right. Felicia *is* out of control."

Gabriela turned, glancing at him over her shoulder. "You're admitting you were wrong?"

"No, I'm admitting you were right. I didn't say anything about *me* being wrong." He flashed a grin.

Lola laughed and playfully jabbed him in the ribs. "You're incorrigible. Have you seen my groom?" she asked, glancing around the bar.

"I think he's in the corner. Save him from his obnoxious cousin, Bill. *Please.*"

Lola nodded and headed that way.

Felicia let out a loud whooping holler as she twerked in front of one of the dancers and he pretended to spank her butt.

Gabriela let out a long, plaintive sigh. "How did she even get them on board?" she wondered out loud.

"I don't know, but she's clearly paid off the bartender," Sebastian said, nodding to the man behind the bar. He didn't seem at all concerned that three of his patrons were dancing around his establishment in their underwear or that Felicia, who didn't seem worried about having lost Sebastian as a dance partner, had moved tables and chairs to the side so there would be more room for dancing. He'd even set the lights to a lower setting and the music got louder.

"I'd better go break all that up," she said.

"What's your hurry, Gabriela Cruz? Why don't you come sit by me? Let's get caught up." He patted the bar stool next to him. She hesitated. Was she really thinking about staying?

Her phone dinged. A few times. Spark connections nearby. She was almost tempted to go find one of them. Quick, dirty sex in some stranger's cabin might just be what she needed to turn the page on this party. Make her feel like a whole woman again, not the insecure girl she'd been in high school.

What was she thinking? She'd shock the entire wedding party. Plus, Lola's parents were on board. They were almost like her own. What if Mrs. Diaz got wind of her antics? She'd call Gabriela's parents immediately.

Then again, she was a big girl now. No need to ask permission for what she wanted to do.

"You getting some better offers than this party?" Sebastian was glancing at her phone's screen.

"None of your business." Gabriela hid the phone against her leg.

"Was that a silver star? Next to your name?"

Gabriela felt her neck grow hot. "It might be."

He slapped the bar with gusto. "Holy shit." A sly smile crept across his face. "You're a platinum Spark dater. That takes some…work."

She knew it, too. That meant communicating with more than a hundred Sparkees. Not all of them ended up with her naked in their beds, but quite a few did.

Gabriela sent him a sidelong glance. "I'm sure you broke that record the first week you were online."

"Maybe." He chuckled deep in his throat and Gabriela almost felt the vibrations in hers.

"But I didn't know you had it in you." His hazel eyes glinted with something more. Respect, maybe?

"Literally," she said, and he burst out laughing. A big burst of a laugh.

"Well, Ms. Cruz…" He moved a little closer so their arms were touching. "What *else* don't I know about you?"

She looked up at him, feeling daring. "Everything," she murmured, voice low and throaty.

He shook his head, slowly, deliberately. "That is what I plan to remedy."

What was she doing flirting with this man? Gabriela wanted to mentally shake herself. Yet…it was fun.

A little bit dangerous. A little bit careless. Like stepping to the edge of a cliff high above a raging sea. He seemed to know it, as well, beckoning her to risk it all with a hint of a smile. *Come on in. Water's fine. It's the jump that'll get you.*

"What are you thinking about, Ms. Cruz?" he asked her.

"I'm trying to figure out if you're worth my time," she said evenly. He didn't seem the least bit put off. She could almost feel the confidence rolling off him like heat from the sun. How could a man be so sure of himself? But then again, she knew why. He'd practically been worshipped as a demigod since eighth grade.

"Oh, I'll make it worth it."

That sounded like a promise. Why did she find herself wanting to see if he could keep it?

He glanced at the dance floor, where Felicia and Liv and their half-clad partners were hogging the makeshift dance floor.

"You know, there's one way to make sure they don't take over this party," he said.

"Really? What's that?"

Sebastian slowly put down his drink and glanced at her, hazel eyes serious. "Let's steal their spotlight."

"How?"

He held out his hand. "Dance with me."

CHAPTER SIX

SEBASTIAN THOUGHT FOR a split second she might turn him down flat, but then he saw the spark of rebellion in her dark eyes. Gabriela liked flirting with him, his whole body told him that. The way she moved. The way she flicked her dark hair back off her shoulder. But he could tell she was also conflicted. Jealous? Maybe about Felicia kissing him? Or annoyed he was injecting life into the party? Either way, he'd find out.

"Okay, but this is just to get back at Felicia," she murmured, as if wanting him to know *she* wasn't doing it because she wanted to.

"Sure," he said. He didn't care why she chose to dance with him. She just wanted to feel her body move with his.

They drifted to the other dancers and started dancing to the beat of the up-tempo song. Gabriela moved with the ease of a cat. He couldn't stop staring at the sway of her hips, the silky fabric that clung to her curves, leaving very little to the imagination. She also had rhythm, not the jerky clumsiness that Felicia called dancing.

Sebastian watched Gabriela sway to the music. She held up her dark hair as she twisted her hips, hot and sultry. He watched the small tendrils of hair curl down the nape of her neck. She was by far the most beautiful woman in the room. He was mesmerized, unable to stop staring at her hips as she shut her eyes and lost herself in the dance. Sebastian had long believed that how a person danced predicted how they'd be in bed. The way Gabriela was swinging her hips right now told him she'd be amazing and his groin instantly tightened with need. *Down, boy*, he told himself. *You're supposed to be on the wagon.*

He took her hand and she let him as he spun her to the music. She laughed, the fabric of her jumpsuit clinging to her as she twirled.

Then the song changed and the tempo slowed down.

Sebastian reached out, took Gabriela's hand and whirled her straight back into his arms for a little slow salsa, his feet guiding hers as he kept her pressed closely to his body. He could almost feel her heart beat, they were so close together. They moved so well, so perfectly, her body against his. The sex would be incredible, that's what he knew. He pulled away enough so their eyes met and, in that instant, he knew she felt the electric connection between them. Their bond went far deeper than the surface; it was primal, animalistic. He knew she felt it, could feel it in the heat of their palms pressed together.

They were going to have sex tonight.

He knew it, even if she didn't yet. It felt destined, an animal magnetism this strong shouldn't be denied.

"You're a good dancer," Gabriela said, her dark eyes on his. She seemed surprised.

"My mother was a ballroom dancer," Sebastian said. He was struck by a memory then. "She used to teach me in our kitchen. Sometimes really late, when she came home from the jobs she worked."

"She worked nights?" Gabriela asked, surprised. "What about your dad?"

"He left us when I was two."

"Oh." Gabriela's face fell a bit. "I'm sorry."

"It's okay. We were a team, Mom and I." He smiled sadly, remembering the fierce woman who'd had no quit in her. She'd never faced a challenge she couldn't overcome. Until she'd gotten cancer.

He rarely talked about his mom because the grief still seemed fresh even though she'd passed three years ago. But Gabriela made him want to share.

"She sounds like an amazing lady," she admitted.

"She was." Before he could talk more about his mom, Felicia and her buff, shirtless dancer bumped into them.

"Hey, watch it," Sebastian cautioned even as Felicia laughed and bounded away. The shirtless man changed tack and headed for Marco and Lola. Sebastian watched as he gyrated between the bride and groom and then tried to steal Lola with a clumsy grab that looked like he cupped her rear. Lola squealed in distress as she scurried away from his hands.

"Hey, stop it," Marco said, holding his ground and pulling Lola back into his arms. "This is my bride."

"Just want to have a little fun," the dancer said. "Isn't this a bachelorette party?"

"Oh, no," Gabriela murmured, stepped back from Sebastian. He didn't hesitate. He flew across the room, clapping the dancer on the shoulder and steering him away from the groom.

"How about we talk about the end of your routine," Sebastian said, moving the man back from Marco and Lola.

"What do you mean? I'm supposed to be on for at least another half hour," he said.

Sebastian escorted the dancer all the way to the exit, the ship lurching slightly beneath his feet. "How about I pay you whatever is left on your tab and you just end the show now?"

"Don't pay him. Just get him out," Marco said, his eyes full of venom.

The man frowned. "What about my tips, man? I need to—"

Sebastian had steered him out the bar door and they were now standing on the ship's hall carpet covered in bright geometric shapes. Marco was hot on their heels.

Sebastian reached into his wallet and pulled out a hundred-dollar bill. "This will handle it."

"Maybe." The half-naked dancer squinted. "But I've got tips, dude. How am I supposed to get them?"

"I don't care. You're out of line," Marco said.

Sebastian ground his back molars together. He was going to have to spell it out for this lunk. "Look, you seem not to understand. This will handle it." If he had to wipe the floor with this guy, he would. "The next tip that's coming is one that you won't like." He held the bill out once more.

The dancer seemed to get Sebastian's meaning. *Good. Don't be a fool.* The two men stared at each other for a beat. *Go on, try it.* Sebastian knew how to maneuver a body. He'd done it a million times on the football field and a few times in real life.

The man grabbed the bill and turned. But then, out of nowhere, swung a wild punch at the groom. Marco easily ducked and Sebastian went in, instinctively rolling the man to the side and then grabbing his arm and slamming him hard against the wall.

"Now you're going to go quietly," Sebastian growled in his ear, as he twisted the dancer's arm so he flinched. "Or I'm calling security and you can spend the night in the brig."

"Okay, man. Okay!" Sebastian released the dancer, not so nicely shoving him along the carpet.

He glanced back, holding up the hundred-dollar bill and grinning. "Thanks for the cash, anyway."

Sebastian, his heart thudding from the adrenaline of the quick fight, felt his pulse pound in his temples. He ought to tackle the man and take back his hundred, but he knew it wouldn't be worth it. Best to keep the peace now and not make more of a spectacle.

"Thanks, man," Marco said, clapping Sebastian on the shoulder.

"Yeah, no problem. What are best men for?" He made sure to watch that the dancer made it all the way into the elevator. He didn't stop watching until the doors slid shut. "He's gone now and shouldn't be coming back."

"I'm going to go check on Lola," Marco said, slipping back into the party.

"You sure did handle that guy," Gabriela said, sneaking up on him as she appeared at his left elbow.

"Just trying to save the bachelorette party," he said and shrugged.

"Well, thank you. You did." Her eyes shone with gratitude.

"It wasn't anything. Just taking out the trash, really," he said. They both turned to head back into the party, but the rolling waves beneath the ship kicked up a notch and the boat tipped to the right.

"Whoa," Gabriela said as she stumbled in her stiletto heels. Sebastian reached out to steady her but before he knew it, she'd fallen straight into his arms.

CHAPTER SEVEN

GABRIELA HAD SOMEHOW gone from walking independently to be pressed straight against Sebastian Lott's very fit, very firm, body. She realized that despite a decade since he'd thrown a football on the field, he'd maintained his physique and was all muscle, not a bit of give in his entire torso, and she was flattened straight against it. She craned her neck upward and his hazel eyes flecked with green seemed amused.

"Are you okay?" he asked.

Was she okay? She hadn't even known what had hit her. She was walking fine and then the boat lurched and now she was close enough to Sebastian Lott to kiss him. On the lips. She felt a surge of adrenaline pump through her body, running hot and then cold as her face flushed. A trickle of sweat dripped down her lower back. No doubt from all the dancing and *not* Sebastian Lott. Though part of her wasn't sure.

"I—I'm fine. Really. I..." Gabriela tried to pull herself away from Sebastian's strong arms, but the boat lurched again and she fell back into them. The drinks plus the rolling seas made for rough walking but why did she keep falling into his arms? The universe was conspiring against her.

Sebastian just laughed. A deep rumble in his belly that she *felt* through his shirt.

"Maybe we should try that again," he said. He glanced at her and for a moment she felt lost in his gaze. Those green flecks. So green. What had he said? Why did it even matter what color the man's eyes were? He was Sebastian Lott, notorious player, and she was the uptight nerd from high school.

Sebastian righted her as she took a step back, keeping a hand on her elbow. She felt even more unsteady on her feet, but that had nothing to do with the rock of the boat on the water. Her face was on fire. God, she hoped she wasn't tomato red, though she felt her cheeks burn.

"Thanks," she managed.

"Can't have the maid of honor toppling," he said. "Who's going to keep the party on schedule with her clipboard?" He grinned a teasing smile, challenging her.

"I think the schedule's blown to hell now," she admitted, shrugging one shoulder.

"Probably," Sebastian agreed, chuckling. He stared at her once more.

Was he coming closer? Were those sensual lips getting nearer to hers?

"Hey, there." Lola's voice broke the spell and Gabriela jumped away from Sebastian. Had the bride seen them doing…what? About to kiss? Lola and Marco were standing at the door now, Marco with confusion across his face. Gabriela had no idea what they must've looked like, bodies pressed together as they fought the sway of the ship.

"The ocean's really wild tonight," Gabriela hedged as she tried to regain her composure, tucking her hair behind one ear. "I nearly fell." Gabriela's pulse pounded in her throat. She felt guilty, like she'd been caught trying to steal a cookie from the jar.

"I saw." Lola's face was a poker mask. Gabriela couldn't read it.

"You guys okay?" Sebastian asked. "Lola, I'm sorry about that dancer."

Lola nodded. "It was so weird—him grabbing me like that!" she exclaimed, shaking her head. "So aggressive."

"Too aggressive," Marco agreed, putting an arm around Lola and pulling her close.

"Should I ask all the dancers to leave? I will," Gabriela offered. She'd be more than happy to kick out the remainder of Felicia's tawdry entertainment.

"The rest are already on their way out," Lola said. "They decided to pack it up." She nodded backward and Gabriela saw the two others putting their clothes back on. "And—" she glanced up at Marco "—I think we're going to head to our cabin, too."

"What? Leave already? It's not even…eleven!" Gabriela exclaimed.

"Yeah, it's early. Have another drink," Sebastian offered.

"No thanks, man," Marco said, clapping his friend on the shoulder. "We've got a big day tomorrow with the snorkeling excursion and then later the rehearsal dinner, so…" He trailed off, glancing at his bride with goofy affection.

"And we need our beauty rest," Lola finished. But she was grinning ear to ear, making it more than apparent that rest probably wasn't on the agenda once the two retreated to their cabin.

"You don't need any beauty sleep," Sebastian told Lola. "But this guy…" He play-punched Marco in the stomach. "Can he sleep from now until the wedding? Hell, I'm not even sure that would help."

"Hey, now," Marco protested but laughed anyway.

"You sure you won't stay?" Gabriela didn't want to imagine the party without Lola. This was *her* night and *her* weekend, and she wanted everything to be perfect.

"No…and Veronica's going to call it a night, too. She told me."

"Well, I'm not surprised. I don't think Veronica's made it to midnight since her kids were born," Gabriela said. "Was the party at least fun? I mean, if that dancer ruined it for you…" Gabriela would stalk him and make his life a living hell. Sweet-as-pie Lola deserved the best bachelorette party of all time and if Felicia and her dumb dancers had messed any of that up…

"I had a great time." Lola broke free of Marco's arm and gave Gabriela a big hug. "Thanks so much for everything you did. It was perfect."

"You're sure?" Gabriela wasn't. Having the bride run out of the party early typically wasn't a sign of a successful party.

"I'm sure," Lola said and pulled back. "I just want to

be with the love of my life." She glanced at Marco, who returned her brilliant smile with one of his own. Their love was so real Gabriela could feel its warmth like heat from the sun. She couldn't begrudge them that.

"Okay, you two, don't do anything I wouldn't do," Sebastian said, giving his friend a one-armed hug.

"Well, considering you're celibate, why don't we just leave that alone?" Marco teased.

Celibate? Gabriela turned so forcefully, she felt her neck muscles tense. Since when was Sebastian Lott celibate?

Marco and Lola moved past them to the elevators. Gabriela glanced up at the tall figure of Sebastian Lott next to her, every one of his dark hairs perfectly in place.

"You're...*celibate*?" Gabriela couldn't stop herself from asking.

"For the weekend." Sebastian sent her a sidelong glance, a sly smile curling his lips. "Why? Disappointed? Did you want to take me to...sexy town?" He wiggled his eyebrows and then laughed a little, acknowledging his own cheesy joke.

"Pffft. As if." They both moved back into the bar and toward the bartender. Felicia, lacking the male dancers to grind with, was dancing around Bill. When she saw them approach, she crooked her finger at Bill and beckoned him closer. Clear ploy to make him jealous—or something, Gabriela didn't know.

"You don't think I'm sexy? Now, my feelings are going to be hurt." Sebastian pretended to pout.

"I doubt my opinion matters at all." What did he

care if she thought he was attractive or not? Did he need *every* woman's approval? Probably. She glanced at him to see if he'd noticed Felicia's gyrating antics. He hadn't. "Besides, I'm sure you can find other women to flatter your ego."

"But I don't want another woman to flatter me."

How did Sebastian make lines like that sound so... earnest? But the way that he was looking at her made her think he was telling the truth. "Want another drink?" he asked.

"Sure." Gabriela didn't have to worry about Lola anymore, or the kind of time she was having. Marco would take care of that. Now she could...relax.

Sebastian held up a two fingers to the bartender, who brought them both another round. Gabriela took her glass, though she was already feeling the vodka humming in her blood. It made her feel bold and it made her not care that she was talking to Sebastian Lott.

"So, seriously, though, what's up with the celibacy vow? I heard you rule Spark. That you like no strings," Gabriela said, taking a small sip of her vodka soda. *Go easy,* she told herself, *you've already had plenty.*

"Eh." Sebastian looked less than enthused.

"What? You're not into hooking up anymore?" Now Gabriela was truly shocked. What was this? A joke?

Sebastian took a drink. "I'm tired of it. The running around. The meaningless sex. One strange face after another every weekend. Sure, it sounds good, but in reality, it gets old." Sebastian focused on his whiskey on ice, knocking the glass so the ice cubes clinked the side.

"You're tired of sex." Gabriela could not believe

this. She'd never heard a man admit he was tired of sex—meaningless or otherwise. "Did you have a serious brain injury? What the hell happened?"

Sebastian chuckled, voice low. She liked making him laugh. She wanted to do it again.

"It all blurs together, one body after another. Nothing means anything."

Gabriela could actually relate. "And then, if you accidentally sleep over..."

"You've got that awkward 'Let's pretend we want to have breakfast but don't have time' excuse."

"Or the 'Oh, got an early-morning work meeting' excuse."

"Or the 'Hey, I need to let my dog out when I don't even have a dog' excuse."

They both dissolved into giggles. What had the world come to when Gabriela and Sebastian Lott had *this* much in common?

"You're like the female me," Sebastian said, looking amazed as he nodded his head.

"I am *not*." The idea was insane.

"You *are*," he persisted. "Except that nobody in Miami knows it. You're me on the down low. Why?"

Gabriela shrugged. "I don't know. Maybe I don't want to be Felicia." She studied the blond as she deliberately shook her boobs in Bill's face. Nothing subtle there.

Sebastian chuckled.

"I prefer to have my fun in New York," Gabriela said.

"I bet you do." Sebastian studied her a moment. "But don't you get tired of all the hookups? I don't want to have sex again unless it's with someone who really knows me. And I know them," Sebastian admitted. "I want something more, like what Marco and Lola have."

Gabriela took a sip of her drink. She doubted Sebastian was really serious. Maybe it was just one more come-on line.

"Oh, sure, use the 'I want to settle down line' to get a woman into bed and then the next morning go back to being your player self. Then it's, 'Oh, I forgot about the sick cat I don't own.'"

Sebastian laughed a little. "It's not a line." Sebastian glanced at her and his hazel eyes looked earnest. She suddenly believed him.

"So, who's your perfect woman, then?"

"Someone sexy."

"I thought you were trying not to be shallow," Gabriela crooked her head to one side.

"Someone smart."

Gabriela sniffed. "Okay, but then, if she were smart, why would she date you?"

Sebastian laughed again. Oh, she liked the sound of that. Liked also that he was tough enough to take her barbs. He surprised her. His ego didn't seem as fragile as she would've thought.

Sebastian gave Gabriela a playful shove. "And my ideal woman has to be funny. Razor-sharp sarcastic wit…" He paused, studying her with sudden serious attention. "Like yours." He stared at her a moment and, for a split second, Gabriela wondered if he were serious. Then she quickly decided he was just pulling her leg.

She threw her head back and laughed. "Flattery will get you nowhere."

"Should I insult you, then?"

"You mean like by ignoring me when your locker was near mine?" She raised an eyebrow and they both burst out laughing.

"We had lockers together?" he deadpanned.

She shoved him. "See? You proved my point."

"I know we had lockers together. It was easy to ask you about what you got on your homework."

Gabriela shook her head. "You never needed to ask me about homework." It was true. He'd always had his schoolwork handled.

"Got me." He raised a glass and she clinked hers against his. "In fairness," he said, staring at the ice cubes in his drink. "You were much different in high school."

"And you were exactly the same." She sipped on her vodka soda, avoiding the lime wedge bobbing in the top.

"Oh, come on." Sebastian glanced up at her, his hazel eyes steady on hers. "I've matured since high school."

"Not according to Felicia and Liv."

A too-loud, brash laugh from Felicia took their attention then. She'd moved closer to Bill and they were now grinding in earnest, the thump of music seeming to grow louder.

"Isn't he married?" Gabriela said.

"You think Felicia cares?" Sebastian downed the rest of his drink. Gabriela studied Felicia as she did her version of twerking. There was a lot of hair-whipping and butt-gyrating.

"Do you get the feeling Felicia ordered the dancers for herself and not Lola?"

"Completely," Gabriela agreed. "There was zero thought about how Lola would feel about dancers. This was all about Felicia."

"What isn't?"

"Agreed." Gabriela glanced at Sebastian's profile, so striking, his straight nose and strong chin. In middle school he'd been almost pretty: too-long eyelashes that made the girls jealous. But he'd grown into a striking man. No doubt about that. Her inner fourteen-year-old, the one who'd once tried out the signature *Gabriela Lott* on her spiral notebook, reminded her that she'd long found the man irresistible.

"Although," she began, "if you ask me, I think she's just trying to make you jealous."

Sebastian nearly spit out his drink. "Me? Why?"

"She's always had a thing for you."

"She hates me. Ever since senior year."

"When you dumped her," Gabriela pointed out.

"Look, we only ever *kissed* and then she started talking about how we should have sex, and how I didn't need to wear a condom, and how she was okay if she ended up pregnant."

"What?" Now it was Gabriela's turn to nearly spit out her drink.

"She freaked me out. Can you blame me for not wanting a date two?" Sebastian shook his head. "I was scared."

"I can see why." Gabriela couldn't think of a worse nightmare. "Did that happen to you often? Women wanting to have your babies?" Gabriela meant that to come out as a joke, but it sounded more serious than she'd intended.

Sebastian glanced at her, a wry smile on his face. "More than I'd like." He studied his empty whiskey glass.

Another loud laugh came from Felicia as she pulled Bill even closer, wrapping herself up in him.

"She's doing that for your benefit, you know," Gabriela said, sipping at her cocktail.

Sebastian sighed. He seemed like he didn't want Felicia's attention, but he would get it anyway. She was nothing but trouble. A new song drifted in through the speakers of the bar and Felicia squealed in delight. She broke free from her partner, clomped on top of a bar table and began to sway her hips, dancing with her hands above her head and beckoning to Marco's brother, James, to join her.

"Didn't we just get her down from there? What is with Felicia and tabletops? Could she be more of a walking cliché?" Gabriela sighed.

"Ah, let her have her fun."

Gabriela watched as Felicia took off her skimpy halter top, revealing an almost-transparent lace bra. The other groomsmen started to whoop and holler, and one even produced a five-dollar bill and waved it in the air. Then she whipped off the bra, too.

"Why did she even need to hire dancers?" Gabriela mused aloud.

The bartender got wind of her near nudity. Apparently actual dancers in skimpy swimsuits were fine, but showing nipple was *not*. Gabriela couldn't hear him but his gestures made it pretty clear that he wanted Felicia off the table.

Liv jumped in to defend her sister and suddenly a whole tumbler of whiskey went sailing off the bar and crashing to the floor.

"Not again," Gabriela groaned and was on her feet.

"Again?" Sebastian asked, surprised.

"They won't rest until they've broken all the glassware on this freakin' ship." Gabriela took a final sip of her drink and grabbed her clipboard. Somebody had to rein in Felicia.

The bartender looked heated as he exchanged words with Liv and pointed to Felicia. Theo was trying to mitigate the situation but it seemed the bartender was having none of it. "You guys need to go," he said just as Gabriela stepped up. Sebastian was right on her heels.

"Hey, man, we'll settle down," Sebastian offered.

"You guys are out of control. You have to go. I'm going to call security." The bartender picked up the phone.

"Like hell you will," Liv growled. Then Liv threw her drink in the bartender's face. He was dripping with margarita and had a slice of lime on his shirt.

Everyone froze.

"Get the hell out of my bar," the bartender shouted as he wiped at his face with a bar towel. "Get the hell *out*!"

"I think we'd better go," Sebastian told Gabriela,

who could feel the heat rising in her face. Felicia and Liv had gotten them kicked out, and the whole incident was mortifying. She hadn't been this embarrassed since…well, since the last time Liv and Felicia had gotten them kicked out of a bar. It seemed to happen more often to them than anyone else she knew.

"Let's go to the pool!" Felicia shouted. The rest of the party followed her out the door.

Gabriela thought for a minute about just letting them go. Letting Felicia make a mess out of the whole evening. But then again, she thought of Lola. How would she react if Felicia got arrested?

"I'm truly sorry about this," Gabriela told the bartender. "I really am."

"You better rein in your friend or I will call security," he growled. "If you knew what was good for you, you'd get her back to her cabin so she can sleep it off."

"I know. We'll stop her." Sebastian remained quiet by her side. Gabriela looked at him. When he still said nothing, she let loose an elbow to his ribs.

"Ow," he cried. Then he glanced at her face. "Uh, right. Yes, of course. We'll take care of it. We promise."

CHAPTER EIGHT

THE LAST THING Gabriela wanted to do was trek around the ship looking for Felicia and a bunch of drunk goofballs who planned to make fools of themselves, but she was also determined that none of said fools would embarrass Lola—not during her big weekend. She'd be mortified if she woke up tomorrow and discovered her bridesmaids had been kicked off the ship—or thrown in the brig. Then again, did cruise ships have a brig? She didn't know. She didn't want to find out.

"There are at least three pools on this ship," Sebastian pointed out. "Do you think they went to the starboard one? Leeward one? Outdoor one with the Jacuzzi?"

"Knowing Felicia, my money is on the Jacuzzi." Gabriela tucked her ever-present clipboard under her arm and sighed. It's not like she needed the party itinerary anymore but something about it still felt reassuring.

They walked down the corridor to the elevator bank and as they stood waiting for an elevator to take them to the mezzanine, Gabriela realized the two of them were completely alone. No party, no bartenders, no other member of the wedding party. He was so tall walking next to her, she had to crane her neck to look at his strong profile. His chin could cut glass. She felt the warm buzz of alcohol in her brain like the low hum of bees. The elevator dinged then and the small gold doors slid open. She felt less angry with him all of a sudden, though she couldn't say why. *He'd forgotten me entirely*, she reminded herself, and yet, maybe it was the cocksure smile on his face, or the way he put his hand on the elevator door, holding it so she could go in. *Gentlemanly*, even though she knew he was anything but a gentleman.

She stepped into the cruise ship elevator—acutely aware that Sebastian was on her heels. As he stepped inside, his broad shoulders took up all the available room in the small elevator. She almost felt pressed up against him, even though there was a good ten inches between them. Gabriela took in a breath and smelled the lingering trace of his shower gel: woodsy with the hint of sandalwood and something sweet. Or maybe that was just how *he* smelled, like the manly outdoors.

Stop it, she told herself. *This is just the vodka talking.* There's no way she could really be attracted to the man, not with his huge ego. He was toxic and she needed to remind herself of that. He leaned across her and she sucked in a breath. Then she realized he was hitting the elevator button.

"You know, we could just let them…be," Sebastian said.

"What do you mean?"

"It's technically not our job to police Felicia." Sebastian glanced at her, hazel eyes steady.

"I promised Lola I wouldn't let things get out of hand." Why did it seem like Sebastian was moving closer to her? She realized she was leaning into him. Leaning into his sweet smell. Cinnamon?

"But Lola is safe upstairs with Marco. You don't have to babysit Felicia. She's a big girl."

Sebastian leaned his arm against the wall behind her head and suddenly he was even closer. But she didn't move away. She couldn't. She wanted to stay right there, the subject of his gaze.

"We have to make sure she doesn't get kicked off the ship. Or ruin the wedding."

"She won't." Sebastian seemed so confident. Gabriela wondered why. How could he know what crazy thing Felicia might do?

"Then what do we do?"

"I don't know." A small smile quirked up the corners of his lips. "What do you want to do?"

Taste you. The thought burst into her mind without her permission. Taste him? What the hell? He was the world's worst player, an admitted Spark addict. A jerk of the first order. Why was she even considering *tasting* him?

But then, she knew why. He was sexy as hell, that's why. The man just oozed primal attraction from his thick, muscled shoulders to his trim, tapered waist. He even smelled good. So very good. He was so close now their noses were just inches apart. She could stand on her tiptoes and kiss him right here, in this elevator. Who would know?

"What did you have in mind?"

"Well, I heard there's Scrabble in the games' room. Is that your speed, Ms. Salutatorian?" He grinned, mocking her.

"I don't even like Scrabble." It hardly seemed like a proper defense.

"No? Well, we could hang out. Party a little. I want to find out about this Gabriela Cruz I don't know. The one who is a platinum dater on Spark. That's not at all the girl I knew from high school."

"I'm still the same person," she protested.

Sebastian stared at her from the corner of his eye. "Are you? A little wilder than you want everyone here to believe." He paused. "I like wild."

Gabriela got the impression that he could see right through her, right to the core, to the woman who'd blossomed since high school, the woman who'd learned to *loosen up*.

"How about we play a game?" he offered.

Naked Twister, she almost wanted to say. Prove to him she wasn't the timid nerdy girl she used to be in high school. She'd long since left that Gabriela in the dust. She thought of the Gabriela on Spark, the Gabriela who'd had dozens of quickies in New York, the Gabriela who had fun. Real fun. *But, seriously, am I going here? With Sebastian Lott?*

"What kind of game?" She retreated a bit and found her back against the elevator door, her clipboard against her chest.

"Truth or Dare." His eyes sparkled with mischief.

"We've got to find Felicia," Gabriela said, her throat suddenly dry as she imagined the kind of dares he might have in mind. Or worse, the truths. Both came with a heaping helping of trouble.

"One round, then. Truth or Dare?"

"Neither," she breathed.

"Truth, then. Tell me—do you want to go back to my room? Right now?"

Yes. The single admission in her head surprised her. But that was exactly what she wanted to do. She felt he knew it, too, could read it all over her face. The vodka really was buzzing around her brain, the hum growing louder. She took a step closer and all she could think about were his amazing lips. Full, sensual, highly kissable. She realized then that she was really considering kissing the man. Seriously considering pressing her lips against his, flicking her tongue inside his mouth. *Tasting him.* The air between them grew thick and suddenly Gabriela forgot to breathe. She was drowning in his hazel eyes, mesmerized by them.

"Won't answer that," she murmured, realizing that answer alone gave him exactly what he needed to know.

"Dare, then," he said. "I dare you to…" He paused as her heart sped up, a rabbit in a cage that desperately wanted out. "I dare you to kiss me."

She froze, every molecule in her body seeming to hold its collective breath. Kiss him? She glanced at his lips, unable to look away. Was she going to do it? Would she accept his dare?

And then came the loud ding as the elevator reached

its destination and the doors slid open. She began breathing again, the spell broken. Sebastian almost looked disappointed as Gabriela moved away from him, out of the elevator.

She laughed uneasily. "I never said I'd play that game," she said.

I can't believe I almost kissed him. What the hell was I thinking?

Hooking up with Sebastian Lott would be the most embarrassing mistake she could think of to make. What if they'd kissed and someone had seen them? What if Felicia had been waiting on the other side of the elevator doors? She'd never live it down. Felicia and Liv would mock her endlessly.

The cool night air hit her as they stepped out onto the sixth deck, with its big, sliding doors open wide to the outer pool deck. Laughter traveled across the open-air patio, along with the distinct sound of splashing. Gabriela moved outside and saw Felicia, Liv, Bill and James in the pool. Bill and James had stripped down to their boxer shorts and Felicia and Liv were wearing just their lingerie. Actually, scratch that, thought Gabriela, Felicia and Liv were topless. Completely topless. In fact, they were all playing some kind of game of Keep Away, trying to keep Bill's drink away from him, even sloshing some into the pool. Their clothes were heaped in a pile on a nearby lounge chair.

"Oh, lord." Gabriela let out a long breath. "Are those sisters allergic to clothes?"

"We could always just pretend we never saw this," Sebastian said. "There's still time to flee."

"No." Gabriela clenched her jaw and tightened her grip on the clipboard. "We have to get them out of there before they make so much noise, the ship security come."

"Whatever you say." Sebastian seemed skeptical but he followed her across the cool, stone tiles surrounding the square pool, the high-pitched giggles and screams of delight washing over them.

Gabriela maneuvered her way around the diving board and called out to Felicia. "Hey, guys, time to get out. Pool's technically closed."

"Oh, look." Felicia narrowed her eyes at Gabriela as she ducked down into the water, her wet blond hair slicked back, and then she stood, deliberately and slowly, showing off her erect nipples, most likely for Sebastian's benefit. It irked Gabriela more than she liked. "It's Ms. Wet Blanket come to spoil all our fun."

"Yeah, Gobstopper. Why don't you move on?" Liv said, wrapping her arms around James. "We're trying to have fun here."

"Why don't you have fun in your rooms? If you get in trouble and ruin Lola's wedding…" She tapped her clipboard for emphasis.

"We're not going to ruin anything," Felicia snapped. She was very drunk and her bloodshot eyes seemed to have trouble focusing, though she was angry enough.

"Guys," Sebastian said, his voice clear and authoritarian. "I think we've probably had enough fun for one night. We've got an early start tomorrow. And cruise ship security is coming."

"Seriously, you, too, Swipe Left?" Liv growled.

"Gobstopper must be rubbing off on him," Felicia murmured.

"Bill," Sebastian said, calling to the man in the drenched plaid boxers who was helping Felicia keep steady in the pool. "Won't your wife be upset if you're…" He paused. "…out this late?"

Bill's mouth worked itself into a thin line. "That's none of your business."

"Hey, guys, why don't we head upstairs?" James offered, trying to help. "I'm getting cold and shriveled anyway. Let's head up before we all turn into prunes."

Liv seemed to consider this a moment. "Yeah, you can come to our suite!"

Gabriela froze. "That's *my* room, as well." Felicia, Liv and Gabriela were sharing a four-bed suite. It was cost-effective, but Gabriela now realized just *how* bad an idea that had been.

"Hey, Gob, you can't have it both ways. Either we stay down here or we go to the room." Felicia climbed up the ladder, her bare breasts bouncing with every step, and her without a bit of modesty. She grabbed her dress from the lounge chair and tugged it on over her head. Liv followed, as did the two men. Liv grabbed a big fluffy towel from a basket nearby and wrapped herself up in it.

"You are literally the antidote to fun," Liv said, shaking her head. "Some things haven't changed since high school."

The foursome walked past Sebastian and Gabriela. "Yeah, you really need to lighten." As Felicia passed Gabriela, she gave her a hard bump, a decided push.

Gabriela was so close to the edge of the pool that there wasn't any correcting herself. Her heel caught the edge and she was free-falling, arms wheeling. Sebastian reached out to her, but it was too late. She fell into the pool, fully clothed, her clipboard launched into the deep end. She came up sputtering and wiping her dark, wet hair out of her eyes, and to the sound of laughter as the group walked toward the elevator. Her clipboard floated nearby, the papers soaked.

Suddenly she was back in high school again, the nerdy outsider, the one who never quite fit in the group. She was surprised by how hard that laughter hurt, how much it reminded her of all she hated about growing up.

"You okay?" Sebastian was kneeling, a concerned look on his face. At least he wasn't laughing, thank God. He reached out a hand to help her get to the side of the pool.

"I'm fine. *Fine*," she growled, though she wasn't the least bit fine. All her anger toward Felicia rushed to the surface. She wanted to take the woman by the hair and drag *her* into the pool. Not that she would. She'd be good for Lola's sake, though she frankly didn't understand why Lola insisted on keeping Felicia in the circle. Misguided loyalty.

"That was a cheap shot," Sebastian said as he helped her climb out. She was soaked, dripping chlorinated water onto the stone tile. She felt like a drowned rat. Her once flowing halter-top jumpsuit now clung to her, sticking to her like cling wrap. Ugh. What a nightmare. And Felicia and Liv were going up to *her* room where *her* clothes were and doing who knows what with those guys.

Sebastian leaned over and grabbed her sopping wet clipboard, a nice gesture she noted, even though the whole thing was ruined. He led her to the basket of towels and grabbed one, wrapping it around her shoulders.

"Wanna go get changed?"

"Can't," Gabriela spat. She looked at the clumped and ruined papers and then leaned over and dumped the drenched clipboard in a nearby trash can. What a waste. "They'll already be in the room. Probably won't let me in."

Sebastian nodded once, pulled the towel tightly around her and then rubbed her shoulders vigorously. His hands felt big and strong and comforting.

"Want me to go roust them out? I will."

Gabriela laughed a bit. "That's not necessary."

"I'll punch Bill *and* Felicia if I need to. Heck, I'd love to punch Bill anyway. I don't like guys who run around on their wives."

"Unfortunately, that's just Felicia's type," Gabriela quipped, thinking about how she'd slept with her married brother-in-law. Sebastian laughed a bit. "Why are you being so nice to me?" she asked as he pulled on the towel.

"Because they're jerks," he said. "You don't deserve that."

"Thanks," she said.

"Was I ever...a jerk like that? In high school? I mean, I know I was a cocky kid but..." Sebastian almost seemed worried.

"No." It was one of the reasons why she'd had a crush on him all those years ago. "You were never like that. You were pretty nice, really. When you noticed me, which wasn't often."

Sebastian looked up at the stars. "Well, I'm sorry about that." He rolled his eyes heavenward, to the big expanse of night sky above them. "I'm sorry. I was an idiot in high school."

"You were a god in high school," Gabriela corrected. "Everybody worshipped you."

Sebastian shrugged one shoulder. "Yeah, and all that went to my head. I've had a lot of time since then to evaluate my life choices… I don't know. I realized I took a lot for granted and I was just starting to expect life to hand me everything I needed. Now I realize I have to work for what I want. And I have to make better choices if I want a more fulfilling life."

Gabriela nodded. The sudden depth from Sebastian Lott surprised her. Maybe it wasn't a ploy at all. She was really beginning to think the man had tired of one-night stands and hookups. Somehow that fact, that surprising depth, made her want to kiss him more. She shivered, the pool water dripping down her back, sending a chill along her spine. She pulled the towel tightly around her.

"I guess it's not always easy to be the guy every girl fawns over," Gabriela admitted, though even to her own ears the words sounded crazy. Though she knew that, from the outside, lives sometimes looked perfect even though they weren't.

"Every girl didn't fawn all over me."

Gabriela barked a laugh as she sat on one of the lounge chairs flipped out in the horizontal position. Sebastian sat next to her, his dry shoes next to her sopping wet ones.

"Sure they did. There wasn't a girl in school that didn't have a crush on you at one time or another."

"You didn't." Sebastian stared at her, hazel eyes probing, questioning.

"I…" Now Gabriela found herself grasping for the right answer. Admit that she, too, once dreamed that the handsome AF Sebastian Lott would notice little old geeky her? "Sure I did." Gabriela shrugged. "Every girl did."

"*You* had a crush on me." Sebastian's wolfish grin grew wider. "Really?"

"Maybe." She was already regretting telling him. "I…I tried to ask you to the prom."

"No." All the color drained from Sebastian's face.

"I tried to ask you…by the lockers. It was stupid." Her face flamed red as she remembered that horrible day, standing at his locker, struggling to get the words out. "All I managed to say was 'Are you going to prom?'"

"I don't remember that." Sebastian wrinkled his brow as if trying to recall the memory. "What did I say?"

"You said, 'Yeah. I'm going with Felicia.' So that ended that."

"A mistake of the first order." He winced. "I'm sorry I didn't notice you then."

The apology went right to Gabriela's center, a salve to a very old wound. "It's okay."

"Well, thank goodness you had a crush on me. I'd worry if not *every* girl had the hots for me. It would damage my ego."

Gabriela rained light blows on his arms and chest, feeling her face flush with heat. "You're an egomaniac."

"Ow, ow!" he cried, holding up his hands. "Help! I'm being attacked!" he called mockingly to the empty poolside.

She kept up the slapping blows to his shoulder and chest, his voice echoing through the empty rafters, the ship's pool long deserted. She wondered if someone would come: a ship worker maybe, someone who would see her drenched, sitting next to Sebastian, beating the stuffing out of his shoulder. Not that she cared. She was enjoying pounding on him. He deserved at least that for being such a jerk. He was full of himself.

"Hey! Hey!" Sebastian started to defend himself, blocking her blows, and before she knew it, he had both her wrists. "Now what are you going to do?"

She wanted to head butt him maybe, but instead she struggled to get her arms free. She twisted her body, losing the towel completely, vaguely aware of how her too thin, now see-through fabric clung to her. "Let me go!" she called, playful but firm.

"Not unless you promise not to hit me any more." Sebastian didn't seem at all hurt or fazed by the blows. It made Gabriela want to hit him again—and again. She twisted, harder this time, and let loose her right foot, kicking him in the shin, harder than she'd intended.

"Oof!" he groaned as he jerked from the impact, flinching. Somehow he was falling backward on the pool lounger and taking her with him. They were sinking against the oversize pillows and Gabriela was right on top of him. In the fall, he'd let go of her wrists, so it was just her body on top of his. Her soaked clothes dripped onto his dry ones and she leaned into the feel of his warm, solid chest beneath her. Now she was so close to him, her heart thudded hard in her chest.

"I see you *have* become a bad, bad girl since moving to New York," he wheezed, pupils growing large.

"You have no idea how bad." That was the truth.

He looked intrigued as he studied her face. "Show me," he challenged, his voice a rumble in his chest.

Every alarm bell in her brain went off at once as Gabriela found herself inches from Sebastian Lott's full mouth, searching his eyes and finding not just shock or surprise there but also...want. A surprising want. Did he want her?

He waited patiently for her to make the first move. Challenging her, almost, as he kept still, their lips nearly touching. All she had to do was to dip down to taste him. She inhaled his scent: sandalwood and something muskier, something dangerous. She wanted that smell on her, she realized. She wanted him on her in every way possible.

An inner voice of warning pinged in her head. *Don't do this. It's a mistake. He says he's reformed, but you know you could never keep someone like Sebastian*

Lott. He'll wake up in the morning and realize how much of a mistake it all was... He just wants sex. He's going to use you.

Not if I use him first, she told the voice.

Oh, she liked that idea. Play the player. Take what she needed...and she would. She needed this. She needed him. She was tired of being polite. What she wanted was a bad boy, someone who was off-limits, someone who wouldn't play nice.

Her inner wild child roared to life. She'd been held down too long beneath the prim and proper, with her pretending to be that timid girl from high school. But she knew she wasn't. Not anymore. Maybe not ever again.

Tonight she wasn't going to be a good girl. Tonight she was going to let the bad girl out. Her real self, finally. Wild, free, a woman who knew what she wanted and took it. *He won't know what hit him,* she thought.

She dipped down and pressed her lips against his.

CHAPTER NINE

SEBASTIAN COULDN'T BELIEVE that Gabriela Cruz was *kissing* him. It was the last thing he'd expected from the clipboard-toting, by-the-book, former high school salutatorian.

All of Sebastian's nerve endings lit up at one time. Gabriela's mouth opened, inviting him in, and he went for it, amazed by how deftly this woman could kiss. This was no awkward nerd from high school. This was a woman who knew how to light a fire in a man. He tried not to think about how she'd learned to kiss like that, learned to tease him with the flick of her soft tongue. How he wanted that tongue all over his body. How he wanted that *now*. He could feel her amazing curves beneath the thin, wet fabric of her jumpsuit, which left absolutely nothing to his imagination. Her nipples pressed against his shirt, hard, wanting, demanding to be squeezed.

His whole body came alive, ready and eager for what came next. He strained against the zipper of his pants, wanting out, wanting to bury himself deep inside this woman. Here on the pool deck or anywhere

else she'd let him. He was acting like a man starved
of sex, not one who'd just had a Spark three days ago,
yet there was something about Gabriela that drove him
wild. Good girl goes bad, maybe? No, he knew what
it was: she'd been the smartest girl in school, the one
who'd always made him feel somehow...lacking. Her
razor-sharp wit challenged him in ways he'd never
been challenged. He'd always been one step ahead
of the women he usually dated. But now? Now this
woman was one step ahead of him. It thrilled and
scared him all at once. This was a woman of substance.

And she was kissing the life out of him. It felt grati-
fying, but more than that, right. Maybe what he needed
was a smart woman, smarter than him, sharper than
he could ever be. Maybe what he needed was a challenge that woman could provide. He kissed her back,
his body taking over, even as he could feel her heart
beat as her chest pressed against his. The woman was
soft and firm all at once. He tasted the sweet sourness
of the vodka sodas she'd been drinking. Her tongue
flicked out, meeting his in perfect unity, as if she anticipated his every move. Her hand slipped down, running the length of his fit chest, and he almost cried
out as she reached below, rubbing his stiffness, making him come even more alive. She knew how to work
him; he could tell even as she stroked him through
his clothing.

Vaguely he remembered some distant promise about
celibacy, but there was no way—with Gabriela's hands
so talented—that he'd honor that promise. Hell, he'd

happily give Marco a bottle of the best whiskey he could find if that meant he could keep tasting Gabriela. She tasted so good, so sweet. Her mouth on his like she was starving for it. Her tongue slid into his mouth once more. Eager, willing, wet. He'd had plenty of women, but something about Gabriela was just…not like the others. She didn't hold back, and she wasn't just putting on a show for him. This woman had passion in her veins. She reached for his fly, nimbly working the zipper. That's when he realized she really did have no compulsion about taking him right there, out in the open beneath the stars, to hell with who saw.

That was unbelievably hot.

She broke free then and hopped off him, as if she'd been electrocuted.

"I didn't mean to do that," she murmured, her face beet red.

"You could've fooled me," Sebastian quipped, rising up on his elbows, his lips feeling bruised from her enthusiasm. "You pretty much attacked me."

She glanced at him and worriedly bit her lip. "I'm sorry. I really am. I didn't mean to do that."

He gave a shrug. "I didn't mind."

"You didn't?" Her question almost came out as a squeak. God, she was adorable. Innocent and chaste one second and then a dirty girl who couldn't get enough another. He was beginning to think there were two sides to Gabriela Cruz. He'd only ever known the tight-lipped good girl. But no good girl had ever kissed him like that.

"I enjoyed it."

His words caused her blush to grow a shade deeper. "Come on." She rolled her eyes.

"I did. I enjoyed it very much. You...surprise me." That was the truth of it. Who knew such a vixen lay beneath that staid exterior? He didn't. His heart still was working overtime in his chest.

"Oh, that? That's nothing." She shrugged and wrapped the towel tightly around her, flipping a wet strand of hair from her face. Her mascara was running slightly, but it did nothing to take away from her beauty. In fact, with most of her makeup washed off, she still looked stunning in the moonlight. If there was even a remote chance of her kissing him again, he'd be up for it. Hell, he'd be more than up for it.

"How about we go to my cabin?" he offered.

"Your cabin?" Gabriela tilted her head back and laughed. "And do what?"

"Whatever you want to do." He sucked in a breath. *More kissing, please. More of everything, please.*

"I'm not going to your cabin," she said, sounding determined. "I'd never hear the end of it if I did."

"From who?"

"Felicia. Liv. Lola. Hell, even Theo wouldn't let me live that one down."

"Why?" Sebastian was almost starting to feel insulted. Was spending the night with him so worthy of derision? He was a good lay. He prided himself on it. Women always came first. Him second. That's the way he did things. He made a point of becoming an expert of his partner's body in a very short amount of time. It was all about her pleasure, not his.

"You are kind of toxic," Gabriela admitted. She sent him a sidelong glance, her dark eyes apologetic.

"Toxic? That's harsh."

"You don't commit to anyone. You're kind of an egomaniac."

"I am not." Sebastian wondered, though. Had he put himself first too often? He could brag, he knew, but was it bragging if the accolades were true?

"Come on. Your Instagram feed is like a temple to your ego."

"Aren't all Instagram feeds that?"

She laughed a little. "You know what I mean. You're always on there with half-clad women, fast cars or your motorcycle."

"And that's bad...how?" he joked. "I'm kidding. Okay, I'm a bit insta-obnoxious. I'll admit it. I should tone it down."

"Seriously?"

"Yeah." He did mean it. Some of his posts weren't in the best taste, but he was just having fun, really. Trying to chase after some reputation that he should've long stopped caring about.

"I guess I'd better try to find some clothes. Maybe Felicia will let me in." Gabriela stood, water dripping into the drenched strappy sandals still on her feet.

"You don't want to even try to get back to your cabin, trust me. They're probably doing things in there that will scar you for life if you see them. The last thing I want to think about is Marco's cousin Bill doing anything with anyone." He stuck out his tongue in distaste and Gabriela laughed. "Come on. You can come to my

cabin. Borrow a shirt at least. First, I won't even stay
in there with you if it makes you uncomfortable. And
we're at least a whole hallway away from the rest of
the bridal party, so the likelihood of anyone seeing
us is low."

"You sure?" Gabriela looked uncertain.

"I promise to be a gentleman. My mom raised me
right."

"But…"

"You're *really* that afraid of anyone seeing you? Seriously?"

She just laughed, her eyes sparkling. "Hey, I have
a rep to protect."

Gabriela's mind wasn't working. That was the only
way she could explain it to herself. The kiss had short-
circuited all logical thoughts in her brain. Or maybe
they were just drowned out by the bad ones, because
she sure as hell loved the feel of his hands on her body
and his lips against hers. Perhaps it was the vodka
buzzing around in her brain, or the fact that Sebastian's
body felt…well, delicious beneath hers on the lounge
chair. She followed Sebastian to the elevators and down
the brightly carpeted corridor to his cabin, wondering
if she should really be doing this at all. Because once
she got on the other side of that door, she was pretty
sure she'd tear the man's clothes off.

What the hell are you thinking? That was her inner,
good-girl voice, the voice of reason that always steered
her to practical choices. Sebastian was *not* a practical choice. Not at all. He was a toxic player. Plus, was

she really going to sleep with him just to prove that she could?

Yes, she thought. *Hell, yes.*

Gabriela felt at war with herself—her good girl versus the woman she'd become: a take-no-prisoners-at-work, do-what-she-wanted-when-she-wanted, full-grown woman. She knew even considering sleeping with Sebastian Lott was wrong, so very, very wrong. Yet part of her didn't care. Part of her, the inner, awkward teen, loved the idea of sleeping with the most popular boy in school, showing him all she'd learned in the last decade. It was wrong. She'd pay for it, too, if anybody ever found out, but at that moment she didn't care.

She would make sure Sebastian Lott never ignored her again. That was for damn sure.

"Here we are," Sebastian whispered, stopping before a nondescript door. She nearly ran into his back, and had to skid to a stop, her still-wet sandals slick against the carpeted floor.

"Whoa," he said, steadying her. "You okay?"

She gave a swift nod. Was she really going to follow Sebastian Lott into his cabin? He slid his card key into the lock and the door swung open. It was a single suite, no roomies for him, lucky dog. But he had a massive king-size bed and a sliding-glass door that opened onto a small balcony overlooking the sea.

"This is huge," she murmured as she stepped inside, momentarily taken aback by the size of his suite. Hers was half the size and it slept four people.

"I like to splurge," he admitted and shrugged. He stepped in and the door slipped shut behind him.

Gabriela's heart beat a little faster. She was drenched still, and her hair dripped cold drops down her back. She shivered, though it wasn't from the cold. She watched Sebastian walk to his suitcase propped on a stand in the corner of the room. He pulled out an over-size concert tee.

"This is probably too big for you, but if you want to change into it, feel free. If you want to sleep here tonight, I can go. Maybe I'll see if Theo is still up."

"No. Wait." What was she doing? She didn't even know. All she knew was that she didn't want him to leave. Not now. "Can you help me with the zipper?" She turned, sure that she wouldn't be able to reach the zipper to her jumpsuit, which began at the middle of her back. She was also very aware that the wet fabric still clung to her, nearly transparent. She saw him stare, his eyes roving down her curves. *That's it. Want me.*

The cabin took a tiny little half spin. Maybe a touch too much vodka, she thought, distantly. *Doesn't matter, I'm in control now.* Or was she? She didn't even care, she had to be honest. If there was one thing that vodka did for her, it was to absolutely and without doubt strip away every last inhibition she had.

He approached, slowly at first, and she turned away from him, her breath catching as she waited to feel his touch. She could sense him behind her, the heat of his body, as he gently tugged at the zipper. She wasn't wearing a bra and when he got low enough he'd find the top of the lacy pink-shell thong she wore. He moved the zipper slowly, deliberately. His finger trailed her back as he went, and she could feel the electric current he created down to her toes. When the zipper reached its end, he stepped back and she turned around to face him.

He seemed to be very still, very quiet, aware of the tension between them. She felt it, too. A sudden urge bubbled up in her. *Be bad*, it said. *Be very, very bad.*

What would he say if prim-and-proper Gabriela got naked right here, right now? Wouldn't he be shocked if she got naked? What would he do? She wanted to find out.

She couldn't think of a good reason not to anymore. It might be the vodka talking, but she sure as hell liked what vodka had to say. Suddenly she couldn't remember why she shouldn't get to know Sebastian in the most biblical ways possible.

Wordlessly, she let the top go and the jumpsuit dropped to a pool of fabric at her feet. Her nipples peaked in the cool cabin air and she wore nothing but her pink thong, its sheer fabric doing little to conceal her bareness. He seemed surprised at first, but then he charted every curve of her body with his gaze, desire growing in his eyes.

That's it. Just like that. Want me.

"You're beautiful," he said, his voice a low growl as he took a step closer to her.

"I want you to touch me," she murmured. God, how could she be so bold? This was *Sebastian Lott*. Yet somehow it felt right. He was right. The two were more the same than different and right now she wanted his hands all over her.

"You sure about that?" His eyes devoured her hungrily, thoroughly, as if trying to memorize every detail of her body.

"Yes," she rasped. Her whole body wanted this, wanted him, wanted to see the ecstasy on his face when she brought him to climax, when he came, hot and gushing.

He took another step forward and touched her nipple, ever so gently, rubbing its delicate pink rim with his thumb. She groaned, leaning into his touch, feeling the delicate nerve endings there come alive. He dipped down, laying a trail of delicate kisses along her bare neck, and she moaned. His touch was so gentle, so sure, like a dancer who knew all the steps. She covered his mouth with hers and melted into him, her bare skin against his clothes, her hands running the length of his soft polo. God, his chest was firm as she put her hands beneath the hem, feeling the ridges of muscle there. Yes, oh, yes. She'd wanted to do this since high school, since she was a teenager daydreaming about the day Sebastian Lott would finally notice her. His mouth was running down the slope of her breast and then it found her nipple. He teased it gently with his tongue. Oh, but her knees went weak at that moment, the softness of his touch, the deliberate swirl of his tongue around her delicate skin. But he wasn't done, yet.

He moved downward, ever downward, and suddenly he was on his knees before her. She sucked in a breath as she looked down, putting her hands into his thick, brown hair. He glanced up, his hazel eyes meeting hers.

"I'm going to make you come," he promised, and she shuddered at the thought. He kissed her, ever so delicately through the thin fabric of her thong, and she groaned at the proximity of it, the whisper kiss against her. Was he really going to do this? Worship her at her feet?

He pushed the delicate fabric to one side and put his lips against her, down there, humming a bit, pushing air through his mouth onto her most delicate nerve endings, and every circuit in her brain lit up. He swept out his tongue but kept it relaxed, delicate, against her, so that she had no choice but to tighten her grip on his hair and groan with pleasure. She'd never had a man touch her like that before, never had a man who seemed to want to feast on her like some exotic delicacy. He kept his tongue against her, moving it ever so gently, ever so slightly, that somehow she couldn't imagine *not* coming. The climax was inevitable and she was helpless to fight against it. She didn't know how she'd be able to keep standing; her knees wobbled and she bent at the waist, holding him for support. God, that was amazing. Whatever he was doing.

"Please...don't stop," she murmured, almost a prayer, as he consumed her, pushed her ever closer to the edge. He was going to take her there. Her heart thudded in her chest and she felt the blood rushing through her ears. *Yes, don't stop. Don't—*

He pulled away and the cool air hit her.

"Not yet," he told her. "I'm going to make you come harder than you've ever come before. But. Not. Yet."

He pulled down her thong and she stepped out of it, clutching his shoulders, her brain spinning. She'd been so close, so very close, and now her pulse thudded be-

tween her legs, crying out for release. He'd built her up
and then just at the moment she thought she'd topple
over the edge he'd withdrawn. She felt her warm slick-
ness between her thighs and the hard disappointment
of thwarted desire. She wanted it all. Now.

"Don't worry," he promised. "It'll be worth the
wait."

He stood then, never breaking eye contact as he
unbuttoned his shirt and then pulled it over his head.
The sight of miles of bare skin and muscle made her
suck in her breath. She reached up to touch him, the
slope of his chest hard beneath her fingers. He found
her mouth again and she kissed him, roughly, tasting
herself and ever so aware that she needed release. Her
blood pounded in her veins for it, her heat beat madly.

He walked her back to the bed, pants still on, and
laid her down on it. She felt splayed, vulnerable, but
ready. He dipped down, licking the inside of her thigh.
She shivered, her pulse threading harder between her
legs. She glanced up at him and his eyes met hers.

"Are you ready?"

"Yes," she murmured, and he dipped down once
more, tasting her again. She almost cried out. The feel
of his smooth, wet tongue was amazing, and the little movements he made immediately ramped her up
to nearly the edge. "God," she muttered, grasping the
sheets on his cabin bed in her fists.

"God has nothing to do with this," he growled, and
then upped his strokes. Gently he probed her deepest
parts with his finger, finding her most sensitive spot
inside. She clenched her muscles around him, eager

for more, as she clutched the sheets harder. Her body tensed with the coming climax as she arched her back, her instincts taking over, and then her whole being exploded with pleasure. She cried out and sank back into his sheets, heart racing, breath coming hard.

"Told you it would be worth the wait." Sebastian grinned, self-satisfied, but this time Gabriela didn't mind the cockiness.

"Your turn," she said, determined to show him her skills. She sat up, him standing between her legs at the edge of the bed. She worked his fly, eager to set him free. Gabriela remembered the rumors about Sebastian, about his size. She wondered if they were true.

Then, suddenly, she'd freed him of his cargo shorts and boxer briefs and his immense erectness stood before her.

"Oh…my." She'd heard the rumors and yet, here in front of her, he was so much larger than she could've imagined. "I've never had one…"

"Had one what?" His mouth quirked up in a knowing grin. So he knew about his size. He had to, right? Any locker room would tell him he was enormous.

"Had one this big," she admitted.

He laughed a little, deep in his throat. "Don't worry. He doesn't bite." He waggled himself a little, so his head bobbed up and down, and that made her laugh, too. "He's friendly. *Very* friendly."

She thought she'd been around enough, but looking at Sebastian she realized how little she might still know about the male anatomy. He was huge. She cupped both hands around him, but they seemed small on him, comically small. Still, they did their best, working his shaft. He groaned and leaned forward, his massiveness before her like a dare. Could she take it all? Would she take it all?

She wanted to. Oh, did she.

She bent forward and licked his tip. He moaned again as she worked her tongue around him. *That's it. Want me. Want this.* She could only get the tip of him in her mouth as she worked the rest with her hands, making him harder, ever harder. Somehow he got bigger.

He moaned once more, leaning into her. Would he come, here in her mouth? He'd love that, she knew, his cum down her throat. But no, not this time. Not yet. She wanted to feel him inside her. Feel him filling her up. She'd have all of him. Gabriela withdrew, freeing him, and he groaned as the air hit his bareness.

"Don't stop," he growled, almost a plea.

"Not yet," she told him, grinning. "I'm going to make you come harder than you've ever come before. But. Not. Yet." She loved teasing him in the same way he'd teased her.

He grinned at her, his eyes glazed with want, his pupils dilated so much that they almost looked black.

"I want to be inside you," he murmured, holding himself with his right hand.

"Condom?" she asked.

"Of course." He reached into the little shaving kit sitting on his bedside table and pulled out a string of condoms—ultra-max in size, of course. She'd actually never seen condoms that big. He opened a package and began rolling it down his immense self.

"Wait," she cried. "Let me do that." She helped him and he bowed into her touch, his eyes never leaving hers.

"Love how you do that," he said. He touched her cheek and then he leaned in between her legs. He was going to take her, and Gabriela spread for him. Eager. Willing. Wet.

Sebastian wanted to be inside her, wanted to be balls-deep *now*. Looking at her, legs spread in a primal offering, on her back, her lips parted with want, he felt like he'd burst right there and spill himself all over her belly. But he had to be careful. He knew he was on the north side of average, and that meant that he had to take care. Not all women were…ready for him.

He nudged his head between her thighs, gently stroking her opening, easing himself up and down. She moaned, anticipation growing as he parted her lips ever so slightly, nudging the tip just inside. *That's it. Tease her. Make her want more.* Before he knew it, she'd be pulling him inside her, taking all of him.

And that was what he wanted so badly. All of him in all of her. But he'd be patient. He'd wait. It was better if he waited. He teased her, just the tip, and then he worked forward, the first third. She sucked in a breath and squeezed around him. God, she was so tight. So very, very tight. He wanted to come right there. But he forced himself to hold it. He wanted to fill all her deepest places.

"You ready for more?" he asked, and she nodded.

He pushed a bit more inside. She groaned louder.

She squeezed around him, her muscles working to accept him, to let him in. *That's it. Let me*, he thought. *Let me in*.

He couldn't believe how turned on he was, how hot he was for Gabriela Cruz. But she wasn't like the girl he remembered in high school. Nothing about her—her dark hair splayed across his pillow, her eyes bright with want—was anything like the girl he thought he'd known.

He knew by how she clutched him that she thought he had no more to give. Oh, but he did. He had more.

"Not done yet," he said.

Surprise crossed her face as it flushed red. "More?"

He nodded. "More." He moved forward, sliding himself all the way in.

"Oh," she squealed, clutching the tops of his shoulders hard. "God."

She felt perfect to him. He could stay here, just like this, and be perfectly happy, but he knew he wouldn't. He began to move. Slowly at first. A gentle thrust. Her legs came around him. *That's it.* He moved again, slowly out and slowly back in. She moaned once more. He marveled at her perfect body: her caramel-colored skin, her pink nipples puckered. Her belly button, adorably an innie. He held her hips, firm and full, as he moved inside her.

For the first time in a long time he thought, *This feels like home.*

Was it because he *knew* her? He'd known her as a person before he'd known her as a sex object? Because they'd had a long history? He didn't know, but something about this act wasn't just sex. Was that why he was so hard? Was that why he felt like coming right then? Was that why he felt a sudden and hot urge to rip that condom straight off? Feel her as nature intended, skin on skin? He pushed the thought away. No, of course he wouldn't do that. But something about Gabriela, staring at him now, desire pooling in her eyes, made him think this was how sex *ought* to be.

He knew himself and knew that often, at this point in the act, he'd be focused on his own pleasure. Yes, he always made sure a woman came first, but after that…after that, it was almost always Sebastian's time. He'd focus on what he needed to do and then it would all be over. It was an equitable exchange, always. Yet, Gabriela made him want to see her come again. One climax wasn't enough. He wanted to see her face when he brought her pleasure again and again. Her pleasure just ramped up his.

"I want you to come," he told her, moving slowly inside her.

"O-okay." Her voice came out breathless. She was focused on taking him, he knew, focused on handling him inside her. But he'd make her forget his size. He'd make her come hard. He licked his thumb and then touched her, gently massaging her clit. She gasped and opened a little more for him.

Take me. Take all of me.

He moved a little faster, and her hips met him in a perfect rhythm. He glanced down and saw himself moving in and out, the perfect primal dance of give and take. He saw her face flush a deeper shade of red as she sucked in a breath. She opened her legs wider for him, and he went deeper, ever deeper. He wanted to come but he held off, waiting for her. She'd come at least once more before he'd allow himself to come. And then, he knew, he'd start all over again. Round two. Followed by round three. He wanted to have her every way it was possible tonight. Every position. He didn't know if a person could get through the Kama Sutra in one night, but he sure as hell would try.

He could feel her muscles tensing as she clenched him and he drove her harder to her climax. He read her body like a book, working her a little bit faster, a little bit harder. She came in a cry as her whole body tensed with the rush of pleasure and then relaxed again. He could feel himself working harder and harder, pushing deeper and deeper, and he could hold it no more. He came, too, in a hot rush, one of the most intense cums he'd had in his life, and all he could think of was how he wanted to do this again and again, and never stop. He wanted Gabriela, not just for this one night, but for many nights to come.

He collapsed, spent, on Gabriela's heaving chest.

What the hell was that? he wondered. He'd never thought about commitment during climax. What was wrong with him? One night with a woman he'd known in high school and suddenly he was thinking about a future?

"Wow," Gabriela breathed beneath him, running her hands through his hair. "That was…"

"Amazing?"

"Eh…it was okay," she deadpanned, but she was grinning ear to ear.

He went rigid and pushed himself up on his elbows in playful shock. "*Just* okay?" He blinked hard, searching her face.

She shrugged. "Yeah, it was pretty good."

"*Pretty good.* Just pretty good?" It was the best sex of his life and she was telling him it was…okay? Pretty good?

"You can't be serious." He withdrew, holding on to the condom as he shrank post sex.

"Well, I mean, you had such a reputation and all." Gabriela grinned and he couldn't tell if she was teasing him or not. "I thought you'd be…well, that you'd last longer."

"I…" *I wanted to come deep inside you and could barely restrain myself as it was,* he wanted to say but didn't. "Oh, so you're under the impression we're done for the evening?"

"Aren't we?" She nodded at his shrinking member.

"Oh, no. We're not done." He shook his head slowly, his blood rising. He'd never had a woman tell him he was just *okay* before. Oh, no. Not on his watch. Not now, not ever. "And you haven't seen all I can do yet."

"I haven't?" Her eyes challenged him.

"You haven't," he promised. He got rid of the condom and worked himself with his hand, already finding he was coming back to life. She thought that was just *okay* sex? He'd blow her mind before this night was over. He was determined to change her mind. She hadn't seen anything yet and he'd prove it. They weren't going to sleep tonight. He'd make sure of that.

CHAPTER TEN

GABRIELA COULDN'T BELIEVE her eyes. He was ready to go. Again. In record time, as if he were eighteen. Not that she'd had sex with an eighteen-year-old anytime lately, but she had had enough hookups to know that going from done to ready again in 1.2 seconds flat wasn't the norm.

"Is that for real?" She nodded toward his throbbing erection, and almost giggled. The question was on so many levels. Was his hard-on real? Was his massive member real? If she weren't sitting here, staring right at it, she wouldn't even believe it.

"Oh, nothing about him is fake." He held his heaviness in his hand and she stared at it, awestruck.

I had all of that inside me. She still couldn't believe she'd been able to take him. Gabriela had come harder than she'd ever come before, probably because he was able to touch parts of her that had never been touched before. Sure, she'd told him the sex was just *okay.* How could she tell him it was mind-blowing? Sebastian Lott's ego didn't need *that.* Besides, she liked teasing him and keeping him off balance. She laughed to herself about how quickly he'd gotten himself up and ready for round two.

"On your hands and knees," he commanded. When she hesitated, he added, "Please." He flashed her a devilish grin. Normally, Gabriela felt self-conscious about that position, but here, with Sebastian, she felt freer. Sure, it was still the vodka at the wheel, but she just felt game. That was all it came down to. Maybe it was all about proving to him—and to herself—that she wasn't that squeaky little mouse from high school. Whatever the case, she wasn't about to back down from a challenge.

"Doggie style?" She hopped on all fours and waggled her butt.

"Woof...wooooof." He slapped her on her bare cheek. She jumped, surprised, and giggled with delight. Oh, this was going to be fun. She heard the condom wrapper rip and then, a few seconds later, he was deep inside her, quickly this time. She gasped, hard, the transition from empty to full so sudden, so quick, that it nearly took her breath away. And then he was riding her, hard. In. Out. Seemingly deeper each time.

All coherent thought left her mind and she was just an animal running on instinct, a dog in heat, desperate to be filled.

"Yes," she moaned. "Yes."

"Harder?"

"God, yes." She gripped the bedsheets, balling them into her fists, holding on for dear life. He grabbed her hips and leveraged himself deeper inside her. She gasped as he reached her innermost depths. She didn't know where he ended and she began. All she knew was that every nerve ending in her body was alive, every bit of her tuned to him. There was something so base about what they were doing, so dirty.

What would her friends say now if they knew she was on her hands and knees? At that moment she didn't care. She just... Loved it. No more responsible Gabbie. No more wet blanket. No more worrying. Here, now, Sebastian was in control and she was riding wave after wave of him. Then he was out of her and flipping her over onto her back.

"Sit up," he told her, his voice leaving no room for argument. God, she loved that. Being told what to do. She spent her entire day ordering other people around, and now, somehow, it felt good to be in the passenger seat, to let someone else drive for once.

He kissed her, hard, his tongue entwined with hers, sending another shock wave of desire through her body. Her nipples felt heavy and ached for his touch. Then he came down on top of her and was in her again, his weight delicious across her breasts. She was so small and he was so very big. She felt like she might come again right there, but after feeling her, exploring her this way, he rolled, flipping onto his back so she was on top.

"I want to watch you," he said.

She sat up, her full breasts heavy as he met her gaze. Something felt irresistibly sexy about being seen by him, being watched. But could she keep this up? Could she keep eye contact? That seemed incredibly... intimate. More intimate than sex itself.

"Reverse cowgirl?" she offered, attempting to turn around.

"No," he said, grabbing her firmly by the hips. "I want to watch you."

His eyes never left hers as she slowly mounted him and began moving ever so slowly. At first she felt self-conscious beneath his gaze, but then, under his watchful hazel eyes, she felt bolder somehow. She moved faster this time and his watching her, his intense focus, ramped up her need.

"Want me." Her words tumbled out of her mouth before she could stop them.

"Oh, God, Gabriela. I want you." His hips moved to meet hers and there, on top of him, as he gazed at her, she hit the top of the peak again, crying out as endorphins flooded her brain. She collapsed on top of his fit chest, breathing hard.

"You're so beautiful when you come," he murmured into her hair. He only let her rest for a second or two and then he'd flipped her on her side. He began moving again, slowly at first and then harder. Somehow he extended deeper with every thrust, filling her up more than she thought possible. Just when she thought she couldn't take any more of him, she managed to swallow him.

"You feel amazing in all the positions," he whispered in her ear. "I don't know how I should come."

"Then maybe you should just come now," she whispered back. She worked him, milking him as she concentrated. He groaned, matching each of her movements with his own.

"No," he said, a whisper against her neck. "We're just getting started."

He moved her so her legs were off to the side and he was taking her even more deeply.

"God, you feel so good." He tilted his dark head back, closing his eyes, seeming to relish the feel of her. She loved the look of intense pleasure on his face. Oh, how he was enjoying her. She wanted him to have the best cum he'd ever had, wanted him to explode inside her, unable to hold it anymore.

Tiring of that position after a few heady thrusts, he pulled her to his side and raised her legs straight up, holding her tightly by the ankles. She'd never had a man who explored her the way Sebastian did, never tried so many positions all at once. He grabbed her ankles hard and moved even deeper inside her and then he pushed her ankles apart, his hazel eyes finding hers.

"I'm coming," he told her.

"Come in me. Come deep," she challenged him, and he met the challenge, pushing ever deeper. She watched his muscles ripple down the front of his abdomen as he thrust once, twice and then found his shuddering release with a shout of satisfaction. She loved the sound. She wanted to hear it again and again.

He collapsed on top of her, their sweat mingling together as he panted.

"That was fucking amazing," he murmured against her bare chest.

The room spun slightly as Gabriela glanced at the ceiling. She still had a heady buzz, not that she could tell if it was the vodka or the sex. Satisfied in every possible way, she felt her eyelids grow heavy.

Just don't fall asleep, she told herself even as a yawn snuck in. *Do not fall asleep.*

Soon after the early-morning light seeped in through the patio doors of Sebastian's suite, Gabriela jolted awake. God, she was sore. So freakin' sore. She felt like she'd been run over by a bus. She blinked the sleepiness from her eyes and focused on the patio doors of the cruise ship suite. Oh, they'd docked, she noticed. The window looked out over the golden shores of Cozumel, ringed by intense blue-green water. Beautiful. Then she remembered: her room didn't *have* a patio. She glanced around the finely furnished cabin and at the unfamiliar suitcase near the foot of the bed, and then it hit her.

Oh, no.

She sat up in bed.

Say it's not so. She glanced over and saw Sebastian Lott sprawled out next to her, naked as a jaybird and snoring. He was on his stomach, firm ass in the air, his tan lines on display for all to see, one arm up over his head as if he'd fallen from a great height and landed straight next to her in *his* king-size bed.

Oh, no. No, no, no.

Her head throbbed, and her mouth tasted like she'd been licking sandpaper all night. What happened? Why was she…?

Memories came back little by little. The many, many vodka sodas. Damn that fine vodka. Then Felicia pushing her into the pool. And the next thing she knew, she was naked in bed, doing all manner of unspeakable positions with Sebastian Lott. Oh, God. The many positions. The many, many, *many* positions.

She moved, trying to get out of bed, and that was when she realized she was sore AF, completely and absolutely sore down there. Then she remembered: he'd been a monster. He did have an eggplant in his pants. Not that she'd minded last night, tipsy on vodka. She'd relished his massive manhood, enjoying it in at least two dozen positions. She had to admit, most men weren't as creative as Sebastian Lott.

But…*no*. This was exactly what she'd told Felicia *not* to do, and she'd gone and done it. Oh, this wasn't going to be good. If she ever found out…?

She glanced at the small bedside table and saw her phone sitting there. She quickly grabbed it but the battery was long dead, the screen black. Dammit. What time was it? She glanced outside once more but couldn't tell from the slant of the sun. Could be early or could be late. The sun was up, that was all she knew. She glanced around the room for her clothes. She saw her jumpsuit—wrinkled from having been dunked in the pool and left to dry on the floor. Where were her shoes? Who knew? She needed to get dressed and get out of there, preferably before the man woke up. She didn't want any awkward goodbyes. What bogus excuse would she come up with on a cruise ship anyway? She couldn't go feed her nonexistent dog.

She slid out of bed, naked, planting both bare feet on the carpeted ground. Lott shifted behind her, murmuring something in his sleep and she froze. *Do not wake up*, she pleaded silently. The last thing she wanted to do was to have to explain why she was sneaking out of his cabin. Then the thought hit her. What if someone saw her? What if she had to explain what she was doing coming out of his room at sun-thirty? No, don't even think about that, she told herself. She just had to get out.

She tiptoed over to her jumpsuit and slid into it one leg at a time, keeping an eye on the snoring Sebastian the entire time. God, the man was gorgeous, even lying on his stomach. He had massively muscular shoulders and the tightest butt she'd ever seen. *Stop gawking and get moving*, her inner voice told her. No time to dally. She pulled up the front of her jumpsuit and glanced around for her wristlet wallet, the one with her cabin key in it. She found it tossed on top of the coffee table near the TV. She grabbed it and made her way to the door.

She paused, hand on the handle. Should she leave Sebastian a note? She glanced backward once more at the sleeping man. No—no need to leave a note. She figured it was easier this way. One and done. Wasn't that the easiest way? Hadn't they talked about avoiding awkward goodbyes with their Spark hookups? Hell, he might even be pretending to be sleeping. No matter. She'd be gone before she could find out. Where was her thong? Her shoes? She searched under Sebastian's cargo shorts lying on the chair and then beside the small desk bolted to the floor. No sign of them.

Behind her, Sebastian groaned and rolled over onto

his side. She froze, glancing up at him, heart thudding. *Do not wake up!* she silently prayed. She stayed completely still until she heard a light snoring begin and then she let out a long, relieved breath. Forget her shoes and her thong, she thought. She didn't need the sandals for today anyway. Her flip-flops would do and she had another set of heels for the rehearsal dinner tonight. Besides, the pool might have ruined the sandals anyhow.

Gabriela glanced through the peephole of the door and saw that the passageway was empty—at least from her limited vantage point. Thank goodness.

"Trying to sneak out on me?" Sebastian's voice was a growl and Gabriela nearly jumped out of her skin.

"Uh, well, it's late and..." Gabriela glanced back in time to see Sebastian, shirtless, hair a ruffled but enticing mess, sitting up on one elbow and studying her with a steady gaze.

"It's seven-thirty in the morning," he told her.

"Right, well..." Gabriela completely lost her train of thought as she glanced down at Sebastian's firm chest. She remembered how those pecs felt beneath her palms.

"Why don't we have breakfast? I'll order something in. And I'm not pretending, either. This—" he grinned "—is a genuine offer." The idea of crawling into bed with a half-naked Sebastian and waiting for the delivery of a plate of eggs Benedict sounded pretty tempting, if Gabriela were honest with herself. But then what? Wait to be found by the rest of the bridal party? Roll down the corridor in the world's worst walk of shame right before the snorkeling excursion in a couple of hours? Try to explain to Felicia how she hadn't actually planned to steal this man right from under her nose? No. Lola didn't need this kind of drama the day before her wedding.

"I don't think that's a good idea." Gabriela kept her hand on the doorknob.

"Why not?" Sebastian raised an eyebrow. Clearly the man wasn't used to rejection. Of course, looking at his smooth bare chest, she could see why.

"Because this..." She motioned between them. "This never happened."

Sebastian sat straighter. "You mean the hundred and one positions and...I think about eight orgasms...and counting? *That* didn't happen?"

"I didn't say I didn't enjoy it," she conceded, remembering how good his hands had felt on her. How very, very good. "It's just that we can't let anybody know about what happened here."

"Why not?" He sat up a bit more, revealing more bare skin. It was like staring at a hot-men-on-cruise-ships calendar.

"Because...because..." She desperately searched for a reason. "Because you were supposed to be celibate. The bet, remember?"

"I don't care about that silly bet. I'll buy Marco a nice bottle of whiskey. It'll be done." Sebastian patted the bed next to him. "Now, what are you doing way over there? Why don't you come here?"

Gabriela hesitated as she pulled her hand from the doorknob. Part of her wanted to jump right into bed with Sebastian Lott once more. But that was insanity. Pure insanity. It was like she felt mesmerized by his bare skin. What was wrong with her?

"I can't do that." She shook her head. "I've got to go. Seriously. I need to get dressed and…" She tugged at her halter top. "And change into clothes that I wasn't wearing for twenty-four hours."

"Well, they spent at least seven hours on my floor, so that's technically not true." A sly smile crossed his face. "Come on. Why are you way over there? It's like you're trying to gnaw your arm off to escape. Come on. This isn't a Spark hookup."

"But it kind of is." She tucked her wristlet under her arm. "I'm going."

He kicked the covers off and revealed his full naked body as he slid out of bed and stood. His impressive abs rippled and that wasn't the only thing she noticed. The man was impressive even when in the off position, she thought. *Endowed* as a word didn't even seem to cover it. *Focus, Gabbie, focus. Got to go.*

"You can't just leave."

"I can't?" She thrust one hand on her hip. Now he was back to his cocky, egotistic self. This Sebastian she could resist just fine.

"No." He shook his head slowly as he moved ever closer to her. "Not without a goodbye kiss." The wall of man muscle kept moving toward her and she couldn't take her eyes off him. When he got to her, she craned her neck to look up at him as he reached out and gently grazed her chin with his finger.

"You're really bolting out of here, aren't you?" he asked, eyes steady on hers.

Her throat went dry. She'd forgotten how mesmerizing the man's eyes were, how strong his hands.

"I can't cause drama for Lola. Not now."

"So you're running out of here because you're worried about Lola?" Sebastian sounded skeptical. "It's not because you had the best sex of your life and it's freaking you out?"

Gabriela stood stock-still for a second. "Nope," she said, though even she thought her denial sounded weak.

He glanced at her, assessing. "Well, then, I've got work to do."

A nervous giggle escaped her mouth. "Oh, you think you get a do-over?"

"Oh, I know I do." He pulled her into his arms then and kissed her, and she felt herself melt into him, even as his desire stirred against her belly. God, the man was such a good kisser. All worries fled her mind as his tongue met hers and she felt her own want grow inside her. He pulled away first. "How about we get that redo right now?"

Gabriela felt her heart thump in her chest. "C-can't right now," she managed to say, even though every fiber of her being cried out for another go.

Sebastian smiled, confident, cocky, not the least bit deterred. He was a man determined to get what he wanted. "Later then," he said, and it felt like a promise.

CHAPTER ELEVEN

SHE FLIPPED DOWN the handle of Sebastian's door and fled, speeding down the passageway, panting. Later then? No, there could *be* no later. This was it, she thought. If Felicia ever found out… But no. She wouldn't think about that now. She had to get back to her room before anyone noticed she was creeping down the corridor in last night's outfit, much the worse for wear. Still, she had to admit, the night had been worth it. God, the man was pure goodness in bed. She bit her lip thinking about all the various positions, all the many ways she'd come. Hell, she didn't even *know* she could come the way she came last night. He was a man on a mission, a man built to please. She tried not to think of all the other women he'd pleased before her and how he'd come to know all those little tricks. Midway down the hallway she realized the numbers were headed in the wrong direction.

Ugh! Wrong way! *Seriously?* She stopped and turned around, only to see Sebastian standing in his doorway, arms crossed. He'd managed to pull on a pair of shorts, but otherwise he was all impressive skin.

"Lost?" he asked, smirk on his face.

"Maybe," she muttered as she quickly hurried by his door.

"You could come in," he offered.

"No," she snapped and padded down the passageway in her bare feet, even as she felt her face turn beet red. She heard his laugh follow her and she knew this wasn't over. Not by a long shot.

She finally got to her room and tapped her key against the lock, watching in growing annoyance as the red light came on each time.

"Come on, work," she muttered, flipping the card over and trying once more. Finally, the green light blinked on. She put her shoulder into the door. It swung open and she was glad to be safely in her room.

Liv was asleep—alone—in her bed. Felicia was nowhere to be found—thank goodness. She shut the door a bit too hard behind her and Liv sat up, groaning.

"Who's that?" she growled, rubbing her eyes.

"It's Gabriela. Sorry, Liv." Gabriela cringed as she plugged in her phone at the cord near her bed. Her phone booted up and she saw that it was almost eight already. The snorkeling excursion on shore happened at nine, which only left an hour to get ready and grab breakfast.

"Is it time for the boat ride yet?" Liv asked, yawning loudly as she stretched her arms to the ceiling.

"Not yet," Gabriela said as she quickly unzipped her suitcase, looking for a change of clothes.

"Wait a minute." Liv blinked at Gabriela, her eyes

ringed with streaks of mascara. "Is that the jumpsuit you wore last night?"

Oh, no. She's putting two and two together. Inwardly, Gabriela groaned.

"Where did you sleep last night?" Liv excitedly bunched the covers up beneath her arms as she sat straighter in bed. "Gabriela *Cruz*. You stayed in a boy's room. Didn't you? Didn't you!"

Gabriela laughed, shifting uncomfortably. "You know I wouldn't do that."

"But you did." Liv clapped her hands together. "Who was he? Tell me!"

"Where's Felicia?" Gabriela asked, trying desperately to change the subject.

"Felicia? I think she's at the gym." Liv crawled to the end of her bed. "Who did you—?"

"This early?"

Liv shrugged. "I'm not her keeper." Liv ran a hand through her messy blue hair. "Who did *you* ride last night is what I want to know."

"Uh, no. Really. I just slept on a chair by the pool, I guess." That might've been the lamest lie she'd ever uttered.

Liv's eyes narrowed. "I'm not buying it. Your hair? That just-got-fucked look? You didn't pass out on any chair." She shook her head as she studied Gabriela further. "Because look at that hickey the size of Wisconsin on your neck."

Gabriela's hand flew to her neck. Sebastian had given her a hickey? Then again, he'd devoured her from head to toe all night long, so she wasn't surprised he'd left a mark.

"You *did* fuck somebody last night! I knew it!"

Gabriela refused to answer. "I've got to shower. Mind if I...?" She ducked into the bathroom before Liv could answer and started running hot water. The last thing on earth she wanted to do was to talk more about where she'd been last night. Of course, pretty soon, the rest of the wedding party would know. Gabriela had no doubt Liv was on her phone right at this minute texting everyone the shocking news that uptight Gabriela maybe *wasn't* so uptight anymore.

Not that it came as any surprise to Gabriela. She stepped into the hot shower and let the water run over her. With any luck, by breakfast, the whole thing would die down and Liv would find something else bright and shiny to distract her. There'd be no more talk about what Gabriela had done last night. She would already be teased for not returning to her room for the night and didn't want to imagine what would happen if Liv and Felicia found out who she'd been with. She'd been warning them away from Sebastian only to fall prey to his charms herself?

Then, as the water streamed down her bare breasts, she remembered Sebastian's hands on them...and his mouth. She felt a surge of heat through her that had nothing to do with the shower and everything to do with his expert hands.

It was just a single night, she promised herself. *Nothing more.* She would be willing to bet anything that Sebastian would pretend nothing had happened between them and that suited Gabriela just fine.

Sebastian was in love. There was literally no other way he could explain how he was feeling. He hummed—actually hummed—while he brushed his teeth, feeling lighter than air. He'd had the best sex of this year... scratch that, of his *life*, last night, and it was all because he'd gotten naked with a woman who actually, finally, had some substance. Gabriela Cruz was smart, sophisticated and, boy, did she know her way around the bedroom. Sebastian had been limiting himself, dating in the shallow end of the pool, but he'd never imagined it'd be so fun taking a dive in the deep end. It's not that he avoided smart women with opinions of their own...it was just that, he had to be honest, he hadn't been so discerning when it came to who landed in his Spark feed. Was she pretty and willing? Then so was he.

But last night...he'd felt a kind of magnetic chemistry he'd never felt before, and it had everything to do with Gabriela's brain. She could challenge him in a way that few women could, and he knew, *just knew*, that if she allowed herself to think about it for a little bit, she'd see that the two were meant to be together. He'd gone to Harvard Law. She'd graduated Princeton undergrad. The only two members of their high school circle who'd made it to the Ivy League? They should be destined to be together.

Sebastian slathered on some shaving cream, ready to shave off his morning shadow. He glanced at his phone, ready at any second for a message to pop up from her. But none ever did. Sure, she'd left in a hurry that morning, but he'd told himself that was no red flag. No woman left his bed unsatisfied. He'd made sure she'd had the time of her life. Gabriela's cries of pleasure still rang in his ears and he could still see her face, flushed with pure bliss. No, she'd been more than satisfied. He'd seen to it. So why had she hurried out? Maybe it was just habit. But he wasn't worried. He wasn't going to let himself worry. No woman could walk away from that kind of amazing sex. Hell, *he* couldn't walk away from it and he'd spent his entire adult life doing just that. He had no problem saying goodbye.

He shaved across his left cheek, assessing himself in the mirror. *You've finally done it,* he silently told himself, *finally fallen for a woman.*

He had to admit, Gabriela was perfect for him. They'd have adorable *and* intelligent kids. She was sharper than his razor, which he now tapped on the edge of the sink, a bit of foam flying into the pool of water there.

He grinned thinking about Gabriela fiercely holding on to her clipboard at the party the night before, how she desperately tried to keep everything—and everyone—in order. *She'd make an amazing mom.*

The thought struck him hard. Was he ready for all that? Wife…and kids? He glanced at himself in the mirror, his hazel eyes steady. He was ready. He'd been ready for a long time. He'd just been waiting for the right woman. He knew this.

He was in love. Sure, he knew it was crazy. He'd

only had one night with Gabriela, but then when he
thought about it, technically, he'd known her for fifteen
years. That wasn't rash. And hell, didn't people fall in
love at first sight all the time? Hadn't Lola and Marco
famously talked about that very first blind date *he* set
them up on and how all the cards seemed to fall into
place the second their eyes met across that restaurant
table? So, falling in love with Gabriela after a night of
mind-blowing sex didn't feel all that outlandish then.

It felt like destiny, he decided. They were meant
to be together, and it was fate that had brought them
back together on this boat. He'd make sure that she
knew it, too.

Sebastian threw on his clothes, checking his phone
once more, noticing there was still no text from Gabriela. Maybe she was…shy? He thought about texting,
but as he debated he walked to ship's main restaurant.
At the main doors, he saw most of the bridal party
standing in line at the buffet, against the window back-
drop of the dazzling blue-green sea.

Gabriela was there, looking radiant in a halter top,
a pair of cut-off shorts and plastic flip-flops, her hair
thrown up casually in a messy ponytail, aviator sunglasses perched on her head. She glanced up and, for
a split second, their eyes met. He felt a smile pull at
the corner of his mouth, but then she quickly glanced
away, focusing her attention once more on Lola in front
of her and Felicia, who stood behind her. Marco and
Theo stood ahead of them, oblivious.

Sebastian didn't understand. He'd spent the night
exploring every single beautiful crevice of her amaz-

ing body and she wasn't making eye contact with him? That had to be a mistake. He walked up just in time to hear Lola giggle and ask, "Seriously, Gabbie. Who *was it*?"

"Who was *who*?" Sebastian asked, sliding into line behind the trio. Felicia frowned at him, but Sebastian ignored her, keeping his attention on Gabriela.

"Gabriela got her rocks off last night," Felicia grumbled, rolling her eyes. "I mean, stop the presses, right? The ice queen gets some! She won't tell us who, so maybe she didn't actually get laid." Felicia shrugged one shoulder to cast her own doubt on the whole story.

Sebastian focused on Gabriela, but she still refused to look at him. Did he have something on his face? Had he missed some shaving cream?

"It's nobody," Gabriela said. "Nobody you know."

"Nobody?" Sebastian asked, feeling his blood rise. He wasn't *nobody*.

"Nobody," she reiterated a little forcefully as she finally, and at last, looked him in the eye. It was there, in that stark stare, that he realized a hard truth: she wanted him to keep quiet. She had no intention of ever sharing with Lola, Felicia or anyone else that they'd spent the night having rock star sex in every position imaginable. He couldn't believe it.

Sure, she'd said something about keeping the whole thing under wraps, but he hadn't realized she'd been so...serious.

"I—" Sebastian began, but she cut him off with a glare. Every curse word he could think of was in that silent stare, as well as every threat. He decided not to challenge her out there, in front of Lola and Felicia. "I bet he was a lucky man," he said.

Confusion crossed Gabriela's face for the briefest of seconds but then she quickly glanced away from him. He couldn't understand what was happening. It was as if...Gabriela was trying to pretend none of it ever happened. He didn't understand. Why was she trying to pretend the hottest sex ever never *happened*? Unless... unless she didn't think it was the best sex of her life. Could it be? He thought back to the night before and to her many, many lengthy and loud climaxes. No woman was that good an actress.

Or was she?

Sebastian was determined to get to the bottom of Gabriela's cold shoulder. He watched her as she grabbed a cup of coffee and a bagel, and seemed to be headed out of line, away from the rest of the group. Back to her room maybe? Now was his chance. He stepped out of line, following her to the elevators.

"Gabriela," he called, but she didn't turn. He knew she must've heard him. He was only twenty feet away. But she kept walking, stiffly and with purpose, away from him. "Gabriela, I know you hear me. Please. Wait."

Gabriela didn't stop. She even bypassed the elevators entirely and hit the stairs heading up to their rooms. He took the stairs two at a time and finally caught her elbow on the second landing.

"Why are you running away from me?" he asked, feeling winded and still off balance.

"Why are you chasing me?" she asked, challenging him as she stopped, one foot on the next step up.

"I wanted to…" *Remind you what an amazing night we had. And plan another one.* "I just…" As Gabriela stared at him, waiting, Sebastian felt all the words dry up on his tongue. For the first time in his life, he was speechless. That had never happened before. He always had something witty to say, always had a snappy comeback. What was it about Gabriela's discerning gaze that made him feel like an awkward teenager again?

"Look, I didn't realize you were really serious. About keeping last night a secret."

Inwardly he wanted to slap himself. Why did he sound like such a needy jerk?

"Deadly serious." Gabriela left it at that. She didn't elaborate, didn't say any more. The look on her face challenged him to probe further.

Now Sebastian started to understand that he might be in trouble. He'd been dreaming up big romantic plans, but looking at her face now, he realized she had *not* been doing the same. *Nice going, egomaniac,* he told himself. Just assuming she'd be on board.

Come on, man, get it together, he told himself. *You're not helpless. This isn't the first time you've ever been with a woman before.*

"Look. I had…an amazing time with you," he said, trying to find his footing again. He reached out and took her hand. "You were…well, you turned my world upside down."

For a second Gabriela froze. "I did?"

He nodded, slowly. "That kind of chemistry…it

doesn't come along every day." Or ever. He'd been with a lot of women. *A lot*. None of them came close to Gabriela. Not even in the same league. He just couldn't believe the chemistry was all one-sided, couldn't believe only he felt the jolt of electricity between them, a current he could feel snapping even now as he held her hand. "I just thought we could explore it. I've never been with someone like you, and I really think this could be something."

There. That sounded reasonable. He wasn't asking for marriage—yet. He wasn't declaring his love or anything as crazy as that. Though his heart, hammering in his chest, told him he was already in way deeper. He wasn't just falling for Gabriela Cruz. He already had.

Gabriela hesitated. "You think we could be something?"

"I do. I really do. I never say this. I really don't. You intrigue me, Gabriela. I want to get to know you better."

She bit her lip. "Come on. We just had fun, that's all."

"It was more than fun." Gabriela felt seared into his brain. Her scent, the softness of her skin, the readiness of her body to meld against his. This seemed to reach her for a minute and her body language warmed slightly. She was hesitating, fighting some inner voice he couldn't hear. "I'd like to try this. Try getting to know you."

"What do you mean?"

"I mean, you and me. Let's see where this goes."

"I thought you were only a one-night guy," she said. "I thought last night was just…one night."

"Why not make it more than that?" Sebastian wasn't going to let her go so easily.

She laughed a little, showing her perfectly straight white teeth. "We can't!" she exclaimed.

"Why not?"

"Because everyone would find out. And Felicia would lose her shit and…and…then we'd ruin Lola's big day, and we can't do that."

Sebastian quirked an eyebrow. "I don't think we'd ruin anything. Felicia can deal."

"Felicia cares about Felicia and she's been wanting to get your pants off since the cruise started. She told us. At the bachelorette party."

Sebastian felt like Gabriela could've knocked him over with a feather. "That's news to me. She hates me."

"No, she doesn't. Or maybe she does. Maybe she wants hate sex, I don't know, but she wants you."

Sebastian felt absolutely nothing about this revelation. Felicia was…not someone he'd ever considered getting involved with again. She was volatile, immature and a walking headache.

Gabriela squirmed beneath his gaze, looking intensely uncomfortable. Then the truth dawned on Sebastian like a load of bricks falling from the sky.

"You're embarrassed to be with me."

"No, I'm not," Gabriela countered quickly. A lie. He could tell by the way she wouldn't look him in the eye. Well, hell, that was a first. There'd been plenty of women who'd been angry with him, furious even, but embarrassed? "Look, I'd just rather not everybody know, okay? We had a good thing, and it was fun, but let's just…you know, move on?"

"Move on," he repeated.

"Yeah?" She looked hopeful. "I mean, don't get me wrong, it was *amazing*. Truly." She was slowly working her way up the stairs—away from him. "But, I mean, casual works better. Like, today if you don't mind, maybe you won't go on the snorkeling trip with everyone? I mean, just pretend you have a hangover or something."

"You don't even want me on the boat?" Now things were getting personal. She wanted him to avoid her? She seriously had no interest in pursuing this further? She was going to light a fire in him and then just let it burn itself out? He couldn't believe she didn't feel the pull, the magnetism, between them. Then he got an idea. He hadn't used all the tricks in his bag of goodies. Not yet. He could show her that what they had was real, with the other ninety-eight positions he hadn't tried last night.

"One more night," he said.

She stopped, hand on the rail. "What do you mean?"

"Tonight. We've got two more nights on this ship, so give me just one more. Just one. Then, if you want to walk, walk." He rubbed the back of her palm in gentle slow circles as he took a step up, so they were both standing on the same step. He saw her hesitate. Time to call this woman's bluff. "Can you truly tell me you don't want a repeat of last night?"

She froze and said nothing, her pupils growing wide. Sebastian moved closer. He inhaled her scent:

something light and citrus, probably from her recent shower. He pulled her closer to him and kissed her on the mouth. She froze at first, making him wonder if he'd been too bold, and then she began to kiss him back. Instantly his groin grew tight as he rubbed against the confines of his zipper. Her tongue found his and suddenly his whole body lit up with desire. How he wanted to know if this kiss was making her wet. He knew he wasn't just imaging their chemistry. He was ready for another night *now*. But he knew he needed to wait. Bide his time. She was breathing heavily and so was he, and they both knew what their bodies wanted.

"One more night," he said, and he turned on his heel and left her, panting, in the stairwell.

CHAPTER TWELVE

ONE MORE NIGHT. Gabriela heard Sebastian's words echo in her head as she sat on the deck of the excursion boat for the snorkeling trip the bride and bridesmaids had planned to take that morning. The sun glinted off the pristine blue water as Felicia, Liv, Lola and Veronica slathered on sunscreen as they positioned themselves on the lounging chairs at the bow of the boat.

They all wore dark sunglasses, Lola bemoaning her hangover while she rubbed sunscreen on her shoulders. Veronica had a streak of thick bright white sunscreen on her nose. She was the only one wearing a cover-up. The other bridesmaids had quickly slipped out of their cut-off shorts and T-shirts, revealing brightly colored swimsuits.

"You can't be too careful," she'd said as a defense. "I burn instantly. I never tan. It's a whole thing in my family. Don't ask me why they moved to Miami. We belong in upstate New York."

"I really shouldn't have had all that tequila," Lola groaned.

"You should've had my hangover cure." Felicia glanced over the top of her sunglasses.

Lola shook her head. "No way am I drinking anything with a raw egg in it," she countered.

The conversation drifted right past Gabriela. She had a hangover but it didn't have anything to do with alcohol. She could still feel Sebastian's lips on hers, the way he'd promised her one more night. Dared her to have one, really. She felt her stomach tingle at the prospect. Would she? Then she thought about how he'd almost outed her at breakfast, and reconsidered. Could she risk it? Sure the sex had been…amazing. Better than she'd ever imagined. But she had to be realistic: what future could they possibly have? He was Swipe Left, for goodness' sake. And when Felicia found out, she'd be livid.

She saw at the other end of the bow that Marco, Theo, Bill and James were huddled there, talking about the snorkeling gear, while Sebastian was nowhere to be found. Thankfully. She didn't want to have to worry he'd say something. A distant headache still throbbed in her temples, and she was regretting that last vodka soda the night before. Would she have ended up in Sebastian's bed if she hadn't drunk so much? She actually didn't know the answer to that. Maybe she would have anyway. She had desperately been trying to prove something—to him, to herself. Hell, to Felicia? She didn't know. Never in a million years had she imagined he'd want a relationship. Maybe she'd overdone it on trying to prove something.

She pulled out her phone, scrolled through her Instagram, and snooped on Sebastian's page. Picture after picture of him and some new girl, nearly every week.

At bars all along South Beach. He said he wanted more than that, but his social media life told a different story. Yet she couldn't forget the intensity in his hazel eyes, the way he'd looked at her on the stairs that morning as if he'd wanted to eat her for breakfast. And she almost wanted him to.

The man had skills, and she was still reeling from his size. No wonder he had a new woman on his Instagram feed every week. She had to admit that one more night was tempting. More than tempting. She'd never come so much in a single night and she was half wondering if she could break that record with another round. The man's body was like the best kind of amusement park. She wanted badly to take another ride.

"Earth to Gabriela," Lola said, waving her hand in front of Gabriela's face. "Hello?"

"W-what?" Gabriela brought herself back to the present, embarrassed to have been caught staring off into space thinking about Sebastian's naked bits.

"I was asking you if you were good to go for the rehearsal dinner tonight? If you want to invite your *mystery man*, he's welcome."

Liv giggled and Felicia snorted.

"N-no, that's okay." *He's already going to be there.* Gabriela wondered how she'd gotten herself into this mess and then she remembered: vodka. It was all vodka's fault. Vodka and the man's damn fine self.

"Speaking of hookups," Liv said, sitting up. "I heard that Swipe Left got him some."

Gabriela stiffened. "How do you know?"

"What?" Felicia was now sitting up, rigid as a board.

Jealous, Gabriela thought. "How do you know, Liv? You *better* have not slept with him, so help me... I called dibs."

"You didn't call dibs," Liv clarified. "You *know* I wouldn't go near that. And besides, I was the one who told *you* not to go near it, either."

"But how do you know he slept with someone?" Gabriela tried to sound nonchalant about it. *Act like you don't care.*

"Marco told her," Lola said, taking off her sunglasses and wiping at them with the corner of her shirt. She held them up to the sun and seemed satisfied with the result as she put them back on. "He went out to get some bottled water last night and saw Sebastian taking someone into his room."

Gabriela felt a cold sweat break out on her back. "Did he see who?"

Lola shrugged. "He didn't say."

Gabriela tried to remember how they'd gotten to Sebastian's room. Had they been loud? Had they kissed in the hall? Could Marco have seen her? But if so, why hadn't he told Lola about it?

Felicia studied her for a minute, the wheels seeming to be turning in her head. "Why do you care so much about Swipe Left's love life all of a sudden?"

"I don't." The sweat and sunscreen combined on her nose, forcing her sunglasses to slip. Gabriela pushed them back up onto the bridge of her nose. "I just don't want...*anyone's* antics to ruin Lola's wedding." *Phew, nice recovery, Gabbie.*

"Well, thanks," Lola said. "I do appreciate that. But,

really, nothing Sebastian does will hurt the wedding. Everyone here is a grown-up, right?"

"Are we?" Felicia joked, and everyone laughed. "Still, I feel sorry for her," Felicia said.

"Yeah, she has no idea what she's in for." Liv shaded her forehead from the sun, which was steadily rising in the sky behind them.

"What do you mean?" Gabriela asked.

"He comes on *strong*," Felicia said. "He's all, 'you're the one for me.' All romantic. All *hot and heavy*."

Gabriela's throat went dry. He'd been acting that way all morning with his *one more night* business.

"Then something else bright and shiny comes along," Liv explained, frowning.

"And he drops you like a bad rash," Felicia said.

"Can you drop a rash?" Lola wondered aloud.

"You know what I mean," Felicia said, waving her hand. "I bet whoever he slept with has no idea he's such a Swipe Left. But she'll find out soon enough."

"Says the person who *wanted* to sleep with him twenty-four hours ago," Liv pointed out.

"Yeah, and that was before I was reminded just how toxic he is!"

Gabriela thought of what Sebastian had told her about Felicia, about how she was so eager to lock him in. She wondered if that was true, but decided it was best not to bring it up. Not here. Not now. She just wanted a peaceful little snorkeling excursion—no Sebastian.

The crew worked to untie the boat from the dock as party music drifted to them from oversize speakers hanging from the wheelhouse. A man wearing a cruise ship uniform walked by them, a clear look-alike for Thor, his blond hair worn longish behind his ears, his strong shoulders tanned from hours in the sun.

"Whoa," Lola said and grabbed Gabriela's arm. "Is it just me or does he look like Chris Hemsworth?"

"Kind of," Gabriela said, barely noticing the toned Viking in the muscle shirt and shorts as he moved to pull up the anchor. Something about him looked a little familiar, but she couldn't place it. Perhaps it was because he did look like a celebrity?

"You're right," Felicia said, watching the man as he worked. "Total Thor over there. Hot guy *alert*."

All the bridesmaids gawked as the Thor look-alike tugged on the rope holding the anchor, his already swollen arm muscles twitching with the effort.

"Wait a minute," Lola said, voice low so only Gabriela could hear. "Wait a second…that's Carson."

"Who?" Gabriela asked, barely paying attention, as she thumbed through more of Sebastian's Instagram photos on her phone. In one he was sandwiched between two bikini models. Seriously? *Two?*

"*Carson.* The weekend in New York?" Lola squeezed Gabriela's arm, suddenly on high alert.

"Uh, what?" Lola now had Gabriela's full attention.

Carson was a guy Lola and Gabriela had met at a bar during one of her trips to New York. That was back when Lola was single. Gabriela had been the one to make out with Carson in the bar, though it hadn't gone further than that. After all, Lola had been in town and Gabriela wasn't going to spend all her time with a guy when her best friend from Miami had flown there to see her. Besides, Carson wasn't the sharpest nail in the box. If Gabriela remembered right, he'd been the one who'd trailed his finger across the bar menu, moving his lips as he read. That was never going to amount to anything. Still, it had been a wild night with one make-out session that had completely changed Lola's view of Gabriela.

"Oh, no." Gabriela shook her head. The last thing she wanted was for New York Gabbie to collide with Miami's Gabriela. Best let those two different personas live in different cities. Except they sure hadn't stayed apart in Sebastian's bed. She shooed the thought away. No thinking about that now.

"Do you think he recognizes me?" Gabriela whispered. She prayed not. Then he glanced up, gave her a tentative smile and a wave.

"Uh, yeah, I think he does." Lola waved back at him, grinning like a madwoman.

"Why is he waving?" Felicia said, leaning into the two of them.

"He must like Lola," Gabriela said, even though she worried about what she'd say to him. After all, he'd texted and called a few times, but Gabriela hadn't made it a priority to get back to him. She'd just hoped he'd get the message she wasn't interested before she'd had to dream up a ridiculous excuse like a sick imaginary cat.

As she worried about how to avoid Carson, she glanced up to see Sebastian at the end of the dock. She stiffened. What was he doing there? She'd told him not to come. She slowly sat up, lowering her sunglasses, hoping somehow it was a trick of the light. But there he was, wearing a T-shirt that hugged all his muscles, worn untucked beneath sleek swim trunks with gray pinstripes, his muscular legs working as he hopped onto the boat in one leap.

"Oh, no. It's Swipe Left." Felicia barely got the words out before the man himself was standing in front of them, grinning.

"Ladies," he said, nodding at each of them, his gaze lingering on Gabriela. He winked at her. Actually *winked*, in front of Lola and everyone.

"Uh, hey… Gabbie?" Carson was suddenly standing beside Sebastian, who for the first time clocked the blond, muscled Viking next to him.

"Uh… Hi." Gabriela pushed up her sunglasses, quickly wishing that somehow they made her invisible. Sebastian, who was taller than Carson, stood a little straighter and frowned.

"How you been?"

"Uh, good. You?"

"I'm Sebastian." He thrust out a big hand and shook Carson's hard. He held it a beat too long.

"Carson. I'm the First Mate on the Royal Harmony. Just here to make sure the excursion goes smoothly for all our passengers."

The two men sized each other up.

Oh, lord. This was all going south and fast. Gabriela glanced up at the sky. How on earth could two hook-ups meet on a tour boat in the middle of the ocean? She shook her head. Only *her* luck. "How do you two know each other?"

"We met in New York," Carson said, and a bright grin flashed across his face.

"Right." Gabriela was less than enthused.

"Well...uh, I need to go check in with the captain, but nice to see you, Gabbie." Carson grinned and scooted away from them.

"Gabbie?" questioned Sebastian.

"Gabbie? Since when?" cackled Liv. Felicia, however, just pressed her lips together in a thin line, unimpressed.

"We just met him in a bar," Lola said. "On that trip a couple of years ago I made to New York. No big deal. He bought us drinks."

"Bought you drinks?" Now Sebastian was completely focused on Gabriela. Was he...jealous? Surely not. Sebastian had a new woman on his Instagram feed practically every weekend. So she'd made out with one Thor look-alike. So what? Besides, *she* was the one who should be mad. She asked him not to come on this little trip and now here he was, crashing the party.

"He didn't seem to remember *you*, Lola," Felicia pointed out.

"Well, I wasn't the one who—" Lola began.

Gabriela jabbed Lola in the arm.

Lola quickly swallowed the end of her sentence. "I mean, er, he talked to Gabriela more."

"*Gabbie*, you mean." Liv broke out into laughter again. "Gabbie! Now we have a new nickname for you. You know, I'm beginning to think maybe we don't know you as well as we thought. A hookup last night and now...Carson!"

Gabriela held up her hands. "Look, it's no big deal."

Sebastian hadn't said a word. He was busy keeping an eye on the retreating figure of Carson as he headed to the wheelhouse to talk to the captain of the excursion boat. Seconds later the engine roared to life and the deck beneath them rumbled as the boat began its journey away from the dock, the wide-open water ahead. She was now trapped on a boat with Sebastian—and Carson—for the next two hours. *Fan-freakin'-tastic.*

On the other side of the boat, Marco beckoned Sebastian over.

"If you'll excuse me." Sebastian walked over to the other end of the boat and Gabriela watched him give Marco a high five.

She felt her blood pressure rise. She'd definitely told him *not* to come. She'd told him to give her some space and yet there he was. She watched as he sidled over to Carson, drumming up some small talk. Ugh. What on earth were they talking about? She prayed not her. This whole little excursion was a complete disaster.

Gabriela stared as Sebastian whipped off his thin T-shirt, exposing his muscular chest to the sun, his muscles flexing as he tossed the discarded shirt onto an empty chair.

"He might be Swipe Left, but damn that man has abs that don't quit," Felicia murmured.

"He's still poison," Liv said, but the way she was looking at him told Gabriela she was admiring the view all the same.

Felicia seemed to notice that Gabriela was being unusually quiet. "Right, Gabriela?"

"What?" Gabriela wasn't really listening. She was too busy worrying about whether Sebastian planned to blow her cover. *Or* planned to grill Carson for details about New York. Either option was horrible.

"She's too busy staring at Carson's ass. Damn, girl. Did you hit that?" Felicia studied her with what seemed to be admiration.

"No, I didn't."

"Pffft. Why the hell not?"

A million reasons, she wanted to say. One of which was the fact that a lack of intelligence was just a huge turnoff. It just always had been for Gabriela. She needed someone who could challenge her in all ways, not just physically.

"Uh, he's not much of a conversationalist."

"Well, hell, honey, for what I'd do to him, talking's not required." Felicia cackled at her own joke, but Gabriela was barely listening. She was watching Sebastian and Carson deep in some conversation. This was not good.

Suddenly the music on deck seemed to get louder. The thump of the bass of a new song rattled their chairs.

"Oh, I like this song," Lola cried.

"Me, too!" Liv cried and began a little dance, still sitting in her chair.

Gabriela stared at Sebastian as he slathered on some sunscreen, acutely aware that as he rubbed in the lotion, his abs shone in the sunlight. Why did Sebastian have to be so gorgeous? How was she supposed to say no to one more night exploring that wonderland of a body? She wasn't sure she'd be able to say no. What

was wrong with her? One night with Sebastian Lott
and now she was like his lapdog, unable to think for
herself?

Then again, would one night really hurt? She
watched as he kicked off his flip-flops and sat in one
of the plastic lounge chairs on the deck. He was talking to Marco, laughing at something the groom said.
Sun glinted off his gold-rimmed glasses. Seriously, he
should be in movies, not litigating corporate cases. He
glanced her way and she froze as a slow smile spread
across his face. He was enjoying making her uncomfortable, that much she knew. She watched as he leaned
over and told Marco something she couldn't hear. Was
he telling his friend about their wild night? Did Marco
already know because he'd seen them?

Why had she even gone to his bedroom in the first
place? This was turning into a ridiculous headache.

He moved to head downstairs. She got up to follow him.

"Bathrooms downstairs, right?" she asked.

"Dunno," Lola said.

"I'm going to go check," she said as she adjusted her
bikini top. She wasn't going to bother slinging on her
cover-up. She'd have to face him in her yellow string
bikini. She jammed her feet into her flip-flops and
headed down the small, single staircase to the floor
below. Lined with four or so benches, with open windows to the sea, there was a small snack bar at the
back. Sebastian was already there, ordering drinks.
Gabriela marched over.

"What do you think you're doing?"

"Trying to get a beer if the bartender ever shows up," he quipped dryly before he turned around. He gave her thin swimsuit a slow sweep and a low whistle. "You look good enough to eat. I love a woman who knows how to own a bikini."

"You agreed not to come today." She tapped an impatient foot on the deck. The engine purred somewhere beneath the floor as the boat made its way out to sea.

"Nope," he said and shook his head slowly. "You told me not to come, but I never said whether I was or wasn't." He grinned slyly and she felt her blood pressure rise. "And now I see why you didn't want me here. What? Would I get in the way of time with Carson?"

"What? No!"

"Really? It just seems convenient you don't want me here and a Spark buddy of yours happens to be here." He gazed at her, his eyes deadly serious. "You think I don't know about games?"

"I'm not playing any. I didn't know he'd be here." This was the absolute truth. And she wished he wasn't.

"You didn't check your app? It tells you when one of your matches is nearby. Surely you knew he was on board. Heck, maybe you even told Lola to pick *this* boat so that you two could meet up again."

"No. Absolutely not." Was Sebastian crazy? "Have *you* been checking *your* app? I bet you have a hundred hookups on the ship alone. I mean, look at your Instagram account."

"You've been stalking me?" He quirked an amused eyebrow.

"No, I haven't."

"You've been checking out my Instagram page, though. That's cyberstalking." Sebastian leaned back on the bar and grinned as he crossed his fit arms at his wide chest.

"I'm not cyberstalking! Ugh. You're impossible." She exhaled a frustrated breath and swept her hair out of her eyes. The man was impossible. "Look, I didn't want you here because I don't want anybody to know…"

"That we hooked up."

"Yes."

His eyes sparkled. "And that we're going to hook up again. Tonight."

"I never said…"

"You didn't have to say." He moved closer and she could smell his scent, something musky and a little bit sweet. "I can read your body, baby."

"You can't say anything to anyone."

"Why? Think Carson will get jealous?"

She craned her neck to meet his gaze. Lord, the man was tall. "I don't care if he's jealous. Carson isn't my type."

"No? Why not?"

"Let's just say talking isn't his forte."

"Dumb as a box of hair, huh?" Sebastian tilted his head back and laughed. "Been there, regretted that. So you're saying you don't have plans with him tonight?" If he wasn't so handsome, she'd want to punch him.

"No, I don't have plans with him. Tonight or any night."

Sebastian studied her a moment. "Good," he said, voice even.

"So you promise, then. Not to say anything?"

"About your plans to break Carson's heart?" He blinked quickly, playing innocent.

"No. You know what."

The bartender arrived, scurrying behind the bar with a big bag of ice. He was clad in a neon-orange hat and wearing the tour boat's T-shirt. "Sorry about that. What can I get you?"

"Would you like a beer?" Sebastian asked.

"I can buy my own." Gabriela lifted her chin. She could theoretically buy her own, except her wallet was upstairs near her towel.

"I'm sure you can. I'm sure you've got money hidden somewhere." He nodded at her bikini. "But how about the first round on me?" He glanced at the bartender. "How about two light beers?"

"Two coming up." The bartender slipped two bottles onto the bar, popping the tops of each one. Sebastian slid one of the bottles closer to her. She hesitated but then took it. She'd need a beer to deal with this frustrating hulk of man.

Sebastian slapped down a twenty-dollar bill and then swiped one bottle, taking a long swig.

"So, please. Promise me you won't talk about us."

"So there's an *us* now?" Sebastian asked. "I thought it was just one night. You made that clear."

"You know what I mean." Gabriela glanced at the beer.

"To *us*," Sebastian said, offering up his bottle.

"No, to *no one finding out*," she stressed, clinking

her bottle to his and then taking a gulp. The ice-cold fizz washed down her throat.

Sebastian watched her slyly as he took a long sip. "You know, you're beautiful when you're hopelessly embarrassed by me."

"I'm not…" She let out a loud sigh. "Seriously, you have to promise not to say anything. Will you promise?"

"Hmm…let me think." Sebastian considered this a moment, rubbing his chin in mock exaggeration. "No."

"Sebastian!" Gabriela slapped him across the elbow. "Seriously. You have to promise."

"No, I don't. I never signed a kiss-and-don't-tell contract." He took another drink.

"Please. Sebastian." She tugged at his arm. She had to get him to promise.

"Why are you so insistent? Why? This can't just be about Felicia."

Gabriela didn't have a good answer for him. She didn't even know herself why she was so determined that no one find out about her and Sebastian. Why not? Why wouldn't she want to lord that over Felicia? Then again, she knew why. Because she was better than that and because this weekend was supposed to be about the wedding.

"I don't want to ruin Lola's day."

"Why would you being with me ruin Lola's big day?" Sebastian stared at her and for a second she lost all ability to debate.

"Because…the drama…"

"There's only drama if you let there be drama."

Sebastian was making a whole lot of sense. Yet why was he pushing so hard? Was this just part of his fall-hard routine?

"Why are you determined *not* to see me again?" he asked her.

Gabriela searched for an answer but couldn't find one. Okay, so maybe it wouldn't ruin Lola's day. Or it might, if Felicia went crazy and tried to throw Gabriela overboard. Or maybe this was really just about Gabriela being embarrassed that she'd spent the last ten years warning people to stay away from Sebastian Lott and then the one single time he'd thrown her a tiny bit of attention, she'd jumped out of her panties. But she couldn't tell him *that*.

Sebastian took another swig of his beer. "Tell you what," he said, placing the bottle on the counter. "How about we go into that little bathroom right there—" he looked toward the door marked with the men and women sign "—and I show you *why* you would want to see me again."

Gabriela giggled, anxious. "Here? Now? Everyone's up on deck!"

"Right. Not down here." He flashed her a devious grin. "Even the bartender's left." He nodded over the bar and Gabriela realized that he had disappeared somewhere. They were all alone. "Just one kiss," he promised.

"One kiss?"

"One kiss." He led her to the door of the bathroom. Was she really going in there? She damn well knew it wasn't just going to be a kiss.

"If I go in there with you," she said, "you have to promise *not* to say anything about…about us."

Sebastian held up three fingers. "Scout's honor," he promised as he flung open the door. The tiny bathroom was hardly bigger than an airplane lavatory, but as he pulled her in, he kissed her deeply and suddenly she didn't care. His hands slipped down her bare back and then cupped her through the thin fabric of her swimsuit. She gasped, forgetting how insistent his hands could be, how well they knew their job, as she pressed herself into him, her tongue lapping at his mouth. God, the man tasted so good. She wanted more of him, not less. Her whole being lit up responding to his touch and she felt like her whole body was a puddle of white-hot need. She couldn't help herself as she threw one leg upward and he grabbed it, holding her just under the knee, pressing his length into her, the only barrier between them their swimsuits.

All coherent thought flew from her mind as well as the distant warning bells. They could be discovered— the whole wedding party was above them, the distant din of the party music playing. Any one of them could come downstairs at any time. She pulled away from him, panting.

"There," she said. "You had your kiss."

"That's not the kind of kiss I wanted." He masterfully tugged at the corner of her string bikini and the entire bottom peeled off to one side. His fingers slipped in deftly, finding her wet and willing. She gasped even as he lifted her and set her on the small edge of the sink. Then he dipped down, his head between her legs. "This is what I meant by a kiss."

Gabriela thought her mind would explode from pleasure. It was the only way to describe what was happening to her in that moment, with Sebastian between her thighs, gently exploring her with his tongue. She couldn't believe it was happening, here, just feet away from the rest of their friends. She knew neither Felicia nor Liv would believe it. Not that she'd ever want them to know.

She grasped Sebastian's shoulders, her whole body on fire. This was different from last night. How many techniques did the man have? Clearly his hands weren't the only things with talent. And if she had to be honest, she was frankly shocked he was so…giving. Given his old reputation, she would've assumed he'd be the one demanding satisfaction.

He worked her faster, his tongue wet and warm and everywhere she needed it to be. She couldn't help herself as she arched her back, pressing into him, wanting more, ever more. Her body was one taut nerve, pulling ever tighter, ever harder. She could feel herself swell with want, with need. She glanced down and saw him looking at her, happily lapping her. She'd never before been with a man so eager to devour her like this. It made her mind spin.

She didn't know if a minute passed, or ten, but all she knew was that she was going to come, and come hard. It was inevitable as he marched her straight to the edge, her body strung tauter than razor wire as he wound her tighter and tighter. She tensed then, every single muscle flexed, her toes curling in her flip-flops as he sent her completely and utterly to the ultimate climax. A moan escaped her mouth. She couldn't help it. Her whole body was awash in the good endorphins as every muscle unwound, throbbing with the quivers of aftershocks.

He stood, a satisfied look on his face, while her whole body was a trembling mound of jelly. What had he done to her? Her knees didn't seem to want to work. She stood, wobbling a little as he helped her steady herself. Pressed against him, she realized that he was more than a little bit excited. She slid her hand down the front of him. Now it was his turn. She gave as good as she got, and she'd make sure he knew it, too.

Someone rattled the doorknob and she froze, hand halfway down Sebastian's swim trunks.

"Hello!" cried Felicia from the other side of the door. "Anybody in there?"

CHAPTER THIRTEEN

PANIC SWEPT OVER HER. Felicia could *not* find the two of them in the bathroom. Gabriela scrambled to get her bikini bottom tied back on.

Now what? she mouthed. Her heart hammered in her chest as all the worst-case scenarios flooded her brain. Felicia would make a scene. There might be yelling. She might have said she wasn't interested in Sebastian, but if she knew what he'd just done to Gabriela in this bathroom… Her jealousy would have no bounds. Then she'd have to explain why she'd told Felicia to stay away from Sebastian only to have him herself.

Gabriela quickly released Sebastian, wondering what she should do. She glanced around the tiny enclave, but found no place to hide. Once that door swung open, Felicia would see them both.

Sebastian placed a finger over his mouth, telling her to be quiet. He pressed his ear against the door.

"Hello?" Felicia knocked harder. "Hello!" She tried the handle again but thank goodness it was locked. "Seriously! Whoever is *in* there, I *need to pee*!"

Classy, Gabriela thought. Sebastian put his hand on the knob, as if to hold it in case the lock gave.

"Ugh!" Felicia hit the door hard one last time and then stomped off, her wooden slides making clomping sounds as she hit the stairs and went up.

With each sound of her retreating steps, Gabriela breathed a little easier. "Thank God," she whispered. Frantically she finished tying off her string bikini. She had to get out of this bathroom.

Sebastian held another finger up and listened once more. He slowly slid the lock to the open positon and pushed the door a crack, keeping Gabriela behind him as much as he could.

"Coast is clear," he whispered and then swung the door wide. Gabriela hurried out, followed by Sebastian. They went back to their two abandoned beers on the bar. Gabriela wondered if Felicia had seen them. She hoped not.

The horn sounded and the captain's voice came over the loudspeaker. "All right, everyone," she said, "we're approaching our snorkeling location for the day, so come to the main deck and get fitted for your masks and fins."

"I guess that's good timing," Sebastian said. He grabbed his beer and had a drink. "You should go on up first. I'll wait a few minutes."

"You will?"

"Sure." He turned to face her, the hint of a smile on his face. "Because you still owe me one more night."

"I do?"

"I think you know you do." He nodded slowly.

"I thought that was the one more time." Even she knew that couldn't be true.

"That?" He laughed. "*That* was just an appetizer. I have twelve more courses at least."

"You do?" Gabriela felt the heat rise in her cheeks. "And what's for dessert?"

He laughed, deep and throaty. "Why, *you*, of course."

Sebastian tried to focus on the snorkeling and the many dozens of beautifully colored fish beneath him as he floated with Marco and the groomsmen around the anchored boat. The bridesmaids were busy using the fish food the crew had given them to attract the fish, schools and schools of bright colors whirling just beneath the surface in a rainbow of bright shades, but all Sebastian could see was Gabriela in her neon-yellow bikini. He could almost still taste her. He wanted to make her come again. And again. And again.

He'd like to spend the rest of his life doing it, actually. He knew he was moving fast, but he was almost thirty and he'd dated so much. He knew what he wanted. Why wait? If it's right, it's right. That's what his mother had always told him. She'd also told him when it's wrong, it can be *very* wrong. Sebastian, of course, knew that firsthand. His dad had skipped out on them when he was just two, moved across the country with another woman and started a whole separate family. It had been Sebastian and his mom most of his life, and with her often working two jobs, it had been mostly just him. Not that he ever threw pity parties for himself. He'd thrown himself into athletics. He'd gotten a football scholarship to a small Florida university and then he'd managed to parlay that into a Harvard law degree.

Sebastian had never backed down from a challenge and he wasn't about to start now. He watched Gabriela and her oversize flippers move away from him, the slim muscles in her legs working as she kicked. She and Lola swam side by side, feeding a school of bright yellow-and-blue Queen Angelfish.

He noticed that the first mate, the pretty, blond boy, was right by her side. He didn't like that one bit. Jealous? Him? No. He didn't get jealous. But he didn't like sleazy tour guides muscling in on women, either. The crewman—Carson—maneuvered between the two women. Sebastian didn't like that some guy who was all muscle and no brain had the hots for Gabriela. It was obvious to him, the man was smitten. The way he stole glances at her, watched her when he thought she wasn't looking. Carson was someone Sebastian would have to keep an eye on.

But keep her coming like that and she'll never look at another Carson again.

Still, Sebastian believed Gabriela when she'd said she wasn't interested. He watched her yellow bikini flash under the water, her taut bare legs kicking hard. He felt himself tighten. The woman was about to make him hard right there in the water. Water trickled into his face mask and he popped up to adjust the rubber strap. From this vantage point, he saw Gabriela's firm round ass bobbing above the water. His groin reacted instantly. He adjusted himself discreetly with one hand, wishing he'd had just fifteen more minutes in that bathroom. Then he wouldn't be aching so hard for her now. The woman was like a drug. He was flat-out addicted after only a couple of hits. It made no sense to him.

Next to him, Lola popped out of the water, flinging her snorkel to the side. "Those fish are beautiful. Did you see them?"

Sebastian nodded. "Yeah, they're cool." But his focus was on Carson, who seemed to be swimming after Gabriela like a shark. He'd have to break that up. *Yesterday.* "So what's the deal with the guy? He and Gabriela dating?"

"Who? *Carson?*" Lola barked a laugh as she dog-paddled, her snorkeling mask on top of her head. "No. He's just one of the New York guys."

Sebastian kicked a little harder as he bobbed in the water. "What do you mean 'guys'?"

"Nothing." She shrugged. "Forget I said anything! Gab would kill me."

"I'm not going to tell anyone. Who would I tell?" Sebastian grinned. "Besides, I already know she's a platinum Spark dater. I saw it on her phone."

"She's just different in New York, that's all. Not like people here know her. You know?"

Oh, he knew. He knew she'd changed. Gobstopper from high school wouldn't have blown his mind in the bedroom like she had last night. Well, that also explained why she knew so many tricks. She'd had practice. He didn't know if he hated that…or loved it. One more layer to Ms. Cruz. Interesting.

Lola shrugged. "I don't think it's even bad, but she's worried people will judge her or... I don't know. She doesn't want Felicia to know."

"I won't say anything," Sebastian promised.

Lola put her mask back on and dipped her face into the water, kicking away from him.

Sebastian watched Gabriela come up for air, her snorkel dangling by her mouth, water dripping off her nose. She caught his eye and then quickly looked away. Well, she could ignore him now all she wanted. He'd have his chance later that evening during the rehearsal dinner. She'd have a much harder time swimming away from him when he was walking her down the aisle.

Gabriela tenderly touched her sunburned shoulder, wishing she'd put on more sunscreen that morning during the snorkeling trip. She and the other bridesmaids sat in the back of ship's open-air veranda overlooking the blue Atlantic Ocean. It was an impressive place to exchange vows. They waited while Marco and Lola talked to the ship's wedding planner.

"Ow," Gabriela groaned as one of the straps from her sundress rubbed against her fresh sunburn. The cool ocean breeze felt lovely on her shoulders, but it wasn't quite like a slathering of aloe vera she desperately wished she'd remembered for this trip. It didn't help that she was acutely aware of Sebastian watching her every move. Now, in fact, he was sitting in a chair across the aisle, studying her. Why did he have to look so gorgeous? He wore a crisp Oxford and khakis, his dark hair swept back from his forehead, those green flecks in his hazel eyes seemingly visible from even this distance. His shoulders seemed too broad for the sport jacket he wore, yet he pulled it off. He looked devilishly good, three buttons open on his shirt that revealed smooth, tanned skin leading to what she already knew was an expansive and impressive chest. She realized she was staring at his neck and chest, and tried to glance away, but somehow ended up staring at the crotch of his pants. She was amazed he wasn't somehow visible through the heavy cotton material. Finally sanity took over and she managed to pull her eyes to meet his.

He raised his eyebrows, amused. God, she hated being caught staring. Might as well have just told him she was thinking about his...everything.

He grinned and mouthed, *One more night.*

She shivered. One more night might kill her. She'd never had so many orgasms, so hard, so fast, before. Could she even *have* another? But then again, she remembered his talented hands and tongue, and knew for a fact she'd be jelly in his hands. He could mold her however he chose. That was what worried her. The more she came, and the harder she came, the more she liked Sebastian. And liking him would just get her into trouble.

He comes on strong at first. Isn't that what Felicia had said? He's hot and heavy and then—poof!—gone. But since when did she really ever believe anything Felicia said? She glanced at him, heart rate ticking up a notch. *One more night.* Would she dare? If she were careful, who would know?

Suddenly he was standing and moving toward her. She realized, with a start, she'd missed some key instructions doled out by the ship's wedding planner, as she saw the rest of the groomsmen also stand, and head for their corresponding bridesmaids. Oh, no. She'd forgotten all about this part, about Sebastian leading her down the aisle.

He was standing in front of her now, as he bent down and offered his elbow.

"Madam," he said, "may I have the pleasure?" His voice was all lightness, his light eyes teasing. She reached up and took his arm and he led her to the back of the aisle of chairs. "So, just which positions *do* you want to try tonight?" he whispered in her ear.

"I…" She didn't know what to say, and everyone else seemed like they were practically in earshot.

"My vote is all of them."

She had to laugh at that. His arm felt warm and strong as she rested her hand on his forearm.

"The music will start and…" The wedding planner, a young woman in her twenties, pointed at Sebastian. "And then you two will start the procession. I want you to walk slowly. Remember *slowly*."

Sebastian and Gabriela began their walk, but all Gabriela could think about was the powerfully muscled man at her elbow—and the promise of tonight.

"I want to touch you *slowly*. All night long," he whispered, keeping his eyes fixed on the captain at the end of the long aisle.

"You sure tonight is a good idea?" she whispered.

"Tonight should be the *only* idea. It's all I can think

about." He sent her a sidelong glance and she felt her cheeks burn with heat. She knew more heat would come once she was in his bed once more. Heat all over. The good kind. "If you can tell me you absolutely, positively, don't want to do it, then I'll respect your wishes. But something tells me you want it as much as I do."

That's because I do.

Gabriela said nothing as they ended their walk and he let her go so she could stand on the bride's side. The beautifully flowered latticework alter stood between them. The rest of the bridesmaids and groomsmen made their way down the aisle, as well, and she watched as Felicia seemed to cling a little too tightly to Bill. She didn't want to know what that was all about. Instead she glanced at Sebastian. Was hooking up with him really so wrong? Sure, she'd spent the last ten years telling all of her friends he was toxic and should be avoided at all costs, but maybe she'd been wrong.

But maybe she'd been right.

She glanced at Felicia and Liv, both of whom were watching them closely. Did they suspect? Oh, she hoped not. She glanced at Lola and Marco standing in front of the captain. Lola didn't look exactly…happy. The thought of the big day tomorrow stressing her out?

"Well, that's it, folks," the captain told them, addressing the wedding party. "Now I believe there's a rehearsal dinner in the private room of the main dining hall down the hall on this floor, here on Deck Five."

Marco, grinning, shook the captain's hand. Lola, however, still seemed a little out of it. She grabbed her phone, thumbing through it. Her parents, who stood nearby, were busy talking to Marco's parents, exchanging pleasantries. Everyone else seemed fine, but Lola was just…off.

"One second," Gabriela told Sebastian. He let her go as she wandered over to the bride, who had already wandered away from the rest of the party and was standing by herself, intent on her phone. "Everything okay?"

Lola's head snapped up in surprise. She quickly pressed her phone to her hip. "Everything's fine." She plastered on a fake smile.

"Come on, I've known you since we were little kids. Something's wrong."

Lola looked uncomfortable. "I don't know. I think maybe… No. It's dumb."

"It's not dumb. Tell me."

Her voice dropped so low that Gabriela barely heard her, even though they were not within earshot of Marco or anyone else. "I think I'm getting cold feet."

"What do you mean?" Confusion rippled through Gabriela. What was her best friend talking about? The two were the perfect couple.

"I…I mean, I don't know. Seeing Carson reminded me of being single and all the fun we had. Am I doing the right thing here?"

"Of *course* you are. Marco is amazing and you love him."

"Yeah." Lola looked a little dazed as she nodded.

"This is probably just stress. And the craziness of the bachelorette party yesterday and just the pressure of it all. But Marco is great. I think you two are perfect for each other."

Lola gave her a weak smile. "You're right," she said. "I'm just overtired. A little hungover from this morning, too. Day drinking doesn't sit well with me, I guess." Lola took a deep breath.

Gabriela laced her arm through Lola's. "You're going to do fine. You'll be the most beautiful bride there ever was."

Lola giggled as the two walked toward the empty dining room. "You're lying."

"I am *not*. Beautiful outside and in, that's you."

Lola squeezed Gabriela's arm but said nothing. "You and Sebastian seem to be getting along well. Something you want to tell me there?"

Sheer panic ran through her. Gabriela felt a drop of sweat trickle down the small of her back. "No. Why? What do you mean?"

"It just looks like you two are in your own little bubble, that's all."

"Us?" Gabriela let out a fake laugh. "I don't think so. We're just trying to get along. You know. Peace for the wedding."

"Yeah. Right." Lola didn't seem convinced. "So there's nothing you want to tell me?"

Gabriela was tempted right in that moment to spill the beans. Admit to it all. *We've been at it like we're competing for gold at the Naked Games.* But what if Felicia overheard? What if Lola got upset? After all, Gabriela had promised her that she'd keep her wedding drama-free.

"Nope," she lied, vowing she'd tell her oldest friend the entire truth…later. Well after the ceremony.

Lola stared at Gabriela a beat, skeptical. "Okay. Then you won't mind sitting next to him at dinner tonight."

"What? Why?" Gabriela's reply came out more forceful than she'd intended.

"I'm not sure if you're sad or…glad." Lola laughed a little. "No matter. It's just that the wedding party is all at one table, and guests at another. That's the lay-out of the dinner."

"Are you two talking about me?" Sebastian stood at Gabriela's right shoulder.

"Just saying that you two made a handsome couple walking down the aisle, that's all." Lola grinned and Gabriela wondered again if her friend had guessed something was going on. Had Lola seen her sneak out of Sebastian's room? Had she guessed what had happened belowdecks on the snorkel excursion? Surely not. *Don't be paranoid*, Gabriela told herself. Besides, would it be the end of the world if Lola knew? Up until now, Lola knew all her secrets.

"I agree. We are pretty photogenic. We'll look good in all your wedding photos." Sebastian put his arm around Lola's shoulders, giving her an affectionate squeeze. "But you'll be the prettiest one in them all. Marco is a lucky man and I tell him that daily."

Lola grinned, a little bit of pink flaring up in her cheeks. "Oh, I don't know about that." A pensive look crossed Lola's face. Wedding jitters? Gabriela wasn't sure but she knew something wasn't quite right with her best friend.

But before she could ask, Marco came and took Lola's hand. He was beaming, happiness spilling out of every pore. "There's the love of my life," he said as he tugged her in close for a quick peck on the lips. "The captain told me cocktails are already rolling out in the next room. We should probably head over."

Lola and Marco began moving into the dining room, leaving Gabriela alone with Sebastian.

"Did you ask Lola to sit next to me?" Gabriela whispered.

"Maybe."

Gabriela stepped onto the small dining area's plush burgundy carpet and took in the several long tables set with rose centerpieces, gold-tinted plates and silverware. It was beautiful, especially with the large windows across most of the room showcasing the port outside. A horn blasted and the ship began to move away from the dock. Soon they'd be out to sea, one more step closer to Key West, where the wedding would take place.

Gabriela glanced away from the windows and saw Carson, wearing his white, first mate's uniform, and looking decidedly more cleaned up than he had this morning. He glanced up and saw her, but she looked away. She saw Sebastian frown.

"Did you know he'd be here?"

"No," Gabriela snapped. That was the truth. The last person she wanted to see was Carson.

Please don't come over here, she prayed, but he seemed not to heed her silent missive. He headed right for her.

Sebastian was going to have to do something about this man. He was always turning up like a bad penny and hanging on Gabriela…like he owned her. Not that Sebastian blamed him. Gabriela looked nearly irresistible in her slinky, leave-nothing-to-the-imagination, shell-pink sundress, her thick, dark hair worn up, showing her delicate neck. How he longed to lay a trail of kisses down that soft skin of hers, feather-soft. Make her moan.

"Gabbie," Carson said. "Just wanted to check in with you about that sunburn."

"Oh, I'm fine, thanks." Gabriela's face looked as sunburned as her shoulders.

"Uh, do you think I could talk to you—" he glanced at Sebastian "—for one second?"

No way was that happening.

"Yeah…uh…maybe in a little bit?" Gabriela blinked fast. She didn't want to talk to him any more than Sebastian wanted him to talk to her. Good. At least they were on the same page about that.

"Um. Sure. Okay." Carson turned, giving Sebastian a look he didn't like. A waiter came by with a tray of red wine and Sebastian took two, handing one to Gabriela.

"What was that about?"

"I have no idea. I'm just glad he's gone." Gabriela took her glass and took a long drink.

"That makes two of us." Sebastian noticed Carson had wandered over to the appetizer table, picked up a small shrimp puff, sniffed it and then put it back down. "So tell me again, why did you hook up with him?"

"I didn't." Gabriela sipped at her wine once more. "And anyway, it's not like you have a bunch of brain surgeons on your Instagram."

He watched as Carson picked up a toothpick meant to stab cocktail shrimp and tried to pick up an eggroll with it. What was the man doing?

"Well, fair enough." Sebastian glanced down at Gabriela. "That's why I think you and I make such a great couple."

"We're *not* a couple."

"We're more of a couple than you and…Carson."

"That still doesn't make us a couple." Gabriela folded one arm across her chest, and held up her wineglass with the other.

Sebastian noticed Carson moving closer to Lola. He was standing right in her personal space. Odd, he thought. Seemed a little forward for a ship's crew member. He told himself he'd keep an eye on Carson, make sure he didn't overstep his bounds. Then he got distracted by Gabriela as she took a tiny drink from her wineglass, her pink lips delicately touching the rim of the glass.

He remembered then what they'd felt like against his: passionate, surprisingly strong and absolutely single-minded. The memory of that, and her delicate pink lips—imagining where else they should be right at this moment, made his groin tighten. What was wrong with him? He was acting like a horny teenager not a grown man who was very adept at getting his own needs met. Suddenly nothing else seemed to matter but Gabriela. He knew on some level he should put the brakes on this madness, but he really, really, didn't want to. Sebastian always had had a reckless streak in him. He wanted to play this out. See where it led.

"I know you don't believe I'm serious. How can I prove that I am?"

She glanced at him, a teasing light in her eyes. "Stick around for more than a weekend."

"You know I want to do that. It's you who seem to want to bolt." Sebastian took a sip of wine, the red not quite as juicy or as fruity as he liked. It was a bit too dry, a bit too harsh on the back of his palate. "Is it just me or does this wine taste like…something you'd buy at 7-Eleven?"

"You're a wine snob."

"Of course I am. I'm an everything snob." He laughed. "What's the point of having good taste if you don't use it?"

Gabriela rolled her eyes. "You're ridiculous."

"Am I? My high standards led me to you, didn't they?"

Gabriela stared at him, a bright, playful look crossing her face. "You're telling me that *you*, Sebastian Lott, are picky about women?" She barked a laugh.

"Sure I am."

"You are not. You're not at all picky."

"I am picky," he said, leaning in so that he was close enough to smell her sweet perfume, something tangy, something spicy and a little bit dangerous. "I'm absolutely picky about the women I fall in love with."

CHAPTER FOURTEEN

GABRIELA STOOD STUNNED, the wineglass frozen on the way to her mouth. Did he say he was falling in love with her? She must've misheard him. There's no way on earth Sebastian Lott used the L-word.

"Did you just say you're falling in love with me?" she managed to croak.

"What if I was?" Sebastian grinned, wide. She couldn't tell if he was joking or not, and that frightened her. Was he serious? How could he be?

"If you were, that would be crazy." Insane. Beyond ridiculous. Love? No way. "We had one night together."

"One night and this morning," Sebastian corrected. "Don't you believe in love at first orgasm? Or, hell, in your case, love at the first nine orgasms?"

"Very funny." Gabriela studied his features but could still not determine if he was teasing or serious.

"You're joking."

"Am I?"

"You have to be." Gabriela shook her head at the absurdity. "You can't love me."

"Why not? I've known you more than half my life."

He took another step closer and now Gabriela could almost feel his body heat through his thin shirt.

"You ignored me almost all of that half."

Gabriela saw from the corner of her eye that Felicia was studying them and moving closer. That was all she needed, Felicia to overhear any of this.

"My mistake," he murmured, voice low. "I plan to remedy that tonight with about six more new positions. By the way, which one so far was your favorite?"

Felicia sauntered over, glass of wine in hand. "What are you two talking about so seriously?"

Sebastian didn't miss a beat. "About which sexual position Gabriela likes the best."

Gabriela froze. What the holy hell? Was he outing her in front of *Felicia*?

But then Felicia cackled a laugh. "Right, good one. Ha. Ha."

Gabriela laughed uncomfortably. "Yeah, right." She gave him a hard nudge to the arm, her warning clear. "We were wondering when we should sit down."

Felicia nodded at the bride and groom, who were making their way to the end of the long table. "Looks like we should sit now, since they are."

Grateful to move away from Felicia, Gabriela did just that, taking her seat on the other side of Lola, with Sebastian taking up the seat next to hers. How he managed this, she didn't know, but she was going to have to set him straight. They were *not* a couple. Of course, then she thought about his knowing hands exploring her body and felt a shiver of doubt. Could sex that good be a sign? He seemed to think so. Gabriela shook her head. Sex was just sex. Just because she'd been in love with Sebastian Lott since pretty much sixth grade, didn't mean a thing. How long before something bright and shiny—or young and shapely—came along to steal his attention away? She knew deep down that Sebastian wasn't loyal to any woman, so why would she be any different?

But then, he was the one who'd said the L-word.

Gabriela tried to focus on the appetizers on the serving trays plopped down at the center of the table, but she was keenly aware of Sebastian's elbow just centimeters from hers. Every little move he made, she could feel in the tiny ripple of nerves in her stomach.

Lola finished the last of her first glass of wine and was already ordering another. "You okay?" Gabriela asked, wondering just how much she'd meant before about having cold feet.

"Nothing that a little wine won't fix." Lola grinned as the waiters swept up the empty trays of appetizers and she dug into her second glass.

Gabriela worriedly watched, until she got distracted by Sebastian's knee nudging hers beneath the table. She felt a little electric shock at the contact.

"Now's the time we're supposed to try for innocuous small talk," he murmured. "But I'd much rather talk about your amazing body."

She nearly spit out her wine as she rapidly scanned the table. Had anyone heard? It seemed not, as everyone was busy in their own conversations, even Lola, who was talking to Marco about something Gabriela couldn't hear.

"Careful," she said, focusing her attention on straightening her napkin in her lap.

"Oh, I promise that I *won't* be careful with you tonight," Sebastian vowed. "We're going to do some very, very naughty things." She didn't move her leg away. Part of her didn't want to and part of her worried that someone would notice. Though, who would be able to tell something was happening beneath the tablecloth?

Sebastian's leg kept firmly pressed against hers throughout the entire meal, a constant distraction. She felt the warmth of his leg and the promise of what it meant: another night in his cabin. Despite her better judgement, she craved the feel of his hands on her body once more. Her mind was clouded with thoughts of the night to come, when she heard the high-pitched plink of a spoon on a glass of wine.

Next to her, Sebastian stood, the warmth of his leg disappearing from hers.

"Excuse me," he said, holding up his wineglass. "I'd like to make a toast."

Across the table, Felicia rolled her eyes. Not exactly fair, Gabriela thought. He was the best man, after all.

"I want to toast Marco and Lola." He raised his glass higher. "I think in some ways, I'm responsible for this little wedding."

"Yep, this is all your fault!" Marco shouted, and most of the bridal party laughed. He hugged Lola a bit closer to him. She sipped at her wine. Gabriela noticed the second glass was nearly gone now. What was up with Lola? Was it really cold feet?

"I first met Marco in law school in Constitutional Law 101," he said. "This guy was late to every class. Never studied and yet somehow blew out the curve on the very first exam. I thought, 'Who was this guy who never studied?'"

The table laughed then.

"But, it turned out, he did study. He worked two night jobs to pay for school, and studied there. And the reason he was late to class is that he was coming in from his bakery job, after having not slept at all the night before."

Gabriela glanced at Marco. He was a hard worker, there was no doubt about that.

"But Marco was more than that, he was an amazing friend. When my mother was diagnosed with cancer…" Sebastian stopped, swallowing back emotion.

Gabriela suddenly remembered that his mother had had liver cancer and had died a few years ago. Gabriela had been in New York, so she'd missed the funeral. Now, it touched her to see how much the death still affected him. She itched to comfort him. Why did it surprise her to see him overcome with emotion? *Why do I sell him so short?*

"It was only just me and my mom when I was growing up and sometimes that was hard. She was my whole world for a long time."

She was? Gabriela realized she didn't know much about Sebastian's family. Then again, sometimes the people you grew up with could be the people you knew the least. Sometimes kids just didn't ask questions, not when they'd known someone since kindergarten.

And it's not like she'd ever been over to his house. She wondered what else she didn't know about Sebastian.

Sebastian swallowed hard and then glanced at Marco. "Marco was always there for me. He helped me get my first internship, and helped me get back on my feet after that." Sebastian grinned. "And I repaid him *a hundred times over*, by introducing him to the other best person in the world, his bride-to-be…"

Everyone, including Gabriela, broke out into applause. Sebastian's toast was pitch perfect and he had the group eating out of his hand. Gabriela hated to admit it, but she was impressed. Then again, it shouldn't surprise her. She knew that charm firsthand, didn't she?

"I want everyone here to know that I believe *this* is true love," he continued. "And I'm also lucky enough to have found someone special myself…"

If there'd been music playing in Gabriela's mind, it would've come to a sudden and irrevocable halt, the needle skipping over the record in the loudest screech possible. What was he saying? Was he seriously, right at this moment, going to out her in front of everyone? And what in the world was he saying? *Found someone special?*

"She's someone I've known a long time and I just want everyone to know—"

Gabriela bolted up from her chair, wineglass in hand. She stared at a roomful of surprised faces. Felicia's mouth had dropped clear open and Lola and Marco stared at her, perplexed. "He wanted everyone to know that he's done *talking about himself.*"

Liv, thankfully, hooted loudly and then everyone else followed.

Gabriela glared at Sebastian but he seemed unperturbed.

"I just want to say that I'm honored to be here to help Marco and Lola celebrate their love for one another, *which is what we should be focused on*," Gabriela said as she gave Sebastian another pointed look. "So, here's to the two best people I know. Lola and Marco."

"Yes, to Lola and Marco," Sebastian echoed. They both raised their glasses to whoops and cheers as she took an unsteady sip of her wine.

"What do you think you're doing interrupting my speech?" he murmured.

"What do you think *you* were doing giving it?" Gabriela finished the rest of her wine and set the glass on the table with an audible plunk. "We need to talk. *Now.*"

Sebastian loved the flare of Gabriela's nostrils as she laid into him, telling him all the various reasons outing their relationship in front of the entire bridal party was a horrible idea.

They were tucked away down the corridor inside the study, a room across from the casino. The study was furnished with a small library of books and two oversize chairs, the oak-paneled walls seeming like something that should be in a house, not a ship, and they had the small reading nook all to themselves. She'd closed the wooden door behind them and he'd taken a seat in one of the plush upholstered chairs. She paced the room, back and forth in front of the bookshelf, gesturing wildly.

Honestly, he was too busy watching her sexy ass move in that dress, her calves flexing as she glided in her stiletto heels. God, she was the sexiest woman on this ship. Hell, the sexiest woman—period. He couldn't remember ever feeling this confident, this fast, that a woman was for *him*. He loved her dual nature: one minute prim and proper and the next…anything but. He liked not knowing what to expect. He liked that she threw him off balance.

"Are you insane?" She thrust a hand on her hip, anger pouring off her in waves.

"Is that a rhetorical question or…?"

"Were you seriously about to out me in front of the entire wedding party?" She stopped pacing and glared at him, her ample chest heaving.

He was having a very hard time concentrating on what she was saying, because he wanted badly to pull her into his lap and kiss the life out of her. "You mean, was I going to tell everyone I'm falling seriously for you? Yes, I was."

Gabriela just stopped and gaped at him. "What are you talking about? You keep saying this, but it just can't be true."

"Why not?"

"Because it can't be. Because…well, people say you come on hot and heavy and then you disappear." She snapped her fingers to show how quickly he ought to be gone from her life.

"You think that's all this is? Some kind of game." He

was truly trying to figure out why she was so against the idea of them giving this a shot. Why wouldn't she want more amazing sex? Sebastian had been with enough women to know that this kind of true connection didn't come along every day.

"Isn't it?" She crossed her arms at her chest and glared.

"No, it isn't."

She hesitated, a split second of doubt, and he reached out and grabbed her by the hips, pulling her into his lap. She toppled there with a half-muffled cry of surprise. Then, once her delectable round bottom was across his thighs, he kissed her, the intensity immediate. It felt as if they'd been expecting this all along. Suddenly her anger turned to white-hot passion. She nearly devoured him like a woman starved.

Well, damn. He ought to piss her off more often.

She ravaged his mouth, her tongue swiping his over and over, a game of endless tag in his mouth. Their heat was like a raging wildfire and, once sparked, it was nearly impossible to control. He cupped her ample, heavy breast in his hand and she groaned into his mouth, driving him nearly wild. He wouldn't be able to control this much longer, as he felt himself grow hard. God, so very hard. She found him with her hands, too, rubbing him through the front of his pants.

He stopped her hand. "Much more of that and I'm going to come right here," he told her.

"That's the idea," she said, a wicked half smile on her face.

Vixen. He loved it. "The door's not locked," he warned. "Someone could come in at any time."

She pulled away, a flash of rebellion in her eyes. "Then we better be quick." She slid down from his lap and her hands were on his fly. Before he knew what was happening, she'd released him and was flicking her tongue across his tip. Those amazing lips, those dark eyes. He wanted to come right now. He'd never before met a woman so talented—and fearless—as she was. She pulled the tip of him inside her wet and willing mouth, and stroked his shaft with two very talented hands. He'd had plenty of fantastic blowjobs and yet, somehow, this one, this woman, was on a whole other level. He felt in that moment he'd graduated from the minor leagues.

"That's…amazing…" He seriously felt like he was sixteen again. He wouldn't be able to hold it. Not with her hot, wet tongue doing…God knows what to him. Short-circuiting every single bit of wiring in his brain. If she'd asked him right now to sign over every single penny in his bank account, he would. "Just don't stop." He dropped his head back as she worked him harder and harder, faster and faster. Amazing. Pure mastery. The sight of her on her knees, working him, her breasts pressed together as she took him deeper and deeper down her throat.

"I'm going to come. God, I can't…" *Hold it.* There was no holding it now, no stopping it now. He erupted in her mouth, a hot explosion of everything he had. He came and came and *came*. It felt like he'd keep on coming forever. As he watched, she took it all deep into her throat as she swallowed every last drop.

This was the hottest cum he'd ever had.

Ever. In his life.

She swallowed and then released him, wiping a drop of him from her now-swollen lips.

"You're the sexiest fucking woman I've ever met," he groaned. "Tell me this isn't love."

She just laughed. "It's sex."

"No." He grabbed her wrist and pulled her close. He smelled him on her. So damn hot. "I've never come so hard for anyone."

"Maybe you've never been with a woman who knew what she was doing."

Outside the study door, voices caught their attention. Gabriela stiffened, rising to her feet, and Sebastian quickly sat up, tucking himself back in and zipping up his fly. He was on his feet, too. The door swung open just as the two had put themselves together. Marco stood there, surprised.

"Oh, I…" He paused, glancing first at Gabriela and then at Sebastian. "Sorry, I…" He seemed flustered. Did he know? Had Sebastian failed to zip up completely? Or was he sticking out of his fly? "Have you seen Lola?"

"Have you lost your bride already?" Sebastian joked.

"Last time I saw her she was in the dining room," Gabriela said.

"Yeah. She's not. Is there a ladies' room near here?" Marco looked like he wanted to make a quick escape.

"It's the other way down the hall—to the left," Gabriela offered.

"Okay, thanks." Marco withdrew from the open door, letting it swing shut.

"That was close," Gabriela said, exhaling beside him.

Sebastian pulled Gabriela into his arms and kissed her fiercely. When he pulled away, she was panting. "Not as close as I'm going to get you right now. You can't just savage me like that and expect me *not* to return the favor."

CHAPTER FIFTEEN

GABRIELA LAUGHED AND pushed against Sebastian's chest, separating herself from his amazing body. She could still taste him in her mouth and it excited her in ways she couldn't even begin to explain. The way she'd made him lose all control, quickly and easily, gave her a thrill she hadn't felt in a long, long time. But then again, part of her knew it was all temporary. Soon he'd tire of it, flip the switch like he did with every woman he'd been with.

"No, we can't," she said, running a hand through her hair, finding a piece sticking up. No wonder Marco had looked at her so strangely. She probably looked like a woman who'd just been on her knees. *No matter. He doesn't know,* she told herself. *But what if he suspects?* "Marco knows we're in here. And if he's wandering around, then other guests might be, too. What if Lola found us? What if her *parents* did?"

That absolutely could not happen.

"You were the one who came on to me," Sebastian said, voice a low growl. "I didn't ask you to…do that."

"I know." Mischief flared across her face. "Are you sorry I attacked you?"

"Hell no."

"Good." She pressed her hands against her dress, flattening out a wrinkle. She glanced down at her knees and noticed the carpet had left temporary indents in them. Had Marco seen them? She hoped not. "Then, you've had your one more night. Still thinking you want to marry me?"

"*This* wasn't one more night. This was literally five minutes in a library." Sebastian gestured to the small shelf of books. "One more night is a *whole* night. In my bed."

The words vibrated through her belly. *In his bed* was exactly where she wanted to be right now. Pleasuring him had left her wanting. She throbbed with need and she knew if he touched her, he'd find her ready. But now wasn't the time. All of the wedding guests were just down the hall, dinner was over and they'd be wandering by the door on their way to the elevators. Marco already knew they were there, and others would soon, probably, as well.

"I still owe you one night?"

"At least." Sebastian stared at her and for a second she was ready to risk everything. Put her hand in his and let him take her straight up to his cabin right now. The way he was looking at her made her believe she *was* special, that she wasn't one of the dozen women rotating through his life. What if he was serious? What if he really was falling for her? Sebastian Lott… In love with her? How did she feel about that? She realized, right at that moment, that part of her—a big part—liked that idea. Maybe liked it too much.

What would they do? Date? Get married? *Yes, and have amazingly beautiful babies with his green-flecked hazel eyes.*

Stop this, she told herself. *None of that is going to happen. You're just setting yourself up for heartbreak.* Sebastian was a man who liked the chase, and as soon as he caught her, he'd tire of her. She knew this in her bones.

"We should help Marco find Lola," Gabriela declared.

Something washed over his face then. Disappointment? Frustration? She wasn't sure. "As you wish," he said. "But *this*—" he gestured between them "—is not over."

Back in the dining room, most of the guests had filtered out and returned to their rooms, but Marco was still there, as was Felicia.

"Where *were* you?" Felicia stormed at Gabriela, who could barely hide her surprise. Why did Felicia care where she was?

"Why? What's up?"

Felicia glanced at Sebastian and then at Marco.

"We can't find Lola." Felicia looked somber.

"What do you mean *can't* find her?" Sebastian asked.

"She slipped out sometime right after dessert. I thought she went to the bathroom, but she didn't come back," Marco said. He couldn't look any of them in the eye.

"What about her room?" Gabriela refused to believe that the bride was missing.

"We looked there." Felicia raised her eyebrows. "Now do you see the problem?"

"She's probably just in the casino…or…with her parents? Maybe they went to get a drink?" Gabriela asked.

"No and no." Felicia shook her head. "We looked all over this floor of the ship. No sign of her. And Liv is in her cabin, and will call us if she comes there."

"Did you try calling her?" Sebastian looked grim.

Felicia nodded swiftly. "Calls go straight to voice mail."

Now Gabriela was starting to get worried. Lola had had more than two glasses of wine at dinner, maybe even as much as four. Gabriela had only noticed how quickly the first two had gone down. She'd been distracted by Sebastian the rest of the time.

"How many people know she's missing?" Gabriela looked at Marco.

"Just you two, Felicia, Liv and me," Marco said.

"Why don't we start looking from Deck One?" Sebastian said, taking charge as he strode from the dining room and into the foyer nearby. The others followed as he walked over to the big diagram outlining the map of the ship near the elevators. He tapped it with one finger. "How about Marco and Felicia take one through four, and Gabriela and I will take six through ten. That way we can check the women's and men's restrooms on each floor, too."

Gabriela glanced at him, nodding, hoping the rising feeling of foreboding in her chest was wrong.

* * *

"She's on this ship somewhere," Sebastian said, almost as much to convince himself as to convince Gabriela as they began searching the long passageways of Deck Six. The auditorium, where the evening's entertainment of a short magic act had already ended, was open, but all the red-velvet seats sat empty. They glanced in, yet only a cleanup crew and a few performers remained. They retreated and walked toward the Italian restaurant on the bow of the ship.

"I've heard of people, though, who...fell overboard." Out loud, the words sounded ridiculous, and yet Gabriela couldn't help but worry. What if Lola had fallen? What if she was out there in that dark water all alone?

"She wouldn't have fallen." Sebastian sounded sure as he strode down the brightly carpeted hallway.

"She had a lot to drink, though." Gabriela hated to admit it, but it was true. She racked her brain trying to remember just how many. "She had at least three. Maybe four or even five."

"That many? But...why?" Sebastian mused aloud.

She hesitated to say. It felt like betraying Lola's trust to mention their brief conversation about cold feet, but what if Lola were tucked away somewhere just freaking out a little bit? What if she'd just needed to take a long walk and clear her head? Or worse... What if she'd really decided not to go through with the wedding?

"I don't know," she lied.

"That's just not like Lola."

Gabriela had to agree on that score.

"How long have you known her?" Gabriela asked.

"Lola? She's like a sister to me. We grew up on the same street. My mom always had to work, and her parents often cooked me dinner."

Gabriela glanced at Sebastian's strong chin. "That must've been hard. It being just you and your mom."

"It wasn't always easy," he agreed. "I got used to fending for myself, though. I guess you have to when your mom works two jobs. But I knew she loved me."

"I'm sorry I didn't go to her funeral." Gabriela hadn't known her well, but she still felt as if she should've gone.

"And fly back from New York? No. Why would you? Besides, what if I'd come on to you at the wake? It would've been in bad taste."

She laughed at the dark joke. She liked his humor: daring, edgy. It was just like her own, provocative.

They ducked into the small breakfast nook in front of the restaurant, but found the doors locked.

"You know, Lola told me that you'd matured."

"Had she?" Sebastian laughed. "Well, when we find her, I'll tell her thanks for that." Then he grew pensive as they walked, their arms swinging so close together they nearly touched. "It just doesn't make any sense to me. Why would she wander off?"

Gabriela didn't answer. She knew one reason Lola might want to disappear.

"Right? Isn't it weird?" Sebastian glanced at her.

"Yeah." Her voice sounded weak, even to her own ears.

"You know something." Sebastian glanced at her as they walked past the second bank of elevators.

"No, I don't. Why do you say that?"

"Because suddenly you've gone quiet. You never go quiet."

They made it to the glass doors of the Italian restaurant, but found it closed and locked. Gabriela blew out a breath.

"You can tell me now, or later, but if it's something that can help us find Lola and help Marco from not losing his mind, now would be a good time to share." He gave the glass doors one last, hard tug.

Sebastian had a point there.

"Okay, but you can't tell Marco."

"I won't."

"You have to *swear* to me you won't." The last thing on earth Gabriela wanted to do was to cause a rift between the couple—especially if Lola turned up to be snoozing on a chaise longue, somewhere, happily passed out.

Sebastian stopped and thrust a hand on his hip, eyes flashing with emotion. "I won't. Now. Tell. Me. Everything." She realized then how intimidating the man must be in the courtroom. The green flecks in his eyes seemed to glow with intensity.

"She might have said something about cold feet."

"What?" Sebastian released the door handle and focused his full attention on her.

"She was just talking about nerves. I didn't think she was serious."

"When?" Sebastian stiffened, suddenly all seriousness.

"Tonight. Right before the rehearsal dinner."

Sebastian thought for a moment. "Well, she wouldn't just throw herself off a balcony, would she?"

"No." Gabriela bit her lip. They walked to the end of the passageway on the other side of the ship and ran into two double-glass doors leading to the outdoor pool where, just last night, Felicia had shoved her in. That seemed like a whole lifetime ago. Beneath the pale moonlight, the deserted pool shimmered. "Oh, no."

Gabriela rushed to one of the pool chairs and saw Lola's strappy stilettos. She'd kicked them off, it seemed, and they were beneath the chair closest to the Jacuzzi. She snatched them up, checked the size—seven—and the rhinestone detailing on the ankle strap. "These are Lola's."

"You're sure?" Sebastian knelt by her, putting his hand on her elbow. She was grateful for the support, because she suddenly felt light-headed. She covered his hand with hers and nodded.

"I was with her the day she bought them."

"Dammit." Sebastian glanced around the pool deck, and Gabriela did the same, mentally cataloging the distance between where they'd found the shoes and the railing. Probably twenty feet. Or more. Could she have stumbled over there? Leaned too far over and fallen?

"She was drunk," Gabriela said. "What if she…?"

Sebastian straightened and helped Gabriela do the same. He walked to the railing and looked over.

Gabriela joined him, watching the waves below them, inky-black beneath the night sky, slosh against the sides of the ship as it cut through the water. The cool night breeze ruffled her hair and she shivered. She prayed her friend was all right. She glanced backward, but only saw the string of white lights on the ship and a very little bit of foamy white wake behind them, the only ripple in the vast sea. She imagined floating in that, in the dark, alone. Horrible. She reached out and took Sebastian's hand, wanting the steady warmth. He squeezed hers hard.

"We need to go talk to the captain," Sebastian said.

"I'll call Felicia and Marco." Gabriela clutched the heels tightly in her hand. She prayed for the best but wondered if they all needed to prepare for the worst.

CHAPTER SIXTEEN

In the small windowless room on the third floor, just off the lobby, Gabriela, Sebastian, Marco and Felicia all sat before several closed-circuit security monitors. The captain, with his head of white hair and his stiff white jacket, stood next to his head of security, an average, middle-aged man in a white cruise ship uniform. They'd let them inside the room to help identify Lola from the security camera video of earlier that night.

Gabriela sat with her hands tightly pressed together. Sebastian stood behind her, his hand on her shoulder. Neither Felicia nor Marco seemed to notice and, at this point, Gabriela just didn't care. She was worried about her friend. Beyond worried. The hard pit in her stomach told her something was very, very wrong. Lola wouldn't just disappear.

Marco rubbed his face, the stress and the fatigue clearly getting to him. "You think she's on this camera?"

"We've got several on the pool deck," the captain told him. "Where did you find the shoes?"

"There." Sebastian pointed to the third screen, second chair from the right.

"Good. Then we should be able to see her. Let's rewind this."

Gabriela watched, feeling as if she were balancing on the head of a tiny pin. She didn't even want to breathe as she watched herself and Sebastian moving backward: first stepping in from out of the frame and then standing by the railing, holding hands. She forgot about that. Well, too late now. Though, instinctively, she moved a little bit away from Sebastian. He glanced at her, noticing. She turned back to the monitor. The video skipped further backward, to when they'd found the shoes, and then soon they were out of frame entirely. The video continued to skip backward until, right about nine, they saw the blurring movement of a woman in pink.

"Wait. That's her," Gabriela said. The security officer paused the tape and they watched as Lola stumbled into frame.

"She's drunk." Marco sounded despondent. "I knew she'd had a lot to drink at dinner, but I thought she was just having a good time."

The group watched as Lola stumbled to the chair and slumped down in it. She wrestled with her shoes and then kicked them off as she lay down on the deck chair. Then, after a minute, she seemed to see someone she knew. She sat up and began talking, but from the camera angle, they couldn't see who she was talking to.

"Who is that? Who is she talking to?" Marco leaned forward.

The captain glanced at the security officer. "Can we get a different angle?"

"I'm trying," the security officer said. He clicked to another camera angle and they could see the back of the man she was talking to. He was in a white uniform, much like the captain's.

"That looks like Carson." Sebastian's voice was low, almost a growl.

Gabriela studied the frame. She had to agree, there was Thor in all his glory.

"Carson? My first mate?" The captain squinted at the monitor. "How can you be sure?"

"I'm not. But it's a pretty good guess." Sebastian took in a deep breath. "I saw them talking at the rehearsal dinner."

"What do you mean?" Marco's head snapped up.

"I mean, they were talking animatedly about something. I thought it was weird at the time but..." Sebastian trailed off. "It didn't seem like small talk."

While everyone watched, the man offered his hand to Lola and she got up, unsteady on her feet. The man put an arm around her and then they hobbled away off camera.

Gabriela felt her stomach sink. She was with... *Carson?* Were they together right now? Her mind whirled with the worst possibilities.

Marco rubbed his face hard, as if to scrub the memory from his head. "Someone tell me *why* that asshole just kidnapped my wife?"

"Hey, we don't know yet—" the captain began.

"I know that I want you to take me to his cabin *now*. Taking advantage of a woman who's had too much to drink...that's a crime."

"We don't know she's been taken advantage of or even where she is. What we know is it's unlikely she's overboard, and that's a good thing," the captain said. "I'll send a security detail to his room and, hopefully, we'll get this all sorted out."

"You'd better." Marco stood and jabbed a finger into the captain's chest.

"Marco, settle down, man." Sebastian clapped a hand on his shoulder. "We have to brace ourselves for the possibility that Lola went with him because she wanted to."

Marco shook off Sebastian's hand. "What the hell are you saying to me right now?"

"She might have been having cold feet."

Gabriela felt all the blood drain from her head. Had he just revealed the very secret she'd sworn he not tell?

"Don't listen to him." Gabriela jumped to her feet and Sebastian whirled, surprised.

"What the hell is going on, Gabriela?" Gabriela glanced at Marco's face, and saw such desperation there.

"You'd better just tell him," Sebastian said. At that moment Gabriela was certain she was going to kill Sebastian. He'd promised not to say a word.

"Lola was having cold feet," Sebastian said.

Marco was inconsolable. His heart was broken, and for what? They didn't even know for sure if Lola had even done what everyone thought she'd done. Gabriela pressed her fingernails into her palms, furious for her friend. They were assuming she was guilty of the worst without even knowing any of the facts. Maybe they'd parted ways hours ago. Maybe he'd just taken her to the dining room to get a snack and some water. Nobody knew anything for sure, but everyone was jumping to the worst conclusions. And this was all Sebastian's fault. The captain sent a few of his security detail to Carson's room, but insisted the wedding party wait in the lobby. Felicia wrapped her arms around Marco's shoulders.

"Lola wouldn't do this to you," Felicia said, sounding sure. For the first time during the whole trip Gabriela suddenly felt a warmth of feeling for her old nemesis. At least someone was standing up for Lola.

"I agree," Gabriela said. "She wouldn't cheat on you, Marco."

Felicia and Gabriela exchanged a look of sisterly solidarity. She wasn't all bad, sometimes.

"I'll be right back," Sebastian declared. He marched down the corridor in the direction of the security detail.

Where the hell was he going? Gabriela jumped to her feet and was after him. "Where do you think you're going?" she challenged, glancing back at Marco, who remained seated.

"I'm going to be there when they open that door," Sebastian said.

"Haven't you done enough damage?" Gabriela tugged at his arm.

"What do you mean 'damage'?" He whirled, his hazel eyes on fire.

"I mean *you* assuming the worst of Lola. Telling her secrets that I *asked* you never to share with *anyone*. Least of all the groom." Gabriela felt her blood pulse in her veins. She was beyond furious. She just wanted to scream at him. "I thought she was like a sister to you? So how can you believe she'd do something like this?"

"Because *all* the evidence points to that. But I know you don't believe in a hard truth even if it's right in front of you."

"What the hell is that supposed to mean?"

"You know what it means. How long are you going to pretend there's nothing between us?" Sebastian's chest heaved, his nostrils flared.

That stopped Gabriela cold. "Don't you think we have bigger problems?"

"Yes, we do, and I think you don't face reality when you don't want to. Your problem is deep denial."

She shook her head furiously. She wasn't oblivious, was she?

"You were worried someone would say something about you holding my hand," he said. "You're embarrassed of me, and that doesn't feel good. Because you and I both know that what we have doesn't come along very often."

Did she know that? She swallowed hard. How could she even think of having a relationship with a man who thought so little of her best friend?

"You think Lola is cheating on Marco."

"I think it's a good possibility."

"She's been a good friend to you, and this is how you repay her?" Gabriela couldn't believe how furious she was. She realized, on some level, this argument had nothing to do with Lola and Marco and everything to do with her and Sebastian. "Is this what you call loyalty?" *And if you're this kind of friend, how could I depend on you to be anything more?*

"Loyalty? Says the woman who loves lying to that same best friend."

"Lying about what?"

"About us."

"This doesn't have anything to do with us." Gabriela felt like she was walking on quicksand. Every time Sebastian opened his mouth, she felt she was losing her footing.

"Doesn't it?" Sebastian shook his head. "Look, so sue me if I'm the kind of friend who is willing to say the unpopular thing if it means being honest. I don't want to be right about Lola. I don't want to hurt Marco. But if she is cheating on him, he needs to know and he needs to know now."

"But you're jumping to conclusions—"

"I'm protecting Marco. Lola was the one who wasn't brave enough to love him." Sebastian's voice had gone an octave lower and somehow Gabriela got the impression he wasn't talking about Lola at all. "They're about to make a promise to love each other forever, and that means something."

"You don't even believe in making a promise to love someone for five minutes much less forever." Gabriela waved her hand dismissively in front of her face.

His face grew stormy all of a sudden, his anger rising as he advanced on her. The sudden change took her by surprise and she stumbled back a step.

"Look, I take marriage *very* seriously. My father didn't. He walked out on my mother when I was just two, and he broke his promise to her—and me. I am not going to do that. When I make a promise, I plan to keep it. I expect others to do the same." His chest was heaving, his hazel eyes flashing with indignant anger.

The man truly did believe in marriage vows. Gabriela was shocked. She just assumed he didn't care for commitment, any more than he cared to have the same woman on his arm in his Instagram account for two weeks in a row.

"I—I'm sorry."

Sebastian regained his calm once more. "No, I'm sorry. I shouldn't have gotten angry. I just… I keep my promises, that's all. I believe that when you *do* agree to marry someone, it's for life, not just when it's convenient."

Gabriela believed him. Could it be that Sebastian Lott respected commitment even more than she did?

She realized then that Sebastian was a good and loyal friend, and he'd done what he thought was right, just as she was trying to do. Could she blame him for that?

Gabriela's phone rang. She fumbled for it in her pocket as Sebastian released her with a sigh. Lola's name scrolled across the screen.

"Lola?" Gabriela pressed the phone to her ear. "Lola, where are you?"

"I'm in your cabin. Please, Gabriela. Can you come? Don't bring Marco."

Lola's eyes were ringed with dark circles of mascara and she smelled strongly of red wine. Other than that, she was fine as she sat on the small chaise longue in the bridesmaids' cabin.

"I know I did a bad thing," Lola said. "I know I shouldn't have gone off with Carson, but I just needed someone to talk to. But I swear to both of you *nothing* happened. We just talked. That's it." She sniffled and wiped at her nose. "I didn't mean to scare anyone."

"You scared everyone," Sebastian said. He couldn't believe Lola—sensible, loving Lola—had done something so boneheadedly stupid. "We need to call Marco. Let him know you're okay."

"Not yet." Lola shook her head.

"Why not?" Gabriela pleaded as she knelt in front of Lola, her knees digging into the carpet. It was closing in on six in the morning and they'd soon arrive at Key West. It was the day of the wedding, which was scheduled at one.

"I'm not sure if I want to go through with the wedding." Tears ran down Lola's cheeks.

"Do you love Marco?" Sebastian asked, studying her face.

Lola nodded fiercely. "More than anyone." She sniffled.

"Then what's the problem?" Gabriela didn't understand. Not one bit. They were perfect for one another.

"W-what if he's not the one? What if I meet someone else even better in a few months, or even a few years? Or worse, what if he does?"

"You really think there's someone better for you than Marco?"

Gabriela handed Lola a tissue and she loudly blew

her nose. "No," she said. "But what if he finds someone better than me?"

"He's not going to." Gabriela was certain on that
point.

"But how can I be sure?"

"You can't be sure," Sebastian said. "It's all just a
leap of faith. That's what love is."

He stared at Gabriela and, in that minute, she knew
he wasn't talking about Lola and Marco. He was talking about her. She realized then how she'd not been
willing to even dip her toe in the water, much less
take a leap.

A beep signaled the sound of a card key opening
the door. Felicia walked in, Marco on her heels. He
looked furious.

"How could you do this to me, Lola?"

Sebastian turned to the door, glancing at Gabriela.
"I think we'd all better go and let these two talk it out."

Gabriela followed Sebastian out. Felicia stood in the
corridor, arms crossed.

"You should give them a minute," Gabriela said.

"Stay out of it, Gobstopper," Felicia snapped. Horrible Felicia was back.

"Hey, don't call her that." Sebastian's voice was low,
the warning unmistakable.

"You're on *her* side now? What? Are you two fucking?"

A long beat followed. Gabriela could deny it. But
why? She realized right in that moment that she wasn't
ashamed at all to be with Sebastian. She also realized
that up until now it had been her own fear that had kept

her from admitting it to herself. She'd been afraid to admit that their white-hot connection was anything more than physical, afraid that if she let herself be vulnerable and admit she wanted him, it would make her weak. But seeing Lola be afraid to take a leap of faith with a man who was perfect for her made Gabriela reconsider her own choices.

Hell, they weren't even talking about *getting married*. Sebastian was talking about dating. Why not? Why not take the leap? She was worried he'd leave her and yet what did that matter if she stopped the relationship before it ever began? Everything she'd seen about him this trip had told her he took commitment seriously. All he needed was a little faith.

"Yes," she said, stepping forward and taking Sebastian's hand. "We are. Have a problem with that?"

"I…" Felicia looked like she might faint. "You can't be."

"We are." Sebastian lifted their joined hands.

"*You're* the one that's been bad-mouthing him to all of us," Felicia declared.

Sebastian released his hold on Gabriela's hand. "What does she mean?" he asked, suddenly wary.

"Oh? You don't know? Gobstopper nicknamed you Swipe Left. Told us all you were toxic. Made us all promise to stay away from you. Was that just because you wanted him all to yourself?"

Gabriela shook her head, feeling a chill seep into her bones. "N-no. I just wanted to keep the peace. This weekend was supposed to be about Lola."

"Why would you think I'm a Swipe Left?"

Gabriela saw real hurt in his eyes.

"Look, it was…before." Gabriela struggled to explain. Two days felt like two years ago. Before she knew he was kind, and determined, and fiercely loyal. "I just thought you were going to be looking for a one-night stand, and so I thought it best if all the bridesmaids stayed away from you."

"So this is what you think of me?"

"No. It's not. It's…"

"You can't trust anything she says," Felicia said and pushed herself from the wall and walked away. "She's been bad-mouthing you this whole trip."

"Stay out of it, Felicia!" Gabriela called, but Felicia just held up a single-finger salute.

Sebastian was also moving the other way down the passageway.

"Hey, Sebastian, wait."

"Look, I get it," he said, the green flecks in his eyes seemingly dulled with pain. "You were just playing me."

Gabriela stood still, feeling helpless, as she watched him walk away.

CHAPTER SEVENTEEN

GABRIELA'S THOUGHTS WERE consumed by Sebastian for the next several hours, and that look of hurt on his face. She'd gone searching for him, but could find him nowhere: not in his room, not at the pool or in any of the restaurants. Even when Lola had let her know that the wedding would be on as scheduled, that the bride and groom had made up just in time, she still felt hollow.

She'd hated Felicia for telling Sebastian and yet she hated herself more for thinking so little of him when he'd proved himself to be so much more. Gabriela had desperately wanted to apologize.

She slipped on her bridesmaid dress, a seashell-pink, A-lined, sleeveless dress that hit at the knee. She glanced at herself in the mirror, nodding at her reflection, her hair up in a tight twist. *I'm going to make this right.*

When she arrived at the staging area, she saw a small alcove near the open veranda where Marco and Lola would be exchanging vows. A harpist stood ready to play the ceremonial music, and the guests had already begun to take their places in the line of white folding chairs covered in white linen tied with pink bows. Sebastian wasn't there. The rest of the bridal party stood crowded into a circle, and they all abruptly stopped talking when Gabriela came close. They were gossiping about her. No doubt Felicia had already spread the word. But, if she were honest, Gabriela found that she didn't really care.

"Is it true?" Veronica whispered, eyes bright. "Did you and…Sebastian—?"

"Have you seen him?" Gabriela cut her off.

"No, but… I mean…is he as good as they say?"

"Better," Gabriela called over her shoulder as she hurriedly left. She had to find him. Where was he? She searched the adjacent corridor and rooms, looking for Sebastian, but saw no sign of him. Eventually she heard the harp begin to play—her cue. She'd be walking down the aisle soon. She darted back to the alcove near the veranda, to find Sebastian standing there, looking stoic.

"Sebastian, I've been—"

But before she could finish, he interrupted. "Let's just get this done today, okay?"

The coldness of his tone took her aback.

"I didn't mean what I said before…" she began, voice low as she stood near him. Ahead of them, Liv and Theo strode down the aisle, followed by Veronica and Bill. Felicia and James waited their turn. Behind them, Lola and her father stood a bit apart.

"Look, I don't need your pity, okay?"

Pity? Seriously? Was that what he thought?

"Look, I was wrong about you, okay? I'll admit it."
Sebastian turned, studying her. "You were wrong?"

"Yes. Wrong. I'm sorry."

Sebastian fell silent. Did he accept her apology?

"Look, if you're truly embarrassed about being with me, then this won't work." Sebastian stared at her sadly. "I thought we really had something, but if for you it was all an act, then it won't work. I want to try, but if you don't, then it ends here."

In front of them, Felicia and James walked down the aisle and then it was their turn. No more time to talk. Sebastian let her go and she took her place on the bride's side. Then, it was the bride's turn to come down the aisle, and all eyes were on her.

The ceremony passed in a blur, as emotions churned in Gabriela's chest. She realized with perfect clarity as Marco and Lola kissed beneath the flower canopy that she wanted to try. She had to try with Sebastian. He was right: something as unique as this didn't come along every day. She realized she'd been too scared to try.

The bride and groom retreated down the path and the bridesmaids followed, Gabriela linking her arm in Sebastian's.

"He's going to leave you," Felicia hissed at her back once they got to the staging area. "He leaves everyone."

"No," Gabriela said, voice stony as she whirled on Felicia. "He left *you*. Get over it. It was more than ten years ago."

"How dare you…" Felicia balled her hands into fists.

"You've *never* been nice to me," Gabriela said.

"Ever. And I've always been nice for Lola's sake, but that stops now. This is my life, I'll do what I want with it."

And with that, she turned to Sebastian, pulled him down by his pink tie and kissed the life out of him. Gasps went up from the bridal party, but she didn't care. She'd kiss him in front of the whole ship if he wanted it.

When she pulled back, she was out of breath. "I want to try…us," she said.

A playful smile tugged at the corners of his mouth. "Oh, there's an *us* now, is there?"

"Hell, yes there is." She tossed her bouquet to the carpet and tugged him down for another kiss.

EPILOGUE

Three years later

THE BRIDE'S HEEL got stuck in the train of her ample white dress as she tried to maneuver down the short aisle on the deck of the *Royal Harmony* cruise ship as it overlooked the bright blue water of the Atlantic Ocean just off the shores of Key West.

"Gabbie! You're stuck," cried Lola, beautiful in an aqua-colored silk gown as she helped Gabriela get untangled. Her own bright gold ring shone on her finger. "And I can't believe you're getting married on my anniversary."

"It's a lucky date." Gabriela laughed a little, nodding at Lola's baby bump, just starting to be visible beneath the silk. She was due in four months. "Besides, this is where it all started. How could we *not* get married on this ship?"

Music drifted into the passageway where they were standing. "Ooh! Almost my turn." Lola helped Gabriela fix her train. "You ready for this?"

She glanced down the aisle at Sebastian Lott, looking gorgeous in his rented tux. She nodded. "I'm ready to take the biggest leap of faith ever."

"When you land on love, the leap's not that bad." Lola grinned and then darted down the aisle.

Gabriela took a deep breath, ready to follow. She saw Sebastian, his hazel eyes never leaving hers, and couldn't wait to start the rest of their lives together.

* * * * *

WICKED
PLEASURE

TARYN LEIGH TAYLOR

MILLS & BOON

For Kim—because I love you. And because you love Max. You'll always be my favourite palindrome.

For Juanita—I put your name in the story as a tribute for getting me through some tough writing battles. Also, because it starts with *J*.

And for Crystal—thanks. *Merci. Gracias. Danke.* I know it's redundant at this point, but I can't say it enough. I couldn't do this without you. #fact

CHAPTER ONE

IT HAD BEEN a long time since she'd crashed a party.

AJ weathered yet another snooty look from yet another glittering society princess, dripping diamonds and sipping Dom. She waited until Socialite Barbie passed before she looked down at herself.

She'd miscalculated a little there, AJ conceded, tugging discreetly at the hem of her dress—short, tight and black. Club wear might get her the right kind of attention when she went dancing—which was to say she never sat out a song or paid for a drink—but tonight, she stuck out like a poor relation. She'd been so busy hacking her way into this shindig that she hadn't paid too much attention to the dress code.

She should have bought something new. Something fancier.

This was a Liam Kearney event, after all. The tech magnate was known for his lavish lifestyle, his womanizing ways and his profligate parties.

Also, his tech was fucking epic.

AJ let her gaze wander over her lush surroundings. Lucrative, too, judging by his fancy digs.

She'd never been to a real Beverly Hills mansion before. The place had the works: tennis court, fountains, greenhouses, indoor/outdoor pool (currently full of bikini-clad models, natch), and most importantly, fancy French doors that led to Liam Kearney's office.

AJ reached into her shiny little purse thing, pulled out a tube of lipstick and did a quick reapplication in the ugly but ornate mirror hanging on the wall beside her. Probably cost more than her rent, she thought with derision, careful to angle the opening of her purse away from the closest of the six hidden cameras she'd located in her visual sweep. She placed the lipstick back inside, surreptitiously starting the stopwatch on her phone as she withdrew her hand.

He might have gaudy taste in mirrors, but his surveillance was expertly placed. Not that she'd expect anything less from the man who'd practically redefined cybersecurity. The whole place was wired up tight, and it was impressive as hell. Good enough to keep most professionals out.

AJ tucked the satin bag back under her arm.

Of course, she wasn't most professionals.

She took a couple of steps before she paused and pretended to fix her shoe, grabbing the doorknob for support. It turned easily in her hand, without setting off any audible bells or whistles. With a quick glance to make sure no one was paying attention, AJ slipped into the room, closing the door behind her.

Four, no five, discreet cameras took immediate notice of her. With that kind of setup, a silent alarm was probably overkill, she figured, sizing up the place, but she wouldn't rule out the possibility yet.

The office itself was modern and stylish with six big, evenly spaced windows that you could see through from the street (provided you were packing a pair of decent binoculars and had the skills to avoid the omnipresent private security patrol), and a computer setup with enough monitors to impress any fourth-rate TV show set decorator, but shit for doing any real work.

AJ stopped at a bookshelf crowded with tech awards and press clippings, careful to make sure whoever was monitoring the feed mistook her for an idly curious partygoer and not the security threat she was.

Despite herself, she was a little impressed by the shiny hardware. From national commendations for tech innovation to entrepreneur of the year, the man had won every accolade there was.

She picked up a heavy silver frame and stared at the photo of young Liam as a newly minted CEO. He looked…scrappy. Determined. Not so much happy as hungry, and she respected that.

He'd been eighteen years old when he'd launched Cybercore.

It was beyond impressive. Also the recipe for a million photo ops.

She set the frame back on the shelf.

No thanks.

AJ preferred to make her mark on the tech industry in less…public ways.

As though she had all the time in the world, she meandered toward the desk.

From the imposing black leather chair to the Cyber-core logo spinning on each of the high-res monitors, everything about the room screamed Inner Sanctum of a Tech Mogul.

AJ didn't buy it for a second.

She was good, yeah. Hell, she was the best, but the fact that she'd just waltzed into this "office" without tripping anything direr than a couple of security cams told her this room was just a showpiece—a quick stop for nosy houseguests who wanted to see where the magic happened.

This was not where Liam worked, and this was definitely not where he stored anything of importance.

Which meant that her gut had been right when she'd spent hours yesterday poring over the blueprints of his mansion.

The office was a decoy; the server was in his bedroom.

AJ rolled her eyes, because *of course* it was.

Rich dudes were so fucking over-the-top sometimes. Honestly…sleeping with it like he was a dragon guarding his treasure or something. Luckily, AJ was a firm believer that the greater the challenge, the more rewarding the heist.

Max would be so pissed.

AJ pushed the rogue thought aside. She might be in enemy territory behind Max Whitfield's back, but she was only doing it to help him. Besides, what her boss didn't know wouldn't hurt him.

Well, "boss" was a bit of a stretch.

She was more of an independent contractor. Ever

since she'd gotten caught hacking into Whitfield Industries by that arrogant dickwad, Wes Brennan. But instead of reporting her like Dickwad had suggested, Max had hired her, and it had really helped her out of a jam. The kind of jam most people went to prison for...

AJ was nothing if not loyal. Somebody was fucking with Whitfield Industries, and that meant someone was fucking with her.

And she was damn sure that *somebody* was throwing this party tonight.

Grabbing the arm of the chair, she turned it so it faced the window and took a seat, unclasping her purse as she set it in her lap. Someone should be here any second now...

As if on cue, the doorknob turned. AJ stole a glance at her phone. Forty-five-second response time, give or take. Conspicuously slow for a silent alarm, so she'd been right about it being just cameras.

The smug smile playing about her lips died instantly as AJ spun the chair around to face the man who'd just walked in on her.

Ho-ly shit.

"I wasn't expecting anyone to be in here," he said.

And she'd been expecting some covert security lackey to be dispatched to check on her, not Liam Kearney himself, complete with a tumbler of amber liquid in one hand and a flute of champagne in the other.

Inconveniently, he was sexier in real life than her Google searches and his television interviews had suggested. She knew he was hot—the man got more press than the latest reality TV starlet's nude selfies—but nothing had prepared her for his presence. There was something about him that didn't quite translate in his pictures, something almost…wild, which was not usually the adjective that came to mind for a man who was known for his savant-like coding and his three-piece suits.

Her lady parts gave a twinge of appreciation, and AJ realized that it had been a long time since she'd gotten her flirt on. And an even longer time since she'd, *ahem*, taken care of things. Why else would she be salivating over a man so completely not her type?

She liked dangerous guys, ones who didn't look like they'd just come from the cover shoot of *CEO Monthly*, with their clean-shaven jaws and their jet-setting tans and their thousand-dollar haircuts, short on the sides, slightly longer on top. In fact, the only thing that kept all that masculine perfection from being completely repulsive was the devilish spark in his hazel eyes. There was an implied dare in them, and AJ had never been good at turning down a dare.

She dropped her gaze pointedly before meeting his eyes again. "The fact that you're double-fisting drinks leads me to believe otherwise."

His grin was lethal, a cocky mea culpa that probably earned the forgiveness of women from six to ninety-six, even though it was completely unrepentant. "Detail-oriented. A quality I admire."

Yeah, she'd figured that out pretty fast. Not often the king of the castle himself came to check on a security blip. AJ wasn't quite sure what that was about. It didn't make sense.

"I was just looking for somewhere quiet, away from

the crowd," she lied with her best damsel-in-a-tiny-dress head-tilt. "These shoes are killing me."

She leaned back in the plush leather chair, propping her heels on his desk, ankles crossed so that her strappy gold stilettos were on full display.

There was a suspended moment as his gaze slid the length of her legs, and she ignored the phantom warmth that followed in the wake of his inspection—an inspection that lingered for a beat too long on her purse. Reflexively, AJ shut it, the snick of the clasp deafening in the silent room. Her breath caught at the snap of awareness as he reestablished eye contact. Something indefinable shifted in the depths of his gaze…and then he pushed the door closed behind him with his elbow, totally falling for it.

AJ exhaled.

When it came to distractions, the classics always worked, though AJ couldn't help a pang of disappointment that she'd won so easily. Liam might be a renowned tactician, but that didn't change the rules of the game: rock beat scissors, scissors beat paper, and penis beat brain.

She let a hint of a smile curve her lips. "So what's your excuse for ducking out of the party?"

"The truth?" he asked, walking toward her. He moved with a lot more grace than your average tech geek. Hell, he moved with more grace than some of the more accomplished pickpockets she'd known.

It took a second before AJ realized she was pressing back against the chair at his approach. She swallowed and forced her muscles to relax as Liam circled the desk, positioning his body between her chair and the desk. A show of dominance that she recognized—she was good at reading body language—but that didn't mean it didn't work. She made a conscious effort not to move her feet even an inch to accommodate his big frame as he leaned a hip against the dark wood surface. The soft material of his suit jacket brushed her bare calf, and she shivered at the sensation.

"I don't believe we've met." His voice was deep. Seductive. "And I was looking for an excuse to rectify that."

He held out the champagne flute.

AJ cocked an eyebrow and ignored the stemmed crystal, relieving him of the tumbler in his other hand instead. "Well then, the first thing you should know about me is that I prefer scotch to bubbly."

He let her see the flare of interest in his eyes. "It's bourbon," he advised, setting the champagne on the desk beside his hip.

AJ took a sip. Potent, but smooth. Much like the man who'd provided it.

He reached into the left side of his jacket, retrieving his phone. His thumb flew over the surface of the sleek, matte black rectangle with impressive speed. It took a moment longer than it should have before the soft whir of the security cameras simultaneously shifting direction penetrated her consciousness, before her gaze cut from his big, capable hand to the reflection of his screen in the monitor behind him. Before she could glean anything of import, he was already tucking his phone back into his interior breast pocket.

Damn.

It took everything in her not to flinch at the wasted opportunity. She'd gotten soft, working for Max, holed up in her cushy apartment and doing everything remotely. She'd been off the front line too long. The old her would have capitalized on a gift like that—a glimpse at the screen of her adversary.

Maybe she still could…

She'd come here to drop a backdoor into his main server so she could poke around at her leisure and figure out how to thwart any further attempts to hobble Whitfield Industries. It was supposed to be a quick, covert mission, under the radar all the way.

Liam had messed up the covert part of her plan by walking in on her, but he'd also presented her with an opportunity she'd never dreamed of—the chance to do the same thing to his phone.

She'd made some mods to the program Max had asked her to look into, the one that had been covertly installed on his sister Kaylee's phone. It had turned out to be Cybercore issue, which put a big red bull's-eye on Liam Kearney's chest. He'd rocketed to the top of the suspect list—douchebag most likely to be responsible for the hack on Whitfield Industries.

After she'd analyzed the malware, she'd tinkered a little. It had good bones, but she'd made it even better. If AJ could get her phone close to his, she could install the spy app remotely and have access to everything: his passwords, his emails, his whole life. Excitement at the prospect bubbled in her chest. There was something poetic about beating Liam Kearney with his own tech.

But to make that happen, she needed him to stay close. Really close.

AJ licked her lips, not missing the quick dart of his gaze to her mouth. Her smile was indulgent.

This was going to be easier than she'd thought.

She waited until he raised his eyes to hers. "How can you be sure?"

"That it's bourbon? I poured it myself."

She smiled despite herself at his dry, offhand delivery. "That we've never met," she corrected.

He searched her face, and her breath caught beneath his scrutiny, trapping her in the moment. She couldn't look away.

"I'd remember you."

AJ's pulse stuttered like Morse code, but before she could parse the hidden message, the door to the office swung open, and in walked a vest-and-bow-tie-clad waiter brandishing a tiny silver tray with a tumbler of bourbon balanced dead center. Liam grabbed it, thanking the waiter he'd obviously summoned with his phone—Kearney was a tech god, not telepathic—and AJ used the distraction to arm the app on her phone with a quick up-down-up-up press of the volume buttons through the satin of her purse.

The waiter removed the abandoned champagne flute before he turned and left as efficiently as he'd appeared, and just like that, she was alone with Liam again.

It was time to initiate Operation Phone Hack.

CHAPTER TWO

AJ TOOK A showy swallow of her drink as she pulled her feet off his desk. She hated to gulp down the expensive stuff, but she needed to move her glass into her left hand, and giving him the impression she was a little tipsy might help sell the next part of her plan.

"Neat trick." AJ tipped her chin in the direction of his bourbon. "Tell me, does everyone come when you call?" she asked, the words low and suggestive as she grabbed her purse in her right hand and got to her feet.

The key to a believable stumble was to commit, trust your mark to catch you, and then keep the response understated. No overwrought flailing or ridiculous exclamations. Even a layman could see the hammy stuff from a mile away.

With a credible slip, AJ widened her eyes—little details were important—bringing her purse hand up and bracing it against Liam's chest in an attempt to catch herself. A quick twist of her wrist ensured the satin lined up right about where that interior suit pocket that housed his phone should be.

The remainder of her drink sloshed perilously close

to the rim of the glass before she fully regained her balance. As far as misdirection went, it was a nice touch, even if she did say so herself. And she knew it had worked by the way Liam's palm had landed on her hip to steady her as he turned his attention from her glass back to her face.

He let his gaze wander down to her mouth and back up. The low hum of arousal between them intensified. "As a rule, they call *after* I make them come."

Her knees went soft, and his hand tightened on her hip.

"You okay?"

Was she okay? Sure, if you ignored the part where she'd spent the last four days figuring out how to break into this man's bedroom without being detected, and now all she could think about was how much she wanted to take him up on the implied invitation to join him there.

God*damn*, she needed to get laid. Usually, when the itch got bad enough, she went out and took what she needed. No fuss, no commitment. But if she was being honest, no one had lit her up for a while.

Not like this.

"Guess the bourbon's hitting a little harder than I thought."

It was a lie, of course. She wasn't drunk. You couldn't run a job if you weren't 100 percent in control of all your faculties. And yeah, matching wits with a worthy adversary always revved her up a bit, but this…this *hormonal glitch* was another level altogether.

"Perhaps a little fresh air would help." He took his

hand off her hip, reaching beneath the lip of the desk, and the twin sounds of music and laughter rushed into the room.

AJ glanced over her shoulder to watch as the window closest to them retracted into the wall, granting them access to a wrought iron terrace.

When she turned back, he seemed closer than he had a moment ago.

God, he smelled good. Warm and sexy. Expensive. Eau de Rich Guy.

Yeah, distance sounded like the smart plan right now.

"Perhaps it would." She meant it to sound mocking—who the fuck said *perhaps* anymore?—but it came out a little breathless.

She pulled her purse back from his chest, tucking it securely under her arm as she straightened. That should have been plenty of time for the malware to install, she figured, turning and stepping through the space where the window used to be, taking a bracing sip of her drink as the warmth of the night surrounded her.

"Some party."

He glanced around the glittering mass of guests amid the fountains and twinkle lights, chatting and laughing while they flitted around. Seeing. Being seen. "You don't like it?"

"Not really my scene." Pomp and circumstance made her itchy.

"Really?" Liam ran a hand over his jaw. "I thought all women loved a reason to dress up and drink a man's bourbon."

Cynical words. AJ's brows lifted as she realized for the first time that he was a little itchy, too. "Huh."

"Huh, what?"

AJ turned to face him, leaning a hip against the balustrade. "Just drinking in the astounding realization that the tech world's most infamous international party boy hates his own parties."

He shot her a what-are-you-talking-about look and he lifted his drink. The muscles in his throat worked as he swallowed. "What makes you say that?"

"Besides the fact that you're up here talking to me instead of mingling? I'm good at reading people. And I have a doctorate in the nuances of cynicism. You just bypassed *world-weary* and jumped straight to *jaded*."

He considered that for a moment. "Some might argue that talking to a beautiful woman is well within the definition of mingling."

"You've purposefully ignored three flirtatious waves and the arrival of a senator."

"Impressive. I could use you on my security team." Liam blew out a breath, and AJ didn't miss that his gaze went directly to said senator, who was holding court next to one of the tiered fountains that dotted his property.

"So is that what you think of me?" Liam asked. "Jaded international party boy?"

She didn't buy the casual spin he put on it. It sounded like a real question, and she let her femme fatale act slip for a minute. "Isn't that what I'm supposed to think?"

The world went still for a second, as though the brief flash of understanding that passed between them in that moment had been captured, a photograph in time. Then AJ blinked, and real life resumed.

"I've always found it a tactical advantage, the ability to disappear into the stereotype." Liam's gaze turned pointed. "Much easier to get what you want when people underestimate you, don't you think?"

Danger prickled along AJ's spine, and for the second time that night, she had to actively loosen her muscles. Rhetorical question. He didn't know anything. First rule of surviving on the street—if you act guilty, you get caught. She might not pick pockets anymore, but she'd do well to remember the lesson. "You don't seem like a man who has too much trouble getting what he wants."

"Not usually." He eyed her attentively. "But I guess we'll find out."

That trickle of lust she'd been fighting since he'd walked into his office upgraded itself to a gush, but before she did something monumentally stupid, his phone vibrated, and they both dropped their gazes to his chest.

"Aren't you going to get that?"

Liam shook his head, and AJ tipped hers to the side, studying him. "I've never known a titan of industry to ignore the siren song of a phone call."

"Do you know many? Titans?"

"A few."

His phone vibrated again. AJ stepped closer, reached toward him, and when he made no move to stop her, she slipped her hand inside his suit and pulled out his phone.

"Dom," she announced, reading the contact info on the display. "As in dominatrix? Are you late for a bit of the whip and tickle?" The phone continued to buzz insistently against her palm. "You must be a good customer. She seems eager for contact."

"Dom as in Dominic. Business acquaintance. He could probably pull off the leather, but judging by his golf game, I doubt his mastery with the riding crop. He's not very athletic."

"Well, color me disappointed." With a twist of her wrist, she held the phone out to him, screen up. "Might be important."

Liam took the phone and tucked it back in his suit without so much as glancing at it. "Work has a tendency to consume you if you let it."

AJ turned back to the balcony, leaning her forearms against the railing. She liked it when work consumed her. Kept that bad shit from creeping into her brain. "You don't let it?"

"As I believe we already established, I live to party."

She laughed at that. "You're so full of shit."

She felt his eyes on her profile, the burn of their focus. Barroom talk was out of place at a cocktail party. She probably shouldn't have said that.

"You see?" he asked, his voice deliciously husky. "I told you."

The tease worked, and she gave in to temptation, looked over at him. He had a tiny jagged scar on his chin. "What?"

His gaze roamed her face in the dim light. "I'd remember you."

Something in his eyes, so dark, ran through her like an electrical current. Her laugh sounded fake, even to her own ears. "Sure you would. Just like you remember everyone else at this shindig?"

Liam flickered a surveying glance at the grounds, teeming with people. His easy shrug of confirmation sharpened her focus.

"There's got to be two hundred people here." Two hundred and twelve, according to her research. All required to RSVP for the code that would grant them access tonight. And another thirteen who'd politely declined, which had essentially nuked their bar codes so they'd been of no use to her. This had been a tough party to crash.

"Give or take," he said, with a sip of bourbon.

She turned toward the terrace railing and rested her elbows on it, staring down at the busy garden below. There were people milling about, but her eyes snagged on a mismatched couple almost directly beneath her, illuminated by the fancy lights strung all over the grounds.

"Who're those two?" she asked, with a head tip at a stout, balding man who'd cornered one of the waitstaff so he could raid the shrimp platter while the gorgeous woman on his arm guzzled champagne with alacrity.

Liam turned to see her pick, and the sleeve of his jacket brushed her upper arm, unleashing a wave of goose bumps across her skin. "Phillip Henderson and his much younger wife, Tara Billings-Henderson."

Her eyes narrowed with suspicion. "You could be

saying any names. How would I know if you're full of shit or not?"

He leaned forward on the railing and raised his voice a little. "Phillip. Tara. So glad you could make it tonight."

The mismatched twosome lifted their heads like a couple of well-trained Labradors at the sound of their names, eager for their host's attention.

"Wouldn't miss it!" boomed the bald guy, yelling much louder than necessary and affording AJ a full view of all his teeth and his mouthful of masticated shrimp. "You always throw the best parties!"

The blonde dropped her husband's arm like she'd been burned, executed a shampoo-commercial-worthy hair shake and waggled her fingers. "There you are! I've been looking for you all night. Save me a dance?"

In a nonanswer, he raised his glass to them, took a sip of bourbon and turned his whole body to face AJ.

"*Super* classy guest list," she complimented, hoping the irony didn't make her sound petty. At least they were *on* the guest list.

A ghost of a smile tugged at his lips.

The sexy pulse of the base-heavy track the pool-deck DJ was spinning spilled through the night, making her want to dance like she did in the club. She wanted to wrap her arms around his neck and sway with him while his hands rode the small of her back, the curve of her ass, pulling her close so she could grind her hips against his while he kissed her neck…

Shit.

She was in big trouble, and the look on his face did nothing but confirm it.

"I'm Liam."

AJ almost laughed. "Oh, I know."

"Then it appears you have me at a disadvantage."

Her hand tightened on her glass at the accuracy of his statement. But it wouldn't be true for much longer if she didn't get her shit together. She wasn't here for his animal magnetism, she was here for his tech.

The reminder gave her the strength to shoot him a cool smile. "Not a position you're used to, I'm sure."

He stepped closer. It was disconcerting, the way his broad shoulders blocked out the view of anything but him.

"On the contrary, I pride myself on being familiar with a wide array of positions."

AJ swallowed, ignoring the urge to mess him up a bit, rake her hands through his hair, tug his tie askew, get him a little bit naked. "You're handsomer than I expected." The thought slipped past her lips and raised his eyebrows.

"That didn't sound like a compliment."

She gave him a once-over and shrugged. "Kind of cliché is all. I mean, hella smart, stupid rich *and* disgustingly handsome? It's a little much. Most people settle for two out of three."

His gaze roamed her face. "I don't believe in settling." His voice was low and intimate and vibrated at the perfect frequency to tighten her nipples. "Tell me your name."

"A—Robin." She remembered her alias at the last

second. *Damn.* Maybe that bourbon *had* affected her a little. She'd been *this close* to saying AJ. That would have been a rookie mistake, giving him her real name. Well, real enough, anyway.

"Robin," he repeated, leaning forward. Or was she leaning forward?

Either way, their breaths mingled, and her breasts ached for his touch, and being horizontal sounded like a way better idea than being vertical because being vertical was highly overrated as a state of being anyway.

It would just figure that the only man to light her up, to really light her up, in the last four years would be the one man who was completely off-limits to her. A mark. Nothing more.

GD sex hormones. This was no time to be all hopped up on dopamine and serotonin and Liam Kearney's mouth.

"Liam! Hey! Awesome party!"

The intrusion was perfectly timed, and AJ took a step back from temptation and sent a cursory glance at the bikini-clad girls beckoning from the lawn below them.

"Why are you hiding up there? Meet us in the pool!"

"Yeah. Come get wet with us!"

When AJ looked back at Liam, his gaze was still locked on her, and she ignored the zing of heat in her belly.

"It seems I've monopolized you for far too long. Your fan club is getting restless." The rueful note in her voice wasn't fully for show. "But it was nice to meet the man behind the legend. Thanks for giving me a reason to dress up and drink your bourbon." She swallowed the final mouthful and pressed her empty glass into his left hand, ignoring the spike in her pulse when her fingers brushed his. "If you'll excuse me, I'm going to go freshen up."

"It was nice meeting you, too." A noticeable beat slipped by before he added, "Robin."

Something about that pause made the hair on the back of her neck stand up.

Liam raised his hand, gesturing toward the house with her glass. "You're looking for the first door on the left at the top of the stairs."

The directions startled her. "What?"

"The bathroom," he clarified, his voice easy though his gaze remained sharp. "You wanted to freshen up. That's what you said, right?"

AJ's smile was deliberately casual. "Yes. That's exactly where I'm headed. Thank you." She knew that, of course. She knew every inch of his sprawling estate, thanks to the blueprints she'd nicked from the city's website.

Not that she couldn't have gotten them through regular channels…but why wait for the mind-numbingly slow wheels of bureaucracy to turn when you could just make the internet your bitch? Instead of filling out forms and weeks of waiting, she already knew where the bathroom was, and where his bedroom was, and where the panic room in the back of his bedroom closet that he'd reconfigured into a server room was.

"It's been entirely my pleasure, I assure you."

Thanks to emphasis, what might have been a bland

pleasantry from anyone else held some heat. Enough to make AJ wish their night could have ended differently.

Ignoring all her good sense, she tightened her grip on her purse and stepped close enough that her breasts pressed against his chest. "Well, if this is your idea of pleasure, it's probably good we stopped now." AJ leaned in, then leaned in a little more, until her lips brushed his ear. "My definition might have killed you."

She pulled back in time to see Liam's mouth tip up at the corner. "It sounds like it would have been a hell of a way to go."

God, it had been forever since she'd felt this...alive. Maybe a little walk on the wild side was exactly what she'd needed. "Oh, it would have been. I assure you."

And with that, she left Liam on the balcony and headed into the house.

Playtime was over. She had work to do.

CHAPTER THREE

LIAM KEARNEY *HATED* being bored.

Sadly, it was becoming the status quo.

His personal life had devolved into a slideshow of inanely shallow parties, forgettably beautiful women and exceedingly nauseating sycophants. Sometimes he got the impression that he'd become the thing he hated most in the world…a black-card-carrying member of the entitled elite.

His mother.

Usually he could bury that irritating thought in work, because his professional life was interesting enough. At least it had been, until a month and a half ago.

That's when Max Whitfield, his rival in the race for the next step in digital cryptocurrency, had grown a conscience and confessed to the world that someone had hacked him, so he was pushing back the release date of his SecurePay app until he'd gotten to the bottom of it. He wanted to make sure that the customers who trusted him with his business were getting the kind of superior product they associated with the

Whitfield Industries name…or whatever PR bullshit his sister had spun for him.

All he'd heard in that press conference was that Max had folded and handed him the win. Liam had been planning on taking it anyway, of course, but it would have been so much more satisfying to do it in a fair fight.

He thought briefly of his past dealings with John Beckett, and his more recent dealings with the dead man's son, Aidan. Max's former father figure and former best friend, respectively. And he knew Max blamed him for the *former* part on both counts. Buying John's code hadn't been illegal per se, but Liam's gut had told him the old drunk wasn't totally on the level when he'd shown up, looking for a deal.

Not his finest hour, but Liam had been young, and hungry, and bent on proving himself to all comers. Passing on John's raw genius and sending him back to Whitfield Industries because it was the sappy, good-guy "right thing to do" was not an option he'd entertained.

Then Beckett Senior wrapped his car around a tree, Beckett Junior had skipped town, and Max's side of the rivalry had turned personal.

A tiny ember of guilt tried to flare, but Liam drowned it with a healthy swallow of bourbon. He couldn't have known how things would turn out when he'd made that deal.

Still, Liam *owed* Max a fair fight, and he'd been looking forward to it, to putting the products each of them had developed to market in a cryptocurrency battle royale and see once and for all who came out on top.

Max's software would be good—why have a rival if he didn't have the chops to push you to be your best?—but it was no match for Cybercore's hardware.

The Shield was a status symbol, one you could display on a watchband, a bracelet, a necklace or a belt. Max could only sell people the SecurePay app once, but The Shield came in seven different colors, a rotating selection of limited-edition prints, and a coordinating line of accessories.

And that was why Liam was going to wipe the floor with him.

Well, he would have.

Now that Max had temporarily dropped out of the game, Liam's inevitable victory was hollow and unfulfilling.

He thrived on testing his mettle against a worthy opponent.

Liam stared contemplatively at the empty glass in his left hand. And speaking of worthy opponents...

He wasn't bored anymore.

Most definitely a party crasher...but *how* she'd done it was what intrigued him most. This was an exclusive bash he was throwing.

He knew she hadn't breached the perimeter. Not only couldn't she have scaled the wall in that dress— *God, that dress*—and those heels, but his new electronic fence tech was unbeatable...which was why the government was about to make him even wealthier than he already was.

That meant she had not just duped a bar code, which would have flagged her for using someone else's invitation, but created a new one that let her through the gates under the alias Robin Capucha, without registering as an extra person and tripping the maximum guest number warning, either.

The cockiness of casually breaching his top-notch security by giving Robin Hood a Spanish flair was… ballsy. And intriguing. And pretty fucking hot.

Someone below called his name, but he pretended not to hear as he stepped back into his decoy office—he kept all the really good tech downstairs—and abandoned the glasses on the desk. Then he pulled his phone from his jacket to check the progress on the facial recognition he was running off the security footage from the front gate, where all arriving guests had to check in. No match on her so far.

Liam tapped a finger against the edge of his phone. "What are you up to?"

As if in answer, his phone buzzed again. This time, he answered it.

"Dom. What have you got?"

"Not sure. All the cameras in your office are now pointed at the ceiling, and I can't get them back online."

Good to know he could still outsmart his employees. "That was me."

"I knew it!" His voice got muffled, as though he was covering the mouthpiece. "I told you it was Liam," he gloated, and then his words were back to full strength. "I told Mina it was you. She and I have a hundred bucks riding on who solves your office cam puzzle first."

"Anything else?"

"Yeah, we just had a camera go out. Nothing but static in the library. Nobody on the feed prior to, so either it's busted, someone hit it remotely or you've got a tech-savvy ghost."

Aha.

The library. It housed a built-in safe behind a false picture frame, like something out of a movie. He'd considered having it removed during the last set of renos, but there was something antiquated about it that appealed to him. And it was a smart hit—a room with a secret was a target that would draw focus.

"Wanted to let you know, but you're a hard man to get ahold of tonight."

Liam's focus drifted to the tumbler on his desk. There was a faint imprint of her lips on the glass, the same deep pink as her lipstick. "I was busy working out a little puzzle of my own."

Dom laughed. "Yeah, I know what you were busy with. I'm the one who told you 'the puzzle' was nosing around your office in the first place, remember? You want me to dispatch some muscle to the book room to investigate?"

"In a minute. First, check the other feeds for looping. Start with the west stairs to the basement and the hallway outside the master bedroom. Work out from there."

"There's no way anyone pulled something as bush-league as a loop with Mina and I on the—Jesus H. Christ in a porno, that's a bingo on the hallway cam. God*damn*, this is clean. It didn't trigger any of the fail-safes."

Liam's blood picked up, like a predator who'd just scented his prey.

Definitely not bored.

"Send someone to the library anyway. Low priority. Tell security not to cause a scene. And get the cameras back online. I'll take care of the bedroom myself."

Liam stowed his phone away, helpless against his own smirk of satisfaction as he hit the button that would close the window to the balcony. It had been a long time since anyone had gotten under his skin like she did. And longer still since anyone had gotten the drop on him.

Gorgeous and brilliant was a hell of a combination.

Liam savored the rest of his bourbon, contemplating the upcoming battle of wits, giving his sexy little interloper a few minutes' head start on whatever she had planned.

Then he pulled the doors to the office closed behind him and returned to the party, placating attention-seekers with a distracted smile and nod as he headed toward the stairs that led to his bedroom.

CHAPTER FOUR

LIAM KEARNEY HAD all the best toys.

A self-satisfied smile curved her lips as the light on the electronic trip wire went dead. With the final booby trap dispatched, AJ shoved her phone back in her purse and slipped into the master suite. Safer to leave the light off, since the giant floor-to-ceiling window across from his bed looked out over the party. All she needed was one nosy guest to report her skulking around and she'd be sunk.

Focus, she warned herself. Quick. Efficient. Eyes on the prize.

No time to indulge in perverted thoughts about his ginormous bed or how good he might look in it. Or on the floor. Or up against the dresser.

This was a onetime deal. She'd known that when she'd hacked her invitation. She'd been all over the security feed since the second she'd stepped onto Liam's property. A second chance at this was never part of the plan.

Might as well hit the main server before she disappeared for good. Right?

You don't owe him anything, she reminded herself sternly, when the answer to her previous question wasn't a resounding yes. He was the enemy. The asshole who'd hacked Max.

And yeah, he was sexy as sin, but their association had the same approximate expiration date as nonrefrigerated dairy in the California sun.

Swallowing her unease, AJ hurried over to the dark mahogany closet, wishing she could have pulled this job in her Doc Martens instead of stilettos. Props to all the women in action movies who kicked ass in heels on the reg. It wasn't easy.

The doors slid out of the way as she approached—the man had a damn spaceship for a closet—revealing an impressive square-footage of meticulously arranged suits, shirts and ties, but she didn't waste time admiring the dark-to-light color coding. Instead, she walked directly to the rows and rows of shoes that lined the wall at the back of the room.

According to the blueprints, the entrance to the panic room should be behind them. AJ ran a hand along the side of the shelves until her fingers caught on a lever.

"Gotcha."

She pressed it, and with a click, one side of shelving came loose from the wall so she could pull it open like a door. But when AJ looked behind it, she encountered the one thing that she hadn't expected from a tech god…

Uh oh.

It was freakin' brilliant, no doubt about it, but there was no way she was getting past the vault door. Three key locks that seemed to be on separate timers, a good old-fashioned combination lock and a manual keypad.

She was a hacker, not an old-timey bank robber.

Touché, she thought with a mental salute to the man who'd won this round. Looked like she wouldn't be using any more of the cool tech she'd loaded on her phone after all.

Good thing she'd gone after Liam's phone when she'd had the chance, or tonight would have been a total bust.

The memory of their dangerous flirtation flooded her body with heat.

Okay, maybe not a *total* bust. At least she had a fun new fantasy to exploit next time she gave her vibrator a workout. Like the second she got home.

AJ pushed the shoe shelf until it clicked into place and hurried back into the bedroom, relieved when the closet door sensed her departure and whooshed shut behind her. She'd just stepped into the hallway when her phone gave two sharp pulses—the signal that some-one had tripped the innocuous little motion detector she'd stuck to the baseboard in the hallway to warn her if anyone was headed her way.

Her heart rate jacked into the danger zone.

Shit.

She'd pushed it coming up here in the first place, she realized as she pulled the door shut behind her as qui-etly as she could, all the while trying to one-handedly unclasp her purse.

Should have gotten the fuck out when I had the chance.

AJ pulled out her phone. She needed to rearm Liam's fancy electronic trip wire, or she was as good as caught. He was a details man, and a deactivated alarm was the sort of detail that wouldn't go unnoticed.

She cursed her impetuousness—always pushing for one more thing, one more score. It was sloppy.

And sloppy gets you caught.

Her thumbs flew over the screen, disconnecting the signal jam she'd deployed to bypass it in the first place. A quick glance at the alarm showed it was still off-line. *What the hell?*

"Come on," she breathed, entering the start-up code again.

Still nothing.

Her eyes darted down the hall. Still clear, but not for long.

Think like the tech god. Liam Kearney was smart. Meticulous. Known for his rotating codes and his attention to detail…

Of course! The sequence changed with each re-start.

It was ingenious. A discreet little counter that let him know how many reboots the alarm had been through. AJ didn't have time to be too impressed, though. Whoever was headed her way would be arriving momentarily.

She made the necessary changes to her approach, and within seconds, the little green light on the trip wire flicked on. AJ jammed her phone back into her purse and turned around just as a figure appeared at the end of the hallway.

* * *

Liam braced a shoulder against the wall and allowed himself a moment to watch her as she stood, unaware of his presence, staring thoughtfully at the artwork in the hallway outside his bedroom.

Her profile was beautiful—the slope of her nose, the softness of her lips, the curve of her neck. Her raven curls brushed her shoulder as she tipped her head to the side, engrossed in the painting, as though he'd come upon her in an art gallery instead of sneaking through his house.

"Find what you're looking for?"

Her gaze didn't waver from the painting, but a slight smile touched her mouth. It was almost as though she was expecting him. She pointed up at the canvas. "Would have put my money on you being more of a dogs-playing-poker-on-black-velvet man."

"I lock up the really expensive stuff during parties." He pushed away from the wall and joined her beside the Pollock. "I thought you might like a tour, but I see you're already taking one."

She crossed her arms, drawing his eyes to the way it pushed up her cleavage. "Just curious," she averred. "I mean, if the bathroom's that nice, what riches must the rest of the house conceal?"

Her voice was full of sarcastic wonder, and yet again, her impertinence made him stifle a grin.

"Well, there's no safe hidden behind this painting, if that's your game."

She cut him a measuring glance at his opaque reference to the library, and Liam watched, fascinated as the suspicious edge that had marked all their interactions thus far relaxed slightly. Like something had changed between them. "Foiled again."

"In that case, I'll call off the cops." Liam pulled his phone from his pocket and keyed in the current iteration of the rotating eight-digit master password that would unlock the room behind them before stowing it away.

"As for the riches concealed behind these doors, only one way to find out."

She glanced behind her, shrugging one bare shoulder in a show of nonchalance before she turned and pushed open the double doors to reveal his bedroom suite. If she was impressed by the room, or the glass wall that looked out over the grounds, she didn't show it.

Despite her nonchalance, his body revved as she stepped over the threshold, wandering deeper inside. At some point after his first million, sex had become an inevitable conclusion. Something easily acquired when and if he wanted it, and much to the disgust of his sixteen-year-old self's fantasies, less exciting for it.

The thread of danger in this interaction, his inability to decipher whether he was the hunter or the prey, had him on edge, primed for action. He'd forgotten how fucking good sexual tension could be.

She clasped her hands behind her back as she explored, taking in her surroundings. "It's not what I expected."

Liam pushed the doors shut, and the click was loud

in the sudden silence as the soundproofing kicked in, blocking out the ambient party chatter and the throbbing bass line of the DJ. "What did you expect?"

"Based on your reputation as a jaded international party boy?" She glanced over her shoulder, and her mocking smile almost undid him. "Manacles on the headboard, some kind of swing in the corner."

Liam slid his hands in his pockets. He wanted her. Against all reason and his better judgment, he wanted her. "I don't need chains to keep a woman in my bed."

"You're awfully confident." She turned back to the window, staring down at the party below.

She was a fascinating study in contrasts. Tough, but vulnerable. Smart, but impetuous. Gorgeous, but oddly reticent to exploit the hell out of that.

"Just hopeful. And for the record, I'm not opposed to chains. I'm just a strong proponent of mutual reciprocity."

"That's encouraging. Although I will admit, I didn't take you for a literal exhibitionist." She gestured toward the window, where a web of party lanterns and the submersible spotlights in the fountains lit the way for the dozens of guests still milling about on the sprawling grounds.

She pressed a hand to the window, and something flared in her eyes, something dark and exciting. He watched in fascination as she pushed it down, resurrecting her cool, mocking facade. "I thought you rich guys tended to show off your penises the old-fashioned way—fancy cars and sexual conquests."

Jesus.

He needed to get his hands on her, his mouth on her.

"Don't let my tech company fool you. I'm very old-fashioned, with a garage full of penis metaphors to prove it. As for sexual conquests," he said softly, letting the words hang there for a moment, "don't tell me this is where your courage deserts you."

She looked over as he joined her beside the window. "I'm not afraid of anything."

The declaration was said simply, as though she thought he hadn't expected her to take him up on his dare to explore this heat arcing between them. But that was only because she didn't realize how much credit he already gave her. And he didn't even know her real name yet.

"Not even me?"

"Why would I be afraid of you?"

He stepped closer, and she shivered, but true to her word, it wasn't because of fear.

Liam reached out and ran the pad of his thumb down her bare arm, from shoulder to wrist. Her pulse fluttered beneath her skin. "Because usually when people want each other this badly, someone ends up getting burned."

She leaned into him, so close that her lips brushed his jaw. Her hand drifted down his chest…lower. Lower still. "I like playing with fire." His knees almost buckled when she stroked the length of him through his pants.

With a quick squeeze, she unhanded him and began dispatching the buttons on his vest with quick efficiency. "Also, for the record," she informed him, before unknotting his tie, "I'm more of an arsonist than a nurse." She reached up and pushed his suit jacket off his shoulders. "So you're probably going to want to be careful."

Careful was the last thing he felt like being with her. He wanted whatever this was, pulsing between them, begging to be let loose.

He swallowed thickly as she slipped his jacket down his arms. "I'm going to need—"

"Your wallet?" she asked, holding it up as the expensive Italian wool blazer hit the ground.

Liam popped the button at his collar. "Impressive sleight of hand."

She pulled the condom he kept inside free and tossed his leather billfold onto his jacket.

"You're easy to please." She tracked his progress as he worked his way down the placket of his shirt, baring his chest to her gaze. "I haven't even gotten started with my hands yet."

She pushed him back against the window and set to work on his belt, the button on his pants. The metal hum of his zipper filled the room, filled his head. His breath came fast, and he swore as her hand closed around his erection, freeing him from his boxer-briefs. He wanted her so fucking badly he could barely stand it.

She licked her lips as she circled her thumb, spreading pre-come over his tip. Liam closed his eyes, letting the pleasure wash over him.

Fuck yes.

The sound of the condom wrapper ratcheted up his need.

He opened his eyes so he could watch, so his brain could sync the pleasure of her touch with the visual of her hand on his cock.

"Let's move this to the bed." His voice was strained as she slid her hand back up his length.

"Why would we do that?"

"Because I want to taste you. Pleasure you with my mouth until you beg me to bury myself inside you so you can come that way, too."

Her hand stopped its methodical stroking, and he used the slight reprieve to take a full breath.

"Look, I'm sure you're a generous and talented lover and the champagne and lingerie crowd goes gaga for your smooth promises and high-thread-count sheets, but in case it wasn't clear, I'm not here for declarations and foreplay. I don't want to make love. I want you to fuck me."

Jesus Christ. If his cock hadn't already been so hard it hurt, that would have gotten him the rest of the way. "Are you—"

"I'm sure." She grabbed the sides of his open shirt and leaned up to cut him off with her mouth, not kissing him, but catching his bottom lip between her teeth and giving it a sharp tug. When she let go, he soothed the slight sting with his tongue. "You talk too much, you know that?"

"Can't say I've ever had any complaints." Liam let himself touch her, resting his hands on the warm curve of her hips. His fingers flexed, as though seeking the warmth of her skin beneath the fabric in their way. If he didn't get her naked and wrapped around him soon, he might lose his mind. "But now you've forced me to defend my honor."

CHAPTER FIVE

AJ'S EYES WIDENED as he tightened his grip and spun
her to face the window.

Something hot and sharp ran through her veins at
the show of dominance.

"Put your hands on the glass."

Yes.

Her breath left her on a shudder, fogging the window for a split second before it cleared.

This was exactly what she wanted. No hearts and
flowers. Just fucking. Down and dirty. Simple. A mistake, maybe, but she was past caring. Her blood always
ran hot during a job.

She placed her palms flat against the cool, smooth
surface as instructed.

Liam stepped close, until the front of him was plastered against the back of her. He tugged her hips back,
as though she wasn't already aware of the hot, hard
length of him pressing against her ass.

"Is this what you wanted?" His voice was a low rasp
against her ear.

She wasn't sure how she'd given herself away, how he

knew this particular fantasy was one of her go-tos. All she knew was that her skin sparked with electric anticipation as she stared down at the unwitting partygoers.

"Does it turn you on to know that one of them could look up and see you pressed against the window, on display?"

The sound that escaped her throat was pure sex.

There was something about the risk of getting caught, of being seen, that made her body burn. It was the perfect combination—the pulse-pounding danger of hacking mixed up with the physical release of sex—a rush that AJ couldn't help but chase.

"Spread your legs."

She followed the orders, widening her stance slightly. Liam was tall, but with her heels, their bodies lined up almost perfectly. His breath caught, as though in agreement with her.

"Can you feel how badly I want you?"

AJ swallowed, unable to resist pressing her hips back against him as she nodded.

God. She was so wet, and he hadn't even touched her yet. She hated to admit it, but Liam just might have the skills to back up his reputation.

He flattened his hands against her hips, tracing the curve down her thighs until the tips of his fingers reached the hem of her dress. It was a relatively short trip, all things considered, and AJ shivered as he fisted his hands in the material and his knuckles brushed the bare skin of her legs.

"Do you want me to pull your dress up and fuck you for them?"

It was like the tech god could read her program-
ming, no training manual required. And so far, he was
doing everything right.

"Yes." She whimpered with pleasure as he dragged
the material up her thighs inch by inch, until it was
bunched around her waist.

He slid his big hand between her legs, tugging her
panties out of the way. AJ almost lost it at the first
stroke of his thumb on her clit, hips bucking as he ca-
ressed and teased but never granted her the relief she
needed more than her next breath.

"You're soaking wet for me."

His voice had her on the edge, and suddenly it
wasn't the party outside she was looking at, but the
reflection of their bodies in the glass. His hand between her legs, the bounce of her breasts as she pressed
back against him.

He did something magical with his fingers that sent
sparks shooting up her spine, and she gasped, her body
arching with pleasure as the world went dark. It took
her a moment to realize why and another to wrest her
eyelids open.

"I want you so fucking badly." Not just dirty talk
now, as their eyes met in the window. A confession.

A truth she felt even through the reflection, because
she wanted him, too.

Her head fell back against his shoulder. Liam
pounced on her exposed throat, and the searing heat
of his tongue on her skin amped up her pleasure.

He groaned as he slid his cock between her thighs,
and she rocked back, desperate for contact, spiraling

closer and closer toward climax, and he wasn't even inside her yet.

"Do it." It was an order. A plea.

"You're not the one in control here."

Judging by the harsh rasp of his breathing and the instinctive rocking of his hips, neither was he, so she let it slide.

And then, thank the sex gods, he was finally inside her, and she moaned as her body stretched to accommodate his impressive erection.

Good boy.

"Fuck." His curse said it all.

Everything in her world narrowed to this—the scent of man and sex and want, and God, did she want.

Then Liam started to move for real.

And it was spectacular.

Combustion was too tame a description for what was happening between them. He wasn't kidding about getting burned. Their bodies fit together like they were two pieces of a whole, built to fuck. And Liam was definitely doing his part.

He rolled his hips, setting up a rhythm that had her *this close* to purring, and her world narrowed to between her legs. Was sex always this good? Had it been so long that she'd just forgotten? Then he slowed his pace and pushed deep, and AJ knew she'd never have forgotten anything like this.

She braced herself against the window with her forearms, pushing back against him as he drove into her, powerless against the wet heat, the buildup of pleasure, the promise of the climax to end all climaxes.

Liam Kearney had mad skills.

She wanted this man, the scrape of his teeth on her neck, the shocking wet heat of his mouth on her skin. It was animalistic, the way she craved him, how much she needed what he was doing to her. His left palm slapped against the window for purchase, right above hers, and the tip of her middle finger touched the heel of his hand. In the heat of the moment, it struck AJ as oddly intimate.

"Christ," he growled. "Once isn't going to be enough, baby."

Under normal circumstances, she might have taken issue with the endearment, but she couldn't stand the idea of him calling her Robin right now, so she'd take baby all day and all night if it meant he'd keep making her feel this way.

"Your thighs are shaking. Do you want to come for me?"

Fuck yes.

And she was close, so damn close she could taste the imminent pleasure like candy on her tongue. As if he sensed it, Liam twined the fingers of his free hand in her hair, pulling tight enough to make her gasp. He pounced on her open mouth, the rough kiss timed perfectly with the plunge of his hips, and pleasure detonated through her, stealing her breath as he drove into her again and again before he shuddered against her, joining her in sweat-slicked paradise.

Holy shit.

AJ leaned her forehead against the cool glass, trying to catch her breath.

It had been way too long since she'd had her world rocked, that was for damn sure.

"Still think I talk too much?"

She bit her lip against the wayward smile trying to escape as she turned to face him, her shoulders resting against the window. He didn't need any encouragement. "Only during the non-sex parts of our acquaintance."

His answering grin stole her breath. Liam Kearney had one hell of a smile. It was a little disorienting when he weaponized it like that, and it threw her off. Otherwise she definitely would have moved before he braced his hands on the glass on either side of her head. At the very least, she would have turned her head when he leaned in and captured her lips in a slow, deep kiss that melted her, softening her knees to the point she had to grab on to his shoulders to keep from liquefying and sliding down the window.

When he finally pulled back, AJ's chest constricted as their eyes met. The intimacy of the moment quaked through her, far more intense than anything that had preceded it. This time when her heartbeat picked up, it had an edge of panic to it. Her hands slipped off his shoulders, but he didn't back up.

"Next time we do this, let's make sure I'm not hosting a party I have to get back to."

He was too close. People saw too much when they were this close.

"Yeah, you have shit for timing," AJ agreed, ignoring the reference to *next time*. Because there was no *next time* for them. Hell, with every second that ticked by, she was more and more convinced there shouldn't have been a *this time*.

"I'm going to shower." He dropped a kiss on her shoulder before he straightened up. "You're welcome to join me."

She shimmied her dress back down her thighs. "Yeah. I need a minute first. I don't think I can walk yet."

The compliment earned her a smug chuckle as he unhooked his cuff links with deft, economical movements that said he'd done the same thing countless times before. "If you promise not to take too long, I'll save you a spot," he teased.

That was the moment AJ realized just how very fucked she was.

Because she wanted to follow him.

In that moment, it didn't matter that she'd risked everything she had getting into this party. If she didn't get the hell out of the mansion that Cybercore built as soon as possible, this unsanctioned mission might end up harming Whitfield Industries more than it helped.

Liam Kearney was a kingpin of the tech industry. Her hacked invitation wouldn't go unnoticed forever. He was too smart for that.

The sound of the shower flipping on drew her attention.

AJ pushed down the resurgence of lust and the even more inconvenient pang of…longing?

Finish the job, she reminded herself.

AJ grabbed her satin purse and headed for the bedroom door, keeping her eyes stubbornly forward as she passed his en suite. She paused only twice as she fled from his house, once to grab her motion sensor from the baseboard in the hallway, and the second time to shoot a quick text to her getaway man—a cabbie who'd jumped at the grand she'd offered to drive her to this shindig and wait until she was ready to bail. AJ pushed through the imposing front door and she was relieved to see the yellow car pull into view as she hurried down to the end of the massive driveway.

AJ slowed as she approached the heavy security presence. She'd been hoping that would have thinned out a bit once the revelry got underway. Keeping her head down, she tried to blend in with the trickle of guests who were mulling about near the big gate, smoking.

If she could just sneak past the—

"Excuse me, ma'am?"

Shit.

AJ smiled blankly at the security guard, trying to look mildly intoxicated rather than guilty as hell.

He smiled back. "I just need to scan your invitation before you leave."

"Oh. Yes. Of course." AJ ignored the way her hand shook as she grabbed her phone and opened the app, hoping the rent-a-cop would chalk it up to too much champagne.

The QR code beeped under his handheld scanner and AJ's heart thudded in time with the heavy bass emanating from the palatial house behind her as she waited to hear her fate.

"Thank you, Ms. Capucha."

She sped up her pace as best she could in heels, dropping the drunk act. She needed to get the fuck out of there before—

"Wait!"

AJ froze, squeezing her eyes shut. *Stay cool.* With a deep breath, she opened her eyes and turned to face the security guard. He was holding out a fancy black bag with the Cybercore logo on it.

"Don't forget your swag bag. It's packed with a bunch of cool tech."

A swag bag? AJ frowned up at the fancy house. Was Liam Kearney fucking kidding? Pasting a wan smile on her lips, she turned her attention back to the security guard as she accepted her party favor. "Nope. Wouldn't want to forget that."

"You have a good night, ma'am."

AJ had never been more relieved than she was when she finally crawled into the back seat of the cab.

The driver looked over his shoulder at her. "That was faster than I expected. Did you have a nice time?"

Nice didn't even cover it. She couldn't remember the last time she'd had that much fun. Or that epic an orgasm. She couldn't bring herself to regret any of it... except maybe the fact that it was over. The realization sobered her.

AJ handed him the swag bag. "This is all yours if you don't talk to me anymore."

His eyes widened as he grabbed the bag and glanced inside. "Deal."

AJ did up her seat belt as the guy pulled away from the curb.

She exhaled.

Her phone buzzed in her hand, startling her, and she looked down just in time to see the screen go black.

AJ frowned.

Then the words *nice try* scrolled across the display, and AJ's fingers tightened on the phone.

What the?

She glanced back at Liam Kearney's McMansion, and when she returned her attention to the screen, it said "SEE YOU SOON" in sharp white text, and a digital clock had begun an eleven-hour countdown.

That fucking bastard.

She couldn't have stopped her smile for all the gift bags in the world.

CHAPTER SIX

TWENTY MINUTES.

Nineteen minutes and fifty-nine seconds.

Nineteen minutes and fifty-eight seconds.

She tried her best to ignore the damn timer, but it was under her skin, just like the man who'd installed it. Liam had rigged the stupid thing so that if she disabled it, it would disappear completely. She'd almost pulled the plug several times throughout her sleepless night, but in the end, her curiosity had won out.

AJ stepped inside the elevator and hit the button that would take her to the top floor of Whitfield Industries. She could count on one hand the number of times she'd been in Max's building. Staying away was part of their plausible deniability deal.

AJ liked to keep a low profile. She worked from home. They could video-chat if required. And they had a very specific drop system to exchange any goods that needed to be passed back and forth. Max had better have a damn good reason for summoning her on a Sunday morning.

Her eyes dropped back to the phone in her hand as the elevator began its ascent.

Nineteen minutes and forty-six seconds.

Also, Max had better talk fast. Because she had somewhere to be.

She just didn't know where it was yet.

AJ bounced the heel of her black Doc Martens against the kickplate, barely paying attention as her fellow passengers came and went during the various stops.

It was actually a pretty ingenious reverse hack. AJ was mildly impressed. She caught sight of her goofy grin in the mirrored wall of the elevator and made a point of erasing it with the dour expression she intended for Max.

The elevator dinged as it reached her destination. Fifteen minutes and seventeen seconds. AJ shoved her phone into the pocket of her leather jacket as the shiny metal doors slid open.

Max was waiting for her in the swanky tiled lobby, with Los Angeles spread out behind him courtesy of the floor-to-ceiling windows.

"Look, if this is about the Cybercore-infected phones Aidan and Kaylee gave you, I haven't gotten through everything yet. I had this thing last night." AJ kept it vague and made herself look directly at the imposing CEO of the eponymously named Whitfield Industries. Eye contact, she'd learned during her grifting days, made people believe you weren't bullshitting them.

And the last thing she needed right now was for Max to find out she'd crashed his arch nemesis's shindig, and worst of all, she'd lost all sense when she'd lost her panties. "So sorry I wasted your time, but next time you should listen to me when I—"

Some movement to her right caught her attention, and for the first time she noticed the two men in suits sitting in Max's glass-walled office. Her skin flushed hot, then cold.

"Oh, hell no." AJ turned on her heel and headed back toward the elevator.

"AJ."

She stopped, not bothering to hide her mutinous expression when she faced him.

"You know how I feel about that asshole." Her lip curled involuntarily as she pointed toward Wes Brennan's back, the pompous dick who'd caught her hacking the Whitfield Industries firewall. "And I thought we decided it would be best if Jesse didn't know I existed."

"We changed our minds," Max said, wryly.

"The less we're seen together, the fewer questions come up."

"A rule you don't seem to mind breaking whenever it suits you."

The reference to the last time they'd met up made her mouth pull up at the corner. "You're just testy because I lifted your wallet and your watch."

Max remained stoic.

"I gave them both back! And for the record, I only came by because I was trying to help you."

"And now you can help me again." Max swept a gallant hand toward his office door. "After you."

AJ glanced at her phone. Fourteen minutes and thirteen seconds. "Fine. But you'd better keep your security dogs on a leash."

AJ didn't wait for Max to open the door for her, just pulled it out of her way and walked inside, standing next to the only empty visitor chair rather than sitting beside her enemy.

The Chief Dickwad of Soteria Security glanced up at her, but he didn't betray emotion one way or the other at seeing her. "AJ."

Wes hadn't been thrilled when Max had brought her on board instead of turning her in. She could still hear the blistering tirade he'd unleashed while trying to convince Max to hand her over to the feds.

She's got skills, but she's impulsive. Lets her ego get in the way of her work. That's how I caught her. She's talented, yeah, but she's fucking sloppy, and sloppy gets you caught. If you're not careful, you're going to end up bailing her out instead of the other way around. You need a hacker, not a hack.

She squeezed her hand around the phone in her pocket, hating that she'd proved the asshole right last night with her little Robin Capucha stunt. Pure ego. It lent venom to her greeting. "Wesley. Other guy."

The VP of Soteria stood, extending a hand and a big smile. "Jesse Hastings."

His cheerfulness was off-putting, so AJ ignored his outstretched hand and gave him a cool nod instead. Then she pulled the visitor chair farther away from Wes and flopped into it before she had to endure the further humiliation of having Max order her to sit.

Jesse and Max also took their seats, and after a dramatic pause, Max placed a small round disc on his desk. It was silver and looked like a miniature version of something a gladiator might carry into battle.

"What is that?" The question was only for show. Because she knew.

Cybercore's tech was legendary. Anyone who considered themselves anyone in the underground tech world kept a careful eye on what Liam Kearney had up his sleeve at any given time. Combined with her affiliation with his biggest business rival, yeah, she knew a thing or two about The Shield, Cybercore's competing entry into the digital cryptocurrency payment ring. The one that was in direct competition with Whitfield Industries' SecurePay app, which Max had intended to launch a month ago. Until he'd discovered someone had hacked him.

"I have a source who provided me with a knockoff version of Cybercore's upcoming product."

Oh, shit. Liam was not going to be happy about that. He hadn't even launched yet.

"As it has just been disclosed to me that Cybercore is in talks with Soteria Security about using one of their products, I feel more comfortable having this piece of evidence examined by a more neutral party."

"Oh. *Ohhhhh*." AJ grinned and sat up straighter as Max's intentions became clear. This wasn't about her at all. He wanted his guard dogs to know they were on notice. "And suddenly the reason for my presence at this very special Sunday morning meeting makes total sense," she gloated. All hail Max's gift for power moves.

AJ winced theatrically. "Well, that's gotta sting, huh, Wes? Having your company's credibility called into question before watching your multimillion-dollar client hire a *sloppy, impulsive hack* to double-check your work?" She grinned, crossing her arms over her chest. Childish? Maybe. But it was fucking liberating, so she ignored Max's warning glance and reveled in the moment. The only thing that would have made it a little better was if Wes had shown any reaction to her taunt at all.

Freakin' robot.

The other half of Soteria Security wasn't looking nearly as calm and collected.

"I really don't think this is a precaution that needs to be taken, Max." Jesse sat forward in his chair. "Cybercore is interested in installing the direct-to-market virus protection we're releasing later this year. The division is completely separate from the private cybersecurity role we play here at Whitfield Industries. In fact, we only disclosed this information as a courtesy. And furthermore…"

Man, this Jesse sure could drone on.

It felt like forever had passed when her phone vibrated in her pocket. She pounced on it.

Thirty seconds.

Twenty-nine seconds.

It wasn't like she was excited to see Liam again or anything.

Twenty-three seconds.

Twenty-two seconds.

This was strictly professional curiosity. And appreciation for another tech guru's work.

Seventeen seconds.

Sixteen seconds.

Besides, she'd always loved a good mystery. Of course she wanted to know what the countdown was all about. Who wouldn't?

Eleven seconds.

Ten seconds.

It didn't mean *Liam* fascinated her. She just had a healthy appreciation for innovation.

Seven seconds.

Six seconds.

AJ's skin tingled as the clock ran out.

Three…two…one.

The black screen turned to a blur of giant pixels, and she didn't blink as she watched the image zoom out until they cleared into a Google map with a pin dropped at the Port of Los Angeles and the words "We leave at noon."

Crap. She had to get to San Pedro. Traffic better not suck. AJ swiped into her ride-share app and booked a car. Thankfully it was only five minutes away.

"Are we keeping you from something important, AJ?"

Max's voice startled her, and she looked up to find all three men staring at her. "Huh? Oh. Yes, actually." She stood up and shoved her phone back in her pocket. "It's been real, boys, but I gotta go. You can finish this little dick-measuring ceremony without me, right?" She reached across the desk to grab the fake Shield off Max's desk. "I'll check this out and be in touch, boss."

She ignored Max's frown and headed for the door, shoving the silver disc into the interior pocket of her leather jacket.

She'd never been on a boat before.

CHAPTER SEVEN

"SIR, YOU HAVE A...VISITOR."

Liam closed his newspaper and glanced over his shoulder at the unflappable chief steward, decked out in the yacht crew uniform of white polo shirt and navy pants. "Is she armed?"

"Sir?"

Liam adjusted his Ray-Bans against the California sun. "Just a joke, McGee. Show her up."

"I tried that already. She's refusing to come aboard."

Liam ignored the rush of relief that she'd taken the bait. Respected the shit out of the fact that even though she'd come, she wasn't going to make it easy on him.

Something heady sparked in his veins—lust, yes, but it was more than that. It was the intoxicating thrill of competition, the driving need to earn the respect of a worthy opponent. No one had ever breached his security before, let alone hacked his phone.

Setting the paper on the table, Liam stood and walked over to the starboard railing. "You came."

At the sound of his voice, she raised her face, and his sharp intake of breath surprised him. He hadn't prepared himself for the sight of her. Black boots, black jeans, black T-shirt, black jacket. So different from the woman who'd crashed his party, and yet exactly like the type of badass who would crash his party.

"Only once," she countered. "I kind of expected more fireworks, based on your rep, but you do get points for quality."

"It's nice to know some people still value crafts-manship."

Shielding her eyes with her hand, she stared up at him and pulled her phone from her pocket. "Quite a production. Most guys would have just asked for my number."

"I'm not most guys." Liam grabbed the railing. "And I thought you might enjoy the novelty of actually being invited."

"Ha. That burn might have held some weight if you'd programmed something that took me longer than twenty minutes to crack. I could have removed it before my ride dropped me off near my place."

Liam nodded, a smile playing about his lips. "I knew you wouldn't."

"Oh, you did, did you?" She tipped her head to the side.

His shrug was careless, in direct opposition to the tightness in his chest. But he took the risk anyway and said what he was thinking, even though he knew she wouldn't like it. "Maybe I know you better than you think."

Her shoulders stiffened and her eyes darted toward land, but she didn't run.

Liam's breath came a little easier.

"Well, I obviously don't know you at all. I would have put money on your evil lair being hidden deep in the bowels of your palatial mansion."

"I prefer a nicer view than mansion bowels when I'm plotting to take over the world."

She scuffed the toe of her boot against the dock. "So now that you've got me here, what are you going to do with me?"

The question was loaded, and answers whirred in his brain like a flip-book of dirty pictures. "I guess that depends."

"On what?"

"On whether you're going to come aboard."

"I haven't decided yet."

"Would it sway you one way or the other if I promise to let you play with my tech?" He lowered his voice conspiratorially. "I don't like to brag, but my hardware is considered legendary in some circles."

Her smile was crooked, pulling higher on the left side, and he wondered how he hadn't noticed that about her before. "Funnily enough, your hardware is one of the reasons I'm not sure my coming aboard is such a good idea."

"Tell me another one."

"How about I barely know you and the Pacific Ocean seems like an excellent method of body disposal?"

He waved it off. "Besides that."

Her laugh was throaty. Sexy.

Liam pointed at himself. "Have you ever tried to get blood out of white linen? Not worth the hassle."

"An argument that would hold more weight if I believed for even a second that you did your own laundry."

Her eyes narrowed, and she stared up at him, not flirtatiously, but contemplatively, and it kicked up his testosterone as he waited to see if she'd deem him worthy.

She jammed her hands in the pockets of her leather jacket, and he wondered briefly how she hadn't melted into a puddle on the dock in all those layers.

"This is a horrible idea."

Liam nodded. "Probably. But I've won a lot more than I've lost by risking it all." His meteoric rise from kid from Encino to reigning tech god was based on taking chances, doing what no one expected, the things other people didn't dare.

"Further proof that you and I are two very different people."

He heard resignation in the cryptic comment, and his stomach dropped at the foreshadowing. He wasn't surprised when she turned and headed back up the dock, but the fact that she was just going to walk away after everything that had brought them to this point... it pissed him off.

"I didn't take you for a coward!"

She didn't look back, just held her middle finger up and kept walking.

Fuck.

Liam banged his palms against the railing and stepped back, raking his hands through his hair. And still it took everything in him to turn away from her retreating form and not watch like a moron until she disappeared into the distance. He wasn't surprised to find the exacting chief steward standing there with a silver tray piled with food.

"Sir? Shall we be on our way?"

Liam gave a brusque nod, and McGee set the tray on the table before disappearing back down the stairs that led to the lower level.

Moments later, the efficient sounds of the crew preparing for departure drifted up from below.

Shouldn't have pushed so hard, he lectured himself.

But the program he'd installed on her phone should still be active... She couldn't have accessed it until the countdown clock played out. And most people would leave the map onscreen until they arrived at their destination.

Liam took a seat and poured himself a coffee while he strategized.

If he sent her another message before she eradicated all traces of his tech from her phone, maybe he could get her to meet him after the—

Several surprised shouts rang out, and Liam stiffened, prepared to go investigate the muffled bang that followed, but then McGee's affronted, "What do you think you're doing? You chose not to come aboard!" stopped him short.

Liam was already grinning before he heard the answer.

"I changed my mind. Sue me."

He relaxed back into his chair. He should have known she'd rather crash a party than accept an invitation. She did things on her own terms. A moment later, a familiar figure in black appeared at the top of the stairwell that led up from below deck.

"I don't think your yes-man likes me very much."

"I don't think he likes me very much, either, if that makes you feel better."

"Seriously? You're gonna try to one-up me right now? I just risked my life, and this sweet leather jacket, jumping over a foot and a half of open water."

"That's on you." He shrugged. "The invitation was clear that we were leaving at noon."

His party crasher walked over and sat down across from him, like she owned the yacht instead of him.

"Newspaper, huh? Really progressive take for a tech magnate."

Liam resettled his big frame against the chair. "The Sunday *Times*, for as long as it exists, is a nonnegotiable ritual. It's important to remember where you come from."

She helped herself to a piece of pineapple from the fruit plate.

"Before he owned the world, a young Liam cut his business teeth with a paper route that taught him the value of hard work?"

His jaw tightened against his will. "Something like that."

He made sure the words held no particular inflection, but her gaze sharpened in a way that brought the hairs on the back of his neck to attention.

He thought for a moment that she might follow up,

and he was relieved when she dropped the subject and snagged a croissant from the elegant pile of pastries.

She lifted an eyebrow. "Still warm."

Her eyes widened when she bit into the flaky, buttery dough to find it stuffed with chocolate.

She was perfect in that moment, and the throaty sound of pleasure that escaped went straight to his balls. *Once isn't going to be enough.* He'd known it last night. He knew it with bone-deep certainty now.

"What?" She swiped the pad of her thumb against her bottom lip. "Do I have chocolate on my face?"

Liam managed a brief shake of his head, though his focus didn't wane. He didn't understand why she affected him like this. She shouldn't.

She licked her lips, like she didn't believe him as she dropped the croissant on the plate in front of her. The move was tinged with the slightest hint of self-consciousness, and the crack in her badass facade intrigued him.

Her eyes searched his face, and Liam kept still, afraid to spook her. Afraid the woman who'd jumped onto his yacht was just as likely to jump right back off and swim to shore if he made the wrong move.

As though she sensed that he'd been admiring the glimmer of vulnerability in her and needed to change the subject, she reached over and grabbed the coffee he'd just poured, and took a large gulp.

"I've never been on a boat before." She looked around. "It's hotter than I expected. Boats always look really windy on TV."

"The guest room is fully stocked with stuff if you'd like to change—shorts, dresses, bathing suits."

"Gross." She scrunched up her nose. "I'm not wearing the discarded spandex of one of your castoffs."

Liam sent her a withering look. "They're all new. I like to have things on hand so that that unprepared yacht guests enjoy their time aboard."

"Yeah, my bad. This is my first time as a hostage." She set the mug down and ripped the end off the croissant. "I wasn't sure of the dress code."

Liam shot her an unimpressed look. "You're hardly a hostage. I tried to leave you behind and you jumped on the boat."

"You commandeered my phone and lured me here with the high-tech version of candy." She popped the flaky, buttery dough into her mouth, chewing slowly. Almost like she knew he was laser-focused on her mouth. She swallowed and gave a little shrug. "At the very least, you've kidnapped me."

"Again, I think you're confusing 'kidnap victim' with 'guest.'"

She picked up his coffee. "Ugh. Bor-ring. At least 'kidnap victim' has some pizzazz to it."

"I understand. Better small talk for the next party you crash. Consider yourself kidnapped."

She took another sip, watching him warily over the rim of the mug until she found the courage to ask the question he'd seen swirling in her eyes.

"How did you know?"

Liam leaned back in his chair. "How did I know what?"

"How did you know I wouldn't just kill your program?"

"Because you like a challenge. Like I do. Once you realized that regaining control of your phone would end our game."

"And what makes you think I like playing games?"

"You're here, aren't you?"

She licked her lips again, but this time, he got the distinct impression it wasn't in search of rogue chocolate.

"And you wouldn't have so elegantly breached my security if you weren't toying with me just a little. I mean, Robin Hood? Tell me that wasn't all about making a statement."

She smiled. "Pure hubris. Signing your work is the kind of sloppy that gets you caught. And I knew I shouldn't have, but your system was so amazing that when I beat it, I just…"

"You wanted me to know you won. You wanted me to know who you were."

There was a shift in the air, the way her throat worked as she swallowed made him remember last night, the way she'd tasted when he'd dragged his tongue up her neck. How good she felt pressed up against him, writhing under his touch.

"So who are you?"

Seconds ticked by in which Liam wasn't sure she'd answer. And then, "AJ. My name is AJ."

"Just AJ?" he asked.

"Well, that proves you haven't been paying attention, Tiger." She got up and circled the table, stopping behind him. Liam's body tightened at her proximity, even before she placed a hand on his shoulder and leaned down, her lips a hairbreadth from his ear. "Because there's nothing 'just' about me." Her soft words raced through his blood as she tugged off his Ray-Bans.

Then she straightened up. "And you can drop the host-with-the-most act. Let's not kid ourselves about what's happening here." AJ donned his sunglasses and walked over to the rail, leaving him no choice but to follow.

The breeze tossed her curls around as she stared out at the sparkling water. She looked out of place in her structured black clothes, like armor, cautioning people not to mess with her.

Despite the warning, he stepped closer, bracing his forearms against the railing. "What *is* happening here?"

She looked over, and he wished she didn't have his sunglasses on so he could see what was going on in those big brown eyes of hers. She didn't know it, but they gave her away, not so much with expressions, but with the suppression of them.

"The same thing that's always happening when two people who have absolutely nothing in common can't stay away from each other, despite their better judgment." A resigned smile tipped the corners of her enticing mouth. "Good old-fashioned lust."

CHAPTER EIGHT

AJ TURNED TO face her smoking-hot adversary head-on. "Why else would you have invited me here?"

Liam rubbed a hand against his rough jaw, and she ignored the answering tingle in her fingertips, the sudden longing to run them across his stubble. Last night, he'd been freshly shaven. Her pulse picked up as she wondered at the tactile differences she might notice if she kissed him now, all disreputable and scruffy.

"I wanted to see you again."

Her pulse thrummed its wholehearted approval of his plan. It was a little embarrassing.

"That's a good answer. It rings true, and yet there's a sweetness to it that keeps you from coming off like a sex fiend. Did they teach you that at the International Playboy Academy? Flirting 101?"

The flash of his smile screwed with her equilibrium a little, blinding her despite her pilfered shades. She had a thing for straight white teeth.

"I wouldn't know. Skipped straight to the advanced course. I'd be happy to give you another demonstration if you'd like."

The wave of attraction was not unexpected, but that didn't make it less potent. AJ squeezed her thighs together. Common sense lost the battle to her baser instincts at the resulting flare of heat, and she pushed him back against the railing.

"Cocky," she mused, reaching out to undo the buttons on his shirt so she could slide it down his arms. She didn't pull it all the way off, though. Instead, with a couple of strategic twists of the material, AJ used the shirt to catch his wrists behind his back and affix him to the handrail. "Maybe it's time I took the reins for a bit. Remind you exactly who's in charge here."

Liam gave a cursory tug, testing his linen bonds. "I would challenge you on that, but this is a new shirt."

She smiled, but not at the joke. Liam's abs jumped as she scraped her nails down his bare chest. Lower. Lower still.

"I know you think you've got me right where you want me."

His eyes grew dark, and something wicked sparked in their depths. "Not *right* where I want you, but you're getting warmer."

"You think I'm here because of your little countdown clock."

"That reverse hack was masterful and you know it," he challenged.

With agonizing slowness, AJ unbuckled his belt, unbuttoned his button, unzipped his zipper. "I'm here because I choose to be here. And don't ever forget it."

He swore as she lowered herself to her knees, and a trill of feminine satisfaction unfurled in her belly.

She'd forgotten the power of this position.

It had been a long time since she'd bothered with a blow job.

Years since she'd cared enough to want to.

No, not cared, she reminded herself as she dragged the elastic of his boxer-briefs out of her way. This was about taking what she wanted, and inconvenient or not, she wanted Liam.

Her breath caught as she freed his erection, and she took a second to appreciate the hot, hard length of him. Male. Primal.

Liam's muscles jerked as she closed her hand around him, air sawing from his lungs as she leaned forward, licking up the length of him before taking him in her mouth. She gave herself a moment there, to familiarize the texture and taste of him, to explore his crown with her tongue, and then she started to move. Took him deep, until her mouth reached the hand she'd fisted around the base of his cock, before pulling back, only to repeat the movement as she settled into a rhythm that worked for her. She placed her free hand on his thigh, for balance, and his muscles bunched beneath her fingers.

"Jesus, AJ."

Her heart jarred against her ribs. Hearing him say her name was so much better than having him call her baby. She looked up at him, reveling in the intensity she saw in his face, the tight set of his jaw as he watched her pleasure him.

"Take off the glasses. I want to see you."

Heat rushed between her legs at the request, at the

harsh need in his voice. Liam had this disconcerting way of taking over situations. Even now, semi-bound in his shirt and at her mercy, he was still…well, if not outright in control, at least equal.

She did as he asked, sliding his sunglasses to the top of her head, applying a little more suction as she reached the tip of him, and his knees buckled as they stared into each other's eyes.

The connection was intense, too much, and AJ dropped her gaze as she dug her fingers back into his rock-hard thigh. She bobbed her head again, taking him a little deeper, testing her comfort level.

He groaned, giving her the confidence to take him deeper still.

"Your mouth is fucking amazing. I'm this close to losing control."

Power throbbed along her skin at the compliment, and she lifted her head, never breaking the rhythmic stroke of her hand. His muscles contracted, bracing against the pleasure she was giving him.

"Maybe I want you to lose control."

"Not without you. You need to stand up." His voice was harsh, edged in desperation, but she'd already given in to one of his demands. She wasn't giving up her tactical advantage again.

AJ smiled up at him. "I don't know if you're really in the position to be giving orders right now." She swiped her thumb across the tip of his erection, and he shuddered under her ministrations.

"I told you once wasn't going to be enough, and I meant it. Get up."

The command sent a shiver of delight through her.
This power struggle they had going on was thrilling.
There was something incredibly potent about over-
seeing his pleasure, holding him captive to the suction of her mouth and the stroke of her fingers. Part
of her wanted to finish him off right now just to prove
she could.

But the rest of her couldn't resist the siren song that
was the throb between her legs, the pleasure she knew
he could give her. With a naughty grin, she leaned in
one final time, dragging her tongue up the length of
his cock before she pulled back, unhanded him with
a final squeeze, never once breaking eye contact. He
might be the one giving orders, and she might be the
one on her knees, but they both knew who wielded the
control in that moment. Her lips curved in a smile that
was heady with power.

Fucking hell.

If he'd thought she'd been spectacular last night,
well, this afternoon was better by far. And he wasn't
even talking about the blow job.

Because last night, she'd been hiding. Dressed to
kill, sure, and so damn sexy it hurt, but there were
only glimpses of the ball-breaker who'd stormed his
yacht.

Liam liked this version of her even more than the
one he'd met last night. And not only because she'd
just taken him halfway to paradise and he was eager
to finish the journey. He liked that she seemed more
real somehow, dressed in black layers and daring him

to back down. More authentic than when she'd been trying to blend in with the dull people at his dull party. He liked knowing her name.

He watched as AJ got to her feet, pulled the sunglasses from her hair and slipped them back on. She was brash, confident, and her warrior stance let him know she thought she'd just beaten him at whatever game it was they were playing.

Lust flooded his veins.

He'd always been competitive; it was one of the reasons he loved business so much. But with success came money, and with money came a bunch of people kissing your ass all the time. It was the part of being rich he hadn't expected…the way people started giving you things once you had the money to buy them. The way you were suddenly granted time and attention as your material wealth grew.

But not AJ.

This woman challenged him, outwitted him, and when he got the jump on her, she'd wrest the power back and the whole dance would start over.

It was exciting. He felt alive in a way that he hadn't for months. Maybe ever.

Of course, that didn't mean he was going to roll over and let her have the upper hand without a fight, either. He stepped away from the rail and shrugged back into his wrinkled shirt, lacing his grin with an extra dollop of the cockiness she'd accused him of earlier.

There was something incredibly satisfying about watching the realization that he'd freed himself from her clever trap dawn on her face. About letting her know this thing between them was nowhere near finished.

Liam reached out and hooked a finger in the waistband of her jeans, tugged her close, kissing her slow and deep, until she melted against him, softening under his hands. It took everything in him to pull back from her mouth.

"You," he told her, pulling his Ray-Bans off and hooking them on the neck of her T-shirt so he could see her eyes, "are the only person who's ever come aboard this yacht and put on more layers."

She looked mutinous at the comment, dropping her gaze to the deck, her shoulders stiff and petulant. "Sorry to disappoint you, but I'm never going to be one of your buxom bikini babes."

"What makes you think I'm disappointed?"

Her head snapped up at the question, and a strangely charged moment descended over them. She stared at him, and something shifted in her eyes— and for a split second, he could see the woman behind the badass. Something vulnerable and real softened her eyes, and Liam's heart lurched in response to the show of trust.

"AJ—"

She attacked his mouth with a ravenous kiss, wrapping her arms around his neck, and Liam grabbed the backs of her thighs, lifting her up so she could wrap her legs around his waist. He walked blindly forward, taking the stairs that led up to the main cabin as quickly as possible as she all but tongue-fucked his mouth.

The woman short-circuited his synapses.

He set her down as soon as they breached the threshold of the room, and it was a race to get naked, yanking off clothes and dropping them where they fell.

There was a quick pause while he donned a condom, and then she was on him again, and they were fumbling their way to the bed, crawling onto the California king mattress.

He followed her down, groaning as his cock nestled against the wet heat between her legs, and she writhed under him, pushing him closer and closer toward climax.

Fuck. He was so turned on. And she felt so damn good.

He knew he was skimping on the foreplay, so he made a half-hearted attempt to lower his head to her breast, to get one of his hands out from beneath her so he could put it to better use, but the second he did, her dark eyes snapped to his.

"What are you doing?"

"Foreplay."

"Fuck the foreplay," she countered. "We're way past that."

He didn't need more encouragement than that. He was so fucking primed from her mouth on his cock, desperate for her. With a growl, he drove into her with just enough restraint to keep from shoving her into the headboard. *Jesus.* He was on fire for her, and she was right there with him, her nails biting into his back, her moans driving him higher as he thrust again and again.

Every nerve in his body begged for release, but even half-mad with pleasure, he wasn't going over without

her. He tried to hold on to the edge of sanity as she
wrapped her legs around his waist, sank her teeth into
his shoulder.

And then finally, mercifully, she cried out, her body
shuddering beneath him, and Liam let himself go, his
hips jerking as he came.

CHAPTER NINE

AJ STEPPED ONTO the deck of the yacht, the gleaming wood warm on her bare feet.

After their shower, he'd lent her a fluffy robe and given her directions to the magical guest room so she could find something more seaworthy to wear. True to his word, it was filled with brand-new clothes, towels, toiletries, anything his jet-setting guests might need. Her hand had stopped on a black bikini as she'd riffled through the drawers of bathing suits. She'd considered it for longer than she cared to admit before she'd pulled her own clothes back on. Her only concession to yachting was that she'd left her socks and her beloved Doc Martens back in the room.

AJ knew better than most that even the simplest offers tended to come with strings, and until she understood Liam better, she wasn't willing to get bound up in any of his.

And speaking of Liam…

His short hair was still wet from the shower and slicked back from his face. Somehow, he was pulling off olive cargo shorts and a white button-down shirt

with the sleeves rolled up his forearms. It looked expensive. Probably some fancy designer. Ralph Lauren,
maybe. Rich guys on boats wore Ralph Lauren, didn't
they? For some reason, he didn't look like a preppy
douchebag. He just looked hot, and completely at home
with his aviator sunglasses reflecting the cloudless California sky. She couldn't help but admire his deft, economical movements as he poured himself a drink from
the bar cart that had been rolled onto the deck.

I could get used to this.

The thought sucker punched her.

Shit. She should never have come here.

She'd known it, had even listened to her good sense
and started walking away from the sex god and his stupid yacht, and then at the last minute, she'd fucked it
up anyway. Jumped onto the boat. Oh, she knew why
she'd done it. Because this game of cat and mouse they
were playing made her feel alive. Really alive. In a way
she hadn't in years.

He fogged up her brain, revved up her body.

Liam fascinated her. And she didn't like it.

She slipped on the Ray-Bans she'd stolen from him
before things had gotten all naked and sexy and took
a step away from the stairs that had brought her up to
the deck.

Liam glanced over so immediately that it made her
wonder if he'd been aware of her lurking the entire
time.

"You're still here."

"We're on a boat. Where else would I be?"

He gave an easy shrug of broad shoulders. "You

took so long, I thought you might've grabbed some tech and made a swim for it."

It was really annoying that he was so charming all the time. Even when he was taking a jab at her for last night.

"Lucky for you, my outfit's not exactly saltwater compatible, and like I said, this is my favorite jacket."

"It must be, considering it's eighty degrees out and you're still wearing it. Did you want a drink?"

"Sure."

He set a short round glass in the middle of the cart. "One bourbon, coming up."

"Make it a gin and tonic."

Liam's laid-back grin was a punch in the estrogen. She didn't like how easily he turned her on, and it lent some snark to her voice. "What?"

"Couldn't have given me that one, huh?" He tucked the glass away on the lower shelf and chose another one.

She strolled toward him as he used fancy metal tongs to fill the fancy tall glass with cubes from a fancy silver ice bucket. "I don't follow."

Liam sent her a sideways glance as he free-poured some gin from a decanter. "Remembering someone's drink is a time-tested way to build rapport."

"Oh?"

He nodded. "Makes them feel seen. Remembered. Special." There was a soft hiss as he twisted the cap off a bottle of tonic water and topped up the glass. "Business is never just business. It's always personal. That's why I could have poured the perfect drink for every single person at the party last night."

"Minus one," she reminded him.

Liam hooked a wedge of lime on the rim and handed her the completed drink. "Minus one," he confirmed. "It makes you difficult to impress."

"How exasperating for you."

"You have no idea." The slight consternation in his voice tugged at the corner of her lips.

"You know what the worst part is?" AJ asked, conspiratorially. "I really love champagne."

His chuckle was warm and low. "To defying expectations," he toasted, and she raised her glass so he could clink his bourbon against it.

AJ closed her eyes as she let the crisp, cold carbonation wash over her tongue. The man knew how to pour a G&T.

"Shall we?"

He followed her as she made her way toward the front of the deck, where a couple of cushy striped lounge chairs were set up, along with a fruit tray and a cooler full of bottled water.

"You've certainly taken care of every detail."

"Business often goes more smoothly when alcohol and food are in the mix."

"Are we doing business?" She took a seat on the lounger. "And here I thought this was a pleasure cruise."

"Considering the way you bypassed my security, I figure it's in my best interest to multitask while you're here. My team worked for two hours to try and get the library camera back up and running."

AJ tried not to let the impressed tone of his deep voice affect her. She didn't need validation. She didn't need anybody. She'd been fooled by the warm feeling in her chest before.

Liam stretched out on the lounger to her right, but his pose was deceptively casual, as evidenced by his first question. "Why did you do it?"

Intrigued, AJ set her drink on the table between them. "I would think, if I had in fact done something, that your first question would be *how* did I do it?"

"*How* doesn't really concern me. *How* is something I can figure out myself. But *how* doesn't explain why you showed up at my party."

"Why Robin Capucha showed up at your party, you mean."

"Potato, po-tah-to."

"Says you. But if you can't prove it, it didn't happen."

Liam pulled his phone out of his pocket and after a couple of swipes, pointed the screen in her direction.

AJ maintained her best poker face as she watched herself, garbed in a black dress, arrive at the party… apply lipstick before slipping into his office…head up the stairs to the "bathroom" so she could "freshen up."

She shot him her best unimpressed look that she hoped he caught, despite her stolen Ray-Bans. "What, no footage of the main event? I would have thought your bedroom would be wired to the hilt."

He lowered the screen. "Some things aren't for my security team's consumption. Footage like that has a tendency to leak for the right price, no matter how well-vetted the team."

The confirmation that she hadn't missed any cameras during her recon was a nice ego boost. That meant he still had no idea she'd infiltrated his bedroom *before* he'd invited her inside and they'd gotten all…carnal.

"Although I could be talked into a home movie if that's your kink."

She ignored the surge of lust in her gut. She would never *ever* film herself in a compromising position— as Liam had alluded, things could, and did, go way too wrong, way too often—but as far as fantasies went…

AJ bit her lip at the sexy mental image of watching herself on-screen while Liam—

"I'd show you some footage of the library around the same time, but it seems to have vanished."

Startled by the intrusion of his deep voice, AJ readjusted herself on the chair and pulled her thoughts out of the gutter. "Well, that's embarrassing, to just lose two hours of tape like that before the camera inexplicably starts working again, as though nothing ever happened."

Liam set the phone on the side table, next to his drink. "Quite a mystery."

AJ kept her outward appearance of smugness intact—years of practice had made her an expert—but inside, something warm and exciting rushed through her blood. It was the same feeling she used to get before a big hack. The exhilaration that came from testing her mettle against the best in the business. The challenge. The thrill.

"You know I can make all that mansion security cam footage disappear, right?"

He shrugged without looking over, a casual challenge. "You can try."

AJ pulled off her jacket, draping it over the armrest of her chair before she leaned back and made herself comfortable.

Yeah. She could definitely get used to this.

"Seriously?" Liam shook his head. "I can't believe I just ate dinner with an insane person."

"I'm just saying that there are inconsistencies."

"The moon landing happened."

"I didn't say it didn't happen," AJ corrected. "I said some of the photos are suspect—the multiple light sources, the boot print discrepancy, the billowing flag. And how do you explain that they taped over the original recordings of the moon landing? That is sketchy as hell."

"You're being ridiculous right now. Please tell me you know you sound like a kook."

"Whatever, dude. You want to pretend the government is all puppies and rainbows so they'll give you that military fence contract, that's on you."

"Shhh." Liam leaned forward and caught her mouth in a soft kiss. "They might be listening," he whispered, before he sprawled out on the double-wide lounger beside hers.

AJ found herself smiling, and it wasn't even against her will.

Fun.

She'd had fun today.

Premium liquor and a hand-rolled sushi dinner

aboard a multimillion-dollar yacht. Lights sparkling on the water softly lapping against the boat as night fell, turning the sky a deep indigo. Laughing and flirting with a brilliant, handsome man.

It didn't take long for her inner pragmatist to ring the alarm bell.

Whatever this was that was happening between them, it wasn't real life. It couldn't last. Perfection never did.

She didn't trust Liam. She couldn't. Her life was littered with proof that her instincts when it came to men were faulty.

"What just happened?"

"What are you talking about?"

"We just had a nice moment. Almost like you lost track of who was the cat and who was the mouse. And now I can feel you retreating. So what just happened?"

"Look, I know most women would be impressed by all this romantic shit—" she gestured around her with a careless wave "—but I know better than to believe in shiny stuff. It always turns out too good to be true. And I didn't lose track. I'm the cat. I survive by landing on my feet. I'm always the cat."

Her last foster father had told her multiple times that she had the finesse of a bulldozer, that she had a talent for leaving destruction in her wake. It hadn't been a compliment, but since he'd only ever said it when he was in full asshole mode, she'd kind of turned it into one in her brain. Her ability to cut through the bullshit was what kept her safe, kept her from trusting the wrong person again.

"I mean, I had a nice time, but let's not pretend this is more than what it is."

To her surprise, Liam didn't look offended, merely curious, and so she answered his unspoken question.

"We're scratching an itch. I'm playing your willing captive. You've squirreled me away like treasure on a pirate ship so you can be sure you're in control of the situation. Because guys like you get off on that sort of thing."

"Guys like me?"

"Walking clichés. Men who ooze charm and wear deck shoes unironically in their quest to appear rich and powerful."

"Says the badass loner with an attitude and a black leather jacket." Liam cocked an eyebrow at her. "Way to buck the stereotype. And for the record, I *am* rich and powerful. And present company aside, I've been told I'm very charming."

He was. Annoyingly so. "Yeah, well. That's what they say about con men and serial killers, too. So kudos on the esteemed company you keep."

"You have an unhealthy obsession with death, dismemberment and body disposal. Anyone ever told you that?"

"Awww. Does the big bad tech mogul not like knowing there's a dark side to life? Sorry I shattered your sparkly illusions."

"You obviously have me confused with someone who grew up in the lap of luxury. I didn't have it quite so good."

AJ couldn't hold back an eye roll. "Oh, Jesus. Is

this… Are you giving me your tragic origin story? Am I going to need a tissue for this?"

Liam's frown was almost quizzical, like he was trying to decide whether he should be offended or not. "Are you mocking me right now?"

"A little, yeah. I mean, trust me here. You do not want to go mano a mano with me on the subject of childhood trauma, guy who owns a yacht."

"Just because I own a yacht, I don't get to have a shitty childhood?"

AJ sighed, and some of the fight went out of her shoulders. "I mean, I guess you can. Just no one wants to hear about it."

Liam's bark of laughter startled her. It wasn't the reaction she'd expected.

"Well, I'll let you in on a little secret. I'll bet about ninety-five percent of yacht owners had a shitty childhood. We're all just trying to prove our worth."

"Okay, I'm in."

He shot her a questioning look.

"Show me what you've got. Let's hear your tale of woe."

CHAPTER TEN

"DEAD FATHER."

His first volley hit her in the heart. Maybe because Liam Kearney was usually so good at playing the wealthy, sociable man about town, happy to field sly innuendo about his dating life and downright charming when it came time to rhapsodize about Cybercore's futuristic tech. His only rule with the press was no questions about his family. Early on, a few reporters had made the mistake of pushing. They never got the opportunity to interview him again.

She covered up the sting with a bland shrug. "Well, who doesn't have one of those? I see your dead father and raise you a dead mother."

"You're an orphan?" Something crossed Liam's face; not pity, exactly. She knew, because pity always made her hands ball into fists. It was subtler than that. Some weird hybrid of understanding and not caring that deflated her usual need to puff out her chest and prove herself, because for the first time in her life, the O-word didn't feel like a weapon. Didn't make her prepare for battle, for that moment when she had to make up for the inherent weakness of that lifelong hurt by proving she was tough without it.

"Car accident." It was the first time she'd ever said the words aloud. Cops had said it to her—"We're sorry to inform you…"—social workers and foster parents had said it about her—"Poor thing lost both of them…"—but she'd never mentioned it before.

And then Liam said the most perfect thing anyone had ever said to her upon finding out her parents were dead. "Man, you're definitely pulling out the big guns."

The deftness of the black humor caught her off guard. He'd somehow understood exactly what she needed. And it was disconcerting as hell.

AJ narrowed her eyes, observing her opponent with new respect. Maybe Liam's playboy persona didn't reach all the way to the core. Maybe he knew something about layers, too.

She lifted her chin. "Damn straight. That's like, automatic twenty-five-point tragedy bonus, and I'm off to the early lead. I told you you didn't want a piece of this."

He took a sip of his drink. AJ glanced out at the darkness around them, took a deep breath of warm, salty air, let the steady rush of water against the hull calm her. She wanted to know more.

"How old were you?"

The question brought Liam's gaze back from the lights dotting the California shoreline. "Four."

She nodded, answering the implied question. "Eight."

Liam finished his bourbon. "So clearly I made up

some points there, because I was so young that I didn't even get the chance to know a father's love."

AJ bit her lip to keep from smiling at the challenge. "No way. It's sad, and I will grant you some general sense of loss points, but I have real memories of my parents, which makes the heartache visceral, because I'm fully aware of what got ripped away from me."

"Okay, I underestimated your commitment here." Liam rolled his shoulders and tipped his head side to side, like a boxer loosening up before a match. "I'm not going to hold back anymore."

The trash talk relaxed something in her chest, and she leaned back in her chair. "Bring it, Kearney. I can do this all night."

"When I was seven, my mom dropped me off at my grandfather's and never came back. Turns out, she'd sunk her fake nails into some sugar daddy who already had grown kids and wasn't looking to commit to a prepackaged family. So she removed 'mom' from her bio and continued her quest for the ring. Just left me there and never came back." His features turned hard and stark in the moonlight. "I waved goodbye to her. I stood there at the door and fucking waved."

AJ winced. "That's cold."

"So add some points to my side of the board, because at least neither of your parents abandoned you on purpose."

AJ started at the comment. She'd never really thought about it like that. "She just…disappeared? You never saw her again?"

"When I turned sixteen, I tracked her down. By

that time, she'd landed her millionaire and was living a life of Botox and caviar. She fucking lost it when I showed up at her door." He chuckled, but it held no humor. "Bypassed their shit security system and rang the mansion doorbell."

"What happened?"

"She told me she'd never forgive me if I ruined the good thing she had going for her. And then she offered to pay me a ridiculous sum of money to fuck off forever." His smile didn't reach his eyes, and he picked up his glass, pausing with it halfway to his mouth as if noticing for the first time it was empty. He set it back on the table with a bang that felt final. "I hadn't gone there to blackmail her. I just…"

Wanted to see her. He didn't say the words, but he didn't have to.

"But I took it. That money paid for college, with enough left over to help me get Cybercore up and running. So I figure I got the better end of the deal."

Liam glanced over at her. "How about you? What happened after your parents died?"

"Seven years in the foster system. Eight different foster families."

"Ouch."

"That's putting it mildly. And without swear words."

"That bad?"

"Some were okay. Some were worse. I was so mad all the time that I didn't care much about the difference. Kept to myself, getting up to no good online, honing my skills. It didn't take long before I realized computers were where my true talents lay. Came in handy when I left."

"You aged out?" he asked.

She shook her head. "My last home, Glen and Nancy, that was hell on earth."

Liam's jaw tightened as he toyed with his glass again. "What happened?"

"You know. The usual."

AJ got up and wandered over to the railing. She needed to move. The water looked black against the twilight.

"Glen used to beat the shit out of his wife on a regular basis. I used to hide in the closet, waiting for it to be over, wondering why she didn't just leave his ass. I was fifteen the first time he was drunk enough to take a swing at me."

"Jesus Christ."

AJ gnawed on her lip, a familiar prickle of guilt burning its way up her spine. "He didn't make contact. Nancy…" She took a deep breath. "Nancy put herself between us. Took the blow meant for me. She told me to run, and I did." AJ shrugged. "I grabbed the laptop and Glen's cell phone and wallet. He used to leave them on his dresser when he got home from work. Then I called 911 and booked it all the way to the bus station. Used the free Wi-Fi at the coffee shop and changed his passwords, withdrew the daily limit from his account at an ATM, and hopped the first bus out of town."

She heard Liam approach, and her hands tightened on the railing, but he didn't touch her.

"To LA?"

The question embarrassed her, and she rolled her eyes at her own naivete.

"My parents took me to Disneyland when I was seven. It was our last family vacation before…" She couldn't make herself say it again. "California was a no-brainer. I just wanted to go somewhere happy, you know?" Her laugh was self-mocking. "Stupid."

"No. Not stupid at all." He set his hands on the railing, and the side of his palm made the lightest contact with her pinkie. It reminded her of the night before, the intimacy when their hands had touched on the window. AJ didn't pull away.

"It was. I learned quick, though. Did what I had to do to survive—some street scams, some dumpster diving. Met a guy. Troy. He took me under his wing in return for my knack with security systems, made me part of his posse. Those gigs paid well, and we started hanging out more. Then all the time. And before I knew it, he'd moved into my place, four years had passed, and I understood. I understood why Nancy hadn't left."

Shit. The back of her throat started to burn, and the inner corners of her eyes prickled. A precursor to the tears she'd so cavalierly mocked.

"I told the lawyers everything. Took him to court. Being on the witness stand was like getting jabbed in the heart over and over with an ice pick, but I answered all their questions." Her voice quavered. "I wasn't going to be like Nancy."

Liam pulled her close and then the tears were just spilling out of her, like the whole sordid story that she'd never meant to tell. She couldn't stop the words. Old anger bubbled to the surface, but it was all tangled up with this weird sense of safety, as though Liam's hold was a force field where she was safe and the old emotions couldn't hurt her like they usually did.

"He got a year in jail. Out in six months because of good behavior. Made my life hell, threatening me and breaking into the apartment while I was out. I had to change my whole life because of him. I moved. I stopped going out. I changed. Hid. And I hate him for that most of all."

Liam's arms tightened around her, not so much protectively, but like he was pissed off, braced for a fight, and the show of solidarity made her feel better. Not pathetic or as though she needed taking care of, but supported, like he was ready to battle beside her. It helped her catch her breath.

"Please tell me you made him pay."

AJ's final sob ended on a slight laugh, and she pulled back enough to wipe her eyes with the back of her hand, without breaking the circle of Liam's embrace. "Credit score decimated, bank account emptied, and some incriminating surveillance footage might have ended up in the hands of the police."

Liam's hand stroked comfortingly along the base of her spine. "You let him off easier than I would have. Where is he now?"

She sniffed, confirmation that her tears were finished. The hollow ache in her chest, the one she feared would fill up with emotions—the twisted, red-hot ones that made it hard to sleep sometimes—wasn't banished so easily. "He died two years ago in a botched robbery. And I'm still…" She trailed off. AJ couldn't make herself admit how fucked up she still was. She'd already said enough. More than enough.

"Hey." She looked up at him, and he cradled her face in his hands. "She'd be proud of you, you know that, right?"

"Who?"

"That girl who hid in the closet. She'd be so impressed to see what a kick-ass warrior she was destined to become."

She could taste the salt of her tears on his lips when he pressed his mouth to hers in a sweet, chaste kiss before he looked down at her again, but this time, something had shifted in his eyes. He was looking at her like he saw her, the real her, and it chilled her to the bone.

The urge to run seized her, tightened her muscles. Desperate to get out of the moment, AJ entertained the notion of jumping into the dark water below, but she settled for her usual verbal parry. "I heard fancy college boys knew how to talk good. Guess the rumor is true."

"I was wondering how you'd trivialize the moment." He thumbed the tracks of moisture from her cheeks. "I should have guessed it would be by taking a swipe at me."

"Well, you're an easy target."

He chuckled as he tugged on one of her curls. The soft touch made her anxious. She didn't confide in people. She didn't want whatever this was. She turned her whole body toward the railing, breaking contact. The lap of waves was soothing as she stared at the lights of the mainland.

"I'm allergic to earnestness. It gives me hives."

"That is such total bullshit, but it might be the most honest thing I've heard you say."

He wasn't wrong. She'd spent her whole life keeping her head down and her mouth closed. That was how she survived. And now, after a blow job, an orgasm and a ride on a fancy boat, she was spilling her guts like she was in a slasher flick. She'd admitted more to Liam Kearney after two days than she had to anyone else in the world. The worst person she could possibly give ammunition to. Hell, she'd loaded the gun for him.

"Well, if I've resorted to honesty, there's only one thing for it."

She ran her hands up his chest, pulled him close. His skin was warm against hers, and she ignored all the shitty feelings in the pit of her stomach and focused on that connection. The one that prickled her skin and warmed her blood.

"And what's that?" he asked.

AJ pressed her hips against his. Liam was right earlier. She was a fucking cliché, a badass in black, distracting a man with sex, but she didn't care. Because she needed the distraction right now.

She needed Liam.

"Time to stop talking."

CHAPTER ELEVEN

L<small>IAM LET HER</small> kiss him, and AJ took full advantage.

She licked into his mouth, nipped his bottom lip, soothed it with her tongue.

She kissed him to distract herself from her bad memories and to remind herself she was a survivor.

She kissed him like she meant it, and Liam stayed right there with her, giving as good as he got. By the time he pushed her back against the railing and anchored a hand on either side of her hips, she wasn't sure if it was the ocean or her pulse rushing in her ears.

She moaned at the loss when he pulled back so they could both catch their breath. "Don't stop."

He laughed, deep and soft. "Not stopping," he assured her as she ran the backs of her fingers along his stomach. She could feel the ridges of his abs through the soft cotton. "Just realigning operations. Because as fucking incredible as your mouth is—" Liam pressed his lips to hers, but before she could gain purchase, he pulled away again "—I have a lot of other places—" he dropped a kiss against her jaw before dragging his lips along her skin "—that I'm dying to get my mouth on."

AJ made a noise in her throat that stopped his intimate exploration of her neck.

Liam straightened up, stared down at her.

"What was that?"

Her frown dripped with disdain. "That was a scoff. I scoffed at you."

"Yeah, I picked up on that, actually. I was looking for the story behind the scoff."

AJ exhaled. "I guess I just gave you more credit than that. I know you've got this playboy CEO reputation in the media, but I guess I didn't think you'd be one of those guys who pretend they give a shit and go around bragging about making their partner come a bunch of times just to bolster their own ego."

Liam blinked. "Please tell me you're kidding right now."

"Why would I be kidding?"

"Because you just made it sound like you think the only reason men perform oral sex is for bragging rights."

Something about the way he was looking at her gave her a sick feeling in the pit of her stomach, and when he narrowed his eyes, she could almost see him putting pieces together.

"Jesus. Have you never had a guy go down on you before?"

"I didn't say that." AJ crossed her arms and jutted out her chin.

"You didn't have to. You sidestepped it last night, and tonight you scoffed."

"So what does that prove?"

"It proves that you don't know what you're missing."

"See? Bragging. And there's nothing wrong with skipping the appetizers. Sometimes we ladies just want to get down to business."

He gave her that assessing look again—like she was a feral animal he was trying to tame. She hated that fucking look. "What?"

"That blow job just makes a lot more sense now. You make a lot more sense now."

"What was wrong with the blow job?"

"Nothing. It was unreal. I'd take ten more just like it. But it was also a hostile takeover."

"What's that supposed to mean?"

"You were asserting dominance. You wanted to teach me a lesson. Right?"

AJ's gaze flickered to her bare feet. A shiver went through her, and she wished she hadn't taken off her jacket.

"You remember when you said you were here because you wanted to be?" He leaned in. "I believe you."

AJ didn't mean to turn her face toward him. She just couldn't help it.

"And I'm asking you to trust that part of you that didn't turn off the countdown clock. The part of you that craves more of whatever the hell this is between us." His breath rushed along her neck, raising goose bumps in its wake. "That part of you that wants my tongue between your legs. Wants the free fall I can give you. All you have to do is take it."

"Pretty words, but I know who has the power in moments like these. It's the person on their knees." There was a quaver in her voice when she spoke.

"I understand your need for control, AJ. You're right about my motivation. You ran out on me last night, so I brought you here so you couldn't do it again. But it's not a loss of control that scares you right now."

He sounded so sure. Dread prickled along her spine.

"It's the intimacy."

AJ rolled her eyes, but she'd deployed her sarcasm shield too late, and the blow landed. It hurt, too. Worse than any black eye or bruised rib she'd ever gotten from Troy. Because those had healed. And when they had, she'd told herself she was okay. That she was still there. That she was tough. But now, standing across from Liam, she understood that she might have survived, but it wasn't without some scars. She might have been a thief, but life had stolen things from her, too, not the least of which was her ability to trust her heart.

Despite the doubt, she couldn't bear the thought of showing more weakness in front of this man, who'd held her while she cried. AJ swallowed down the terror crawling up her throat. "I told you last night. I'm not afraid of anything."

Liam stared into her eyes. Stepped closer. Tucked her hair behind her ear. Each move was slow. Precise. He gave her time to adjust. It was sweet…caring, and she loathed him for it. She wasn't fragile. She didn't want his pity.

"Then prove it." They were the perfect words—a life raft. Action in a sea of overthinking.

She stared at him as she reached for the hem of her

T-shirt, breaking eye contact only when the black cotton obstructed her view as she pulled it over her head.

He didn't move. Her mind was spinning. Too many warring emotions, grappling for dominance. Guilt over this betrayal of Max. Fury at Troy. And Liam, she didn't know what to feel about him. And that made him the worst of the three.

As though he could tell, he swooped in and pressed a hard kiss to her mouth that stopped the spinning in her brain. Focused her scattershot emotions.

Lust.

She could deal with lust.

"I'll stop whenever you want me to." His voice was low and rough, and so damn sexy.

Even so, she almost pressed the escape button when he popped the button of her jeans open. And again when he dragged the zipper down inch by inch.

Liam kissed the hollow of her throat, dragging his lips down her sternum, between her breasts, pressing a kiss just above her navel as he settled onto his knees.

She could hear her heart thudding in her ears, drowning out the surf as the boat cut through the water below. Liam peeled her jeans past her hips, down her legs. Arousal diluted her earlier panic. Her pulse was heavy between her thighs. She could feel his breath on her stomach as she balanced so he could tug the denim off one foot, then the other.

AJ's knees shook, a weird mix of lust and panic, but when Liam's fingers slipped under the waistband of her black undies, the panic won out, and her hand clamped over his.

He looked up at her, and when their eyes met, she felt a connection there, an understanding she didn't expect. There was no recrimination in his hazel eyes. None of the guilt or jeering that a guy sometimes used when *no* wasn't the answer he wanted.

Liam was still. Solid. And he didn't look away.

Slowly, her grip on his hand relaxed.

"You okay?"

"Yeah, I just…"

"We can leave them on."

AJ nodded.

It was stupid, the way that calmed her. She had the strange feeling that he'd somehow known it would. Layers. He'd mentioned them earlier, with the sunglasses. She'd shed a lot of layers today, but stupid as it might be, a pair of black boy-cut panties felt like security right now.

Liam glanced up as he ran his fingers along her right ankle, up her calf, to the back of her knee. AJ shivered at the light touch as he lifted her leg over his shoulder. Her muscles drew tight at the new position, at the heat that flared in his eyes as she looked down at him. It was as though her body already knew what to expect, was already desperate for a release that only he could give her.

His stubble brushed her inner thigh, unleashing the most exquisite ache between her legs.

He pressed a kiss to the sensitive skin beneath her navel, and her abdominal muscles retracted in shocked delight.

She closed her eyes tight in preparation, clenched

her hands around the wooden handrail as she braced for impact, but he didn't attack her like she'd expected.

"AJ."

The sound of her name startled her, and she looked down at him.

"I won't let you fall."

And then he pressed his mouth against the wet cotton of her panties and she cried out as the sensation overwhelmed her, sizzling along her nerve endings like Liam was the human equivalent of a downed power line.

Her leg tightened reflexively, her heel digging into his back, and he growled. AJ thought she might pass out from the pleasure.

The sound of the waves under the boat filled her head and she tipped her face to the inky sky, her hair blowing in the breeze as Liam drove her higher, and then higher still.

And then, when she was certain things couldn't get any better, Liam tugged her underwear to the side, and the shock of his tongue against her clit sent her free-falling into orgasm.

And true to his word, he didn't let go.

AJ was panting as she leaned against the railing, using it to support her as she eased her leg back over his shoulder, so she had both her feet on the deck.

It took a minute for her to catch her breath, for her pulse to slow, for her brain to reengage. But when it did, it went full bore, cutting through the aftershocks of pleasure still dancing along her skin.

What had she done? Shit.

She'd come here for a reason. And she could pretend all she wanted that she'd changed her mind and jumped onto the *SS Overcompensating for Something* for altruistic reasons. Out of loyalty to Max. To find out if Liam was the one who'd hacked Whitfield Industries. But in the aftermath of a truly phenomenal orgasm, she realized the truth was much more selfish.

Last night, she'd gone to Liam's for Max.

But today, she was here for herself.

And as a result, she'd betrayed both her boss and his biggest rival.

"I need to get off."

CHAPTER TWELVE

LIAM GRINNED AT her as he got to his feet.

"I thought you just did," he teased, but before he could lean in and kiss her, she ducked down and grabbed her jeans, yanking them on.

"We need to land."

"Dock," he corrected absently, distracted by the way her breasts bounced as she shimmied the black denim up her thighs. She'd melted for him, given herself to him, to the pleasure, and it had been...incredible. There was some caveman pride there, about being her first, yeah, but it wasn't just that. There was something else, too. Something all bound up in the story she'd told him about that asshole who'd hurt her. The one who was fucking lucky he was already dead, by Liam's estimation.

Trust. She'd trusted him. And it had made what just happened between them bigger somehow. More.

He dragged a hand through his sex-mussed hair, a little embarrassed by the quixotic bent of his thoughts. He was still hard for her, obviously not thinking straight.

"I don't give a shit what you call it. Let me off the boat."

Something about the heat in her voice penetrated the haze of his arousal. He could see the gleam of panic, like she was trying to come to grips with what he'd done, what she'd let him do.

"AJ?"

There was a hint of cornered animal to her, and he could almost see her assessing her options in the quick dart of her eyes.

"Not until you tell me what the hell is going on with you right now." He walked toward the loungers, where he'd left his phone.

She pointed menacingly at him. "I will hack your systems and send you straight into an iceberg if you don't let me off this goddamned boat."

"We're in the Pacific, about a dozen nautical miles off the coast of California. If there's an iceberg, then we're dealing with apocalyptic levels of climate change, and you crashing us into it is going to be the least of our worries." Still, he pressed the buttons that would summon McGee before stowing his phone in his pocket.

AJ grabbed her shirt from the deck and dragged it over her head.

"Sir? Is everything okay?"

Liam looked at his steward, then back at AJ.

Determination had fisted her hands. "I'll swim to LA if I have to."

He exhaled. "Take us back." He glanced at McGee, and the man nodded before leaving to let the captain know about their change in course. They weren't far out.

She set off across the deck. He didn't follow. Just watched as she took the stairs on the starboard side that led to the guest cabin and disappeared from sight.

Liam exhaled, wandered over to the railing.

Her walls were back up, full force.

He didn't know her well enough to figure out if he should go to her or give her some space and wait for her to come back. Indecision kept him rooted there, watching the lights of the Port of Los Angeles get closer and closer, until they were about two minutes from docking. She hadn't come back.

Liam raked a hand through his windblown hair.

If he wanted to figure out what had just happened, it was now or never.

Liam stopped in the wide-open doorway of the guest cabin, leaning a shoulder against the jamb. She was sitting on the edge of the bed staring blindly at the window. He waited a minute for her to notice him, wondering if she'd spent the entire journey like that. Lost in thought. Just like he had.

Finally, he rapped his knuckles on the jamb.

She jerked at the intrusion, sending him a sharp glance as she set to work, pulling on her socks. "What?"

"Are you going to tell me what this is all about?"

"I shouldn't have come here." She jammed her feet into her boots. "This was stupid. We're not… This can't… I should have shut down your countdown clock and disappeared."

He watched, oddly fascinated, as she laced them up with sharp, precise movements, like a general suiting up for battle. If not for the slight shake in her hands, he might have bought the resurrection of her badass facade, missed the cracks in her usually inscrutable smirk.

She kept her eyes averted as she approached him, obviously intending to blow right past. The air between them vibrated, despite the coolness she was trying to establish.

At the last second, Liam put his hand out, blocking the doorway. She glanced up sharply. "AJ—"

"Sorry to interrupt, sir, but we've arrived. We'll be ready to disembark in a few moments. We're just tying up."

Liam closed his eyes. Exhaled. Dropped his arm. "Thank you, McGee."

When he opened his eyes, AJ hadn't moved. A slight frown marred her brow, and Liam thought for a second, for just a second, that maybe she'd changed her mind. But then she shook her head, like she was clearing it, and hurried down the stairs. With a sigh, he pushed off the doorframe and followed her back to the deck.

She was standing at the railing, feet from where she'd tied him up earlier and blown his mind.

Liam shoved his hands in his pockets and walked over to stand beside her as she watched the crew finishing up on the dock below. "So that's it then?"

Her breezy shrug confirmed it. "What more was left? Fights? Resentment? Breaking up? We already got all the good stuff, right? Why ruin a perfect…"

She reached out and grabbed his forearm, and he ignored the crackle of awareness as she tugged his left hand out of his pocket and checked his watch. "Twenty-two hours?"

"I could've sworn my reservation was for the whole day."

Her fingers slid along his arm as she lowered it to his side, and then her touch was gone. She smiled, but it lacked the spark of her earlier ones. "It's all about craftsmanship, right? Quality, not quantity. So let's stop trying to make this more than it was. We had a couple of great orgasms together. It was fun. Now it's over."

He stepped close, too close, and she lifted her chin defiantly. *So fucking stubborn.* He swooped in, capturing her mouth in a kiss that went from zero to sixty faster than his Bugatti. Her head tipped back under the pressure, and she clutched his shoulders for balance, kissing him back angrily. Hungrily. Desperately. And still, he didn't let himself reach for her, tucked his free hand back into his pocket even though every part of him wanted to drag her closer, feel her pressed against him.

He bit back a groan as he lifted his head, watching the desire swirl in her eyes before she regained her senses and tamped it down, tugging her arms back from where they'd ended up twined around his neck. He rested his hip against the rail. "If you say so." Liam tipped his head toward the dock, where several crewmen were milling about. "McGee can give you a lift wherever you're going."

"I've got my own ride," she informed him, rather haughtily, as she walked away.

He forced himself not to turn, though mentally he kept track of her progress, past the table, down the stairs, she should appear on the dock right…about… now.

Liam turned back toward the deck. He didn't want to be caught staring if she decided to look back, he wasn't going to wave, but as though fate knew how much he wanted to check on her progress and was mocking him, something on the lounger caught his eye.

He sauntered toward the bow of the yacht, stopped beside the chair with the black jacket slung over its arm.

His jaw tightened in response to the feeling that spiraled in his chest as he reached for the leather. It was a little too much like relief for his peace of mind, but before he could analyze it further, something fell out of her jacket and bounced on the deck.

Liam frowned at the small silver disc.

What the…?

He reached down to pick it up and his throat went dry. It wasn't his. He could tell by the shitty plastic case, but it was a pretty credible knockoff. Why the hell would AJ have…

Their entire acquaintance flipped through his mind, but without the haze of lust, it looked far more incriminating.

He riffled through the rest of the pockets, but they were empty.

His hand fisted around the fake Shield and he stalked back toward the table where he'd left his laptop. First, he was going to upload this counterfeit and see what kind of trouble his upcoming product launch was in, and then he was going to light up the fucking tracker he'd embedded in the countdown clock code and pay his little thief a visit. He chucked her jacket on the chair she'd sat in earlier that day, eyeing him warily over his coffee.

Unlike usual, McGee hadn't cleared away the remnants of their breakfast or the *Los Angeles Times*, because Liam had made it clear that he and AJ didn't wish to be disturbed.

Which was why, when Liam lifted the newspaper, he'd been expecting to find the ultra-slim, ultralight portable computer that he'd developed still on the table where he'd left it.

It wasn't there.

And the sick feeling in his gut let him know exactly where it was.

Scratch that, exactly who it was with.

Well, fuck.

AJ crawled into the cab and gave the driver the address of the bar down the block from her place. Not much of a cover, but if Liam tried to track her down, at least he'd have to do more than bribe someone at the cab company.

Speaking of Liam…

She leaned forward and tugged his laptop out of the waistband of her jeans and placed the almost weightless silver rectangle on her lap. The Cybercore logo was etched into the top, and she traced her finger over it.

It had been stupid to take it, a whim as she'd passed by the table where he'd been reading the newspaper, where she'd eaten a chocolate croissant. Proof that she didn't want what he was offering. Her version of burning the bridge on the way out of town so she couldn't cross back in a moment of weakness.

She wasn't sure what the hell had just happened back there, but it wasn't sex. Not the sex she was used to.

Liam Kearney had made her feel things. And that wasn't a euphemism for orgasm. She'd been empty for so long, just a void, operating on base instincts. When she was hungry, she ate. When she was horny, she fucked. She buried the rest of her emotions in work.

But tonight, she'd felt them all, inextricably bound up in the physical, until she couldn't discern the difference between feeling happy and having an orgasm. And in her world, those were two distinct categories that shouldn't ever cross paths. Fucking him was one thing, but liking him? Not okay.

AJ blinked against the sting of tears that prickled at the bridge of her nose.

No.

She didn't owe him anything. Her loyalty was with Max, with Whitfield Industries. She'd lost sight of that. It was better that Liam knew exactly who he was dealing with. She was a thief. A hacker. And she worked alone.

And now she had the holy grail. The laptop of Cybercore's CEO. With any luck, once she'd finessed her way past whatever booby traps he'd loaded onto it, she'd have free access to the specs for The Shield. She could check the coding of the original against the counterfeit.

Hell, she could check them both against the program that had been used to hack Whitfield Industries. Prove once and for all that he was the one who'd screwed up the launch of SecurePay.

Hackers left traces, even the good ones. You just had to know how to read it. Once she uploaded the fake version of The Shield, she'd be in business. AJ reached for the inner pocket of her jacket and...realized she wasn't wearing it.

Shit. She bolted upright, eyes searching the darkened back seat, as though she'd find it beside her. But she wouldn't find it beside her. Because she hadn't taken her jacket off in the cab. She'd taken it off hours ago...

Shit, shit, shit.

She looked out the back window like an idiot, as though they hadn't been driving for ten minutes already. All she could see were other cars on the 110.

"You okay, lady?" the cabbie asked.

She was so. Very. Screwed. And not the good kind.

"You know what?" AJ flopped back against the well-worn seat. "I've been better."

CHAPTER THIRTEEN

LIAM STRAIGHTENED HIS tie as he stepped out of the elevator and into Cybercore's head office. He'd slept like shit and had no luck with the tracker he'd planted in the countdown clock code. She'd wiped her phone clean, and she'd done a fucking good job of it, too, which meant finding her again was going to take longer than he wanted.

In addition to running a comparison between the real and knockoff versions of The Shield, he'd deployed every weapon in his arsenal—tracking his laptop, trying to reestablish the link with her phone, reexamining the way she'd hacked into his party, in case there were any clues there.

He'd known she was a threat the instant he'd realized someone had sneaked into his party, but he'd been thinking with his dick. Let himself be intrigued instead of wary. And when she'd shown up at the yacht…fuck. He'd been a fool to let his guard down.

"Good morning, sir. I wasn't expecting you in until tomorrow."

The familiar voice pulled him out of his dark musings, and he walked over to his executive assistant's desk.

"Was there a problem with the yacht?" Krista asked.

Without conscious volition, he touched the left side of his suit, where he had the fake Shield tucked away in the interior breast pocket. He assured himself it was just to make sure it was still where he'd put it, and not because he couldn't shake the feeling that letting AJ, if that *was* her real name, off that boat might have been the biggest mistake of his professional life.

"You could say that," he answered cryptically, accepting the envelopes Krista held up for him, as was their morning custom. "Anything I need to know?"

"Henry Mitford got called away on business, so he had to cancel tomorrow's meeting. The soonest I could reschedule it was next Monday, which he agreed to, and he asked that I tell you he's looking forward to seeing you at his party on Friday. On that front, your tux is ready for pickup. Did you want me to send someone for it?"

Liam shook his head. "I'll take care of it."

"Also, Jesse Hastings of Soteria Security arrived about an hour ago to upgrade the four computers running the antivirus software that you've been testing. I gave him access to the three computers that were on-site and explained that you had your laptop with you. He's in the boardroom now, finishing up."

"Sounds good. I do have one question."

"Yes, sir?"

"Am I paying you enough?"

Krista smiled. "I can promise you I wouldn't be this efficient if you weren't."

"Excellent." Liam slapped the envelopes against his hand and made his way to the boardroom.

He arrived to find Soteria Security's second-in-command hunched over a laptop at the head of the oval table. "Jesse."

"Liam. Good to see you." The man stood, and they shook hands. "Krista said you were out of the office today."

"My plans fell through. I'm sorry for the improvised setup. I didn't know you were coming by."

Jesse grinned. "Join the club. But Wes insisted I come take care of the updates right away. Between you and me, I think he wants to make a good impression."

"I appreciate the attentive service."

"You should see what we do for the companies who've signed with us." Jesse closed the laptop on the table in front of him. "I did the two desktops in your testing lab, and I'm done with this one." He pulled out a notebook and flipped through to the page he was looking for. "Wes said you had four computers with the antivirus installed?"

Liam nodded. "It's on my laptop as well."

"Cool. Well, now that you're here, I'd be happy to install the update before I go."

He forced himself to unclench his jaw. "I'm afraid I don't have it with me."

"Oh. Okay, no problem. Wes made it clear it's important to get this updated as soon as possible. When do you think you might bring it in?"

For the second time that morning, Liam's hand drifted automatically to his left breast pocket. He covered the tell by pretending to pick a piece of lint from his lapel.

"To be honest with you, Jesse, I have absolutely no idea."

Liam was in a foul mood. He'd accomplished virtually nothing at the office today, aside from giving in to a near pathological need to monitor the progress of the programs he was running in his home office—still no lead on his sexy thief—and enumerating a list of all the ways that giving in to the intense sexual attraction with such a formidable rival had been the stupidest thing he could have done. He'd finally given up the pretense of working at five, ludicrously early, because he couldn't concentrate on anything anyway.

The Ferrari hugged the final bend in the road, but as Liam approached his driveway, he noticed a lone figure, dressed all in black, leaning against one of the pillars that flanked his gate.

No fucking way.

His pulse echoed in his ears, like he'd taken a syringe of adrenaline to the heart.

Liam set his features into a more neutral expression as he glided the car to a stop in front of the wrought iron gate that guarded his driveway.

His trespasser pushed away from the stone support and walked toward the car.

The passenger-side window descended with the push of a button, and AJ leaned forward. She was wearing his Ray-Bans. "I just came for my jacket."

He hated the surge of lust that assailed him despite the anger bubbling in his veins. Liam's fists tightened around the steering wheel, and he reminded himself to breathe.

He hit the button that unlocked the door. "Get in."

The order came out soft and low. She took off the sunglasses, but despite the mutinous look on her face, she did as she was bidden. AJ shoved his sunglasses in the pocket of her black hoodie as she slipped into the leather bucket seat, staring at him with critical eyes.

"You came for your jacket?" he asked silkily, reaching into his suit and placing the silver disc on the dashboard in front of her. He was vindicated by her slight flinch. "Or you came for what was inside your jacket?"

Her shrug wasn't quite as disaffected as he assumed she'd been aiming for. "Both would be best."

Ballsy. Even now.

"Neither is a more realistic expectation."

He stared at her profile, and though she did an admirable job of keeping her expression disdainful, the slight flattening of her mouth let him know that she'd just come to a big decision. And she wasn't happy about it.

She leaned forward, hiking up her sweatshirt in the back, producing a familiar silver rectangle. Ultra-slim. Ultralight. Ultrafast.

Rather than being relieved, all he could see was the curve of her back, the color of her skin.

She tugged her hoodie back into place and gestured toward the gate with his laptop. "Maybe we can negotiate once we're inside?"

Now he was the one scoffing. "You think I want you anywhere near my house after what you did?"

She rolled her eyes. "Please. If I wanted to be inside your house, I'd be inside your house."

Possibly true, he decided, thinking of all the other things she'd managed to pull off. Although he had some tricks up his sleeve as well, things that would surely trip her up, make her work for it and even impress her a little bit.

"I'd love to see you try."

He frowned as he realized that he meant it, that he was curious about her hacking style, wanted to watch her work.

She glanced over at him, and he hoped she hadn't heard the truth in his words, and just assumed that it was a dismissal of her considerable skills.

"Give me your phone."

"Forget it."

He held his hand out. "It wasn't a request."

"You could at least ask nicely," she chastised, shifting against the seat so she could tug it from her back pocket. There was venom in her eyes when she handed it over. "And you're being paranoid. I'm not recording anything."

He gave the phone a cursory check and powered it down before tucking it inside his suit, ignoring the way the warmth from her pocket seeped through his shirt. "You'll forgive me if I don't take your word on that."

Liam grabbed the silver disc from the dashboard, palming it before he pressed his thumb to the panel he'd installed on the dash. The wrought iron gate swung out of the way as the screen recognized his thumbprint and he punched the gas, guiding the Ferrari up the long driveway toward the garage.

CHAPTER FOURTEEN

AJ TIGHTENED HER grip on his computer, her heart racing wildly as they sped toward the garage. She knew
he'd be furious at her arrival, but the change in him
was staggering. Gone was the easy, laid-back charm
of the man who'd plied her with expensive alcohol and
flirted with devastating precision. She understood now
how he'd taken the tech world by storm. He was good
at lulling, at making you believe he was tame enough
to pet, but a tiger lurked beneath the gregarious surface. One that might not want to rip your throat out,
but would have no qualms about doing so should the
situation require it.

With another swipe of his thumb, the big door lifted,
and Liam parked inside.

AJ was already out of the Ferrari and three cars
away, past the Corvette and the Maserati, staring contemplatively at the vintage Jag, by the time her "host"
caught up with her.

"I thought you were bragging when you said you had
a garage full of penis metaphors," she said.

His smile slipped out, like he'd forgotten he was

mad at her. The sudden white glamour of it was a jolt to the chest. "I was."

She nodded, lamenting that his grin disappeared as quickly as it had come. "Well, it's not bragging if you can back it up."

They meandered past the Aston Martin and the Porsche, toward the door that led into the main house.

"So does that mean you're not bragging when you talk about your computer prowess and how good you are?"

Now it was her turn to grin. "Pure fact."

Liam looked contemplative at that, tossing the knockoff Shield in the air and catching it, twice, three times, before stowing it away inside his jacket.

She tipped her chin at where it was hidden. "I can help you solve that problem."

"I have an inconvenience, not a problem. The Shield will launch as scheduled. There's no real value in releasing the knockoff tech until it does, so the worst that happens is that the fakes flood the market a week before they normally would." He gave a shrug of broad shoulders. "So you can let Max know I'm sorry to disappoint him."

Her eyes snapped to his, and Liam frowned at her unwitting confirmation. She swore under her breath.

"I knew it. I fucking knew it. Of course it would be him."

"You think Max did that?" She gestured again to the pocket that hid the knockoff from her view.

Liam's eyes were focused just over her head, a slight

frown on his handsome face. "Who would want The Shield to fail more than the guy I beat to market?"

At her continued silence, he finally lowered his gaze. "No, wait." His face cleared with sudden realization. "That's not why you came to my party. You were trying to get him proof that I was the one who hacked SecurePay so I could fuck up his launch."

Her eyes narrowed. "Max doesn't know I'm here."

"So I think Max hacked me, and he thinks I hacked him."

They both stood there, facing each other, letting that sink in for a moment.

"Now what?" she asked.

"Maybe we can help each other out."

"You didn't seem so into this plan a few minutes ago when it was mine."

"Because the game has shifted. This isn't about trust anymore. It's about skill. You breached my security, probably would have made it into my bedroom if I hadn't interrupted you in the hallway, and managed a semi-credible job of hacking my phone with an elegant dupe of my tech."

She frowned in refutation of the understatement. "What I did with your tech wasn't a dupe. It was a fucking revelation."

"Well, whatever you call it, now you're going to use that talent to help me."

AJ crossed her arms at his imperious tone. "How do you figure that?"

"Because until ten seconds ago, my suspect list for this consisted solely of Whitfield Industries. If Max thinks the delay in launching SecurePay because of the hack was costly, wait until he feels the full brunt of me filing an injunction against him so he can prove his innocence in court."

This time, AJ managed to keep her expression neutral, but it didn't lessen the threat.

Whitfield Industries couldn't survive another scandal. The media was still having a field day with the fact that Max had ratted out his father to the Feds and his sister, Kaylee, the company's PR director, had been outed as a burlesque dancer. The family business had been in the news too much lately.

The last thing they needed was someone else questioning the honesty of their current practices, even if the story didn't have an ounce of truth. Public confidence would only stretch so far.

"Somebody leaked the specs for The Shield. That means somebody fucked me over, and I will figure out who did it, even if I have to raze Whitfield Industries to the ground and walk through its ashes to do it. So if you're so sure this wasn't Max, it's in your best interest, and his, for you to aim my retribution at the rightful target."

Liam's voice was thin, like a razor's edge, and she had no doubt that he meant every word.

AJ felt the familiar itch she got when she was onto something, when a night full of hacking or code analysis loomed before her, when she got to test her mettle against an opponent and see exactly how she stacked up.

It was a character flaw, the little thrill she got from doing the wrong thing.

Her eyes dropped to his mouth.

And worst of all, she wanted to do him again.

"So is that a yes?"

"Okay, here's how this is going to work. First, I charge double whatever you planned to get around to offering me."

"Who says I was going to offer you anything?"

"Time is of the essence here. You really want to waste time on something we both know is going to happen anyway?"

Liam conceded with the slightest tip of his chin.

"Second, I'll report here every day by noon and—"

"Deal's off."

AJ scowled at him.

"You're not leaving this house. We're working from here. End of story."

His imperiousness raised her hackles. "What do you mean 'we'? In case it hasn't become infinitely clear in our short acquaintance, I don't play well with others. And I always work alone."

"Not this time." Liam motioned at the computer she'd forgotten was in her hands. "You've had access to something I have never let anyone see—"

"Ha!" She sent a derisive glance at his crotch. "Not according to the tabloids."

"—and you hacked into my systems once already. You have enough knowledge in that pretty little head of yours to do some serious damage to me...to Cybercore," he corrected.

"Awww." AJ tipped her head and batted her eyelashes in parody. "You think I'm pretty? Well, that just makes everything okay then, doesn't it?"

"If you think I'm going to hold the door open and wave while you run back to Max with everything he'd need to destroy my business, you're delusional."

The phrasing, so reminiscent of the story he'd shared about his mother's abandonment, deflated her anger.

I stood there at the door and I fucking waved.

AJ held the computer out to him. "I didn't poke around in there. And I know you probably don't believe me, but it wasn't why I came to the yacht. I was just…" She exhaled. "Sometimes when I feel cornered, I do stupid shit." She shoved it at him again. "So take it."

His hand closed around the edge of the laptop.

"And fine. I'll stay," she relented, before he said something to make her regret what she'd just done. "But I get my own room for the duration of our arrangement. I sleep alone."

His nod was sharp.

Something smug and satisfied spread through AJ's chest at the realization that he wasn't a fan of the revised rule number two. Not that she thought he intended to make her his sex slave or anything. It was just a relief to know that this reckless, wicked heat that invaded her blood when he was near wasn't flowing one way.

"And lastly, I find our hacker, and Max never knows about me showing up at your party."

Liam's jaw flexed. "Unless I'm right and it turns out that my hacker is Max."

"It's not Max. And I'm serious. If you ever tell him, if you tell anyone, the fires of hell will rain down upon you. I can make that happen. You ruin my life, I'll ruin yours right back. I am not above mutually assured destruction."

Their silent standoff ended with a brusque nod of his head. "I accept your terms."

She extended a hand, and Liam reached for it, but before he could clasp it, AJ drew back. "Wait."

They stared at one another.

"As soon as we shake, things are going to get very complicated."

The truth of that settled between them. Because things were already complicated.

He knew she was affiliated with Max.

He had the power to make her body hum like a voltage meter.

He'd already proven himself a cunning adversary. She'd be a fool to take him solely on his word. For the thousandth time, she wished she'd deleted that stupid countdown clock from her phone on the way home and erased Liam Kearney from her thoughts that first night.

And then, for the thousand-and-first time, her conscience called her a liar.

CHAPTER FIFTEEN

"I want my phone before we make a deal. And my jacket."

Liam shook his head. "Now you're just adding shit to see how far you can push me. Stop while you're ahead."

"Nonnegotiable. I'm not stepping into this fortress without all of my possessions." She held out her hand, not for a shake, but with her palm up, mimicking his actions in the car when he'd confiscated it in the first place. "It wasn't a request."

She smirked as she threw his words back in his face.

Fine, she wanted to push buttons? He could push buttons. He gave her his most patronizing smile. "You could at least ask ni—"

She grabbed him by the tie, giving it a sharp jerk so that their mouths were inches apart. "I swear to God, if you tell me to ask you nicely, I'll fuck you up."

Her eyes flashed with heat as she stared up at him, the threat hanging between them. He'd missed this, the intensity of her. The crackling heat that always sprang up when she was close.

"I was totally on board until you added the 'up.'"

She swore as she pushed him back against the wall beside the door, crushing her mouth against his, and he pulled her close, trying not to lose his grip on the computer as he hoisted her up his body. Liam groaned as she wrapped her legs around his hips and ran her hands up his chest, winding her arms around his neck.

It wasn't enough, and he spun around and pushed her against the wall, reveling in the hitch of her breath as their bodies slammed together with the pressure he craved.

In response to the rock of his hips, AJ bit his bottom lip, laving the sting with her tongue.

He'd never felt anything quite like what she did to him.

He held her, pressed against the wall, staring at her as their breath slowed, as his heart rate returned to normal.

She unhooked her legs from around his waist, and Liam closed his eyes briefly at the heavenly sensation of her body sliding against his. He stared down at her kiss-stung lips, soft and tempting. He had to take a step back to keep himself from reigniting the flame that licked along his nerve endings, so close to the surface.

They might have come to a truce, but a quick fuck against the garage wall was just the sort of thing that could burn their uneasy alliance to the ground. He needed to figure out who had sold him out as quickly and efficiently as possible. He had some big military contracts on the line for his new fencing tech, and if word got out that he had a leak, he could kiss them

goodbye. And AJ, despite their rather complicated...
relationship, was good at what she did. Almost as good
as him, and he could use all hands on deck.

Still, he was relieved that she looked as disoriented
as he felt by the hard punch of lust that had just consumed them, and she glanced down at her feet for a
moment, as though checking that she was back on solid
ground. When she raised those cynical brown eyes,
Liam could see that sanity had returned, and it kept
him in check. He straightened his tie as he stepped
back from her.

AJ extended her hand. "So we have a deal?"

"We have a deal," he confirmed, and for the first
time, the buzz of skin-on-skin contact didn't take him
by surprise. He wasn't sure AJ could say the same, as
she pulled her fingers free of their shake with more
force than was necessary.

"Next time give me my phone when I ask," she said,
turning to open the door to his house. There was a
phone-shaped item in the back pocket of her jeans as
she stepped across the threshold.

A quick touch revealed that his inside left breast
pocket was now empty, a wry smile touching his lips
as he followed her inside the house.

"If you want to head to the library, it's——"

"I know where it is."

He raised his eyebrows at her certainty.

"You think I broke into your party without going
over the blueprints?" she asked, heading off down the
hall. "What am I, an amateur?"

No. No, she wasn't. And that made what he was

about to do all the more stupid. But The Shield was launching in three weeks, and the more information he had about the knockoff, and the asshole who had leaked the specs, the better he could prepare. He could use her on this.

"AJ."

Her name on his lips stopped her progress, and she turned to face him. He tipped his head in the opposite direction.

Her brows drew together over sharp eyes. "The stairs through that door only go up."

She really did know her stuff. "On the blueprints that were filed with the city they do. What good is a false panel if everyone knows about it?"

AJ sauntered back toward him, managing to look seductive and superior and far too tempting for his peace of mind. She poked him in the chest as she passed by. "Mansion bowels. I knew it."

Liam smiled despite himself.

"You coming?"

"I'll be right there. I'm just going to slip into something more comfortable."

She stopped in the doorway to say, "Fair warning— if you show up in a silk robe with an ascot and matching slippers, I'm out of here, our deal be damned," before she disappeared from sight.

After he'd changed and grabbed the black leather jacket from the foot of his bed, Liam swung back through the kitchen to grab a couple of bottles of water from the fridge and made his way downstairs to his favorite room in the house.

A big fireplace, red walls, floor-to-ceiling bookcases accented by a big wood desk and a brown leather couch; it had an old-school vibe that appealed to him. He liked the dichotomy of the classic setting tricked out with the most up-to-date Cybercore-made tech and gadgets.

AJ looked up from the computer when he entered, and his body was not immune to the once-over she gave his jeans, T-shirt and bare feet.

"Do I pass inspection?" he asked, dropping her jacket on the back of the couch as he passed.

"Very man of the people." She rested her chin in her hand, and the look she gave him was too sweet by half. "I see you've been studying the masters."

She spun the monitor that displayed his analysis of her party invite hack.

Liam handed her a bottle of water and set the other one on the desk in front of him. "Okay, don't choke on those canary feathers."

Her crooked smile was in full effect as she leaned back, cracking the seal on the water. "Just savoring a compliment from a hot guy with some mad tech skills."

"Nice try, but I won't be distracted by completely true statements. Did you find anything?"

"Mmm-hmm." AJ swallowed a mouthful of water as she recapped the bottle and set it on the desk. "Well, technically, your computer did most of the hard work. The analysis you were running between The Shield and the counterfeit seems to have finished up. Check out that last line of code."

Liam circled the work station, bracing one hand on the desk, the other on the back of her chair so he could lean over her shoulder. The familiar scent of her teased his nostrils.

He frowned as his eyes scanned the computer screen. "But what does it do?"

"As far as I can tell, it serves no purpose. But it's the only thing that distinguishes the knockoff from The Shield. So I figure that's gotta mean something, right?"

He hoped so.

"But as I'm looking at it, trying to figure out why counterfeiters would bother adding this shit, I realized there was something familiar about it. Like I'd seen it before." She gestured toward the monitor below the one they were looking at, and he dropped his gaze.

A tingle of recognition flared at the base of his skull. "Same garbage code."

"*Exactly* the same garbage code," she stressed.

They grinned at each other, but the moment of discovery was swallowed by something else. Something darker. Hotter. AJ was so close he could feel her breath on his neck. Every part of him ached to kiss her. But if their short acquaintance had taught him anything, it was that he needed to keep a cool head. He wouldn't give her the power to destroy him again. She was a runner, and this was not a game he could afford to lose.

Clearing his throat, Liam straightened up. Took a step back. "Why do I get the feeling you're about to tell me this code I'm looking at isn't actually from my hack?"

She smiled approvingly, and he felt his good intentions slip a notch. "Because you're smart. Not as smart as me or anything, but I like that you can keep up."

He smiled despite himself. "High praise. So what's this from?"

To his surprise, her face grew deadly serious. "This code is from the hack on Whitfield Industries."

"What?" Liam couldn't hide his surprise. That was a big fucking deal, that she'd uploaded such sensitive information to his machine.

"I brought it as a show of good faith," she confessed softly. "In case you wouldn't talk to me."

Trust. It was the third time she'd gifted him with it—first with her past, then with her body, and now... it was a huge risk, her showing him the inner workings of Whitfield Industries. The profundity of it had weight as it settled around them.

So of course, Liam wasn't shocked in the least when she plowed through it with a reckless lack of finesse.

"How was I supposed to know you were such a shitty negotiator that you'd let me in without even putting up a fight? Also, I'd like the record to show that I told you Max wasn't your hacker."

"Has anyone ever told you how incredibly gracious in victory you are?"

"What can I say? I've had a lot of practice winning."

He shook his head, telling himself it was exasperation and nothing else. He definitely wasn't charmed. "So now what?"

"Now we wait for the computer to finish running all

the supersmart analyses I told it to do while you were getting all prettied up. Should take at least an hour." Her eyes turned sultry as she got to her feet. "How ever will we pass the time?"

CHAPTER SIXTEEN

LIAM DIDN'T STOP her when she flattened a palm against his chest. Or when she started walking him backward in the direction of the couch.

"I thought you said no sex," he said, reaching over his shoulder and dragging the T-shirt he'd just put on back off.

"I said I wasn't going to sleep with you. I didn't say we weren't going to fuck."

Her hand was back, warm against his bare skin, and he let the pressure of her touch guide him around the coffee table. Once they'd cleared it, she gave him a hard shove, and he landed on his ass on the brown leather couch. "Works for me."

AJ pulled off her hoodie and her T-shirt in one go. "Before we do this, I feel like I should confess that I made it into your bedroom the other night." She bent over at the waist to work her jeans down her thighs, giving him the most perfect view of her breasts, spilling over the cups of her basic black bra. "You caught me on the way out."

"The trip wire was still on," he countered, reaching down to adjust himself as she finished stripping off her jeans.

"Better check your secret counter there, Tech God. Should be up one unauthorized entrance."

"You figured that out?" he asked, as AJ crawled onto the couch, planting a knee on either side of his hips. "That's so fucking hot." He groaned as he ran his hands up her torso, palming her breasts. No finesse, but he needed to get his hands on her. Her nipples were hard peaks beneath the fabric of her bra, and she leaned into the caress.

"Jesus, I love your breasts."

She ran her tongue over his bottom lip, getting his mouth wet, ready for a kiss that was part desperation, part hostile takeover. His hips surged at the blatant sexuality of it, the expert blending of teeth, tongue and suction. Liam dropped his hands to her ass, yanking her closer, grinding against her until she gasped into his mouth. When she pulled back, they were both panting. He used the moment of disorientation to unhook her bra, and she helped him pull it the rest of the way off.

He groaned at the sight of her, bared to his gaze. "How are you so gorgeous?" Liam pressed a kiss to the slope of her breast. "All caramel skin and nipples like mocha."

"Focus there, big boy. Are we having sex, or do you want dessert?"

She gasped as he caught her nipple in his mouth, laved it with his tongue.

"You taste plenty sweet." He traced the bottom curve of her breast with his thumb.

She tucked a raven curl behind her ear, stared down at him with indecision in those dark brown eyes, and then surprised the hell out of him by giving him an answer.

"My dad was half British, half Puerto Rican." Her fingers toyed with the hair at the nape of his neck. "And my mom was part Filipino and part Italian, with a little Jamaican thrown in."

"Wow." He ran his fingers along the edge of her panties, and she shifted her hips in retaliation, teasing his cock.

"Yeah. I'm a walking DNA-test commercial."

"Well, it looks good on you." Liam returned his attention to her spectacular boobs, kissing and licking his way to the other peak, until she was clutching his hair and rocking against him, driving him out of his mind, getting him hard.

When he couldn't handle it anymore, he grabbed her around the waist and executed a quarter turn, so he could lay her down on the couch.

Body primed for action, Liam got to his feet and shucked his jeans.

"All my ancestors are from Ireland," he offered, pulling a condom from his wallet.

She laughed up at him, shimmying out of her panties. "Really, *Liam Kearney*? Shocker."

She was so goddamn sexy, all soft and curvy, breasts jiggling when she moved, that he stroked himself a few times before he got down to business. He didn't miss the way her eyes tracked his progress as he rolled the condom on.

"Fun fact—" Liam braced an arm on either side of her head as he lowered himself onto the couch, onto *her*, "—the name *Kearney* means 'warlike or victorious.'"

"How interesting." Her eyes were dark, more pupil than iris, and heavy-lidded with arousal. "Does that mean you have experience handling this weapon?" she asked, and all the breath left his lungs as she wrapped her hand around his cock. Squeezed. His balls were tight with need, and he thrust into her hand, desperate for more of this pulse-pounding desire that sparked between them.

"Some experience," he told her, then gritted his teeth against the pleasure as she twisted her wrist and stroked up the length of him. "But you're going to make me look like an amateur if you keep that up."

She giggled as she took pity on him and let go, and something about the innocent sound, devoid of bravado or cynicism, coming from the kick-ass, take-no-prisoners woman beneath him left him stunned, grabbed him by the chest.

Liam leaned forward and caught her mouth in a deep, spiraling kiss that felt less like physical satisfaction and more like he'd fallen into an emotional vortex.

AJ was a little dizzy when Liam pulled back.

There'd been a surge, something hot and bright and blinding, like she'd looked directly into the sun and it had singed the synapses in her brain. She blinked against the disorienting sensation.

It was a kiss, sure, but not a kiss like anything she'd ever experienced.

She glanced toward the power source, and goose bumps flooded her skin.

The look on his face was so intense it crackled along her nerve endings. It was like he was looking through her skin, to the heart of her. Like somehow, she was suddenly more naked than she'd been before his mouth had touched hers.

She licked her lips, and his eyes cleared. Liam looked more like himself again, and that made her feel more like her. She was suddenly vibrantly aware of the throb of his cock against her thigh, and she moved her leg, reveling in the resulting clench in his jaw.

"Your aim's a little off there, warlord."

The challenge sparked something exciting in the depths of his eyes, dark and passionate, more brown than green with his arousal. "You can't just rush into the fray, swinging your sword," he counseled. AJ shivered as he dragged his fingers from the side of her torso to her navel before shifting direction and heading south. "At least not until you're sure everyone's ready for battle."

His fingers dipped into the moisture at the apex of her thighs, and she moaned as he circled her clit, sending sparks of need racing along her limbs.

"Do I pass muster, sir?" AJ reached up, wrapping her arms around his neck and drawing him closer.

"Slow down, soldier." He pressed his lips to the pulse point at the base of her throat, and she tipped her chin up, granting him better access. He dragged his lips up the side of her neck, nuzzled her ear. "I'm not finished with my inspection."

AJ bit her lip as his fingers stroked through her slick heat, driving her to the brink of madness before retreating, only to attack again. Her hips moved restlessly beneath his ministrations, trying to get closer.

Finally, he put her out of her misery and sank two fingers deep inside her.

Liam pressed a kiss to her jaw. "I love the sounds you make, the way your breath catches when I touch you in just the right way…"

The pad of his finger skated over her G-spot, and AJ's body jerked with pleasure.

"God, yes. Right there."

He obliged, and AJ's arms tightened reflexively around his neck and she pressed her forehead against his shoulder.

And then he did it again. And again. Until she couldn't deny the build of pressure and expectation, undulating against his hand, desperately seeking that burst of pleasure that was so close…

Liam twisted his wrist, driving his fingers deep and flicking his thumb against her clit, and AJ cried out, tasting the salt of his skin as she broke, lifting her hips as heat radiated through the core of her.

It took her a second to catch her breath.

"Yeah, I'd say you're ready."

The dry observation startled a laugh from her. "Understatement. Come 'ere."

She kissed him as he shifted on top of her, and his weight pressed her deeper into the cushions.

He reached between them, and there was nothing wrong with his aim this time.

AJ's breath stuttered at the aftershocks of her orgasm as he filled her. His back muscles strained under her fingertips as he pushed up so he wouldn't crush her. She'd just come, but at the feel of him deep inside her, something rolled under her skin, like thunderheads gathering for an impending storm.

It took her a moment to realize he wasn't moving. Just staring down at her, the planes of his face harsh with need. "Are you ever going to tell me?"

"Oh, baby, your cock's so big and hard and good at sex."

Liam rolled his eyes. "What AJ stands for," he clarified.

"Seriously? That's your most pressing concern right now?" She wiggled her hips, gratified when he groaned, and his thighs flexed against hers, pushing him deeper.

It took a few hard thrusts before he caught on to her diversionary tactic and frowned.

"Hey, no distractions." In retaliation, he pinned her to the couch with his hips, cutting off her entire arsenal of sexy lower-body movements.

"Why are you stopping? Things were just getting good again."

"Just tell me what I want to know, and this will all go away."

She laughed at the bad-guy refrain. "What am I? Your sex hostage?"

He leaned close, nipped her bottom lip with his teeth. "Tell me your name, or I'll kill the orgasm."

There were two answers to his question, so she picked the one she'd made up. The one she hoped would impress. "Arctic Jade."

Liam's eyes widened at the mention of her old hacker handle, so she used the element of surprise to her advantage and shoved on his chest.

He rolled obligingly onto his side, helping her reverse their positions on the couch.

"No shit?" he asked as she straddled him. "*You're* Arctic Jade?"

"In the flesh." AJ shifted her weight, started to rock against him. "Did you dabble?"

He growled at the friction, his hands coming up to ride her hips, spurring her on.

"I *may* have dissected a few of your hacks back in the day."

"Oh, yeah?" She rewarded that confession with a squeeze of her internal muscles that made his eyes roll back in his head.

"Jesus, AJ."

"And?" she asked, leaning forward and bracing her hands on his chest. "What did you think?"

"I think you were good. I think you're better now. And I think if you don't finish me off soon, I'm going to take over and fuck you senseless."

The last word ended on a groan as she circled her hips, catching him off guard with the change of pace. Electricity surged through her veins, lighting up her body. He was so hard and strong, and she liked that she didn't have to be careful with him. She didn't feel like being careful.

He might be worth hundreds of millions, more if his new fence tech got picked up by the military, but he had the body of a warrior, not a desk jockey, and it turned her on so much to have him pinned on the couch, his body growing harder under her questing hands.

She couldn't get enough of him—of each flex and thrust of his hips as he tried to get deeper inside her. She tightened her thighs around him, biting her lip as she rode him faster, grinding against him until she felt the deep throb of his cock, so hard and hot inside her, pushing her toward ecstasy. She tumbled over the edge a second before his hips bucked and he joined her there.

It was a good three minutes of panting before she could summon enough energy to slide off him. "Nice work."

Liam exhaled and tugged her closer. "Back atcha."

AJ tucked into his side, genially stroking her fingers against the smattering of dark hair that covered his chest before arrowing enticingly downward.

Postcoital glow was the shit. At least the way Liam did it, it was. She'd never stuck around long enough to have a comparison.

"Why do you work for Max?"

The question didn't surprise her, not really. You could only push things off for so long with sex. They always caught up with you, sooner or later.

She lifted herself up on her elbow, resting her head in her hand so she could see his face. "Oh, you know. The usual reasons. Money, food, shelter."

"But why tie yourself down?"

She poked him in the chest. "Are you trying to poach me, Mr. CEO?"

"Sure. You want a job at Cybercore, say the word. But if you ask me, you should be doing your own thing."

The words, hearing the idea aloud, made her antsy, like a million bugs were swarming beneath her skin, but Liam didn't seem to notice her plight.

"There's big money in forensic hacking. And if you play up the mystique of the whole Arctic Jade, vaguely criminal past, there's some cachet there. Bad girl gone good. People love that shit."

AJ shook her head, thoughts racing a mile a minute. "I can't… I'm not… I couldn't…"

Liam reached out, caught her chin in his fingers and tipped her face toward his. Stilled her. "I've known you for forty-eight hours. I have no idea what your favorite color is, or how you like your eggs. Hell, I don't even know your last name. But despite all that, there is one thing about you that I'm absolutely certain of."

She didn't want to know, but she wasn't sure she could stand not knowing, either. It took everything in her to ask. "What's that?"

"You can do anything."

The answer stole her breath.

CHAPTER SEVENTEEN

THREE DAYS.

Three days in Liam's basement, staring at code, with the odd break for food and sleep, and slightly more regular breaks for sex and more sex, but they were no closer to figuring out who their asshole was.

AJ scraped a hand down her face. At times like this, when she was stuck, Wes Brennan's words often came back to her.

Sloppy gets you caught.

Sloppy got everyone caught. So all she needed to do was find the sloppy.

"Okay, just think," she counseled herself. Going after Whitfield Industries and Cybercore took balls. Big fucking balls. "You pull off something like that, you're going to want to tell someone about it. Leave a clue. Sign it." But how? "Think, Alyssa…" Maybe a—

"Alyssa?"

Fuck.

Fuck, fuck, all the fucks.

She'd forgotten about him. Though when she looked over to where his big body was slung out on the couch, she had no idea how that was possible. The man was sex personified, surrounded by a bunch of Chinese take-out boxes, looking like a lounging god.

"Well, now we're getting somewhere."

Nowhere good. How could she have let her guard down like that? She was usually so careful. Her survival had depended on it for a long time. But sometimes, when it was just her and Liam, she got lulled into this place where the really bad stuff felt far away. Like it couldn't touch her. Like she was...safe.

He sat up and swung his feet to the ground, setting the laptop on the couch beside him. "So the *J* is...Jane? Johanna? Jillian?"

"I need to focus if I'm going to save your billion-dollar company and figure out who leaked the product specs before you launch The Shield."

"Janine?"

"You're not even close."

"Jocelyn?"

She pushed her curls back from her forehead. "Seriously, Liam. I'm trying to work here."

"Jordan? Jordyn with a *y*? Juanita?"

"You're not going to let this go, are you?"

"Hell no. In fact, I'm prepared to read every single *J* name off a Google baby name list until I figure it out." He reached menacingly for his laptop.

With a sigh, AJ stood up and stretched. A quick glance at the time showed it was two thirty in the morning. No wonder she was so stiff. She rubbed her eye as she made her way over to the couch, grabbing a container of cold moo shu pork and a set of chopsticks before she sat down beside him. "It's James, okay? My last name is James. Mystery solved."

"Alyssa James, huh? I was expecting something more…"

She shot him a glare. "If you say *exotic*, I'll be forced to kick you in the junk."

"Actually, *Alyssa*, I was going to say *badass*."

She sat up a bit straighter as she selected a piece of pork. "In that case, your junk and I both thank you."

"So why AJ?"

Her sigh deflated her shoulders, and she shoved the chopsticks back in the box before tipping the container in his direction. He accepted the offer.

"Just wanted a change, I guess."

She watched Liam expertly wield the chopsticks she'd just used. His jaw was shadowed with a few days' worth of stubble, and it flexed as he ate some moo shu pork.

The fact that he didn't push her on her nonanswer should have been great. But it wasn't great. It made her feel vaguely restless. Like that swarm of bugs was back, burrowing under her skin.

"I didn't want them to call me Alyssa," she blurted, reaching for the pineapple chicken so she didn't have to meet his eyes. "My parents called me Alyssa, and I didn't want their replacements…strangers…" She cleared her throat. "I just liked AJ better."

The chopsticks made their way into her peripheral vision, and she took the offering, glancing at him as she did. There was nothing annoying on his face. No recrimination. No pity.

It made her feel a little better.

"Thanks for telling me." He put the moo shu box back on the table.

"Yeah, well." She dug into the box of chicken, looking for the best piece. "You probably would have just sexed it out of me later anyway. Figured I'd save you the trouble. But just so we're clear moving forward, my name is AJ, which means if you call me Alyssa, I'll kick you in the junk."

He leaned back against the couch and closed his eyes, fingers linked over his belly. Well, his abs, she corrected herself. "You seem pretty obsessed with my junk. I like that about you."

She gave a huff of annoyance but let herself smile since his eyes were closed anyway. "You would." She reached out and gave his shoulder a shove with her chopstick hand. It was hard beneath her knuckles, warm, and he barely moved. If not for his grin, she might have thought he hadn't felt it at all.

She chewed thoughtfully on a hunk of chicken as she stared at him. "Why do you suppose that I'm always spilling my guts around you?"

It was embarrassing. She didn't like it.

He cracked his eyes open, angled his head toward her. "Okay, go ahead."

AJ shoved the take-out box and chopsticks beside the moo shu. "Your sex talk really goes downhill after two a.m., huh?"

"You get to ask one gut-spilling question. That's it. You want to waste it on bad jokes, that's on you."

Her eyes widened at the offer. He was letting her even the score, and there was no way in hell she was going to pass on his offer. "Why do you throw those parties if you hate them so much?"

Liam's chuckle was self-deprecating, and he pulled a hand down his face. "Sure you don't want a second to think about it?"

In answer, she pulled her feet up on the couch and sat cross-legged, facing him, her knee brushing his ribs. "I'm good. Say all the things."

"Okay, so you know all that stuff I told you about my mom?"

"Yeah."

"That's why."

AJ shook her head. "I don't follow."

Liam blew out a breath and held his arms open wide. "That's what all this is about. The house, the cars, the parties, the photo shoots." He dropped his hands into his lap. "Hell, even Cybercore, if you want to get deep about it."

His meaning hit her all at once, as though someone had adjusted the focus in her brain. "Revenge," she breathed.

He nodded, looking distinctly less than pleased about it. He shifted on the couch, and his elbow came to rest on her knee.

"The day she gave me that check, I promised myself that I was going amass a fortune that made her wish she'd never walked out. Launched the company when I turned eighteen, put everything I had into making it a success. And when it was, I made sure everybody knew it. Dated famous women, hosted lavish parties, said yes to every interview request that came my way."

"You wanted her to see you."

"Damn straight I did."

His hand had drawn into a fist in her lap, and AJ covered it with her own. His gaze snapped toward the unexpected touch, but he didn't pull away, so she kept stroking his knuckles until his hand relaxed.

"You know what the kicker is?" he asked, twisting his wrist and lacing his fingers through hers.

"What's that?"

"It took me so many years to realize I wasn't actually trying to hurt her."

"No?"

Liam shook his head. "I was trying to get her to come back. To pick me."

AJ squeezed his hand, and a sad smile touched his lips.

"By the time I figured that out, my international party-boy rep was well established. And the networking opportunities are usually worth a couple of hours of hatred, so I persevere."

Liam let his head fall back against the couch, closed his eyes. "If you ever tell anyone any of this, I know people who can make you disappear."

"I should hope so," AJ agreed. "Otherwise they'd have to revoke this sweet supervillain lair you've got." The reminder of where they were, and why, crept back into her head. The computer was probably done with the latest round of code. "I should get back to work."

His fingers tightened around hers when she tried to pull free. "Uh-uh. Sleep first."

AJ stifled a yawn and glanced over at the desk. Something flitted at the edge of her brain, like a spasmodic butterfly, but she couldn't quite catch it. There was a familiarity about the code that wouldn't quite reveal itself.

She blinked, and her eyelids were heavy. Maybe if she just took a quick nap, things would make more sense when she looked again. Just twenty minutes, she decided, lifting their linked hands and ducking under his arm, readjusting her body so she could use his shoulder as a makeshift pillow. Twenty minutes, and she'd be good as new.

Shit.

AJ knew before she opened her eyes that something really bad had happened.

She could tell by the warmth of the muscled shoulder that her cheek was pressed against. She could tell by the soft rise and fall of the chest her arm was resting on. And she could definitely tell by the soft blanket that covered her and the man she was suction-cupped to, because that meant that at some point during the night, he'd been completely aware that she was using him as a body pillow.

God. She had one freakin' rule. She slept alone, and all it took was a few nights in his sexy spy den and she'd broken it.

AJ stifled her groan as she attempted to extricate herself from Liam and the couch without waking him up, but by the time she lifted her head, it was too late. Because Liam was already awake.

CHAPTER EIGHTEEN

AJ DIDN'T WANT to kiss him.

No, she corrected, staring down at his gorgeous face. She didn't *want* to want to kiss him.

She swallowed back the claustrophobic tightness that gripped her chest at the threshold she'd just crossed. Fucking someone was one thing, but *sleeping* with him? Sleeping *on* him? That way lay Girlfriend City and Commitment Island. Better to keep things light. That way feelings didn't get mixed up with the hormones.

But here she was.

And in that moment of suspended animation, where everything was still and quiet except the magnified beat of her blood against her pulse points and the synced rasp of their breathing, *want* was everything. The only thing.

Hyperawareness prickled along her skin, focusing her on their bodies—the way her leg rested across his rigid thighs, the softness of his skin and warmth of his chest beneath her hand. Heat pooled in her belly as she gave in to the inevitable and leaned down to press her lips to his.

His hand came up to cradle the back of her head, and something about the restraint of that melted the last of her resolve. She got caught up in it, the slow, hazy magic of the early-morning kissing, touching, unhurriedly pulling each other's clothes off.

"Let's take this upstairs."

AJ shook her head, tamping down panic at his suggestion. The change of location felt too purposeful, too intimate. Couches were spur-of-the-moment. Hormones getting the better of you.

"I need you inside me now," she countered, pulling Liam close.

"There's more room in my bed."

"I'm sure we'll manage just fine."

Relief washed through her when he gave in, kissing her into mindless insensibility as he rolled her onto her back, donned the condom.

Even though she was desperate for him, she let herself savor the preshow, the weight of him, the shift of his back muscles beneath her palms as he settled himself between her legs.

And then he finally slid inside her, and they rocked together in a dreamy buildup of mutual pleasure that was like nothing AJ had ever experienced. She grew restless under his seeking hands and insistent lips, desperate for release.

When she couldn't take it anymore, she pulled her knees up, dragging her heels along the couch so she could dig them into the cushion by his thighs, and Liam grunted in pleasure at the position change.

That was all it took for the sweetness to turn sharp. Liam sped his pace, driving into her with quick, insistent strokes, and AJ clasped him to her, circling her hips until finally, the current sizzled through her, overtook her, and she cried out his name as wave after wave of sensation racked her body.

She pulled Liam close as he joined her in ecstasy.

As she lay there, in his arms, AJ trembled at the realization of what had just happened. The magnitude of it.

Somewhere along the way, she'd let Liam in. The worst thing she could have done, really, considering who she worked for. But it wasn't just Max, she realized. She'd spent the last five years hiding. She stayed under the radar. Worked alone from home as much as possible. Wore layers of black to pass unnoticed. And Liam…he lived his life out loud.

Flashy cars, mansion parties and stylish clothes. He had the kind of bank account and businessman street cred that made sure people took pictures of him when he was out in the world, whether his dates were famous or not. People noticed him. And AJ wasn't looking to be noticed.

They had nothing in common.

"Hey." The sound of his voice startled her. "You're shivering. Come here."

AJ let him pull her closer, let him rearrange the blanket over their bodies. It was stupid, taking comfort from the cause of the problem.

Then the problem tightened his arm around her,

stroked his fingers soothingly against her skin. This was no big deal, she assured herself, stifling a yawn and tucking her head against his shoulder. Just good sex. That's all there was between them. Her eyes drifted shut. Nothing wrong with that.

AJ had no idea how much time had passed when her hard, muscled pillow shifted under her, but judging by her grogginess, it had been a while. She moaned in protest. "S'too early to move."

"Go back to sleep." Despite the whisper, he disentangled their limbs, and her skin grew cold now that they weren't touching anymore. He readjusted the blanket to cover her, and she snuggled in.

"Stay."

"I have to get to work."

"What?" The statement banished all of her sleepy disorientation.

Liam, who was gathering his clothes from the floor, paused in the act to shoot her a questioning look. "I... don't really know how to clarify that any further."

"You're leaving me alone here?" She pushed herself up to a sitting position.

It was one thing for her to feel like something had shifted after what had just happened, but she didn't want him to feel it, too. Not good. Bad, even.

Liam straightened to his full height. "It's not haunted or anything."

"Four days ago, I was persona non grata and you basically stopped going to work so I wouldn't snoop in your stuff," she reminded him.

Remember? she wanted to yell. *How I hacked your party invite and swiped your laptop?*

"I've got a meeting this morning that I couldn't move. I'll be back around noon."

He was honestly going to leave her here. Trust her here.

"I could steal so much stuff by then."

He shrugged. Fucking shrugged! "I mean, you could try, but the house is full of security cameras. I'd definitely catch you."

AJ pulled the blanket up to cover her breasts and anchored it under her arms. "Again with the pervert cams."

Liam rolled his eyes. "They're connected to the security system. They're not on unless I turn them on."

"So say all the amateur porn kingpins."

"Don't sell us short." He surprised her, dropping a quick kiss to her lips. "That felt pretty professional to me. I think we could make it in the big leagues of porn."

She gave him a dirty look, but it had no effect. He remained unrepentant as ever. Just standing there, gorgeously naked, semihard, with his arms full of clothes that she wanted to knock to the ground so she could drag him back on top of her.

His house might not be haunted, but it was terrifying. Because for all the outrage she was mustering, she knew she wasn't going to take anything.

"Whatever. I'm going back to sleep."

She lay back down, made a big production of closing her eyes and getting comfortable, but she watched through her eyelashes as he walked his spectacular naked ass up the stairs.

Pretending to be asleep after he'd disappeared seemed pointless, so she tugged on her clothes, grabbed a room-temp piece of leftover pizza from a box almost buried under Chinese take-out cartons and tried to distract herself with the mysterious junk code.

Might as well run it through the next decoder on her list, even though it was starting to feel futile. She'd already run it through a bunch of code breakers, trying to figure out if it was a taunt, or a signature, or both, but so far, no luck. If she could just find one little clue, something to tie it to someone...

She was still watching the computer churn through its analysis a half hour later when Liam reappeared, freshly showered and shaved, clad in gray pants and a white button-down, his gray vest hanging open. He laid his suit jacket on the arm of the couch and turned to face her with a red tie in one hand, a black tie in the other.

The man was like one of those human evolution posters, a masterpiece in every state between naked and fully clothed.

"Which one of these ties will help me achieve peak pretentious douchebag?"

"The red one. But only if you drive the matching Corvette."

"Consider it done." Liam tossed the black one on the back of the couch, and AJ watched in fascination as he made quick work of fashioning the perfect knot before adjusting his collar and buttoning up his vest. Lethally handsome. A woman could probably die of lust just watching him put on clothes and take them off again.

"So listen, I have this work thing I need to go to. Tonight."

AJ glanced back at the computer screen to check the progress on the deciphering. "I like cats."

"What?" Liam looked up from his vest.

"I thought we were just stating random facts about ourselves."

"I was easing into inviting you to my work thing."

She cocked an eyebrow and pulled her feet off the desk, so she was sitting properly in the chair. "A work thing. Like a company barbecue?"

"It's a *little* fancier than that."

Semantics were never a good sign. "How much fancier?"

"Black tie."

AJ brought a hand to her chest, affecting her poshest accent. "Oh, I'm certain I don't have a thing to wear."

Liam grabbed his suit jacket from the couch and pulled it on. "We can go shopping this afternoon."

Panic reared in her chest, trampling her lungs with a flurry of hoofbeats. She couldn't breathe, couldn't move, couldn't think.

And Liam just stood there, adjusting his cuffs, like everything was normal. After another beat of silence, he looked at her. "You know I'm being serious, right?"

"I had a bad feeling you might be." AJ toyed with the zipper on her hoodie, up, down, up, down. The sound of it sawed away at the conspicuous silence in the room and helped drown out the blood rushing through her ears. "I don't really do parties. Or crowds. That sounds more like supermodel socialite time."

"Except I know that's a deflection, because we met at a party. And I didn't invite a supermodel socialite. Because I want to take you. So say yes."

He meant it.

Something in her chest loosened, as though her resistance had grown brittle and splintered apart. As though what had happened between them that morning had changed things. As though fear's mighty fist wasn't lodged in her chest anymore. Free.

"If I say yes, will you stop pestering me?"

"You know what the best thing is?" Liam shifted his shoulders and buttoned the top button of his suit jacket. "Your excitement makes me even more excited."

AJ's smile seeped out against her will. "I said I'd go. You didn't stipulate I had to like it."

"This is why I have lawyers go over all my contracts. I'm garbage with minutiae." He glanced at his watch. "I have to get to my meeting."

"Okay." She got to her feet, rounded the desk. "I'm gonna shower, and then I'll just keep trawling the depths. See if I can connect this code with anyone active on the dark web."

"You know that makes you sound cool as hell, right? Text me if you get a hit?"

"Yeah, sure. Have a good day at work." The words were out before she realized she'd said them, and the domesticity gave her some serious icks. She needed to get the hell out of the vortex before she did something insane, like kiss him goodbye. She tried to walk by him. Thought she'd made it, too.

"Hey, wait a minute."

"I've got stuff to do," she countered, but Liam caught her fingers in his.

"I'll be quick," he promised, and tugged her close, then closer still. She clutched his lapel like some golden age movie heroine as he claimed her mouth, slanting his lips over hers. The contact jolted along her nerve endings, pulling a low, desperate sound from the back of her throat, and Liam responded with one of his own as he licked into her mouth, ratcheting the kiss up another level. Suddenly she didn't want to let him go.

The thought was scary enough to make her pull back, and as she stood there in the circle of his arms, trying desperately to catch her breath, the look on his face did nothing to ease the prickle at the base of her neck. Because the way he was looking at her made her think that maybe he didn't want to let her go, either.

"I'll see you later."

She stood there, stock still, and for the second time that morning, watched him until he'd disappeared up the stairs. When she heard him close the door, AJ took what felt like her first normal breath since she'd woken up in the middle of the night, plastered against Liam's big, hard body.

Focus.

She needed to concentrate on this mystery code, and not think about Liam, or his fancy suits, or his magic kisses, or his hard parts. That decided, she headed back to code-breaking.

But, she supposed, first she should probably google "black tie" and see just what kind of trouble she'd signed up for.

CHAPTER NINETEEN

Rodeo. Fucking. Drive.

She should have known.

"You're joking, right?"

"I have to pick up my tuxedo right over there."

AJ didn't bother to look where he pointed. She was too busy staring down the store in front of her. She tugged the cuffs of her hoodie out from under her leather jacket, so that they covered the heels of her hands.

"I'll be right back."

She nodded distractedly, vaguely aware of the knot of snakes forming in her stomach. After several more minutes of psyching herself out, and then up, AJ set her shoulders and strode purposefully toward the door.

You can get further than you think just by acting like you belong. One of the first rules of running a successful con. Apparently, it didn't apply to posh stores with pinch-faced women in uncomfortable shoes who hadn't ingested carbs in the last decade.

The closest harpy swooped in before she'd made it to one of the racks. AJ did not miss the cool once-over, or how it lingered on her boots.

"Can I help you?"

"Just looking right now," AJ informed her, feinting left before passing her on the right. Cautiously, she approached a shimmery silver gown displayed to perfection on one of the faceless, avant-garde mannequins at the center of the shop. It was gorgeous, like liquid metal. Strapless. Strong. Sexy.

"That's very expensive," her new shadow cautioned.

"I assumed." AJ turned to face her, thumbing at the dress. "Do you have anything like this in black?"

The blonde's eyes hardened. "Perhaps I didn't make myself clear."

"Oh, no. You did." AJ walked farther into the store, stopping beside a long, floaty black number with kind of a rhinestone shoulder holster thing at the top. Well, probably not rhinestones. Swarovski crystals or something.

When she reached out to touch it, the woman made a strangled sound deep in her throat, so AJ followed through, just to be a pain in the ass, sliding her finger along the jewels. "Quality craftsmanship," she said. "I'll give it a try."

"Ma'am, I really must ask you to refrain from…" Her voice trailed off, and her glower turned into wide-eyed astonishment. "Good afternoon, sir. I'm Ashley. May I hang that up at the counter for you while you look around?" she asked, plowing past AJ with the force of a heat-seeking missile.

The analogy proved even more accurate when AJ turned to see the object of her attention. Liam surrendered his garment bag, scanning the boutique, as though unaware that every woman in the store had turned to ogle him. His eyes stopped on her, and AJ ignored the hit of pride and lust that swirled in her blood as he started toward her. She was not unaware of the surprised looks that accompanied his approach.

"How's it going?"

"Better now." AJ shot him a flirty once-over before grabbing his tie and tugging him close. She ignored the questioning raise of his eyebrows right before she indulged in a soft, slow, vaguely-inappropriate-for-public-consumption kiss.

"What is happening right now?" There was a rasp in his voice that hadn't been there in his previous question. His hand had come to rest on her hip during the tongue-wrestle, and now his index finger slipped under the hem of her hoodie and moved upward until he found skin.

AJ leaned close to his ear. "Revenge."

For the sake of their audience, she let a saccharine smile drift across her lips as she pulled back and fiddled with his tie like she gave a shit about wrinkles, or crookedness, or whatever television housewives were trying to fix when they did this.

Her little helper reappeared at AJ's side. "I was just assisting your...uh, we were just picking the perfect gown. Is there anything in particular you'd like to see her in?"

A different, non-Liam-related heat worked its way through AJ's veins as she turned on the blonde. "I've been picking out my own clothes since I was eight years old, so I think I've got this under control without him. If you could just get me the dress I already told you I wanted to try on, that would be awesome." AJ soaked up the eye daggers being shot her way like a power source. "Or perhaps I didn't make myself clear."

A faint buzz interrupted their glare-off, and they both turned as Liam reached into his suit and produced his phone. "If you'll excuse me for a moment, ladies, I need to take this."

Liam greeted the caller as he stepped away to take care of business.

With a pouty look on her face, Ashley reached for the dress, but at the last second, AJ stopped her. "You know what? I changed my mind. I think I'll try on the silver one instead. And I'll need some shoes, too."

"Of course, ma'am. Right away."

AJ did not miss the snide tone of voice. She was grinning as she followed Ashley to the dressing rooms. Shopping was not nearly as bad as she'd remembered it.

AJ stared at the incongruous sight of herself in the slinky silver dress. It was…a lot. Like something a femme fatale in a spy movie might wear to kill a pervy head of state with her poisoned lipstick. Which, if she was being honest, made her like it even more.

She grabbed her phone from her jacket, which she'd abandoned on the fancy antique-looking chair in the corner of the dressing room with her jeans and shirt and bra, and sent a quick text. Three letters. SOS.

She tucked her phone back in her pocket and stared at herself in the mirror. Front. Side. Front again. Over her shoulder.

"AJ?"

Liam's voice startled her from her inspection, and she shoved her curls back from her face and took a deep breath. "Here."

She shoved her hand through the split in the heavy velvet and beckoned him over.

"What's the emergency?" he asked from the other side of the curtain.

"Get in here," she whispered. She hoped it sounded insistent, rather than panicked.

After a moment in which she assumed he was waiting for the coast to clear, he ducked into the dressing room.

"Is this okay for tonight? Or is it way too much? You said you're wearing a tux, right?"

He stared at her. And stared at her. And stared some more.

The cubicle, which had seemed rather spacious before Liam's arrival, suddenly felt like it was shrinking. She grew antsy as she waited for the verdict.

"Well?"

"Holy shit."

She tried to look at herself in the mirror, but he blocked it completely from her view. "What?"

"I was expecting black."

AJ's eyes widened as she looked down at herself. Maybe she should have—

"This is better."

She glanced up. "Yeah?"

His gaze roamed over her, and her nipples tightened in response. It was very inconvenient.

"You shouldn't hide all that from the world."

There was too much sincerity in his voice. It made her cheeks hot and tugged her focus to anything but his eyes. "Boob man, huh? Should have guessed by your bevy of interchangeable tabloid beauties."

"I'm not talking about your boobs. I'm talking about you."

She risked a glance at him, and what she saw turned her knees spongy. Lust, yes, but something else gleamed in the depths of his hazel eyes, and when she recognized it, her brain got hot, like emotion was short-circuiting her motherboard. "Don't look at me like that."

"Like what?" he asked, his voice low. "Like you're so fucking gorgeous that I'm going to have to keep my jacket buttoned all night?"

She shook her head, and her tongue darted out in an attempt to moisten her lips even though her mouth was dry. "Like you're proud of me. It's just a dress."

"It's a hell of a dress," Liam countered, "but that's not why I'm proud of you."

Don't ask. "Then why?"

"Because you stood up for yourself against what's-her-name. Because you chose a dress that wasn't black. Because you're out in the world with me."

The reasons hit with devastating precision, as though someone had fed him a script of the most perfect things to say. It was as though he knew how much she wanted to blend into the shadows where things were comfortable, but also how much she'd missed the light.

"I'm glad you said yes."

"Oh, yeah?"

His eyes lowered to half-mast as she stepped close. "AJ..."

It sounded kind of like a warning, but she ignored it.

"How glad?"

He swooped in and captured her lips, walking her backward until she was pressed against the wall that divided her cubicle from the one beside it. He braced a hand against the fancy embossed wallpaper on either side of her head, licking into her mouth, and she savored the taste of him, the mastery of his tongue, as she picked his pocket, liberating the condom from his leather billfold before tucking it back into his suit jacket.

They were both panting as he broke the kiss. He glanced down as she ripped open the foil, then back up at her. Connection crackled in the air between them, high voltage, like always. Maintaining eye contact, AJ grabbed him by the waistband of his pants and pulled him a step closer. Liam obliged her, pressing his forearms against the wall instead of his hands, cutting the distance between their bodies as she undid his pants.

The sounds from outside the dressing room seemed muted and far away compared to the beat of her heart and the rasp of her breath. Still, the rise and fall of conversation, the clop of high heels against polished wood floors, the metallic scrape of curtain rings on metal rods, all danced around the edge of her consciousness, ratcheting up her need as she freed him from his underwear. He was hot and hard in her hand, and his stifled groan as she wrapped her fingers around his pulsing cock sent heat rushing through her.

This was what she craved. Danger. Excitement.

Risky, dirty sex in a dressing room with a man who fucked like he was born to do it.

This morning had been an anomaly. It didn't mean anything except that she was horny and he was willing. Sex hormones masquerading as feelings. A little weirdness because she hadn't spent a whole night with another human being in years.

But now, things were back to normal. Or at least they would be, she decided, working the condom down the length of his shaft with a long, slow stroke that made his breath catch in his throat.

Liam dragged his hands down the wall on either side of her body, close, but not touching her. Anticipation made her restless, and she shifted her shoulder blades against the wall. When his fingers finally brushed against the flare of her hips, her breath came out in a rush. Leaning his forehead against hers, Liam inched the expensive material up, then up some more, so that it bunched around her waist. The tight fit around her hips loosened as the thigh-high slit finally reached waist level. He took quick advantage of the newly provided access, tugging her panties far enough down her thighs that gravity took over.

And then she was wrapping her arms around his neck and he was lifting her up his body, bracing her between him and the wall as she wrapped her legs around him. The first rock of his hips, the intense friction of his cock between her legs, sent pleasure spiraling through her. His breath unleashed a wave of goose bumps against her neck, and the deliciously slow grind of their bodies had her all keyed up. But it wasn't enough. She reached between them to reposition him, and she gasped when he slid inside her.

Liam caught the sound with his mouth, and she was lost. In his kiss, in the drive of his hips, in the pressure building between her legs. She didn't understand this thing between them, how he could turn her on, light her up, with so little effort. It might have pissed her off, the power he had, if he wasn't right there with her, on the brink of sanity.

"Are you doing okay in there?"

They froze at the sound of Ashley's bored voice, a mere black velvet panel away, eyes wide as they stared at each other.

"Hello?"

Oh, sure. *Now* she was going for salesperson of the year?

"Um, yeah." It was a bit strained. AJ cleared her throat and tried again. "Yep. Fine."

"Just fine?" Liam whispered, and she shot him a warning look—the one that said *shut the hell up.*

"It fits okay?"

Liam raised his brows as if seconding the question, but before AJ could roll her eyes, which was no more than he deserved, he canted his hips, unleashing a shock wave of electrical pulses deep in her belly.

AJ bit back a moan. She wanted to come so bad. "I'm good." AJ tightened her ankles, her heels digging into his ass, pressing him closer. At least she would be soon.

"Okay."

God, why wouldn't Blondie leave already so Liam could finish what he'd started here and put them both out of such exquisite misery?

"I just thought it might be a little small."

AJ ignored the implied insult, distracted by Liam's cocky smirk. She glared at him. "It's adequate."

He flexed his hips, driving slow and deep, a refutation of her understatement, and AJ almost lost her grip on his shoulders at the overwhelming sensation.

I hate you, she mouthed.

Liam leaned close, flattening her aching breasts against his chest, ramping up the level of her need. Every part of her was on fire for him. "Liar," he whispered, before nipping her earlobe.

"I'll be done in here in just a minute," AJ managed.

Liam thrust again. Again.

Thirty seconds, she revised.

"Whatever. I'll be out front."

AJ attacked his mouth with a desperation she couldn't understand, let alone control. His left hand tightened against the back of her thigh, his fingers digging into her skin, and she writhed against him as he sped the pace of his hips.

Then suddenly, his right hand was between them, and his thumb circled her clit and she imploded, her orgasm flashing through her like heat lightning, sparking through her veins. Liam's hips jerked, and he kissed her harder, muffling his groan against her mouth as his cock pulsed deep inside her.

She was trembling as she unhooked her legs from around his waist and found her footing. Liam didn't let her go right away, as though he, too, didn't quite trust himself to stand without support.

AJ sucked air into her lungs and let her heart rate even out. She tugged the silver material back down her hips as Liam straightened up, taking care of his own situation.

Somebody walked past the dressing room, and AJ waited until the sound of footsteps faded into the distance before she spoke. "So, I think I'll get the dress."

His grin was downright rakish. "Well, it obviously has my vote."

"You'd vote for a paper bag if it made my boobs look this good."

"If you think the only reason you just got fucked to within an inch of both our lives in a fitting room is because your boobs look great, then you're not giving yourself enough credit. And if you think all it takes to make me risk my business reputation with a scandalous charge of lewd conduct in a public place is great boobs, then you're not giving me enough credit."

And on that incredible confession, he lifted her chin with a finger and took her mouth in the softest, most sensual open-mouth-but-no-tongue kiss she'd ever experienced.

She wanted to make out with him until they both died from lack of oxygen.

Sadly, Liam pulled back before that became a viable option.

"I'll wait for you out there." He moved the edge of the curtain ever so slightly to check if the coast was clear, and a moment later, he ducked out of the dressing room. When he was gone, AJ leaned back against the wall and closed her eyes.

What had he said when he'd first seen her in the dress? Holy shit?

Yeah, she seconded that.

CHAPTER TWENTY

"YOUR LIFE IS RIDICULOUS. You know that, right?"

He exchanged the key to the Aston Martin for a valet ticket and tucked it into the interior pocket of his tux. Liam let his eyes wander over her profile, while she stared at the formidable Bel Air mansion before them.

She'd worn her hair down. Her makeup was minimal, though her eyes seemed more defined than usual and her lips seemed shinier. The dress, well, the dress set her off to perfection.

"It looks pretty good from where I'm standing," he countered before extending his arm.

Her startled smile was pleased as she accepted his elbow. He liked surprising her, knocking through her cynicism and witnessing glimpses of her enjoying herself. She'd been through a lot, trauma he couldn't even begin to understand, and her strength and resilience was incredible.

"Ready?"

"As I'll ever be," she returned, and they started up the lantern-lit walkway. Two liveried doormen pulled open the imposing wooden doors as they approached, and classical music spilled out into the night.

AJ's gaze drifted up to the ornate chandelier above them as they stepped into the marble-tiled foyer. An efficient-looking woman with a wide smile approached them. "Mr. Kearney. Welcome. The Mitfords are so happy you could make it. If you and your date will follow me, I'll take you to the ballroom."

"Pretentious much?" AJ muttered under her breath, and he smirked at her as they followed their guide down the cream-and-gilt hallway. "Who lives like this?"

He leaned closer, lowering his voice. "Just your run-of-the-mill rich guy and his wife."

"Are you sure they didn't die in 1842, and now they're trapped in this creepy Victorian fun house? I mean, this place has evil written all over it. Everything's so...*gold*, and I think the naked angel babies are staring at us."

Liam glanced at the cherubs on the closest wall sconce and couldn't dispute AJ's theory.

"It's like a horror movie."

Liam chuckled. "I'm glad you're having a good time."

"Oh, no way. A fancy gold freakhouse doesn't count as showing me a good time. I dropped nine grand on this outfit, and these shoes already hurt my feet." She gave a dismissive flick of her wrist to signify their opulent surroundings. "You're going to have to do way better than this."

"I offered to buy the dress."

"First of all, I don't need your charity. I'm fucking good at what I do, and I make sure I'm paid accordingly. And second, the price tag was almost worth the look on Ashley's face when I pulled out my credit card."

Before Liam could comment on that, their guide turned that overly bright smile back on them. "Here we are. Please enjoy yourselves. The balcony is through the French doors near the stage. Facilities can be found at the end of the hallway that's through the doors near the bar."

Liam nodded his thanks to the woman before ushering AJ inside the impressive room with vaulted ceilings. Waitstaff circulated with large silver trays of champagne and hors d'oeuvres. The stage, currently hosting the piano trio responsible for the classical music soundtrack of the evening, and the aforementioned bar dominated either end of the space. In the middle, men in tuxedos and women in gowns of all colors mingled, danced and imbibed.

"So this is how the one percent get their freak on, huh?"

Liam grinned at her observation, but it faded when he caught sight of their hostess for the evening, issuing orders to one of the waitstaff while her husband, Henry Mitford, laughed genially with a couple to her left. Though Liam's step didn't falter, all his muscles drew tight.

AJ's fingers flexed against his forearm. "Hey, you okay?" she asked.

The fact that she'd noticed his change in demeanor brought him back. "Yeah. I'm good. Just a little busi-

ness to get through before we get on with the night.
Let me introduce you to our hosts."

Their hostess finished up with the waiter as they
approached.

The smile she donned as she turned to greet them
turned brittle as recognition set in. "Liam. You came."

"I did." He tipped his head in a mockery of a bow.
"Sorry to disappoint you. AJ, I'd like you to meet Cynthia Mitford…"

AJ had already put on her best party smile and was
in the act of extending her hand when Liam gave in to
the perverse whim and added, "My mother."

AJ jerked her hand back, which made him want
to drag her off into a dark corner and kiss her senseless, but his mother didn't even notice the slight as she
turned to make sure that her husband was still otherwise engaged before her razor-sharp gaze cut toward
him. He assumed, if she weren't Botoxed to the level
of marble, she would be frowning at him.

"If Henry had heard that, I would never have for-
given you," she spat.

"My sincere apologies. I keep mixing up which one
of us it is who should be seeking forgiveness in this
relationship."

She stole another furtive glance at Mitford before
unleashing a very cold and unwelcoming "Why did
you come?"

"The same reason you invited me in the first place.
Appearances."

"You could have declined."

AJ's fingers dug into his arm almost painfully, as

though his flesh was the only thing keeping her from forming a fist, and he appreciated the way it stole some of his focus.

"I could have, but what would your husband think if I did? He's been begging me to attend one of these soirees of yours all year. And speak of the devil."

His mother's retort, whatever it might have been, withered on her tongue as she fixed her thin mouth into a practiced smile. The effortless transition to perfect wife was almost impressive.

"Kearney! Glad you could make it." The welcome held genuine warmth, and it made his mother's frosty greeting sting more in retrospect than it had in the moment.

"Henry." He accepted the man's hearty handshake. "I was just thanking your wife for the gracious invitation. I'd like to introduce my date. This is AJ."

"A pleasure, to be sure." Henry shook her hand as well. "What do you do, AJ?"

"Well, my socialite-ing keeps me very busy."

Liam watched in awe as she leaned conspiratorially toward the woman beside her.

"You know how it is, right, Cynthia? Barely enough time left in the day to take care of the little ones, what with all the rich-people things going on."

His mother turned deathly white.

Unaware of the subtext, Henry tried desperately to right the sinking ship. "Oh, how lovely. You have children?"

"God, no," AJ replied as she plucked a flute of champagne off the tray of a passing waiter. "I do a lot of supermodeling on the weekends, so pregnancy isn't really on my list of to-dos right now."

Henry's bushy eyebrows drew into a confused frown. "I thought you just said—"

"Cats," Liam interjected. "AJ likes cats."

AJ's dark eyes sparkled at his save, and to his surprise, his chest loosened a bit.

"I do. They're much easier to deal with than humans, don't you think? Besides, there are so many kids in the world who are just abandoned on doorsteps, left to fend for themselves. It's really tragic. I don't plan on having children until I'm responsible enough to take care of them."

Cynthia's mouth twisted sourly.

Henry looked like a man adrift at sea with no clue what to grab for buoyancy. "So, you're a model?"

"Actually," Liam cut in, taking pity on the man, "AJ is a brilliant forensic hacker. If you hear of anyone in the market for a top-notch security consultant, put them in touch with me."

"Of course." Henry's smile cleared now that they were on a page that made sense to him. "Well, now, I'm not surprised to hear that. I'll bet being high-tech helps you keep up with this guy."

AJ took a sip of her drink. "You'd think, right? But the truth is, I'm way ahead of him. Liam's actually a huge aficionado of old-timey stuff. Bank vaults. Vests. Newspapers."

"Newspapers? Really, Kearney? I'm surprised to hear it."

"My grandfather used to read the Sunday *Times*

without fail." His mother's shoulders stiffened at the recollection. "I like to keep up the tradition."

"What a great memory." Henry patted his wife's hand, which was perched on his forearm. Her knuckles were white. "Cynthia and I believe very strongly in family."

"I'll bet you do." Even to his own ears, Liam's voice sounded sharp, like the edge of a knife. It was in direct opposition to the light, personable tone he usually struck at gatherings like this one.

A light smattering of applause filled the room as the current concerto drew to a close.

He wasn't sure why he'd gotten so defensive. He'd been to dozens of parties with Cynthia and Henry over the years and never cared much one way or the other, just exchanged a couple of stiff formal pleasantries with Cynthia if they met head-on and couldn't avoid it. And while they'd been running into each other more and more frequently since Henry had set his sights on becoming a subcontractor for Cybercore, this marked the first time Liam had let his resentment bubble to the surface.

The first time he'd mentioned anything as personal as his grandfather.

He supposed it had something to do with the fact that he'd never had a champion fighting in his corner before.

As if on cue, AJ leaped back into the breach as the piano started up again, shooting him a syrupy smile that was completely out of character.

"Liam, did you do this?" Before he had to figure

out what she meant, she turned to their host. "They're playing our song. Isn't that romantic? Sorry to steal him away from you like this, Henry, but this guy promised me a dance tonight, and I aim to collect."

By the time the violin and cello joined in, it was all Liam could do to tamp down his grin.

"Mozart's Piano Trio in G Major is your song?" his mother asked, words dripping in acid.

"What can I say? I'm super classy like that. Take care of this for me, would you, Cynthia?" AJ thrust the champagne flute into his mother's hand before grabbing Liam's elbow.

"We'll talk Monday, Henry," Liam assured him as he let AJ extract him from the farce that had just played out. She didn't stop until they'd cleared the French doors by the stage and made their way out onto the balcony. There were a dozen or so people milling about, so they ducked around a corner, using a huge potted plant as a shield.

Even in the shadows, Liam could see that her eyes flashed with ire.

"Just a rich guy and his wife, huh? You might have warned me." She gave the bodice of her dress a sharp upward tug, like she was adjusting her armor, as she paced back and forth, two steps south, two steps north. "You know my inner bitch gets rowdy when shit like that gets sprung on her."

"Hey." Liam reached out and touched her arm. She stopped, but when she looked up at him, all her agitation and anger faded into something so deep and sincere that it almost brought him to his knees.

"God, I hate what she did to you."

He was overwhelmed with emotion. His throat constricted with it. "You're fucking amazing. Do you know that?"

Without waiting for an answer, he pulled her into his arms and kissed her.

With gratitude. With hunger.

She wrapped her arms around his neck, and memories of their afternoon tryst ignited beneath his skin. Liam let the scent of her, the taste of her, the feel of her, drive all the other shit from his mind.

CHAPTER TWENTY-ONE

THEY'D ALREADY HAD sex twice that day, and still AJ's body seemed happy to gear up for round three. When she finally pulled away, it was because she needed oxygen, not because she wanted to.

His eyes were dark with passion, and her heart rate accelerated at the roguish intentions she could read in their depths. He wanted her, just like he had in the dressing room. Just like he had that morning, on the couch. He wanted her beyond reason—she knew because she felt the same.

"This can't happen here." Liam's voice held a note of regret as he reached up to cup her jaw in his palm.

"I know."

His thumb stroked her cheekbone. "I can't wait to take you home."

The words, the softness of his touch—it knocked the breath from her lungs. *Home.* He said it casually. Simply. Like she belonged there, too. No one had ever taken her home before. She'd never let them.

She wanted to let Liam, though, and it was...terrifying. Too close. He kept getting under her armor, kept taking control she couldn't afford to give up. This was exactly why she should never have let what happened on the couch that morning happen. "Why wait?" she asked, directing the action the way it should be going. The way she needed it to go. "I mean, we've already proven the dress can take it."

He raised his eyebrows, but it wasn't an outright no, so she laced her fingers through his and tugged on his hand. He let her pull him forward a step.

"It's my understanding there are some *facilities* that might be perfect for our wicked intentions through the set of French doors near the bar."

She loved his attempt to look vaguely disapproving even though he was just as turned on as she was. "You want to fuck in the bathroom?" he clarified.

"Sure. I'll bet it's all decked out in gold and marble or some shit. It's probably nicer than my place."

He took a step back and tugged her with him.

"I wouldn't know. You haven't invited me over." He kissed her, nipped her bottom lip.

AJ laughed. "Oh, so that's how it's gonna be, is it? I didn't liberate you from that ballroom so you could give me a hard time, you know."

"Really?" Liam turned her and pressed her back against the wall, nudging her with his hips. "I thought that's exactly why you brought me out here."

She moaned low in her throat as their lips met, dragging her under as another wave of desire overtook them. She could drown in him and not even care. AJ had never known anything like it. His hand drifted up her side, and when he palmed her breast, she thought her knees might give out.

They were both panting by the time Liam lifted his head again.

"I'm not wearing underwear."

Liam's eyes flared at the announcement. "Where did you say that bathroom was again?"

AJ grabbed his hand and sent him a naughty smile over her shoulder, intending to set a new land speed record as she dragged him through the party. The second they rounded the giant plant they'd been using for cover, though, she collided with another partygoer. The collision knocked her off balance and she yanked her hand free of Liam's so she could grab the man in front of her. His strong hands steadied her, closing around her upper arms.

"Shit. Sorry," AJ muttered, clutching his lapels as she tried to regain her footing on her stupid strappy heels. The buckle of one seemed caught in the hem of her dress, and she kicked her foot a few times, trying to get it free.

"AJ?"

The sound of her name, the familiarity of the voice, the tightening of the man's fingers against her arms; it all combined to send a foreboding shiver skittering down her spine.

It took everything she had to raise her eyes, to confirm the one thing she didn't want confirmed.

"Max."

She yanked her hands back from his jacket.

He let go of her arms just as quickly, but his amber

eyes swirled with questions, and their eye contact wasn't as easy to break. At least not until something behind her distracted him, and his gaze shifted over her left shoulder.

AJ didn't have to wonder what had caught his attention. The air buzzed as Liam stepped closer to her, that low hum of awareness between them still strong, even in the chaos.

"Are you okay?" Liam asked, and she managed the barest hint of a nod as his hand came to rest at the small of her back. But she couldn't bring herself to look away from her boss.

Max's jaw tightened and his gaze cut back to hers. "What the fuck are you doing with him?"

It wasn't the question she'd been expecting. Not from Max. It had heat, and Max was known for his icy control. His poker face was legendary, and the fact that he was so angry that he hadn't even bothered to mask it proved that AJ's actions had cut deep. Like a knife to the back, judging by the accusation in Max's leonine eyes.

Max's girlfriend, Emma, stepped forward, blond hair in an intricate updo, looking downright stunning in a green dress with short sleeves and a plunging neckline.

AJ had never met her. Not officially, though she knew her pretty intimately if you factored in the extensive spying and background check she'd done on the woman back when she'd been the number one suspect in the hack on Whitfield Industries.

Emma twined her fingers with Max's before

placing her other hand on his biceps and giving it a squeeze. The action drew his attention, and Emma gave a subtle chin tip toward their growing audience on the balcony. The animosity between Max and Liam was hardly a secret, and the fact that neither of them had addressed its origin story meant that it had become the stuff of legend among a certain crowd of people. And a lot of those people were in attendance tonight and trying very hard to look like they weren't paying attention to the altercation unfolding—and failing miserably.

At the reminder that they were in public, Max's impermeable mask slipped back into place, and Emma smiled brightly.

"AJ. It's nice to finally meet you. Max has told me wonderful things."

AJ got the feeling the introduction was more a reminder to Max than a compliment for her, but she liked the *stand by your man* vibe of it.

She accepted Emma's hand. "Yeah, he likes you a lot, too," she said, but her attention remained on Max. He was giving her nothing. Ice cold. Guilt swirled in her chest and dread reared in her belly, colliding near her heart in a weird, torso-centric case of vertigo. She'd hurt the only person in her life who'd ever given her a chance. She'd hurt him in the worst possible way. Betrayal. It was the one thing Max would never forgive her for. Not after what had happened with his father. Charles Whitfield's duplicity had almost ruined Max. And now she was no better.

AJ was only vaguely aware that Liam and Emma

were now shaking hands. Keeping up appearances. A twisted version of real life where the two men AJ cared about most in the world had to play nice because she'd gotten carried away by her hormones and made a huge mistake.

She'd let herself get caught up in Liam's version of life, this facade of a place where everything was beautiful and decadent, and although the hyper glamour and casual riches weren't exactly real life, there was something…nice about being out in the world again. Finding pieces of herself she'd thought long dead. She'd been seduced by pretending she was something she wasn't. And now they were all paying penance for her fantasy.

"Max, I—"

He shook his head, and though he kept his voice low enough to foil any eavesdroppers, the words still struck like lashes on AJ's skin. "You know what he did to John Beckett. How that affected Aidan. How it affected me."

Liam's voice was tight. "I bought information that was offered to me."

Max spared him the barest glance. "I have nothing to say to you."

"You seem to have something to say about me, though, and I'm not going to stand here while you assassinate my character in front of AJ."

"She deserves better than you, Kearney. All I'm doing is stating facts, and if your character can't withstand the truth, maybe that's something AJ should be aware of."

"Stop it. Both of you. Don't talk around me like I'm not here. I don't need either of you deciding things for me. I make my own choices."

Max's gaze slid to Liam, then back to AJ. "Obviously you do."

Before AJ had recovered from that, his eyes turned hot with rage. "I swear to God, AJ. If I find out you're the one who hacked me..."

"Watch it, Whitfield."

Liam stepped forward, coming to her defense, and for a second, AJ thought they might actually trade blows, but Max iced over again. "I wouldn't give you the satisfaction. If you'll excuse us." He and Emma headed for the French doors that led to the main ball-room.

"Max, wait." AJ hadn't managed a full step before Liam caught her hand.

She looked down at their fingers before meeting his eyes again.

"AJ..."

She knew what he was asking. He wanted her to choose him. To stay. To take a chance on the unknown.

But the unknown had never been good to AJ.

Max represented the status quo. Safety. She knew how to live this life, the one she'd painstakingly cobbled together so the pieces wouldn't shatter out from underneath her again.

She looked at Liam, willing him to understand. "I have to. I owe him an explanation."

AJ tugged her hand free, and the second she did, it was like the tentative thing between them, whatever it was, whatever it might become, cracked in two. She saw it in Liam's eyes.

A sense of loss that she hadn't let herself feel in a really long time started to well in her chest, but she pushed it down through sheer force of will. It helped when she turned away from Liam. It helped more when she hurried toward the doors that led into the ballroom. Distance. Distance always helped.

She scanned the ornate room, catching sight of a woman in a green dress and a raven-haired man heading toward the front entrance.

AJ dodged through the hoity-toity crowd as best she could in her silver gown, desperate to catch up to her boss, to explain, to erase the look of betrayal that had crossed his face when he'd seen who she was with.

The doorman dragged an ornate door out of her way, and AJ skidded to a halt on her stilettos outside, but it was too late. The valet was already stepping away from the vehicle Max used for business and personal events alike.

She called his name, a last-ditch effort that proved fruitless as the sleek black town car pulled away.

Liam leaned against the stone balustrade, staring down at the pool. He hated this fucking house, though he'd never been inside it before. He'd thought seeing it as an adult might make it more palatable, overwrite his teenage memories of the way Cynthia had looked down her nose at him when he'd rung the doorbell, when she'd chosen Henry Mitford and handed him that goddamn check as a parting gift.

For the first time since she'd walked out on him, Liam wished he'd given Cynthia exactly what she wanted and declined the invitation to the party.

In this case, it seemed, Mother really did know best. The irony wasn't lost on him.

He should never have brought AJ here, although he supposed there was no more fitting location for her to choose Max over him.

"Hey."

As if her name had conjured her, she appeared beside him. Despite everything, his body stirred at the sight of her, clad in silver.

"Hey."

"I'm… I had to take care of that. I had to try."

"Sure."

The word came out a little testier than he'd intended, and he felt her grow tense beside him, saw the way she set her chin in defiance.

"What, are you jealous? He's my boss, Liam. And my friend, okay? The only one I have." Her bluster faded when she exhaled. "Max believed in me and gave me a chance when most people would have turned me in. He fronted me the money to take Troy to court. He gave me a life. And I owe him."

"Bullshit!"

AJ flinched at the anger in Liam's voice, but he couldn't help it.

"Stop selling yourself short, okay? You don't owe him anything. Do you understand how good you are at what you do? Max is a lot of things, not all of them complimentary, but one thing he's not is stupid. He recognized your talent, and he did what any good businessman would do—he hired you. He didn't put Troy in jail—you did that." Liam raked his hand through his hair. "You say Max gave you back your life. But what kind of life is it?"

She glared at him. "Stop making it sound like I'm a prisoner. Max doesn't keep me under lock and key."

"I didn't say he was the problem."

The words detonated. AJ looked shocked by the force of them, but Liam couldn't stop.

"You run and you hide. And Max is just one more way for you to stay where you're comfortable. You do just enough to convince yourself you're doing okay, and he lets you. He doesn't challenge you. And you know why? Because unlike you, he's got a real fucking life!"

"What the hell is that supposed to mean?"

"It means that he's running a company. He's dating Emma. He's spending time with his sister, attending parties, being out in the world." Frustrated, Liam pulled a hand down his face. "Look, I honestly don't give a shit if you're friends with Max. I'm just saying that you can't keep acting like he's the only thing in your life, because you're sure as hell not the only thing in his!"

They stood in the shadows, together and miles apart.

"I'm leaving."

"Of course you are. Just like always. Serves me right for falling for a woman who equates closeness with hostage situations."

She rounded on him, eyes bright with fury. "Fuck you."

"Fuck me?" Liam laughed. "Jesus, AJ. You won't even do that unless you're sure there's an escape hatch. I have to beg you to be in public with me. And even then you've always got one eye on the door, so you can run before things get too real."

"Oh, that's something coming from you! You want to keep things real, Liam? Real like throwing lavish, glittering parties that you hate? Real like the playboy reputation you cultivated by serial dating models who mean nothing to you? Just because you hide in plain sight doesn't mean you're not hiding."

Liam frowned at the accusation, watching as she crouched down, lifting the hem of her silver gown enough to expose one of her strappy shoes. After a couple of tugs, the buckle came loose, and she kicked it off, before doing the same thing with her other shoe.

She grabbed them both in one hand before she straightened up to her full height, three inches shorter than a moment ago, and yet more formidable for it.

"Did you ever think that maybe the reason I'm always looking for the exit is because you keep trying to lock me in? Yachts, and gated mansions, and security fences. Everything you have, everything you build, is to keep people from leaving like your mom did. But none of it's going to make me stay."

It was a debilitating punch. The kind that bruised deep and made it hard to breathe. But AJ wasn't quite done with him yet.

"And just so we're clear, this isn't me running. This is me walking the fuck out."

As far as parting shots went, it was a knockout. But going down for the count wouldn't hurt enough, so Liam made himself stand there and watch her leave.

CHAPTER TWENTY-TWO

AJ STARED OUT the window of her condo at the concrete jungle below, watching cars glide by, people scurrying around. People living their lives as though the world hadn't tipped off its axis a week and a half ago. Like nothing had changed.

But everything had changed.

She couldn't sleep. Barely ate. And there was a dull ache in her chest, like a piece had been ripped out. She'd let her guard down a little, and now she couldn't get it back up.

Work, she decided. Work always focused her, keeping the thoughts she didn't want to deal with at bay.

AJ got up and pulled the phones out of her safe. The ones Max had given her because they contained Cybercore spyware, which had been the reason Liam's name had jumped to the top of the suspect list in the first place. Without these phones, she would never have ended up in Liam's mansion, in Liam's office, in Liam's bedroom.

Her heart cracked a little at the thought, as though there was a jagged fault line down the middle of it, but she ignored the fissure. She needed to keep her mind occupied. Focus on the code.

Grabbing the phones Max had asked her to look into, she set them in front of her on her desk. As she always did when approaching a forensic hack, she took a moment to lay out the facts as she knew them.

On the left, the silver phone that Aidan Beckett had purchased from Liam with the intent of spying on Whitfield Industries. The Cybercore-issued phone contained Liam's impressive spyware, the same program she'd tweaked and tried to use on the man himself the night she'd crashed his party. Aidan had used it to remotely install said spyware on Kaylee Whitfield's cell.

AJ turned her attention to the black phone on the right. Kaylee's phone had been given to her by none other than security dickwad in chief, Wes Brennan. According to Kaylee, it had started glitching the same day she'd received it, which coincidentally, was the same day Aidan had installed the malware.

Problem was, the Cybercore malware was clean. She analyzed it a dozen different ways and it always came back the same—straightforward, elegant code, with a dash of Liam's trademark charisma. Built for one thing. Built to do its job. Built to bring the target—in this case, Max—to his knees.

Logic said that meant Kaylee's phone was the snarled one. The one that had caused the problem. And maybe, just maybe, those glitches had nothing to do with the Cybercore spyware at all.

Working that hunch, AJ plugged the black phone into her computer, and subjected it to her newly developed analyzing program, but instead of investigating the spyware again, this time she scrutinized the phone itself. She'd expected it to take a while. She'd expected a slog. But that wasn't what she got.

AJ's spine snapped straight as the issue revealed itself to her. It couldn't have been more obvious if it had flashing arrows pointing at it.

There was another bug, built right into the phone.

The exact line of junk code that was etched into her brain from her forensic hacking marathon at Liam's stood out starkly on her screen.

Holy shit.

Sloppy gets you caught.

If it meant what she thought it meant, then she'd just blown this case wide open. All she needed to nail the perpetrator of Max's hack, of Liam's hack, was some corroborating evidence. The final puzzle piece. And she knew exactly who could help her with that.

AJ's hands shook as she grabbed her phone. Her heart was in her throat when she hit Send on the text she'd composed.

And now, she waited to see if Liam would answer.

It took forty-five minutes before there was a knock on the door.

She ignored the rush of…something that flooded through her at the sight of Liam. He was handsome as ever in his black pinstripe three-piece suit and a red tie.

"Driving the Corvette today, huh?" It was a dumb joke. An olive branch. Something to remind him of their history, but it fizzled.

Liam dropped his gaze to the floor, and AJ's heart fell with it. "You said you needed this? It seemed kind of urgent."

She accepted the computer he handed her and forced a smile. "That depends. Did Jesse upgrade the virus protection software like Wes told him to?"

Liam shook his head. "No, we haven't managed to connect on that yet."

AJ sighed with relief. She'd kept her text vague, hoping to intrigue Liam into answering the summons. A rational person would have asked about the virus protection upgrade in the text. So that Liam didn't have to drive all the way over if there was nothing for them to find.

But there was nothing rational about how much AJ wanted to see him.

"Well, in that case, yeah. It's urgent." She let the tease hang there for a moment as she opened his laptop and placed it on her desk. Finally, after what felt like a lifetime, Liam stepped inside her loft and shut the door. She held her breath as his gaze skated around the exposed brick walls and dark wood floors. "This is where you live, huh?"

AJ managed a nod. Normally she would have called him out on such an obvious question. But this was what they'd been reduced to now. Banal small talk. Besides, she was still adjusting to seeing him here. Around her stuff. Her first houseguest. The only person she'd actually given her address to.

"It's nice. I wish you'd invited me under different circumstances."

So did she, but there was no time to dwell on missed opportunities and regrets.

Obviously, Liam felt the same way, as he was much more brusque and businesslike when he joined her beside his desk. "So, what does this have to do with the software update?"

"Yeah. Business." She nodded. "Let's do it." AJ motioned toward her desk. "Max gave me two phones to analyze—the one you sold Aidan was clean, but guess what I found on the one Wes gave Kaylee Whitfield?"

Liam's gaze snapped to hers. "The garbage code."

AJ nodded. "And that got me thinking about how Soteria Security is the one link that Cybercore and Whitfield Industries share."

"Whitfield Industries has been using Soteria for years."

"Sure, but that just makes it even more conspicuous that after you consider using one of their products for the first time, both Whitfield and Cybercore end up with leaks involving your competing products. And you said Wes was eager to upgrade your software protection, right? Sending Jesse after you to the point of annoyance? It's one thing to offer great customer service, but what if there's another reason he's pushing this upgrade so hard?"

"What are you thinking?"

"I hacked your party and broke into your bedroom to drop a backdoor into your main server so I could poke around later. What if Soteria's security program has a backdoor built right in?"

Liam swore. "Sell me the software to score Cyber-core as a client and then collect again by peddling the specs for The Shield to some overseas counterfeiter."

"And that doesn't even count all the extra hours they've been putting in at Whitfield Industries since the hack. Cause the security breach, and then rake in the cash when your clients order you to fix it." It was brilliant. And unethical to the extreme.

"Swoop in with a bunch of upgrades, but really all you're doing is removing the backdoor once you're done with it," Liam offered.

"Yes! Wes sends someone in to do a little spring cleaning, before sloppy gets his ass caught."

Liam pulled off his suit jacket and started rolling up his sleeves. "It's worth a try." She could feel the excitement radiating off him at the possibility. She was brimming with it, too.

They fell back into the rhythm of the days they'd spent working together side by side, just like this, at his house. AJ realized how much she loved digging into this stuff with him. She'd always worked alone, but there was an energy to having a partner, someone to bounce things off of. Someone brilliant. And handsome. And…this was not the time, she reminded herself.

It took the two of them less than an hour to isolate what they were looking for. A backdoor, just like she'd hypothesized. AJ couldn't stand still. She was too hyped. They'd just uncovered a cybersecurity scandal of epic proportions.

Liam shook his head, double-checking their results. "Why would he put the exact same string of code in the exact same place? It's almost like he was trying to get caught."

AJ couldn't wipe the grin off her face. "Well, I guess he got his wish then, because we just nailed Wes Brennan! Who's sloppy now, bitch?"

Liam laughed, and the sound rumbled through her.

"What's so funny?"

"Asks the woman whose extreme gloating includes the phrase 'Who's sloppy now, bitch?'"

"I'm not gloating. I'm...reveling in poetic justice."

"Oh, is that what it was?"

Liam got to his feet, and AJ stopped in front of him.

"You're damn straight! I just took down the dickwad who caught me five years ago. If I can't revel now, then when?"

"Touché." He smiled down at her, and AJ was swamped with a pang of longing so deep that she couldn't breathe for a second. He was too close. Or she was too close. Either way, the familiar thrum of attraction started up between them as they stared at each other. And she wanted it. Wanted to lose herself in the heat of it. To forget all the shit that hung between them. All the obstacles that stood in their way.

She made herself say the words that she knew would pop the bubble of intimacy that seemed to engulf them whenever she and Liam were around each other.

"We have to tell Max."

Liam's smile dimmed, but he nodded, stepped away

under the pretense of grabbing his suit jacket from the chair.

Her heart ached at the graceful, familiar way he tugged it on.

When Liam looked back at her, the intimacy they'd shared a moment ago was gone. "I'll drive."

CHAPTER TWENTY-THREE

MAX WAS TAKING the news better than Liam had expected.

"Son of a bitch."

Or not.

"You're sure about this?"

AJ nodded. She was slung out in the visitor chair beside Liam, lounging carelessly. "Am I ever wrong, boss?"

For some reason, Liam liked that despite her dogged loyalty to the prick on the other side of the desk, she treated him with the same amount of deference she'd always spared Liam—which was to say, none.

He almost laughed at himself. *For some reason.* Right.

He'd all but blurted out that he loved her, and she'd walked away. She'd made her choice.

"—FBI. What do you think, Kearney?"

Liam's head snapped up. Since all he'd been thinking was how much he wanted to drag AJ into his arms, for the first time in his life, he was glad Max was on top of things. "Yeah. Sounds good."

Jesus. He needed to stay focused.

Max hit a button on his desk phone. "Sherri, get Special Agent Behnsen on the phone for me. Tell her it's urgent and see if she has any time to meet this afternoon. And send Vivienne up to my office, too."

"Vivienne's not back from vacation until Thursday. Greg Chapman is the interim lead for the legal department."

"Right. Send him up."

"Legal?" Beside him, AJ straightened up in her chair. There was an edge of panic in her voice, and it took everything in Liam not to touch her, remind her to breathe.

"What are you... The FBI is coming? Why?"

"If he gets word of this, Brennan could be in the wind in minutes. We need to strike hard and fast."

The answer did nothing to dissipate any of AJ's sudden nervous energy.

While Liam agreed with Whitfield's approach—Wes Brennan wouldn't know what hit him by the time his lawyers were done with him—the cold, robotic part of Max was too focused on calculating the next move. Which was great for nailing Brennan to the wall, but not quite so good for the woman trembling beside him.

Liam glanced over at her, and the fear on her face had him turning in his chair. He ignored Max and his own better judgment and placed his hand over hers—the one white-knuckling the armrest. Her skin was freezing. "Hey. AJ. Look at me."

It took a second for his voice to penetrate her consciousness, and another second after that for her eyes to focus in on his.

"I won't let you fall." But he knew those words were just a stand-in for the three he really meant. The three she didn't want to hear.

Relief washed over her face, and she let go of the chair to grab his hand instead, eyes pleading.

So he gave her the one thing he knew she really wanted—an escape hatch. "It's okay. You don't have to stay."

"What do you mean she doesn't have to stay? She's the one who found everything. Who else is going to present the evidence to the FBI? You're staying."

Liam got to his feet, lamenting the loss of her hand. "I thought you cared about her."

Max's glare said he'd overstepped. "What the fuck is that supposed to mean?"

"It means look at her, for Christ's sake! You of all people should know what she went through to put her scumbag ex in jail for what he did to her. The trial was invasive as hell, and that one barely made the news.

"This one is going to be a circus when the media get ahold of it. And not just because we're business rivals, and not just because Wes Brennan is the king of security, but because you just turned in your father. They'll figure out where she lives. They'll hound her for comments, shove cameras in her face and stalk her everywhere she goes. They'll eat her alive."

Max frowned. "And we're going to do what when they ask how we figured all this out? How strong is our case going to be if we all get charged with perjury?"

"Jesus, Whitfield. We're tech magnates. You think we can't convince a bunch of laymen whose eyes glaze over the second we open our mouths about code that we found the anomalies ourselves?

"AJ might have put the evidence together, but it's all still there. I can explain the coding anomaly that shows up in the knockoff version of The Shield, and the Soteria antivirus program on my laptop. You found the same chunk of code in the program that got loaded onto one of your employee's computers, and your sister is going to need to vouch that she got that phone from Wes anyway if we're going to tie this up."

Liam pulled a hand through his hair. "Everyone saw our blowout at Henry Mitford's party. We just say that you accused me of hacking SecurePay, I accused you of leaking The Shield to a counterfeiter, and we figured out that we'd both been victims of the same scam.

"Jesse Hastings will be so desperate not to have his business fall apart when this breaks that he'll turn on Wes in a hot second. It's a slam dunk without her."

Max looked over at AJ. It wasn't a big tell, but Liam knew that if he didn't have the man convinced already, he was close. So he pressed the final advantage.

"Think about it. Wes is the one who caught her hacking your company. If anything, bringing her into this will give Brennan's attorney a case to play this off like revenge."

"Fine. We do it without her."

Something shifted in Liam's chest, and when he turned to face AJ, she was staring at him, brown eyes bright with unshed tears. "You should probably get out of here. The fewer people who notice you leaving the better."

She nodded, pulling the hood of her sweatshirt up as she stood. To his surprise, she stopped as she drew level with him. Her fingertips brushed his, and he closed his eyes to memorize the touch.

"Thank you." It was barely a whisper. But he heard it. And then she was gone.

Liam opened his eyes, but he didn't turn around to watch her leave this time. He couldn't bear it. Instead, he turned his attention back to Max to find his business rival appraising him with a calculated interest.

"Is there a problem, Whitfield?"

Max shook his head. "No. It's just a little surreal to have you in my office. Guess it struck me for the first time that we're on the same side."

Liam understood the dissonance of it. He and Max had been at odds for a long time. Although Liam couldn't deny that knowing Max had kept AJ out of prison, helped her nail her scumbag ex, offered her a job that had improved her life, had softened his opinion of his rival. A little.

"You might not believe it, but I am sorry for John's death."

Max's jaw flexed, and his gaze dropped to the little statue on his desk—a horse with a flaming mane. "Thank you. I am, too."

"I know it doesn't help, but if I was faced with the same opportunity today, I wouldn't dabble in such a gray area. He assured me there was no conflict of interest with his job at Whitfield, and because I wanted it to be true, I didn't vet his claims. If there was a way for me to retroactively fix it, I would."

Max shoved his hands in his pockets. "You could always postpone the release of The Shield until SecurePay is ready for release."

Liam smiled despite himself. "Not fucking likely."

"Worth a try," Max said with a shrug. "I guess I'll have to settle for you helping me rain fire and brimstone on Brennan."

Now that was a plan Liam could get behind. "It would be my pleasure."

CHAPTER TWENTY-FOUR

THREE DAYS OF hiding out and psyching herself up later, AJ found herself back at Whitfield Industries.

Max looked up as she stepped into his office.

"What are you doing here?"

Oh, just jumping headlong into the unknown without a parachute, she thought wryly. *Thanks for asking.* But what she said was, "I'm your three o'clock appointment."

Max frowned. "I don't have a three o'clock…" The denial faded into a sigh. "I thought we discussed that hacking my schedule was not a sanctioned use of your skills."

"I didn't want you to have any excuse to brush me off." AJ took a deep breath and screwed up her courage. "There are a couple of things I need to say, and I didn't want us to be interrup—"

"What the hell is going on?"

Max surged to his feet and AJ whipped around as a statuesque brunette with a razor-sharp bob and hellfire in her eyes stormed into his office. Another person she'd never met, but AJ knew Whitfield Industries' top-dog lawyer by sight. Vivienne Grant was even more intimidating in person than she was in her security clearance photo.

"I was gone for three days. Three days! And I come back to this?" She strode toward Max's desk, holding her phone in front of her. The screen was playing some news footage of Wes Brennan's arrest, the money shot of the FBI marching him out of the Soteria Security building in handcuffs as the newscaster filled the audience in on the scandal.

"You honestly think Wes betrayed you? He would never do something like that!"

"Vivienne—" Max's voice was low and even "—I know it's a shock. I'm still processing it myself, but if you'll just take a seat, I'll ask AJ to leave and we can discuss—"

Vivienne's eyes flickered dismissively over her, like she was noticing AJ's presence in the office for the first time. Obviously, she'd been judged beneath notice, as Vivienne returned her attention immediately to Max.

"There's nothing to discuss. The fact that you would team up with Liam Kearney, of all people, to ambush Wes with all these heinous accusations when he's done nothing but try to help you. His business is security, Max. You've ruined him."

Max's eyes turned cold and icy. AJ had seen it happen before on-screen, but it was much frostier in person. "Before you say another word, I caution you to assess where your loyalties lie on this issue."

"I know exactly where my loyalty belongs." The

woman reached into her purse and pulled out a lanyard filled with keys and security passes. It hit Max's desk with a clatter of finality.

"That's why I quit."

Max stayed dead still until Vivienne had stridden out of his office and the glass door swung shut behind her.

"Fuck."

As far as outbursts went, it was the appropriate amount of subdued that she'd expect from Max Whitfield, given his cold-as-ice reputation.

"Take a seat, AJ. I'll be right with you."

AJ figured he could use a break, so she flopped into the nearest visitor chair as Max called security and gave a couple of instructions about ensuring Vivienne Grant left the premises and revoking her security clearance.

Then he straightened his tie.

"Okay, what can I do for you?"

"Well, that's kind of a hard act to follow," AJ ventured, "but, uh…I quit, too."

She pulled the phone that she used solely to contact Max out of the pocket of her leather jacket. It felt weighty in her hand, bogged down in symbolism and the last five years of her life. Years she'd considered the best of her life. Until she'd met Liam. Until he'd made her see that hiding out wasn't enough anymore. Until he'd made her want more. A real life. No more layers. AJ held her breath as she set the phone on the edge of his desk.

"Of course you are. First Emma, then Kaylee. Now Vivienne." Max sighed. "Why not you, too?"

"Yeah, it's kind of starting to look like you're the common thread, huh?"

Her joke fell flat, and she was treated to that frosty gaze he'd just used on the lawyer.

"But, I mean, you live with Emma now, so workplace sexual harassment policies being what they are, her quitting was probably best-case scenario. And your sister ended up changing her mind, so you dodged a bullet there. Really, it's just Vivienne and me, so, you know. Could be worse."

"How delightfully glass-half-full of you." Max leaned back in his fancy chair.

"Yeah, I'm toning down the cynicism. Trying something new."

"Liam Kearney, huh?"

His name made her chest tight. "I'm sorry you found out the way you did. I never meant to betray you. I was trying to help you, to prove he did it. And then somewhere in the middle of it all, it just…" She trailed off, because the rest of that speech was for Liam, and she wanted him to hear it first.

Max shook his head. "You don't need to apologize. I was… You caught me off guard, that's all. Now that I've had time to adjust, it's… I just want you to be okay."

"I am okay. I mean, I'm going to be. Actually, I thought I might look into starting my own thing. Contract work. Do a little security here, a little forensic hacking there."

Max stared at her for a long moment before he spoke, and even though AJ braced for his verdict, his words still made her heart stop.

"It's about time."

"What?"

"You're incredibly talented. I knew it the second Wes...the second you were brought to my attention. When we met... Christ, AJ. You were so broken and bruised. I understood that you'd need some time. Some space. That was a lot of shit you went through. More than anybody should. And it leaves marks."

Something about the way Max said it caught her attention. And to her surprise, her boss, her ex-boss, dropped that inscrutable poker face for a moment, just long enough to let her see that he understood what she'd been through. He wasn't just a witness to her pain that day. He'd survived some of his own.

She blinked against the burn of unshed tears. "It does. I'm... I've let it make decisions for me for a long time, but I'm working on it. I've been talking to someone recently. A therapist. She thinks it's time I started being more direct about what I want."

"Hence the quitting."

"Hence the quitting," she confirmed.

"I always knew you wouldn't stay forever. If I weren't such a selfish bastard, I would have shoved you out into the world a long time ago. I'm proud of you. It's a good decision."

AJ thought her chest might burst. She hadn't realized how much she'd needed to hear the words. How much Max's opinion really meant to her. He was a big part of her life. But Liam was right. He couldn't be her whole world.

"Starting your own company, I mean. Verdict's still out on Kearney."

With a sniff, AJ tugged the cuff of her hoodie over the heel of her hand and wiped her eyes. "I think I'm allergic to your ugly corporate office."

"Well, that's going to be a bitch when you open your own business."

"I'll stock up on antihistamines."

Max nodded. "Probably wise."

AJ got to her feet. "I should get out of here. You've got a lot to deal with. And there's someone I need to go see."

She'd only managed two steps before Max's voice stopped her.

"AJ. Keep the phone." He tossed it to her, and the relief that clogged her throat was overwhelming. "Give me a call when you're up and running. I don't know if you've heard, but I'm in the market for a new security firm."

"Was that a joke?" She affected her best scowl. "Not cool. Just because I won't see you as much, doesn't mean you get to fuck with our dynamic. You're the inflexible hard-ass. I'm the funny one. And don't forget it."

Max actually smiled. A little. "I'm sure we'll see each other plenty. And I'll expect the friends and family discount, obviously."

That made her pause. "And which one are you? Friend, or family?"

Max contemplated that for a moment. "I like to think a little of both."

It was AJ's turn to nod. Those stupid tears were back. "Yeah. Me, too. But don't think for a second that means I'm giving you a double discount."

CHAPTER TWENTY-FIVE

LIAM STRODE ACROSS the parking lot, adjusting his sunglasses against the California sun.

Logically, he knew he should be on top of the world. He'd just locked down the government contract that he'd been after for the last two years.

Several shipments of the counterfeit version of The Shield had been seized coming into the country.

Wes Brennan had been arrested.

Business was good. Better than good.

And he was miserable.

The Corvette unlocked with a quiet beep, and Liam crawled inside. He'd just turned the key in the ignition when his phone buzzed against his chest.

He pulled it free of his pocket, but before he had a chance to unlock it, the screen went black.

Liam frowned.

Then the words *I'm sorry* scrolled across the display, and Liam's grip tightened on the phone.

Large white text flashed on the screen. SEE YOU SOON. Then it disappeared, only to be replaced by a countdown clock. It was set for eleven seconds.

Liam's chest got tight as the seconds ticked by. Three…two…one.

The black screen turned to a blur of giant pixels. Against his will, a slight smile touched his lips. She'd done a pretty good job of duping his original. Thrown in a few nice touches of her own. He watched the image zoom out until he was staring at a Google map with a pin dropped in the last place he'd expected.

Liam threw the Corvette into gear and headed home. His chest was full of something that felt suspiciously like hope.

He slowed at the last bend, expecting to see a black-clad figure leaning against the stone pillar, but there was no one there. With a frown creasing his forehead, Liam pressed his thumb to the panel so the gate would swing open, and drove up to the garage.

He keyed in the current iteration of the rotating eight-digit password that would unlock the door. As Liam stepped into the house, his phone buzzed again. The perfect timing of that let him know that she was tracking him, so he checked the screen, expecting the next piece to whatever puzzle she'd designed. Instead, it was just a simple text.

I'm upstairs.

He knew he should be pissed that she'd managed to bypass his security. Not just blow it up, but reset it, and all without his knowledge. And he was. But much like the first night he'd laid eyes on her, he was impressed, too.

That was the thing about AJ. She'd gotten into his brain as well as his blood.

She could tease him all she wanted about his history with supermodel socialites, but none of those women had ever affected him like she did.

Liam's heart was in his throat as he took the steps that led toward his bedroom. But when he turned the corner, expecting to see her standing there, fake-admiring his hallway art in a pantomime of that first night, his expectations were subverted yet again.

The doors to the master suite were thrown wide open.

What he saw when he stepped inside stole his breath.

AJ was standing at the window with her back to him. She wore fancy lingerie—not her usual cotton. This was exquisite black lace with some kind of patent-leather harness thing, a sexy bra-and-panties combo that seemed to hide as much as they revealed, tricking the eye with shadows, making him wonder what was skin and what was lining. Apt, he supposed, that even now, almost naked, he couldn't quite figure her out.

In total contrast to the tease of that, she wore her scuffed-up black Doc Martens. A riding crop dangled from her right hand.

She was desperately, quintessentially AJ right then, standing in front of the window part dominatrix, part warrior, and all defiance.

Liam leaned his shoulder against the doorjamb.

"I assume the boots are symbolic of the way you stomped through my security."

A wry smile touched her lips as she turned to face him. She was so fucking beautiful. His abs clenched like he'd been punched in the stomach.

"You know I can't resist a challenge. Putting a kick-ass security system in front of me is basically a giant dare. As for the boots—" She shrugged. "I just like them."

Liam pushed away from the door and walked toward her. Every part of him wanted to lose himself in her, to not ask the question he needed to ask, but he realized that would get them nowhere, so he stopped, leaving distance between them so that wouldn't happen.

"What are you doing here?" he asked.

"I'm here because you were right. I run when things get hard. And I was hiding behind Max. But I finally realized that if I keep doing that, if I don't let myself be part of the world again, then I'm going to miss out on all this amazing stuff. Like annoying snooty sales-girls and telling off shitty moms."

Until that moment, Liam hadn't thought it was possible to love her more than he already did.

"And I don't want to miss any of it. So I broke into your house and I, uh…I took off all the layers for you." She looked down at herself, then back at him. "Basically, I'm standing here in some slutty underwear with a riding crop to tell you that you make me want things. Good things. Like cunnilingus. And sex in a bed. And to stay the night."

He couldn't stay away from her for another second.

She was like a magnet, pulling him forward. "Well, I don't like to brag—"

She arched a contrary eyebrow. "Yes, you do."

"I mean, sure, a little. But I heard it's not bragging if you can back it up," he reminded her. "And I figure if I can knock off all three items on your list by tomorrow morning, that's got to count for something, right?"

To his surprise, her face turned serious. "Did you mean what you said at the party? That you're falling for me?"

Liam shook his head. Giving in to the urge to touch her, he rested his palms against the flare of her hips. "Sometimes, it's a smart business move to hedge your bets, leave a little wiggle room. Understate things a little so you can exceed expectations."

"So lie?" she asked with a knowing look.

"Not lie, just bend the truth a little. Like in this case, I said what I meant. I just played a little fast and loose with the verb tense. Because I'm not falling in love with you, Alyssa James. I already fell."

Her wayward smile did funny things to his pulse. "Well, that's pretty fucking embarrassing for you, isn't it?" She poked him in the chest with the riding crop. "What will the supermodel socialites say when they find out?"

"Uh-uh. You don't get to joke your way out of this one." Liam tugged her a step closer. "After everything we've been through, don't tell me this is where your courage deserts you."

She licked her lips. Met his gaze. "I'm not afraid of anything."

Liam grinned down at her. "Prove it."

AJ kissed him as he hoisted her up his body so she could wrap her legs around his waist. But as incredible as it felt to have her in his arms again, it was nothing compared to the look in her eyes when she pulled back.

"I love you," she said simply.

"I love you, too." Liam tightened his arms around her, but when he tried to capture her lips, she wouldn't let him.

"I feel like I should probably make it clear that if we're really doing this *us* thing—"

"Oh, we're definitely doing this *us* thing," Liam assured her.

"—that I'm gonna fuck it up so many times in so many ways. But if you're willing to be patient while I work through some of this baggage, I promise I'll do everything I can to make it worth your time."

"You're worth everything to me," he said solemnly.

AJ kissed him again, but this time with a heat that wouldn't be denied. Liam let the flame consume him as she shoved his jacket off his shoulders. He did his best to help her out, pressing her back against the window so he could let go of her with one arm, then the other, until the Italian wool slipped past his wrists and fell to the floor. She was already tugging at his tie, but after a couple of attempts, she ripped her mouth from his so she could see what she was doing.

"The pretentious douchebaggery of your three-piece suits is really getting in the way of you getting laid right now, you know that, don't you? Man, and you accuse me of hiding under layers."

He reached up with his right hand and with a practiced pull, the blue silk came free. "And you accuse me of talking too much, but now you're the one who won't shut up."

She set to work on the buttons of his shirt. "Guess you'll have to make me then."

Liam's grin felt downright wicked. "I was hoping you'd say that."

* * * * *

COMING SOON!

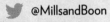

MILLS & BOON

THE HEART OF ROMANCE

A ROMANCE FOR EVERY KIND OF READER

MODERN

Prepare to be swept off your feet by sophisticated, sexy and seductive heroes, in some of the world's most glamourous and romantic locations, where power and passion collide.
8 stories per month.

HISTORICAL

Escape with historical heroes from time gone by. Whether your passion is for wicked Regency Rakes, muscled Vikings or rugged Highlanders, awaken the romance of the past.
6 stories per month.

MEDICAL

Set your pulse racing with dedicated, delectable doctors in the high-pressure world of medicine, where emotions run high and passion, comfort and love are the best medicine.
6 stories per month.

True Love

Celebrate true love with tender stories of heartfelt romance, from the rush of falling in love to the joy a new baby can bring, and a focus on the emotional heart of a relationship.
8 stories per month.

Desire

Indulge in secrets and scandal, intense drama and plenty of sizzling hot action with powerful and passionate heroes who have it all: wealth, status, good looks…everything but the right woman.
6 stories per month.

HEROES

Experience all the excitement of a gripping thriller, with an intense romance at its heart. Resourceful, true-to-life women and strong, fearless men face danger and desire - a killer combination!
8 stories per month.

DARE

Sensual love stories featuring smart, sassy heroines you'd want as a best friend, and compelling intense heroes who are worthy of them.
4 stories per month.

JOIN US ON SOCIAL MEDIA!

Stay up to date with our latest releases, author news and gossip, special offers and discounts, and all the behind-the-scenes action from Mills & Boon...

 millsandboon

 millsandboonuk

 millsandboon

It might just be true love...